REELIN' IN THE YEARS

CARL L. BOST

REELIN' IN THE YEARS

Carl L. Bost

Owl Songs, LLC

Do not say,

"Why were the former days better than these?"
For you do not inquire wisely concerning this.

Ecclesiastes 7:10 (NKJV)

For my other family, the Goekes:
Gene, Ginny, Scooter, & Brett

Contents

A Note from the Author

Rather than a memoir, my book serves as a memorial. It reflects my recollections from those tumultuous years between high school and my enlistment in the US Navy, all compressed into the summer of 1979.

Books may be the only viable vehicle that allows us to time travel. *Reelin' in the Years* is my first foray into the work of literature as an author. The book I began writing more than three years ago was birthed from adolescent memories: some pleasant, some embarrassing, and some only a figment of my imagination. It seems that I am not alone in discovering later in life that sometimes the things that happen to us in high school carry over into adulthood. Although I am blessed with an overthinking neurodivergent mind, wrestling with thoughts while trying to connect emotional dots with a lot of missing data was exhausting. Writing stories and scenes down was therapeutic and connecting them became a bittersweet experience.

In several chapters, additional flashbacks are used to demonstrate how remote events ripple across time and impact the story. To be sure, the book is based on people I have known, but all the characters have been altered and changed by my imagination to fit the narrative.

My story takes place in 1979. Why 1979? The last year of that decade was the twilight of a new era. The zeitgeist of the '70s I grew up in was drugs, sex, and rock and roll.

After 1979, analog gave way to digital, pinball gave way to video games, and movie theaters and drive-ins gave way to VHS tapes and strip malls. Stay-at-home moms began working. Television programming, which once consisted of three major networks plus PBS, had to compete with countless stations due to the rise of cable and satellite television. TV stations no longer went off the air; news coverage went from just a couple of hours in the evening to a twenty-four-hour never-ending cycle. Japanese companies began to import more than motorcycles.

After 1979, DJs had less to say in the music we heard as program directors dictated playlists. Some DJs got paid more to say shocking things than spin records. Rock concerts that were once cheap to attend became more expensive. While disco and punk music were abominations to the rock and roll crowd, both influenced the music soon to flood the airwaves. In 1979, MTV was less than two years away.

My book is a coming-of-age story about a young man with no sense of direction, meaning, or purpose, doing all he can to fit in with like-minded friends. The story takes place mainly in Jefferson County, Missouri—a county bordered by two rivers, rivers that seemed at times to make Jefferson County a remote and disconnected island.

The central theme of this work is actions have consequences. We reap what we sow. There is misery to vain pursuits, and even the pleasures of youthful vanity do not last and rarely satisfy. We might yell and scream for more, but we often regret it when we get our heart's desire. Sometimes, in our quest for the temporal, we miss out on the things that would have mattered most. Life in a broken world often appears random and uncontrollable, but in writing this book, I have affirmed there is an underlying purpose and grace for all. In the end, my characters get away with nothing. Neither do we. Some of us see the lightning and begin counting…anticipating the thunder of the coming storm.

Map of the Meramec River

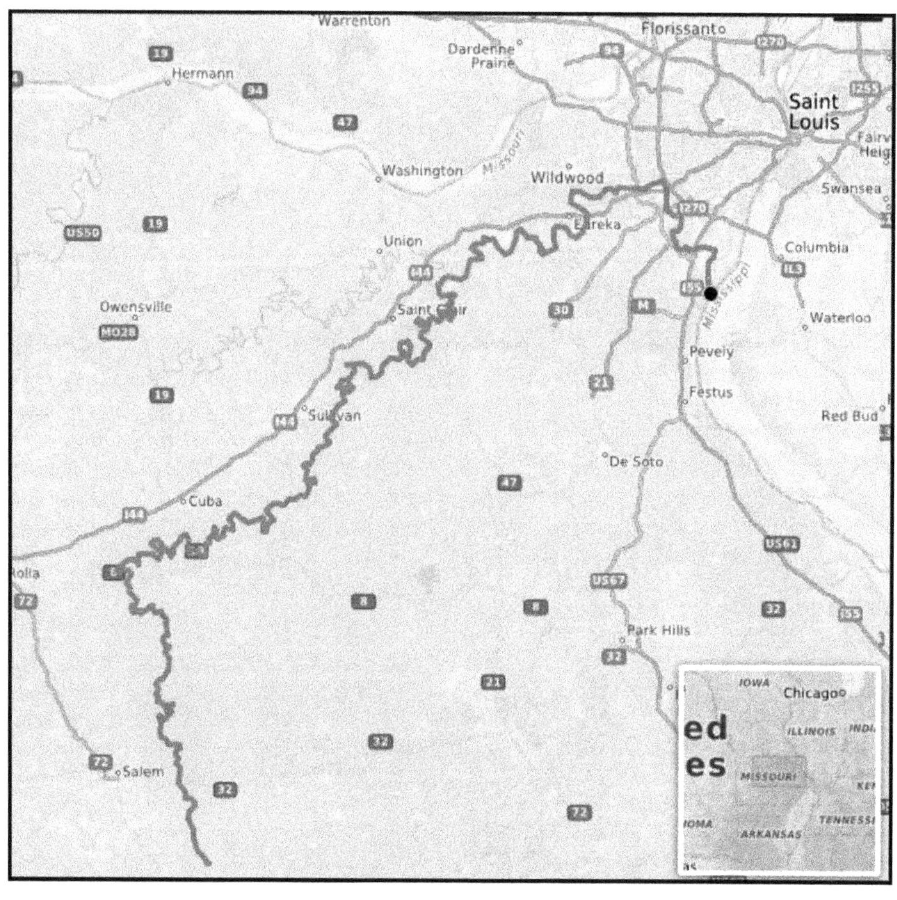

Chesley Island, Jefferson County, MO

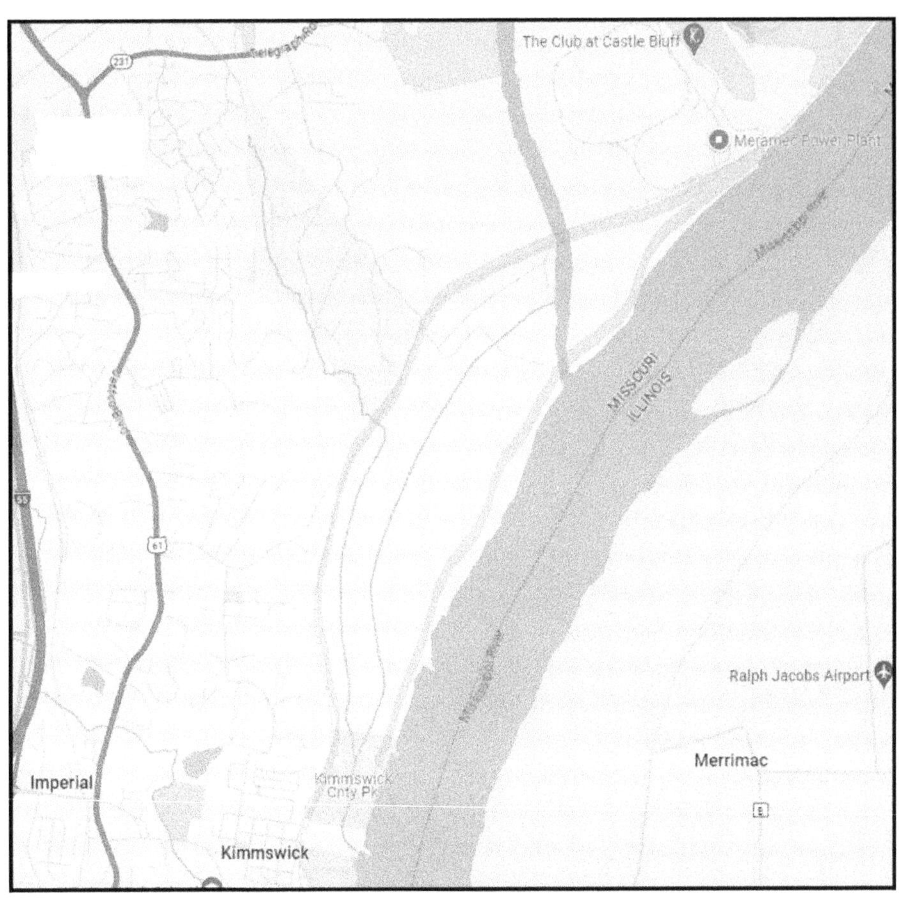

Map of Jefferson County – 1979

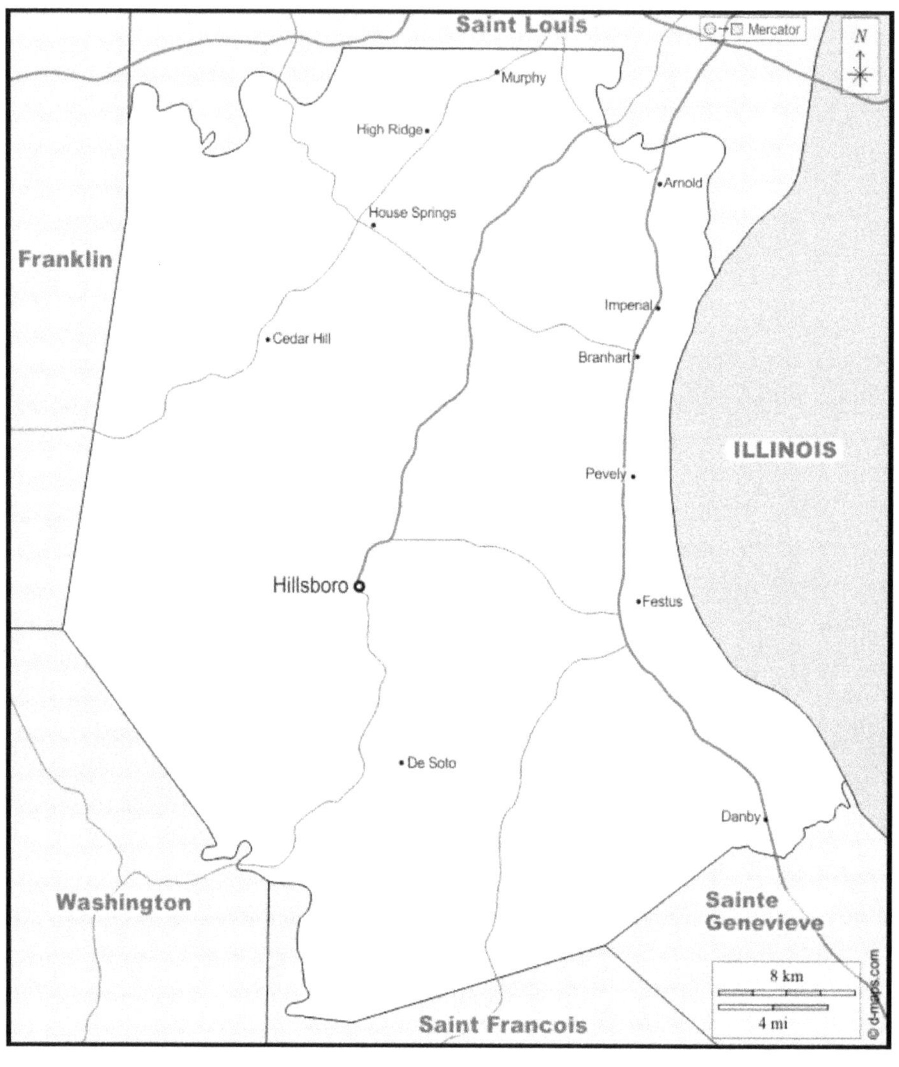

CHAPTER 1

A Friday Night in Jefferson County

Flashing blue and red lights filled the night sky, and a spotlight flooded the cab of the 1965 Ford pickup with brilliant white light.

"Damn it," Curtis muttered as he rolled down the window and turned off the music in anticipation of the inevitable interrogation.

"How many beers did you drink tonight?" asked Marty, riding shotgun.

"Just a few," he replied.

"Yeah, right…a few, my ass."

The patrol officer approached the truck with the swagger and confidence police officers have when confronting teenagers on a Friday night. The cop had a giant flashlight powered by half a dozen D-sized batteries. He shined a bright beam into the faces of the two teenagers inside the truck.

"I need to see your license," he barked.

When Curtis handed him the requested state-issued card, the officer snatched it from his hand. Their eyes were granted momentary relief when the officer turned the light from their faces to examine the license.

"Is this your truck?" he asked, redirecting the painful beam toward Curtis's face.

"Technically, it's my dad's truck," Curtis replied with squinting eyes. He did not mean for the sarcasm to come out that harshly, but there it was. He tried to recover by adding, "But he lets me drive it whenever I want."

"Do you know why I pulled you over?" the officer asked.

"No, not really…"

Curtis had barely uttered his response before being jarred into reality. The officer, now slightly red in the face with one hand on his service revolver and the other waving the flashlight, shouted, "Keep your hands up where I can see them and get out of the truck…now!"

Immediately, severe anxiety set in, coupled with a moment of clarity. Curtis was painfully aware he was in serious trouble. The police officer aggressively yanked Curtis out of the truck, manhandled him to the front, and ordered him to put his hands on the hood.

"Spread your legs apart," the cop yelled. He kicked one of Curtis's feet, nearly knocking him off the truck.

"You know where you're going tonight? You're going straight to jail." The patrolman bent Curtis's right arm backward, placing a cuff restraint on his right wrist. "Do you have any alcohol, drugs, or weapons in that truck that I should know about?"

"No, sir, it's just me and my friend."

"Now, let's try this again… Do you know why I pulled you over?"

"Because I burned some rubber leaving the 7-Eleven?"

The confession brought immediate relief to his arm, and the policeman's voice lowered a few decibels.

"Son, that is what we call reckless driving, and I should write you a ticket for that." There was a moment of silence before he asked, "Where were you two headed anyway?"

"We were just heading into town to get something to eat."

"No, you're not going anywhere. You need to get back in your truck, turn around, and go back home. Do you understand?"

"Yes, sir."

"If I see you again tonight, you will go to jail. Do you understand me?"

"Yes, sir."

He removed the handcuff without regard to the pain inflicted while taking it off.

"Now get the hell out of here and learn to drive safe."

Curtis rubbed his wrist gingerly and returned to the truck with shaky knees. The cop returned to his car and turned off the flashing lights and spotlight while talking into the radio.

It was around ten o'clock, and there was hardly any traffic on the four-lane road. After checking both ways several times, Curtis carefully maneuvered his truck into a long, swung-out U-turn to head back south toward Imperial, mindful of the acceleration and not to make any squealing noises from his tires. He wisely showed restraint by not waving goodbye as he drove past the menacing glare of the Arnold patrolman, who probably still had another eight hours left on his double shift.

Once they were out of Arnold, Marty lit up a doobie and grabbed two beers from under the seat.

"Do you want a hit of this?" Marty offered the rather large, hand-rolled fatty.

"No, not right now. I can't even see straight. All those lights made me dizzy."

"Are you okay to drive?" Marty laughed as he popped the tops off two cans of beer. He said, "I really thought you were going to jail."

"Yeah, I did too."

Marty handed Curtis a cold beer, and the two friends continued toward Imperial. It grew unbearably quiet, which prompted Curtis to push the cassette back into the player and rock the truck's cab with the Sammy Hagar live album, *All Night Long*.

"I'm still hungry," Curtis said as he drank from the can of Busch beer.

"Screw it then. Let's just go to the McDonald's in Festus," Marty replied.

Jefferson County, Missouri, is one of twenty-plus counties in the United States named after Thomas Jefferson, the nation's third president.

In 1979, Jefferson County fell under the responsibility and leadership of Sheriff Walter "Buck" Buerger, who would hold that position for an unprecedented twenty-eight years from the county seat in Hillsboro. Under his authority, he had a few dozen deputies and auxiliary deputies to cover the 650-plus square miles.

Many of the towns, like Arnold, had their own municipal law enforcement, and there were always a few Missouri State Troopers patrolling the region. In addition, many people in Jefferson County owned at least one dog and one gun, just as they did in 1818 when the county was organized into existence.

Few things were as enjoyable for restless, carefree teenagers as cruising around on cool spring Friday nights with the windows rolled down and the music turned up. They traveled by the lit-up Rock Roll-O-Rena with the remnant of the Friday night crowd lingering in the parking lot, saying their goodbyes or waiting for rides. The post-skate live music and sock hops were long gone, replaced by the occasional "all-night skate."

Curtis and Marty made it to Imperial, and as they approached Jerry's Market, Curtis inquired if they needed more beer.

Marty looked at the store and said, "I can't. Rico isn't working tonight."

They continued their southward journey on the state highway toward Barnhart. They drove past Kohler City and the treacherous curve that molded into one of the long straightaways between Barnhart and Herculaneum. It was always tempting to see how fast you could go on that long stretch of highway, but the Jefferson County Sheriff's Department and Missouri State Troopers were also aware of the temptation. Local and state governments profited from the numerous fines they collected, probably saving innumerable lives with their routine patrols.

As they approached Pevely, the lights of the giant glass manufacturing facility lit up the night sky. Marty turned down the volume.

"Do we have something else to listen to? This is the twentieth time we've heard this tape tonight."

Curtis dug around to find another cassette tape as they passed the darkened drive-in theater. Summer was right around the corner and that meant no school, drive-in movies, and swimming at Springdale. He popped the tape out of the cassette player and pushed a different tape in without looking. The bass introduction indicated they had struck sonic gold with Van Halen's recently released second album.

"Thank you, April," Curtis shouted out loud.

"What are you talking about?"

"You know April Weaver?"

"The weird girl who doesn't talk to anyone and draws pictures all day?"

Curtis said, "She's not weird, she's different. She talks to me."

Marty replied, "Well, that explains a lot."

"I like her. I find her interesting."

"You would find any girl that talks to you interesting," Marty teased.

"Seriously, Marty, she's cool. She's smarter than people think. I never even heard of Van Halen until she told me about them."

Marty said, "That's bullshit. They've been playing their music on the radio for the last year."

"I know, but April told me about them before they were on the radio," Curtis replied.

"That's impossible. How could she know about someone before they're famous enough to know?"

"Marty, sometimes I think you like to argue just to hear yourself talk."

"Well, I think you like this weird chick and would say anything to get her to like you or make me think she is interesting or someone special."

They drank their beers as they drove through Pevely toward Herculaneum and Festus.

It was ten forty-five when Curtis turned the truck into the McDonald's parking lot.

They left a short time later and ate their food as they cruised down Main Street. Because it was a typical Friday, it took thirty minutes to go half a mile before turning around. It was an exercise in vanity, but it was what weekend cruising was all about. Unless you knew someone, you didn't speak to them. The guys traded a lot of verbal teasing while the girls endured harassment, which they mostly ignored. Generally, guys only paid attention to the other guys if they had a flashy vehicle or liked the music. Curtis and Marty felt ignored by everyone they passed, reinforcing the futility of driving around to nowhere.

"This is bullshit," Curtis said. "Let's get out of here." He turned off Main Street, got on the interstate, and drove north.

They got off at the Imperial Main Street exit and made a right-hand turn toward the state highway. At the light, Curtis asked Marty, "Which way do you want to go? Do you want to drive down to the auto auction to see if they're playing poker tonight?"

Marty sighed and shook his head no. "They cheat too much down there. I don't want to play cards with no chance of winning money, and I sure as hell don't want to lose the money I have."

"Seriously?" Curtis asked, wondering why friends would cheat friends in friendly games of poker.

Marty said, "That's what my brother tells me. He told me he lost a hundred dollars on a large pot. Afterward, he found out the dealer was passing cards."

"Yeah, that's not cool. That guy needs to get his ass kicked."

"Oh, he did," Marty assured him. "I was so pissed when Ricky told me, I nearly kicked his ass for not telling me about it sooner. Once I found out who it was, I went and beat the crap out of him and made him promise to pay my brother back. Just take me back to the Gradys' house to get my car. I'm riding down to Cape Girardeau tomorrow, looking at some cars. They might need me to drive one back. Do you have to work tomorrow?"

"Yeah, but I don't go in until five o' clock."

Curtis stopped the truck about a tenth of a mile from his house.

"What are you doing?" Marty asked.

"Screw the Arnold police," Curtis replied as he applied the brake and floored the accelerator before releasing the brakes. The driver-side truck wheel spun loose on the asphalt, the engine roared, and the tire squealed as white smoke billowed from under the wheel well. Curtis proceeded to leave a strip of black rubber about twenty-five yards long.

Marty released his grip on the dashboard when he felt safe and said, "I hope you have some money put away for new tires."

They returned to the Gradys' house, just up the street from where Curtis lived. Marty's car was just one of many parked in the large gravel driveway.

"I wonder what's going on here tonight."

Curtis parked the truck. He entered the basement door with Marty carrying two warm, unopened beers behind him. The radio was tuned to KSHE 95, one of the better FM rock radio stations in St. Louis. The Alan Parsons Project's "I Wouldn't Want to Be Like You" filled the air.

Steve Grady was home from Mizzou for the weekend and was shooting pool with Travis, one of the kids who lived up the street. Everyone referred to Steve by his nickname, Gunner. Brad, Gunner's younger brother, sat in a giant lounge chair nodding off. Marty exchanged the two beers for cold ones from a fridge by the door.

"Where the hell have you two losers been all night?" Gunner mocked after finishing his shot.

Marty jabbed his thumb in Curtis's direction and said, "Doing my best to keep this dumbass out of jail."

"What?" Travis's face brightened with surprise.

Brad, stirred by curiosity, opened his eyes.

Marty detailed the exploits of the evening, with Curtis offering commentary.

They hung out for about thirty minutes, just enough time to drink another beer and shoot a game of pool. In disgust, Marty dropped the pool cue onto the table after Travis sank the last ball into the corner pocket. He waved both middle fingers goodbye and left. Gunner turned the stereo off and said it was time for everyone to clear out because his dad would be home from work soon. Brad yawned and went upstairs without saying a word to anyone.

Curtis drove three hundred feet home with his headlights off and parked the truck as far away from his house as possible. He quietly opened the door to the house, removed his boots, and walked into the kitchen only to be met by the angry eyes of his mother, wrapped in a robe.

"Where have you been? Do you know what time it is? Have you been out drinking tonight?" she asked through gritted teeth, somehow yelling and whispering at the same time. "Please tell me you weren't out drinking and driving that truck. If you get arrested and go to jail, I will tell them to throw away the key."

Curtis was smart enough not to argue with his mom when she was like this. He mumbled some words, walked past her, heading to the bathroom, and closed the door, hoping she would return to bed.

Her bedroom door was closed when he came out, so he crossed the tiny hallway to his bedroom and crept in. His younger brother was fast asleep on the top bunk. He undressed, crawled into the bottom bunk, and turned on his reading lamp. He picked up the Piers Anthony book he had started earlier that week and read for about thirty minutes before turning the light out and falling asleep.

It felt like he had just fallen asleep when his mother woke him up.

"Curtis, I'm doing laundry this morning, and I need your sheets and pillowcase."

He mumbled something as she walked out of the room. She returned ten minutes later, yanked the blanket off him, and demanded that he get up so she could take the bedding to the basement to be washed. When she returned a third time, she had a large glass of cold water, which she poured on his head.

While he sat on the edge of the bed with a headache and upset stomach, she left with his wet bedding. He grabbed his blanket, laid his damp head on the bare, wet pillow, and fell asleep.

"Are you going to sleep all day?" his mom asked when she came back a few hours later.

"Mom, I have to work late tonight."

She set the laundry basket with clean bedding down on the floor.

"Well, before you leave for work, I want you to make both beds."

"Why do I have to make his bed?"

"Because he's not tall enough to make it himself," she answered. "And because I told you to. I'm going to Herrell's to get some lunch meat. I'll be back shortly."

When Curtis was sure his mom had left, he got up, went to the kitchen, grabbed one of his dad's Dr. Peppers, and drank it, hoping it would make his stomach feel better. He poured the remainder of the soda into a glass of ice and buried the can deep under the trash in the can in the foyer.

He went into the living room, turned on the television, and watched the end of an episode of *The Bowery Boys*. When his mom came home from Herrell's Market, he snapped the television off and helped carry in the groceries. Then he got dressed, made the two beds as asked, and brought the empty laundry basket downstairs to the wash area. His younger sister, Helen, was playing school with her friend Lynn. They ignored his intrusion into their classroom.

He went back upstairs and saw it was nearly three o'clock. He really did sleep his day away. He would have to leave for work in a little over an hour. He did not particularly like working in a restaurant, but it was Saturday. He would be busy, and the time would fly by.

"Would you like a sandwich before you go to work?" his mom asked.

"Sure, thanks," Curtis replied as he watched an installment of Charlie Chan already in progress.

A few minutes later, she brought him a bologna and cheese sandwich with chips and a glass of milk.

"Thank you, Mom."

"Thank you for making the beds like I asked," she replied.

Chapter 2

Riccardo & Lorenzo's Restaurante

There isn't a boy alive who, at some point in his life, didn't need to gain respect from his father. Curtis bore the heavy burden of being the eldest child in the family, but he also carried his father's names—all of them, as he was a junior.

His father was a passive man in many ways. Curtis Sr. worked late nearly every day of the week. It was not unusual for him to spend half his day driving to and from central Illinois to work on a piece of construction equipment. When he came home from work, he would go straight to the deep sink in the basement to clean up from a day spent in oil, grease, and grime.

The petroleum distillates and the propylene glycol of Joe's Hand Cleaner would fill the basement with a unique, sweet smell. He spent the better part of his first hour at home getting cleaned up. After his shower, he would put on a clean work uniform, go upstairs, and eat his warmed-up dinner alone.

Sometimes, JoAnn would sit with him. Her inquiries into her husband's day were met with a sad stare and few words. The kids seemed to intrinsically know that this was a special time for their parents and would disappear.

Curtis Sr. worked many hours. There were weeks when Curtis Jr. would only see his dad in passing. It is difficult to gain the respect and knowledge of a man who is a virtual stranger.

Curtis Sr. earned excellent wages as a union diesel mechanic. His hard work and personal sacrifice put a roof over their heads and food on the table. JoAnn made sure every birthday and Christmas was memorable.

As a card-carrying member of the International Union of Operating Engineers Local 513, he provided good benefits for his family. Every

Tuesday night, he would toss his paycheck on the kitchen counter. He never bothered to sign it. JoAnn took care of everything: shopping, cooking, cleaning, paying the bills.

Curtis Jr. was eight years older than his sister, Helen, and eleven years older than his brother, Garrett. For the longest time, Curtis felt like an only child. In many ways, he was. He got away with much more than a child should have gotten away with because his mom would rush him outside to play elsewhere.

Since Curtis Sr. was away at work most of the time, and JoAnn was busy raising two younger children, Curtis Jr. spent much of his younger years on his bike, looking for someone to hang out with. Most days, he only had to ride three hundred feet up the gravel road to the Grady house. Brad and Gunner were like brothers to him. Their exploits were many and would raise the hair on the back of the neck of any parent who knew a fraction of what they did.

For all his faults, when properly motivated, Curtis Jr. had a decent work ethic. Once he gained knowledge of the value of a dollar, he began looking for ways to earn money. He started hustling for cash at the age of twelve. His first job was passing out Bingo cards on Wednesday nights at the American Legion Hall about a half mile from his house. He would ride his bike up to the Legion Hall with Brad and hand out cards to elderly, chain-smoking Roman Catholic women.

At any given moment, but usually between games, a gray-haired woman would grab one of the boys by the arm and ask, "Young man, would you please find me a card with a two on one corner and a sixty-three on the other?"

It could be done, and the young boys were tipped generously for the sodas and cards they delivered. One time, Brad found a card for a woman, and she won a large jackpot the next round. After collecting her cash, she was so excited that she waved him over and gave him a ten-dollar bill. After Bingo, the boys would ride their bikes back to their homes with heavy pockets of loose change jingling around. The first time Curtis walked into the house, he got an earful from his mom because he had come home so late smelling like an ashtray. Instead of arguing, he dumped all the loose change from his pockets onto the kitchen counter.

She sorted and counted his earnings while he was taking a shower. She was impressed with how much he'd brought home, working only for tips.

She would swipe the loose change into ziplock bags, which she would take to the bank the following week when she deposited Curtis Sr.'s paycheck. She tried many times to convince Curtis Jr. to open a savings account to prepare for college. "You want to use your brain, not your back," she was fond of saying. Curtis Jr. would have none of it, so she relented and withdrew the cash.

In the summer, he could also find lawn mowing jobs and odd jobs like cleaning and hauling things away with his dad's Sears riding mower and trailer. When he was in junior high school, he would offer his services to write book reports and essays for lazier students who didn't like to read or write.

At four o'clock, he grabbed his wallet, truck keys, and jacket before attempting to sneak past his mom, who was standing at the kitchen sink with the water running.

"Are you leaving now?" she inquired without turning away from the sink as she washed vegetables. It was like she had eyes in the back of her head. She stopped what she was doing, turned the water off, and turned around. She looked her son over and gave him a kiss.

"Please drive carefully," she pleaded, as all mothers do when their teenagers have car keys in their hands. "And do not stay out too late after work. Also, please don't waste your money. You still need to get your truck inspected. Those license plates are due for renewal."

Curtis reached the foyer door when she said, "Hey, if you could, would you see if you can get another block of that Provel cheese for me?"

"Sure. I'll see you tomorrow, Mom." After getting in his truck, he drove up the gravel road. He saw all his friends hanging out as he passed the Grady residence. He honked his horn and waved. He did not see Marty's car there, so he wondered if he had made it back from Cape Girardeau. He felt regretful because he knew their Saturday night would be more exciting than his. Curtis had an agreement with his parents; for the privilege of driving the truck, he had to pay half the insurance premium. There was no way around it; he had to have a steady part-time job to pay for it. He found one at an Italian restaurant in South St. Louis County.

As Curtis drove down Lincoln Drive, he spotted his burn mark and laughed. He thought the asphalt would absorb most of the rubber, and the stain would disappear in a few weeks.

It was a quick quarter-mile ride to Montebello Road. He glanced to his left and, seeing no cars, drove straight through the stop sign. It was a habit every resident succumbed to, one that surprisingly caused no accidents. He passed the American Legion parking lot. It was the school bus pickup location and a perfect place to do donuts whenever it snowed. He looked forward to driving himself to school and no longer having to walk to the bus stop. The school only allowed juniors and seniors parking privileges. He turned north on the state highway and drove up to Arnold. He saw the other long burn mark as he drove by the arcade next to the 7-Eleven. It began midway in the southbound lanes and made a sharp swoosh as it turned into the northbound lane and extended a reasonable distance. He regretted doing that. The scare he'd received awakened him to be careful when cops might be around. And in Arnold, they were always around. And that went for double whenever he crossed the bridge into South County.

He drove to Richardson Road and turned left at the flashing yellow light. He saw the older couple tending to their spring garden as they had for as long as he could remember. He waved to the woman whitewashing her large produce stand. She smiled and waved back. Her husband worked the soil with a rotor tiller going in the opposite direction. The long rows of tilled earth indicated he had been at it all day.

Curtis soon made it to the interstate and used the on-ramp like a quarter-mile racetrack, mashing the accelerator and bringing the Ford engine to life with a roar. He merged onto the highway littered with other northbound vehicles and headed to the far-left lane. Curtis spotted the large green Arnold water tower in the distance and wondered why they hadn't stayed with the "golf ball on a tee" design incorporated on every other water tower in Jefferson County. He didn't give a second thought to the water tower as he zoomed by it.

He crossed the Meramec River, the physical boundary between St. Louis and Jefferson Counties. He was familiar with the Meramec and Mississippi Rivers, as both were a couple of miles from his home. Many hours were spent with his friends near the confluence, contemplating all manners of mischief on the Mississippi and carelessly flirting with death. As he crossed the interstate bridge, he looked to his right and saw another bridge less than a mile away, allowing traffic on the state highway to cross. He had crossed both bridges numerous times.

He arrived at work thirty minutes before his shift. He knew he could not go inside yet. The waiters and busboys would be having their briefing on specials, menu changes, and whatever else the dining room manager wanted to impose into their minds before a busy Saturday night. Curtis sneaked in early once and clocked in fifteen minutes too soon. When Steve, the kitchen manager, found out, he was livid. As policy and law prescribed, they had to pay overtime for anything more than eight hours. Curtis had plans and had wanted to get out early that Friday night, and Steve had no choice but to let him leave with verbal threats of termination "if you ever pull that stunt again."

He sat in the car until he saw the other guys pull up and get out. Curtis was the youngest of the entire group and the only one still in high school. The first guy to get out of his car was Tiny. He stood almost six feet tall and weighed nearly three hundred pounds. He had a round face with dark, squinty eyes and hands that always looked swollen. He had a short, dirty blonde ponytail sticking out the back of his ball cap. Nobody messed with Tiny.

Curtis fell into Tiny's good graces, and the much larger and older line cook shielded Curtis from abuse from the other workers. Curtis found it refreshing to be on the receiving end of kindness from someone older and sizable. Curtis had suffered a lot of bullying in school, particularly while in junior high. Young alpha males aimed to dominate anyone they considered passive or prepubescent. Whoever came up with the idea for community showers for teenage boys in public schools obviously did not take this into consideration.

Tiny would offer him insights to survive working in a restaurant, but more importantly, he taught him how to approach and handle people. He spent time explaining the hierarchy and the rules, both written and unwritten. Tiny was incredibly smart; no matter how hungover or stoned he was, nothing got by him when he came to work. He had a memory like a steel trap and would not take any grief from anyone.

Curtis strolled over and greeted him with a high five. "Tiny. What's going on?"

"Hey, Speedy. You know, same shit, different day."

Speedy…yes, that was Curtis's nickname at work. Most of the kitchen workers had nicknames. In the six months Curtis had worked there, he never inquired about his coworkers' real names. It was a rite of passage to be given a nickname. Dishwashers usually didn't get nicknames because they rarely lasted more than a few weeks. Many never made it through their first night. It was a physically challenging, thankless, and often painful job.

When Curtis started, he was told he would be eligible for a promotion and a raise to work on the line if he stayed with it for six months. Curtis demonstrated he was reliable because he never called in on a Friday or Saturday night, which was extremely uncommon for a teenager still in high school. When one of the regular evening cooks transitioned to the day shift, Curtis was immediately promoted to the kitchen to toss salads and help with evening prep work. The work was a lot more interesting than washing dishes and scrubbing pots.

Curtis and Tiny were talking when "Mouse," the pizza cook, pulled up. Curtis never figured out if he got his name because he was so quiet or because he nibbled on cheese all night. Mouse got out of his car and nodded at the other two but stayed over by his car alone. Tiny pulled a small roach out of his pocket and lit it up. Curtis watched the end cherry up as Tiny deeply inhaled the illegal smoke.

"Do you want some?" Tiny offered, struggling to talk while still holding his breath.

"No, man, I have to work tonight."

Tiny busted out laughing and started coughing as the sweet smell of the smoke exited his lungs. "You fuckin' crack me up, Speedy."

Five minutes later, two more cars pulled up. Two guys got out of an old Dodge Dart, and another young man got out of his little brown Ford Pinto. Sidney and Laurence shared an apartment and rode to work together. Laurence made the mistake of telling people his real name when he started.

"My name is Laurence, but everybody calls me Larry, and I prefer to be called Larry." That's all it took for Larry never to be called by his shortened name. The more he fought it, the more entertaining it was. He eventually relented and accepted that he was Laurence at work.

The young man who got out of the Pinto was Nate. He was tall and fierce-looking with reddish-blonde hair. Nate was the pasta chef for the night. He was the younger brother of Leo, the other pasta chef. One brother covered Friday nights, and the other brother worked Saturday nights. They had the most demanding job in the kitchen. A tremendous amount of responsibility was placed on them to quarterback the onslaught of orders and coordinate them with the assistance of an assortment of misfits who wanted to be anywhere but where they were. The pasta chefs and managers were the only workers in the kitchen who made real money. The rest had to supplement their income in other ways, some of which were illegal.

They saw an old, rusted-out Chevrolet pickup pull up and park in the front row at five minutes to five.

"Aw, fuck, here we go…" Tiny muttered as he pinched off the hot part of his joint and put the roach in his pocket.

The small group started to migrate toward the restaurant's front door. The kitchen manager, Steve, waited for them so he could walk in with them. "How's everybody doing tonight?"

"Just peachy," Tiny replied.

Steve pulled Nate away and had a private conversation with him as everyone else clocked in.

The number of quality, affordable meals that went out of that kitchen on a Saturday night was astonishing. Nate was amazing to watch. It was not uncommon for him to have eight pots of pasta dishes cooking simultaneously. All it would take was one small error—the toss-in of a wrong ingredient, adding an ingredient too early, or plating the pasta too early—to lead to a dish being returned to the kitchen and an unhappy customer. Only when Nate got overwhelmed did things spiral out of control. It only happened a few times, and it never was his fault. One time, for example, a waitress returned with a change request for an order she had just placed but said it incorrectly. Nate already had two pots going for her, then four, and the order was still wrong. As a result of spending all the time trying to clear the matter up, other orders kept piling up, and he exploded on the waitress. Steve came back to the kitchen and sent Nate to the bar for a while to calm down. Denny, the floor manager, had to intervene and console the crying waitress before she could return to her tables. Steve stepped in and assumed control over the kitchen to get the kitchen caught up.

Saturday night was underway, and everyone's mood, even Nate's, was lighthearted. Mouse was quietly making pizzas, and Sid was singing and talking to himself, making salads to order. Tiny and Laurence debated whether Ronnie James Dio would be a better frontman for Black Sabbath than Ozzy. Curtis was happy after being tasked with making fifty gallons of marinara sauce in the large steam kettle in the back of the kitchen. He loved that job because he enjoyed working in solitude.

Curtis was in the middle of opening one of several cases of #10 cans of tomato sauce when Sid came over to him and asked, "Hey, Speedy, would you mind cutting a cheesecake for me so I don't have to stop and clean up?" He waved his hands back and forth, showing that they were coated front and back with oil, parmesan cheese, and bright red specks of pimento.

"Sure, Sid, no problemo," Curtis responded.

Curtis crossed the kitchen to the freezer, where boxes of whole cheesecakes were stacked. He grabbed a box and the cutting template and went back to the kitchen.

"Hey, Tiny, can I borrow one of your large chef's knives?"

"Say please.

"Say pretty please…

"Pretty please with sugar on top your highness and keeper of the never dull blade?" Tiny enjoyed making trivial and banal things fun.

"Just remember where you got it and bring it back clean," Tiny directed.

Curtis moved a case of cans on his workstation to set the box down and carefully removed the cake. He set the template down on the cake and began to press it into the softening cake that was quickly thawing in the warm kitchen. He was interrupted by a familiar voice.

"Whoa there, dude," Tiny called. "What the hell are you doing?"

"I'm about to cut a cheesecake for Sid."

"Get out of the way, amateur. Let me show you how a professional does it."

He took the chef's knife back from Curtis and tossed the template aside. Tiny free cut the cake into eight pieces, one noticeably smaller than the others. "See, if we did it your way, there would be eight perfect pieces of cheesecake. This piece is way too small to sell to a customer and must be disposed of immediately." With that, he took a bite of the cheesecake and walked into the cooler. He shut the door behind him to prevent anyone from seeing him finish it off.

He came out of the cooler and handed Curtis the knife. "Go wash this thing off and bring it back to me."

After Curtis cleaned and returned the knife, he opened the smaller cooler door and counted seven small, chilled plates. He carefully plated the remaining cheesecakes, wrapped them with clear wrap, and placed them in the walk-in cooler.

"Your cheesecake is cut, Sid."

"Muchos gracias, señor," Sid responded with a massive grin.

Curtis had just opened the last case of #10 cans of tomato sauce when Nate returned to grab a few trays of pasta to restock his drawers. "Speedy? What the fuck? You haven't got this sauce cooking yet?" He disappeared into the large walk-in cooler and came out carrying trays of covered pasta. "We might need to change your name."

Curtis was about to defend himself when Tiny came around the corner and almost collided with Nate. "Chill, dude. He's helping with other things you know nothing about."

"Well, I do need to know. If you were in charge, you would want to know we're almost out of marinara sauce," Nate yelled back as he carefully maneuvered around the big guy and rushed back to his station with his trays in hand.

Tiny followed him back to his station, barking, "Well, go yell at the day crew because they're the people that are fucking you, not Speedy. Besides, if you need to know, I'd never be in charge of this hellhole."

Curtis went back to his task, filling the pot and stirring all the ingredients to make the much-needed sauce. The steam kettle did not take long to bring the large volume of sauce to a nice, steamy simmer. The smell was delicious.

Special orders were always a pain, but the restaurant owners catered as best they could to their patrons.

Tony, one of the younger waiters, came back to the kitchen.

"Hey, I have a guy wanting me to add some pepperoni on top of his cheese garlic bread. Is this something we can do for him?"

Nate replied, "Yeah, we can do that, but it's going to be two dollars more." The waiter disappeared momentarily and then returned with the special order.

Laurence was the line cook who handled the items going into and out of the baking oven. If an order called for a baked pasta dish, Nate would prepare it, and Laurence would take his tongs and place the steel dishes in the oven. Both his arms were marred with burns and blisters in various stages of healing.

Every time he yelped, Tiny would add insult to his injury by saying, "Careful, that's hot," or "Hey, Laurence, don't fucking touch the oven, it's hot." Even when he wore the large oven mitts, he still managed to burn his arm. Laurence hated the insulated gloves; they were cumbersome, and he couldn't handle the tongs while wearing them. He hated being cussed out by Nate or Leo when he dropped a dish of lasagna or baked rigatoni. So, he suffered his burns along with Tiny's taunts.

Laurence reached into his drawer and grabbed a loaf of bread, cut it into the appropriate-sized pieces, slathered it with melted garlic butter, then sprinkled it with a generous portion of grated Provel cheese.

"Hey, Mouse, can you bring me some pepperonis?" he yelled over the counter in the direction of the pizza oven. Mouse walked over with a large handful of pepperonis, much more than Laurence needed. Out of habit, he tried to take a piece of pepperoni out of his closed hand, but a couple of them stuck together, and one fell onto the floor unnoticed. He set the rest of the pepperoni down on Laurence's workstation, and when his back was turned to Nate, he stuffed the few pieces of pepperoni into his mouth.

Curtis had just finished breaking down the boxes, disposed of all the cans into a couple of large trash bags, and set them beside the door. Steve returned to the kitchen and yelled, "Everyone, stop what you're doing right now. I need every station wiped down and the line floor swept and mopped."

At just past seven, the evening rush was in full swing. All the workers stopped what they were doing to brush down their workstations, the debris falling to the floor. Curtis, a heavy-duty commercial whisk broom in hand, quickly swept under the workstations, moving from the front of the kitchen to the back. Steve directed two dishwashers to fill the mop bucket with hot water, with instructions for one to wet mop and the other to follow with a dry mop. When the first dishwasher tried to push the mop bucket, it almost tipped over when it transitioned from the elevated portion of the large black floor mat at the dishwashing station to the red brick tile of the kitchen floor. Nate lost his patience with the young kid, grabbing the wet mop from him.

"Watch how I do this." Nate swiftly and expertly swabbed the entire length of the kitchen as most of the other cooks scurried out of the way.

Tiny stayed put and observed with critical eyes. When Nate finished mopping, Tiny backed away before yelling, "Hey, Nate, you missed a spot."

Nate ignored Tiny and looked at the other dishwasher.

"What's your name? Marcus?"

The kid nodded.

"Did you see what I did there, Marcus?"

When the kid nodded yes, he said, "Now do the same thing with the dry mop."

The young man did as Nate instructed. When Steve was satisfied, the kitchen went back to cooking.

The waiters continued to place orders, and the food left the kitchen at a remarkable pace. "We still have a twenty-minute wait," one of the waitresses informed the kitchen.

A few minutes after Steve left, Lorenzo came back into the kitchen. Lorenzo was one of the owners of the establishment and the face of the company. He was a short middle-aged balding man. To say that Lorenzo was trying to compensate would be a gross understatement. He always wore an open, button-up silk shirt that revealed gold chains around his neck and nestled in his chest hair. The shirt was bloused into his flat-front, medium-rise trousers with belt loops, side pockets, and plain-hemmed trousers. He had one of those classic coke-dusted '70s mustaches and wore expensive Italian leather topsiders. If you got close enough to talk to him, you could close your eyes and imagine you were in an Aramis factory. He drove a brand-new white Porsche 911 Turbo. If you didn't know he was a successful restauranteur, you might think he was a successful porn star.

On this night, he came back into his kitchen to show it off to his girl-friend. She, of course, was tall and stunning, but everyone was smart enough not to stare at her for too long. He asked Nate to step aside for a minute and personally made his date shrimp scampi with linguini while she watched. He asked Tiny to prepare him two medium-rare steaks. When their food was ready, they took their plates to the bar to eat their meal.

About an hour later, Lorenzo came back to get a cannoli. "Are these fresh?" he questioned Sid.

"I didn't make any tonight, so I'm pretty sure the day crew made them. We have fresh cheesecake though," he offered.

"I don't want cheesecake, Sid, I want cannoli, and I just…" He stopped midsentence when his eyes found something on the floor that required his full attention.

"Sid? What the fuck is this on the floor here?"

Sid peered down at the floor but couldn't see anything.

"I don't see anything, sir."

"You've got to be kidding me. Seriously, you do not see this?" Lorenzo was pointing at the floor with a violent stabbing motion of his index finger. "You don't see a quarter of my goddamn money on the ground?"

By then, Tiny and Curtis had walked over to inspect the floor, and they couldn't see anything either. Fearful that his employer was having a coke-fueled hallucination, Curtis backed away slowly. Lorenzo, mean-while, was growing redder in the face, angrier with each passing moment. "Nate, get your ass down here now and tell me what this is all about," he commanded.

Nate got down on his hands and knees, bent his face as close to the floor as he could, and carefully peeled up a flattened piece of pepperoni perfectly camouflaged into the red brick tile. Lorenzo was livid, ripping into the kitchen staff. Waiters who wandered in immediately walked right back out during the tirade.

"This is why I don't give you guys raises. You don't care about my food or my money." He went on for several minutes until the fire of his rage dissipated. Once thoroughly quenched, he grabbed his cannoli and left. The workers all relaxed, taking deep breaths when he left the kitchen, and returned to their workstations to catch up on their orders.

It was right around ten o'clock when the word reached the kitchen that there was no longer a waiting line. Steve sent Mouse home and told Tiny to handle any incoming pizza orders. The announcement was what everyone was waiting to hear. Everyone knew all that was left was their prep work and reasonable cleaning effort while keeping up with the dwindling orders before they could all go home. It also allowed them time to grab a bite to eat.

The rule, as explained to Curtis when he started, was that employees could get a free meal when working a complete eight-hour shift. Employees who worked less than eight hours only got an appetizer. It was also specifically stated that a free dinner was a pasta dish or a small pizza but not steak, shrimp, or chicken Parmesan.

"Hey, Nate, would you make me an order of carbonara, please?" Curtis asked.

"Sure, if you take all these pots over to the dishwashing station and restock my pasta drawers while I make it." Curtis thought it was a fair exchange and agreed.

While everyone enjoyed their pasta as they cleaned and prepared for the next day, Tiny had his own dinner routine. Since he primarily worked the grill and deep fryer, he patiently waited for a waiter or waitress to order a rare steak. He would then grill it medium rare and send it out. If it came back, he would blame the waiter for letting it sit in the window too long: "It was perfect coming off my grill. You let it sit too long and cook in its own juices." Then, he would set it aside and make another one while the server waited. When he got hungry, he grabbed a piece of bread from Laurence's drawers, cut it down the middle, made himself a steak sandwich, and went inside the walk-in cooler to eat it while Nate was preoccupied with all his orders.

Curtis finished eating his pasta then emptied the steam kettle into ten white but red-stained five-gallon buckets. He wrote "Marinara" and the date, "SAT, 4/21/79," on the lids with a grease pencil before securing them onto the buckets. Then he carried two buckets at a time into the walk-in cooler and placed them on the lower shelves. He diligently organized and rotated buckets by content, with the oldest date moved to the front. As he scanned the walk-in cooler to ensure everything was in order, he spotted dozens of boxes of Provel cheese carefully stacked on top of the far-end shelves. He felt the rush of adrenaline countered by a sense of dread and anxiety. He pushed the cheese out of his mind for the moment. When satisfied with his efforts inside the cooler, Curtis returned to the prep room to clean the steam kettle until the stainless steel shined inside and out.

"That looks good, Speedy." Nate offered a rare compliment, and Curtis beamed with pride and was thankful that his effort was noticed.

He added, "Would you help Sid with his prep work so we can get out of here in an hour?"

The last hour was the fastest of the night. So much needed to be cleaned, mopped, scrubbed, and put away. The focus was cleaning, but preparing food for the next day was also necessary. Curtis was glad it was Saturday night because prepping for Sunday was a lot easier than preparing for Saturday on a Friday night.

"What can I help you with, Sid?" Curtis asked.

Sid was at the table, slicing a hundred pounds of onions he had already peeled. The tears and puffy red cheeks were real, and just walking into the corner by the large slicer was enough to make Curtis's eyes water.

Fortunately, Steve walked through the kitchen and opened the back door. The fresh air brought some relief to Curtis's eyes. Steve smoked a cigarette as he stood guard watching the busboys and dishwashers carry dozens of trash bags that had accumulated throughout the evening. Management had to carefully monitor the back door and the trash leaving the kitchen. It was not unheard of for someone to try to sneak food out the back door and pick it up later. A dishwasher once tried to sneak a bag of steaks out and not only lost his job but also got a ride in the back of a St. Louis County police cruiser and a weekend stay in the county jail. Curtis shuddered to think what Lorenzo would do to someone he caught taking more than a piece of pepperoni from him. Then he thought again about his promise to his mom concerning the block of Provel cheese, weighing the pros and cons of what he should do.

While Sid finished slicing and putting away all the sliced onions, Curtis and Tiny peeled five pounds of garlic. They bitched and complained to each other the entire time. Misery does love company.

It was five minutes to midnight when Denny locked the front doors to the restaurant. The few remaining guests would not be rushed to leave. While the restaurant closed at midnight, the bar remained open for another hour. The last remaining dishwasher pushed one more load of dishes into the cleaning machine, pushed the button, and called it a night. Nate inspected all the equipment, floors, and stock levels of all the drawers before giving Steve the thumbs-up that released the kitchen crew.

Curtis sat in the back, talking to Tiny and Sid, clutching his jacket and watching the clock. As soon as Tiny and Sid heard it was time to go, they headed to the time stamp machine to clock out. Curtis rapidly entered the cooler, reached in one of the boxes of Provel cheese stacked on the top shelf, and—rationalizing they would never miss one—rolled a block up inside the sleeve of his jacket, folded the jacket just so, and tucked it under his arm. He held it to his side, firm enough that he would not drop it but not so laborious as to indicate he feared dropping it. Curtis then clocked out and headed straight for the front door. He knew nothing would look out of the ordinary, for even in the dead of winter, nobody in the kitchen wore a coat when leaving. Getting out of the hot kitchen and into the cool evening air always felt great.

Nate and Tiny were sitting at the bar; they were the only workers from the kitchen old enough to drink legally. The bartender, Rich, was busy wiping down the bar, stocking shelves, and cleaning glassware. A few people sat around the bar at the small tables, eating appetizers, drinking, and talking quietly.

When Curtis passed Lorenzo, he gazed into Curtis's eyes and said, "Thank you for all you did tonight, Curtis. I really appreciate it. Enjoy your weekend. Drive safe going home."

"Thank you, sir. You have a good weekend too." Curtis noticed the attractive blonde was no longer there and, strangely enough, felt bad for the guy.

He traversed the mostly empty parking lot, brightly lit by numerous lampposts, and got in his truck. He breathed a sigh of relief as he dropped the jacket onto the large red bench seat. He put the key in the ignition, started the truck, and sat there for a few minutes.

The quiet bothered him. All he could think about was the cheese sitting next to him, the trust Lorenzo had in his workers, and the decision he had made. A part of him wanted to go back in and confess, with a promise never to do it again. However, another part of him wanted the twenty dollars his mom would give him, and he knew his mom liked the cheese.

To quiet the stinging of his conscience, he turned on the radio and immediately recognized the song. He turned the volume way up to hear Tarney/Spencer Band's "No Time to Lose."

Curtis struggled to sing along, so he raised the volume to drown out his screaming conscience. He drove through several flashing yellow lights with a devil-may-care attitude, found the highway entrance inviting, and accelerated past the posted speed limits. The hard-rocking drive back to Jefferson County was an enjoyable one. He looked forward to showering, going to bed, and reading until his mind was as tired as his body.

Chapter 3

Day Shift

Curtis woke up late Sunday morning to the sound of the Statler Brothers, not quite able to drown out the hum of a vacuum cleaner. The windows were open, and a cool breeze filled the home with a slight chill and the pleasant aromas of spring. He lay in bed with a rumble in his belly that told him it was time to get up and eat breakfast.

He walked in a daze into the living room with sleep still in his eyes. His mom turned the vacuum off, making the Statler Brothers song deafening. She walked over and turned the volume down.

His mom said, "Good morning. How was work last night?"

"It was okay… I got your cheese; it's in the refrigerator."

"I saw. Thank you. I put the money on the counter. Don't forget to take it with you on Tuesday. There's some leftover bacon on the counter. Would you like for me to scramble you some eggs?"

"No, thanks. I'll just make some toast."

She turned the vacuum back on then reached over to turn the volume up on the stereo. The Statler Brothers song "I'll Go to My Grave Loving You" resounded through the modest traditional house with more hardwood than carpet and more plaster than wood paneling.

Curtis finished his breakfast and went into the bedroom to get dressed. His mom followed him with the vacuum and a dust rag.

"Before you go anywhere, you need to make the beds, dust, and vacuum for me."

Curtis knew better than to complain and did his chores without much enthusiasm.

Meanwhile, singing along with the Statler Brothers, JoAnn went to the kitchen and cleaned up. It amazed her just how big a mess a boy could create by making a peanut butter and jelly sandwich on toasted bread.

After the tasks his mom gave him were complete, Curtis hiked up to the Gradys'. Marty and Travis were playing pool. Brad was upstairs watching television, and Gunner was gathering his things to take back to Columbia.

When Curtis entered, he opened the fridge and grabbed a beer.

"It's a bit early for that, don't you think?" Marty asked as he lined up his shot.

Curtis popped the top and replied, "Nope."

Gunner came downstairs with two bags he had packed.

Curtis asked, "What time you heading back?"

"In a couple of hours," he replied, walking out the door. Gunner put his bags inside his Impala. He grabbed a beer and turned on the stereo when he came back in.

The four guys played a few games of pool while talking and listening to KSHE. During one of the commercial breaks, the DJ announced: "There are still plenty of good seats remaining for the Van Halen concert this Saturday night at the Checkerdome. Tickets are available at Peaches..."

Curtis asked the group, "Hey, guys, what are you doing this Saturday night?"

Gunner was the first to speak up, "I can't go. I won't come back home until after finals."

"How are you going to go to the concert? Don't you have to work Saturday nights?" Marty asked.

Not to be dissuaded, Curtis answered, "Where there's a will, there's a way."

Travis bailed on the proposition. "I can't. I don't have any money."

"Dude, you need to get a job," Marty yelled.

Travis shouted back as he cleared the table, "Fuck you! I'm gonna work for my dad this summer, ya prick."

Marty held his pool cue up in the air like a baseball bat. "I'm about to smack a knot on your head."

Curtis backed away so he wouldn't get hit by the wavering pool stick.

"Marty? Do you want to go or not?"

"Yeah, sure, I'll go. Rack them up one more time, then I got to get the hell out of here before I whup this kid's ass." He laughed at Travis.

After a long commercial break, the DJ came back on air and said, "And now, here's 'The Logical Song,' new music by Supertramp, and you are hearing it first on KSHE 95 FM."

Monday morning, Curtis picked up two ten-dollar bills lying on the counter and put them in his wallet. Combined with the cash he had from his last paycheck, he had just over sixty dollars. He headed for the bus stop.

Marty and Curtis skipped lunch and walked to Marty's house for the last half of the day. Marty drove them to South St. Louis to buy their concert tickets. People from Jefferson County rarely bothered to drive up to South County, much less go into the City of St. Louis. While jobs were the primary reason people left the county, there were other reasons to go into the city: sporting events, an afternoon day cruise on the *Admiral*, a visit to the zoo, or purchasing tickets for a Van Halen show.

Curtis and Marty drove to Peaches, a popular record store in South City. They perused the aisles, and Curtis picked up a cassette of the new Supertramp album, *Breakfast in America*. Marty asked where they could buy the tickets, and a store employee pointed to the customer service counter reserved for returns and exchanges. The tickets were only $8.50 each, but the ticket fees raised the price to ten dollars. The cassette tape was six dollars plus tax. Marty handed Curtis a ten-dollar bill, and Curtis paid the clerk thirty dollars. He dropped the change and receipt into the bag with his new cassette. He handed Marty a ticket and put the other ticket in his wallet.

Marty drove Curtis back to school. Curtis had time to go to study hall and complete some homework before catching the bus.

When Curtis got home, he cut the grass. His parents had five acres of heavily wooded property with a huge yard. Even though the Sears tractor could cut strips of grass nearly four feet across, it still took several hours to mow.

While he finished trimming, his mom grilled hamburgers on the charcoal barbecue pit. Then she went inside and hand-cut potatoes for homemade French fries. She cleaned and cut lettuce and tomatoes for the burgers, salads, and then cut up a cantaloupe.

After JoAnn fed her family, she sat down to eat her supper. Curtis excused himself, grabbed his plate, and headed for the kitchen.

"Please leave those French fries for your father…"

Curtis placed the dirty dishes into the sink.

"I'm going up to the Gradys' for a while."

"Is all your homework done?"

"Yes…well, most of it anyway."

"Be home by seven, please. I meant to ask you if you got the truck inspected. Your plates are due at the end of the month."

"I'll take care of it," he promised.

Curtis had to go to work after school on Tuesday. He left for work early enough to have time to stop at B. Dalton. He browsed the fantasy section and found a book by Stephen R. Donaldson titled *Lord Foul's Bane*. The title and cover art intrigued him enough to buy it.

He drove to Riccardo & Lorenzo's but only had enough time to read the story summary and glance through the Tolkien-like map before Steve arrived. Curtis jumped out of his truck and intercepted Steve before he reached the front door.

"Hey, Steve."

"What's up, Curtis?"

"Listen, I have a ticket for Van Halen this coming Saturday night."

"Van who? What the hell is a Van Halen?"

"They're a rock band from Los Angeles I really like. I was able to get good seats for the show yesterday."

"Are you going on a date?" Steve inquired.

Curtis answered, "No, I'm just going with a friend."

"You really need to check with me before you do something like this once you're on the schedule."

After an awkward silence, Steve relented, "Let me see what I can do for you, okay? You're a good worker. I don't want to bust your balls on this, but I can't promise anything yet."

It was close enough to four o'clock for them to go inside.

Tuesday was "all you can eat" pasta night at Riccardo & Lorenzo's. The promotion would bring families from all over, filling the restaurant for several hours to eat massive amounts of spaghetti and Alfredo. Countless loaves of Italian bread were sliced, slathered with garlic butter, and baked with Provel cheese.

St. Louis was the home of Provel cheese. Most residents within a 200-mile radius of the City of St. Louis preferred it over traditional mozzarella. Provel combines Swiss, cheddar, and provolone cheeses, which is processed into a butter-like mixture. The cheese firms up into a semi hardened state before being wrapped and shipped as loaves. At Riccardo & Lorenzo's, Provel was shredded into gooey ropes and was a key ingredient on their pizza, garlic bread, and baked pasta dishes. Restaurants all over the metro area bought and sold tons of it every year. And occasionally, a few boxes fell off the back of the truck.

Tuesday night was the one night both Leo and Nate worked together. The sheer volume of pasta served required two pasta cooks. As Curtis got ready for work, he was approached by Leo, the older and, some would say, meaner of the two brothers.

"Bad news, Curtis. We're short a dishwasher tonight, so you're back on dishes and pots tonight." The grin on his face indicated that he was delighted with the bad news.

Tiny piped up, "Show 'em how it's done, Speedy."

Curtis looked at the bright side: he wouldn't have to cut and prepare trays of garlic bread and run pasta pans all night long.

Curtis walked back to the dishwashing station. Since he was senior to the other two guys, he sprayed and made the other two guys run and scrub. One dishwasher would run clean dishes out to the bus area and return pots and cooking utensils to the kitchen; the last dishwasher, usually the newest one, scrubbed pots in the deep sink.

Curtis didn't mind washing dishes. It didn't require much thinking. He just had to be mindful of the placement of his hands while he worked. The large single-handled flow nozzle could release over four gallons of near-boiling water per minute. It took little effort to spray off plates, dishes, and flatware. The only work was stacking them in one of the carriers. Dozens of them were stacked and littered all over the floor. The busboys would push full tubs of dirty dishes onto the heavy-duty chrome wire shelves, and the dishwashers cleaned them and returned them to service.

The cycle would continue until the manager locked the doors and the last customer left.

The pots were the worst. The sauces would sometimes bake and adhere to the steel pots, seemingly at the molecular level. Water pressure alone would not undo the enigmatic chemistry; neither would the enchantments of the colorful obscenities that streamed from the dish-washers' mouths.

The pots and pans needed elbow grease—and lots of it. Soap and high-pressure hot water would only do so much. Only a robust effort with scouring pads and tough hands attached to powerful arms could produce an acceptable result.

Anything returned to the cooking line not appropriately cleaned and unsuitable for use was sent back to the dishwashers with great force and a verbal assault. These outbursts occasionally resulted in an angry dish-washer storming out of the restaurant to seek other means of employment.

The most crucial thing Curtis learned from his restaurant experiences was that he knew he definitely didn't want to work in a restaurant all his life.

Steve came to the back after the dinner rush to tell Curtis he had worked it out. He said Curtis could have Saturday night off, but he had to come in and work the day shift instead. Curtis realized it was the best he could hope for and thanked Steve for getting him the night off.

The week went by fast. Fortunately, all Curtis had to focus on was school until Friday. He worked Friday night, and Mouse agreed to stay late so Curtis could leave early. Curtis went home, showered, and spent the evening reading the rest of his Piers Anthony book before falling asleep.

On Saturday morning, his mom woke him up at seven and made him waffles and sausage links for breakfast. He left for work and arrived at the same time as the day crew.

Curtis looked forward to working with them. He had seen them as the shifts overlapped, but no pleasantries were usually exchanged. Curtis assumed it was because one group was happy to leave with an evening to look forward to, while the other group seemed envious because their shift was just starting.

The daytime pasta cook was Frank, a well-groomed young man who would have gone largely unnoticed in a university classroom. Curtis thought he looked like Peter Frampton with his loose-fitting sky-blue dress shirt and long, dirty blonde hair.

Frank crammed his curly locks into a hairnet before putting on an apron, then strode around the kitchen, making sure everyone else had theirs on. He was the only pasta cook with a nickname; everyone called him Frenchie.

Frenchie aspired to be a chef and hoped to save enough money to attend culinary school. Two other cooks handled the rest of the kitchen for the lunch crowd.

Zero worked the pizza oven and handled desserts and salads. Zero was a tall, lazy-looking fellow with disheveled hair and sleepy eyes. Everything was drudgery to him. He dragged his feet when he walked and mumbled when he talked. The nickname fit him perfectly.

Gonzo worked the oven, grill, and deep fryer. He was a short college-aged student with dark, wavy hair. He also had a scraggly Fu Manchu mustache nearly down to his chin. Gonzo grimaced when he found out Curtis had tickets to see Van Halen. He tried to convince Curtis that King Crimson and Frank Zappa were far more interesting to listen to than any club band from Los Angeles.

Curtis spent most of the day preparing food for the Saturday night crowd. First, he had to put away the large grocery delivery that filled the back storage room. Then he made fifty gallons of meat sauce in the steam kettle and handed Gonzo cooking sheets filled with baking potatoes throughout the afternoon. Curtis also prepared desserts before he left for the day. Using the template, he cut up a few cheesecakes and stuffed enough cannoli to fill a couple of trays.

When the day crew clocked out, Curtis left with them. He passed Tiny.

"Oh, I'm so envious. Have a good time at the show tonight. It should be killer."

Curtis laughed, happy to be getting out of there. He just had to go home, get cleaned up before picking Marty up, and drive back downtown for the concert.

CHAPTER 4

Van Halen

Curtis made a beeline for his truck. The plan was working perfectly. It occurred to him that he enjoyed working the day shift. There were fewer uptight workers, and the lower customer volume made the job less stressful. There was no yelling; even a radio could be played if it wasn't heard in the dining area. It was strange not to see a manager come back into the kitchen throughout the shift. Curtis fit right in because he did what was asked and did it quietly. As a result of his hard work the past two days, he could enjoy the sweet fruit of his labor. He climbed into his truck, fired up the engine, and took a deep breath. He sat there for a minute deciding what Van Halen album he would listen to.

It was barely a year ago when Curtis had been daydreaming in English class, staring at a girl sitting across from him engaged in an artful endeavor. Her name was April. She was a comely girl with long, slick-backed hair and dark eyes. She was quiet and kept to herself. She never talked to boys at school. Thinking about it, Curtis realized she didn't really speak to the girls either. Or teachers, for that matter. It was her clothes that stood out. She never wore dresses or skirts; instead, she wore faded bell-bottom jeans with T-shirts and black boots. Her boots reminded him of black-and-white photos of days gone by.

As he intently gazed at her work on a notebook page turned sideways, she drew a large, slanted V on the paper. It was so big it took up half the sheet of paper. From the V, she added three horizontal lines extending from the top left side. Then she carefully drew an equally large H, slanted the other direction, as if the two letters met in a mirror. She slowly drew three horizontal lines from the H. Then she began shading with her pencil, using lead, an eraser, and a wet finger to complete her artwork before the class ended. When the bell rang, she started gathering her things, and Curtis couldn't help but ask her about her work. April smiled at him, tore the sheet of paper from her notebook, and handed it to him. "This is the greatest band in the world, ever."

Only a month before April handed that drawing to Curtis, Van Halen, a relatively unknown band from Los Angeles, released their self-titled debut album. April had got in on the ground floor and quietly enjoyed what many were missing. And of all the people she didn't talk to, the day she opened up to someone, it was Curtis. Two months later, nearly half of the songs on that album were in regular rotation on local FM rock radio stations. The young guitar player, whose last name was Van Halen, captured the awe and inspired his generation with a sub-two-minute guitar solo called "Eruption" that faded into a blistering cover of The Kinks' "You Really Got Me."

Coming out of his reverie, Curtis went back to contemplating his choices of album: the tried-and-true debut album he had heard at least a hundred times or the recently released second album. He chose the latter.

Van Halen's sophomore offering contained some of the hardest-hitting music Curtis had ever experienced. His other favorite bands, like Rush and Styx, were fascinating to listen to and think about; Van Halen did not appeal to the mind as much as it did the gut. It hit hard and was relentless with its sonic assaults. If there was an appeal to the mind, it was not about thinking but about experiencing life. It was a simultaneous release of a teenager's primal "4 Fs" for survival.

As Curtis pulled out and headed to the interstate to go home, he thought about April's picture. He had carefully folded it in half four times so it fit comfortably in his pants pocket. To his horror, he forgot about it when he got home. When his mom washed his jeans, the paper melded into a solid piece after it hardened in the dryer.

He pushed the cassette into the player and listened to the end of "Bottoms Up!" The song faded out to make room for an all-out sonic beating as the unworldly sounds of "Outta Love Again" invaded his truck. The eccentric sweeping, noisy guitar suggested shrieking birds being stung by angry bees as the controlled feedback gave way to a single hard-hitting snare drum pop that prompted a rapid firing of a repeating bass line as if the drummer was counting down with a high-hat tap, like falling dominoes—five, four, three, two, one—and go!

It was so easy to become focused on the guitar because Eddie Van Halen had come along and established himself as the most innovative American guitar player since Jimi Hendrix. It was equally rewarding to listen to the controlled drumming of his brother, Alex. His performance on this song was a clinic on syncopation as he moved in and around his kit with some uncanny and crazy fills that the late Keith Moon would have envied.

Yet for all the displayed genius of the brothers Van Halen, the wild card of the bunch was the unconventional frontman and singer David Lee Roth. There was no denying his essential and unique role as their spokesman to fans and critics alike. Arguably, he was more entertainer than vocalist, but he could carry a tune and improvise as if his career depended on it. His trademark wails, whelps, and shrieks are peppered throughout their songs. It was a matter of attitude over ability. Say what you will, but the girls wanted him, and guys envied him for it. Eddie and Alex were larger than life with their musical abilities, but Dave did everything he could to match them with his effort and dedication to hard work.

Then there was Michael Anthony, the hidden hero of the group. His playing was firm enough to build a world-class band on—the rhythm he laid down with Alex was rock solid. Like the instrument itself, the bass player is so much a part of rock and roll and so integrated into the music that nobody even notices it's there. There is no denying the Van Halen sound would not be complete without his tenor background vocals.

Lyrically, "Outta Love Again" resonated with Curtis. David Lee Roth's "piss and vinegar/take no prisoners" style bled through his lyrics. No longer were guys required to sing the blues when their hearts were broken or a woman mistreated them. They no longer had to get angry and turn their pain into hate. It was refreshing to see there was a third alternative: simply get up, say goodbye, and move on.

The song, like the album, ended too soon. It was like a roller coaster ride that you waited so long to get on, but it's over before you know it. Roller coasters may be the best analogy for Van Halen: you get in, you hold on for dear life, you yell and scream, then it's over.

Curtis was driving well over eighty miles an hour when he glanced down at his speedometer. The song was barely three minutes long, and he could already see the Meramec River bridge ahead in the distance. A ticket would cost him time and money, so Curtis slowed down before crossing the river into Jefferson County.

Curtis strolled into his house as happy as he could be. It was Saturday afternoon, and he didn't have to work again until Monday after school. He knew the concert would be a fantastic experience, and then he could stay out as late as he wanted because he could sleep in Sunday morning.

JoAnn was in the kitchen making dinner. "Please take your shoes off. They're always full of grease, and I just cleaned the floors today. Also, Marty called and wants you to call him back immediately."

Curtis kicked off his shoes and flung them into the breezeway; wherever they landed, they would stay until JoAnn moved them. Curtis called Marty and found out he wanted to drive to the concert. Marty said he would leave in about thirty minutes to pick him up. Curtis was disappointed because Marty's car was raggedy and used as much oil as it did gas. However, what bothered him was that the car only had an AM/FM radio with a single speaker on the dashboard. On the plus side, he would probably save money on gas, so he didn't make an issue of it.

After dinner, Curtis took a shower and got dressed. He pulled out his favorite jeans, which he hid from his mom so she couldn't wash them. Every time she washed them, they shrunk a little, and it was difficult to put them on and make them feel comfortable again. He dug out his Jack Daniels T-shirt purchased from Spencer's in the mall and put on his waffle stomper hiking boots. Curtis splashed on some of his dad's Old Spice aftershave for good measure. When he was ready to go, he grabbed his wallet and put forty dollars inside. He put the wallet and the ticket on the kitchen counter and waited for Marty to arrive.

It was a little after five when he heard the horn honk.

"Curtis, you should take a jacket with you. It's going to be much cooler later this evening."

Curtis considered grabbing his blue denim jacket but reasoned that nobody would see his Jack Daniels T-shirt if he wore it, so he declined his mother's advice. JoAnn stopped Curtis as he grabbed his wallet and hugged her son. "Please be careful," he heard her say as he walked out the door.

As they drove away, Marty asked Curtis if he had his ticket. Curtis looked down on the seat and saw two bottles of Jack Daniels. One of the bottles was a partial fifth, and the other was a new half-pint.

"Yes, it's right here in my wallet."

They stopped for gas, and Curtis went inside and bought a six-pack of Coke. When he went to pay for it, he noticed his missing ticket and began to panic.

He grabbed the soda and his change and went out and told Marty. Marty scowled, saying, "You got to be kidding me." Marty was agitated and banged the fuel nozzle accordingly before going inside to pay for the gas. Curtis took a quarter out, went to the payphone, and called home. His mother confirmed that the ticket was still on the kitchen counter.

"I even asked you before we left…" So, for the next twenty minutes, Curtis got a lecture from his friend about having shit for brains. Curtis knew he deserved it and kept his mouth shut. He could handle the verbal abuse from his friend, but what aggravated him was listening to all the stupid commercials on the radio. He wished he was driving so he could put in a tape.

"Why don't you get a real stereo for your car?"

"Why don't you buy me one?" Marty replied.

Curtis ran inside and grabbed the ticket off the kitchen counter. The show didn't start until eight, so they still had plenty of time to get there. Marty made up for the lost time by speeding up the interstate as fast as his car would go. They soon crossed over the Meramec River into St. Louis County, and fifteen minutes later, they crossed River Des Peres into the City of St. Louis. Marty picked up a piece of paper with some scribbled notes and then handed the paper to Curtis, telling him to navigate.

Curtis told Marty when to change lanes, when to turn, where to merge, and what exits to use. Once they got off at Hampton Avenue, Curtis quickly got his bearings on the landmark of a large Central Hardware down below them on Manchester Avenue. They turned off the road, descended the hill, and parked as close as possible to the parking lot without technically being on it. For the effort of walking about five blocks, they would save five bucks. It was still early, barely thirty minutes past six. The sun sank fast in the west as they drank Jack Daniels and Coke. Marty took the half-pint bottle, tucked it into his sock, and pulled his pant leg back over his boot. A gentle bump could still be seen, but it had worked before, so there was no reason to doubt it would work again.

By seven, streetlights replaced the sunlight. Both boys felt good and relaxed. At the top of the hour, they heard on the radio that the concert was an official sellout. "Let's roll," Marty said as the station went to another commercial.

Marty and Curtis were not the only ones to park away from the venue, and with each passing block, individuals, pairs, and groups filed in, so by the time they reached the south entrance to the parking lot, there was a large group of people. The walk up through the Cheltenham neighborhood was not without stares from residents looking out their windows. Some residents would use the arena events to make a few dollars by letting people park in their driveway or in front of their houses. Homeowners put up with a lot from strangers passing their homes. It wasn't bad now, but when the crowd returned to their cars in a few hours, they would have to contend with some urinating in the streets or vomiting in their yards. Still others would laugh and yell without regard for interrupting the quiet, peaceful evening. On occasion, uninhibited horny couples would engage in sex acts in the shadows or in the semi privacy of their cars.

As Curtis and Marty entered the parking lot with the crowd, the large building revealed itself at the top of the hill. The beloved Checkerdome, as it was called after being purchased by Ralston-Purina a couple of years earlier, was still referred to by many as "The Arena." Old-timers simply called it "The Barn." It had been around for decades and had been the home of the St. Louis Blues since they entered the National Hockey League in 1967.

The building was built during the Roaring Twenties and opened to the public during the Great Depression. It was among the nation's largest indoor venues for decades. Only Madison Square Garden was larger. St. Louis was a fraction of the size of the Big Apple and was fortunate to have such a magnificent building to host events.

The Arena was used for conventions, concerts, political rallies, and circuses. It was also used for professional wrestling, boxing, roller derby, and ice hockey. The Chicago Blackhawks played games there for many years before the St. Louis Blues became an NHL franchise. It was one of the loudest arenas in the league, and it would certainly be loud tonight.

Curtis and Marty made their way to the south entrance. A long line formed as people waited for the gates to open. Marty suggested they go to the north entrance, thinking fewer people would be in line there. They soon discovered they were not the only people with such incredibly gifted minds.

They walked around the far side of the building and could see the tractor trailers backed into the dock area. In front of them were a couple of large buses, and as they passed by, a young man with a head full of black curly hair exited a bus, jumping down the steps. He briefly turned to observe the gathering crowd.

Marty punched Curtis to get his attention. "I think that's the guitar player," he said. Curtis stopped walking and stared. Standing a mere fifty feet away, in plain clothes, was their generation's most innovative, virtuoso guitar player. All they could think of doing was wave, and the guitar player waved back and smiled before heading toward the private entrance of the venue.

That smile and wave meant more to Curtis because he could forever hold it in his memory. It was more precious than any autograph that could have accidentally made it into his mom's washing machine. Even a handshake would have implied what was not real, but the wave and smile were genuine, just like the music they were about to experience.

When Curtis and Marty made it to the north entrance, they found themselves in a shorter line, but it was only faster because the gates were open, and people were already going inside. When it was their turn, they handed the agent their tickets before going through the turnstile. As soon as they were through, Marty was pulled aside by one of the security men wearing a bright yellow T-shirt. Marty was patted down, and the half-pint of Jack Daniels was promptly discovered and confiscated. The security man didn't say a word; he just tossed the bottle into a large plastic bin filled half full of other glass bottles of assorted liquor and beer. No protests were made, so they weren't hindered in proceeding to find their seats.

Marty lamented the loss of his bottle, so Curtis tried to cheer him up by pointing to a pair of scantily clad women walking ahead of them. A dark-haired woman, who appeared to be college age, was wearing open-toe sandals, low-cut, tight-fitting shorts, and a yellow tube top that exposed her midriff. The other woman was a little taller and thinner and wore a mini-skirt with a lace cami top, fishnet stockings, and heels. Marty and Curtis picked up their pace, and as they drew closer to them to step through the opening to get to the seats, Curtis reached over and smacked the denim-clad butt cheek in front of Marty. Unfortunately, he was too slow returning to his spot behind the other girl and was caught. Flushed with anger, the woman yelled at Marty, "Control your jack-off friend."

Marty glanced at Curtis in confusion. Marty, who hadn't seen what had happened, asked, "What the hell was that about?"

The two women sat several rows ahead of their seats and kept turning back and pointing. Curtis felt the shame and embarrassment he deserved and wondered if he would get thrown out of the concert. Marty could do nothing but shrug his shoulders, saying, "I don't know."

People continued to pour into the arena, and the empty blue seats disappeared under the growing crowd. It was interesting to observe the activity on the floor. Someone had snuck in a colorful beach ball that was bounced all around the stands until, finally, one of the ushers confiscated it, letting the air out to an enormous chorus of boos. People paraded around as sound checks were done on the stage, with a round of applause given with each drum strike or guitar chord. After some time, the lights finally went out, and a man named Robert Fleischman came out and performed some Journey songs he had cowritten when he was with the band. Forty-five minutes later, he left the stage, and the house lights came on so the stage could be rearranged. Thirty minutes later, the house lights dimmed again, and the roar of the crowd was deafening. For a time, live music and a full-blooded, engaged audience would breathe life back into the old Arena. Twenty-thousand lit joints and cigarette lighters glowed like Burmese rubies in the sunlight as the sweet-leafed incense filled the air and rose toward the altar of Dionysus.

In 1979, people were still generous with their pot. It was not uncommon for a large fatty to be passed down the row from aisle to aisle. And sometimes, it was significantly better than Jack Daniels.

Lights and sound erupted to the euphoria of the crowd, and the band launched into a stunning, faithful rendition of "Light Up the Sky." Barely one song into the set, Curtis had a blister on his thumb from holding the lighter too long. The song ended with a huge standing ovation, and David Lee Roth greeted the fans and thanked them for their support. "I think I'm getting ill," he shouted before quickly adding, "Somebody get me a doctor." Alex counted off as the band ripped into the song from their debut album. They ended the song with a blistering drum solo. The evening continued with their popular songs "Running With the Devil," "Dance the Night Away," and "Beautiful Girls."

Curtis couldn't help but watch the young woman he had assaulted earlier having so much fun, dancing and singing along to the songs. He thought of April and wondered if she was somewhere in the Arena enjoying the show. Until this moment, Curtis did not consider Van Halen to be dance music. Curtis now believed that the music of Van Halen was there to incite a riot within the soul. It was music to persuade young lust to come out of hiding and blow rooftops off old buildings. The young woman proved him right about one, but he was wrong about the dancing. He had to discipline himself not to stare. He had already invaded their privacy one too many times. And someone would still have to examine the roof of the Arena the next day.

As lively as the old Arena was in the rocking environment, now filled with smoke and half-naked dancing women, wonderful things about it were easily taken for granted. The seats were marginally comfortable and spaced apart without feeling like someone was crowding you out of your seat, and ample elevation allowed for unobstructed viewing. The lamella roof eliminated the need for internal support pillars, which would have obscured the view for some people.

If there was a problem with the Arena, it was its poor acoustics. Bass frequencies tended to growl and hum. Dreadful standing waves sustained the lower tones and absorbed the higher ones. Curtis watched Alex Van Halen violently strike his cymbals, but they weren't heard clearly. However, they mixed the piercing wail of David Lee Roth with the delightful crunch of the Frankenstrat. Only by the amplified power could those sounds break through. Concerts at the Arena were loud because they had to be. There was no other way to be heard than to amplify and reproduce with as many speakers as a couple of tractor trailers could haul.

Something else breaks through standing waves: bass guitars. Michael Anthony was the first bass player Curtis had ever heard who played a bass solo. It wasn't a bass fill—it was a bass solo that lasted several minutes while the rest of the band took a short break. When the band returned, the solo went right into the Linda Ronstadt cover, "You're No Good."

"Feel Your Love Tonight" got the girls out of their seats again to dance, and "Jamie's Cryin'" brought tears to the young girls' eyes as they swayed to the song.

It is said that the greatness of a whole is greater than the sum of its parts. Curtis reckoned this to be true, and twenty thousand people were bearing witness to incredible greatness in this moment of history. The nuances and subtleties of that greatness would take years, if not decades, to unpack. Unbeknownst to everyone there, they were defining the rock of the new generation. Unless, of course, April was there. She knew this more than a year ago. Curtis hoped she was there. He wished he could get a chance to talk to her about the band she introduced him to.

Even as the band launched itself into "Ain't Talkin' 'Bout Love" from their first album, what struck Curtis was how effortless Eddie appeared playing his guitar. Seeing a man use both hands to play an instrument without even looking at them was stunning. He just smiled that same smile he had shown in the parking lot a couple hours earlier. Anyone who has ever picked up a stringed instrument knows that playing with such ease and confidence did not happen by accident. The show ended with a spectacular performance of "Eruption" and "You Really Got Me."

A brief break occurred, and the band returned to perform two encores, one from each album. "Bottoms Up!," a double entendre that appealed to drinkers and lovers alike, gave Dave the opportunity to invite the crowd into a sing-along with him. The band finished the evening with a sizzling performance of "Atomic Punk" before taking their final bow and sending the crowd home with a smile, a buzz, and a little tinnitus.

When the house lights came on, the crowd migrated toward the exits. Curtis noticed the lovely dancing ladies staring at him. He wanted to apologize, but when he started toward one portal, they went to the other.

It grieved him to know that he directly put a black mark on their otherwise fun-filled evening.

Leaving the Arena, they were hit by the cold night air. The temperature had dropped twenty degrees since they went inside. Curtis thought of his mom and regretted not bringing a jacket with him.

Curtis and Marty stopped at a gathering of people and saw a man dressed in Army fatigues. He was selling Van Halen "World Vacation Tour" concert T-shirts from duffel bags stuffed with them.

A voice in the dark yelled out, "How much for the shirt?"

"Five bucks."

Curtis gave the man a ten-dollar bill for two large shirts and handed one to Marty. Marty said, "I really don't want one."

Curtis replied, "It's free for you. Thanks for driving."

Marty balled the shirt up, tucked it under his arm, and said, "Let's get out of here. I'm freezing."

Curtis put his T-shirt on because he was freezing too.

As they walked back to the car, they were intercepted by some street evangelists handing out gospel tracts with warnings about the dangers of rock and roll music. The one young man looked at Curtis and said, "There are consequences for running with the devil."

"It's just a song," Curtis objected.

"It's just your soul," the man replied. "Life is short, and eternity is long. We will all be judged by what we say and do. You should be ready because you don't know the hour of your departure."

Curtis took the tract because they made good bookmarks.

They stopped at White Castle on the way home and talked about the show. Curtis confessed what he had done to the girl in tight-fitting cutoffs. Marty just shook his head.

It was after midnight when Curtis got home. His mom was waiting at the door when he came inside.

She asked, "How was your show?"

"It was really good."

"Are you hungry?"

"No, we stopped at White Castle on the way home."

"Yuck, those things are nasty." She noticed his new shirt. "Do you really need another shirt? You have a whole closet full of shirts you never wear."

"It was only five bucks. I thought it would be a nice souvenir. Please do not wash it in hot water or dry it in the dryer or I won't be able to wear it again."

"I'm just glad you made it home," JoAnn said as she hugged her son good night.

Chapter 5

My Old School

A storm rages in the form of teenage angst, causing restless sleep, but the storm relents and yields its strength against the rugged, rocky shoreline in solid and rhythmic pulses of cosmic bliss. Now broken free, the waters rest on the damp, peaceful shore. The salty seawater deposits tiny life-forms on the sandy beach, which will soon die from exposure outside their natural element. Life goes on, and a weary soul in desperate need of rest finds peace.

Curtis thought he heard the click of the alarm clock before he heard music. He opened his eyes but saw only darkness. He listened to a heavenly choir of voices over an electric piano and the faint sound of a heartbeat. The surreal experience confused him, and he wasn't sure if he was still sleeping and dreaming or partially awake in another world. Fifteen seconds seemed like a lifetime, but a singing voice finally broke through the fog, and Curtis was aware he was, indeed, awake. He got lost in the whispery, ethereal lyrics of 10cc's "I'm Not in Love."

Curtis rolled over to see what time it was. The G.E. flip clock on the nightstand displayed 6:33. He did the math: The bus picked up at five after seven, and it took ten minutes to walk to the bus stop. Curtis only needed five more minutes. Next year, he thought, he would be able to drive to school and would be able to sleep in until after seven. As he listened to the end of the song, the thought of thirty extra minutes of sleep relaxed him even more, so he shut his eyes. His relaxation ended when his mother's intruding voice reverberated throughout the house from the kitchen: "Curtis, get up. You're going to be late…again!"

Curtis rolled over, pulling the covers up over his head. Then he felt it. "Oh no, not again," he murmured with chagrin. He felt seminal fluid ooze down his inner thigh. Stricken with mortifying fear of stains on the sheets, he jumped out of bed. Curtis opened the dresser drawer, grabbed a clean pair of briefs, and cracked the bedroom door just enough to see where his mother was. When he saw her at the sink with her back turned, he darted to the bathroom and slammed the door shut before locking it. He turned the shower on, stripped down, and cleansed himself under the stream of water, vigorously scrubbing himself top to bottom.

Seconds later, a pounding on the door startled him. "Curtis," his mom yelled, "you should have taken a shower last night. You're going to be late, and I will *not* drive you to school if you miss the bus."

Curtis quickly rinsed off and hand-washed the underpants. Once out of the shower, he wrapped himself in a towel and rung the underwear out over the sink. He sprayed on deodorant before going back to his bedroom. He dropped the towel and dressed as fast as he could. He wrapped the wet underpants in a hand towel, stuffed it inside his gym bag, and threw it under the bed. He'd deal with it later. He glanced at the clock, calculating he had fifteen minutes to catch the bus. He spent five minutes getting his shoes on and gathering his schoolbooks and folders containing partially completed homework assignments.

He walked briskly to the front door, passed his breakfast on the kitchen table, and tried to ignore the overly concerned look on his mother's face. When Curtis opened the door, the cold morning air greeted him. He turned around and nearly bumped into his mom, standing there with his jacket in one hand and his breakfast stuffed between two pieces of toast.

"Hurry or you'll be late. I love you."

Curtis took the jacket and sandwich, ran up the hill, and walked briskly until he spotted Elizabeth and Fern a few houses ahead. The two sisters were always five minutes early to the bus stop. Seeing them, he knew he would be fine. Relaxing his pace, he ate his cold bacon and egg sandwich.

He caught up with the girls and walked with them the last hundred yards to the American Legion parking lot.

"Good morning," Curtis said as he approached them from behind.

"Hey," Elizabeth replied.

"Good morning, Curtis," the younger sister echoed.

It was a cool morning as the early spring still wrestled with winter in the skirmish of seasonal change. Elizabeth was stunning, wearing a form-fitting black leather jacket and a pleated, olive-green skirt that landed below her knees. Dark pantyhose covered her legs, and she wore a pair of black Mary Jane flats. Fern wore a red hoodie, blue jeans, and sneakers.

Even though Elizabeth was a year younger than Curtis, she stood three inches above him and appeared three years older. Curtis imagined her as an Amazon because she was tall and robust. Elizabeth's long black wavy hair accented her soft honey-toned skin.

Fern was a year younger than her sister and languished in her prepubescent state, worsened because she waited in the shadows of her sister's seemingly overgrowing womanhood. Both girls seemed to enjoy talking with Curtis when they strolled together in the mornings or afternoons. At school, it was a different story. Elizabeth wouldn't even make eye contact with him around the other girls at school. On the other hand, Fern never failed to wave and yell at him, even if she was a hundred feet away in the cafeteria and called attention to herself with her screaming.

When they arrived at the bus stop, a handful of kids were already waiting and dancing about, trying to keep themselves warm. They didn't have to wait long because the bus rounded the corner, sped down the street, and turned into the parking lot.

Mister Earl, a retired Korean War veteran and member of the Marine Corps, drove for the school district and worked in the maintenance building. He swung the big yellow bus around the parking lot, as he'd done twice a day for the last ten years. Mister Earl was a towering figure of a man, but the bulk of his frame remained hidden in his seat. He was mostly silent, but his steely gray eyes saw everything inside his bus—and woe to anyone who angered him to the point that he got out of his seat. Curtis's thoughts drifted back to last year.

Billy Reeves was a troubled young boy. He was a year older than Curtis but a grade behind him. Billy was always angry and lashing out at students and teachers alike. The boy received paddlings, suspensions, and eighth hours, but nothing changed his disposition to meanness. Billy was not a bully; he was *the* bully. Billy was a walking, brooding fisticuff looking for a reason to hit someone.

Billy wasn't a big boy and didn't care about size or age. He didn't even care if he got beat up. He punched a fifth-grade teacher for taking a ball away from him during recess. Billy also held onto grudges. If he did get beat up, which he did regularly, you can bet it was not the end, for his revenge knew no limits. In seventh grade, Billy received a paddling from the junior high principal. Afterward, he snuck into the office and stole the principal's paddle. Nobody could prove he did it until he got caught cutting it in half on the band saw in shop class. That same year, Billy was beaten to a bloody pulp by a sophomore named Gary Griggs. It happened off the school grounds, so the school didn't get involved. A few days later, Gary's dog got sick and died.

Billy was usually the first to get on the bus and the first to leave. Everyone avoided him, and Curtis made sure not to make eye contact with him. Anything could set him off. And one day, that is exactly what Mary Plath did..

Mary was an introverted girl, neither ugly nor pretty. The simple truth was Mary was an only child who lived alone with her mother in a small house across the street from the bus stop. Her mother was a waitress, and all she could do was put food on the table and pay rent. Mary wore secondhand clothes and had unruly hair. She had overly chapped lips, making it appear like she drank nothing but cherry Kool-Aid. She was quiet and kept to herself. Her rides to and from school were spent staring out the window. She was an easy target for gossip and ridicule, both in front of and behind her back.

On this day, Billy got on the bus after school and decided he wanted Mary's seat. Curtis was two seats back and saw the entire exchange take place.

"Get up!" Billy barked. "That's my seat."

Mary leveled a stare at him and said calmly, "I was here first. You may sit next to me or go sit somewhere else." Mary turned her head and stared out the window.

Billy stood there dumbfounded. When the last student got on the bus, Mister Earl yelled, "Take a seat, Billy." He would not shut the door until all the kids were seated. After a minute of glaring back at him through the sizable rearview mirror, Billy sat behind Mary and made her ride home unpleasant.

Billy tormented Mary for the next fifteen minutes pulling on her hair and calling her names until the bus circled around the American Legion parking lot and came to a stop.

Usually, Billy would rush to be the first one off, but on that day, he waited until everyone was off the bus and waited for Mary to leave so he could follow her. Mary clutched her books, lunch box, small canvas with flowers she had painted in art class that day, and a small box of acrylic paint tubes. She stood up from her seat to exit the bus, carefully descending the steps, and then headed for the security of her home, right across the street. Billy was behind her. After getting off the bus, he waited for the door to close. As soon as it did, he smacked Mary's arm so hard she screamed and dropped her canvas, books, and box of paint tubes. To the horror of everyone there, Billy picked up the box of paints and the canvas painting and tossed them under the rear wheels of the moving school bus.

Mary sobbed uncontrollably as everyone stared at the bleeding rainbow of colors and broken wood and ripped canvas flattened into the blacktopped surface of the parking lot.

Nobody offered Mary any comfort, nor did anyone champion Mary and challenge the bully. Curtis felt shame for being weak when he should have been strong for the girl who had nothing, and now, less than nothing. For all the misery that Billy seemed to thrive in, the day he was exceedingly cruel to Mary Plath seemed to be the happiest day of his life.

Now, Curtis got on the bus with a polite nod to Mister Earl. As Curtis stared out the window, he thought of Mary. It was sad that she no longer went to Windsor. If there was any comfort in her absence, it was that wherever she was, Billy wasn't. The last Curtis heard, Billy relocated to Mexico, Missouri, to attend a military academy.

Windsor School registered students from kindergarten through twelfth grade. The kids enrolled predominately lived in Kimmswick, Barnhart, and Imperial. The Windsor campus was small but starting to show a measure of growth. For most of the ten years Curtis had attended the school, the campus consisted of three old buildings, one for each of the three levels of public education. A few buildings had recently been added, including a newly constructed building with a massive cafeteria with two serving lines to accommodate all the students. Above the cafeteria were numerous classrooms on both sides of a lengthy hallway and many lockers for underclass students.

The mascot of Windsor School was an owl. The "raptor of the night" was an unusual symbol to represent a school. The owl was probably chosen for its representation of intelligence and insight or possibly because of the wisdom and knowledge associated with Athena, the ancient Greek goddess of wisdom whose symbol is an owl. Then again, it might have been chosen because it is an apex predator that can see in the dark and is full of mystery.

The wisdom or hunting prowess of the extraordinary and comical bird was lost on the public. The cheerleaders and pom-pom squad fought an uphill PR battle when the school engaged the Hillsboro Hawks, Festus Tigers, or the Herculaneum Black Cats. While Windsor could remain competitive against the smaller schools, they were usually fodder to the Fox Warriors or Northwest Lions, as they were huge schools.

Curtis arrived at school almost twenty minutes before his first class. It aggravated him that his bus route was the closest to the school. His bus was one of the first to arrive and the last to leave, making his day longer than most other students. It was just another item on his never-ending list of things that made life unfair.

Curtis sauntered down the hill to his locker in the cafeteria building and ran into Marty. Seeing Marty in the morning was rare because their schedules were on opposite sides of the campus. Marty was wearing his Van Halen T-shirt, and Curtis immediately regretted not wearing his. The two boys briefly talked before Marty headed up the hill to the high school.

Curtis had his first two classes in the new building. He started his day with Biology at 7:35. The wall clock indicated 7:40, and he waited with the other students gathered around the locked classroom door. It was 7:48 when the high school secretary, Marge Grady, appeared with a younger, well-dressed man. The kids parted ways for them as Mrs. Grady sorted through the large key ring to find the right key to unlock the door.

The class poured into the dark room. Mrs. Grady looked directly at Curtis with fierce eyes and said, "You better behave yourself, or I will whip your ass." She handed the key to the young man before walking back up the hill to the high school.

The man said, "Good morning. I'm Mr. McDonald. I apologize for the late start." He turned on the lights and hung up his coat as the kids made their way to the various lab tables in the room. He got their attention again and told the class, "Mrs. Borman is not feeling well and will be out the rest of the week. We will not do any labs, but she has provided reading assignments. I'll try to have some worksheets printed out for you by tomorrow. So, for today, use the time as a study hall." Curtis was relieved by this unexpected good news, allowing him to complete his unfinished homework assignments.

Curtis worked diligently on his term paper for Mr. Englewood's second-hour English class. The English class was the first of three class periods he had with Mr. Englewood. He would return after lunch for English Literature and do his best to stay awake as they digested *The Mayor of Casterbridge*. Mr. Englewood also hosted a study hall at the end of the day, which Curtis used to his advantage to minimize the schoolwork he had to do at home. He hated homework unless it was a reading assignment. Curtis made every effort to take care of schoolwork at school. He found reading enjoyable, excluding the Thomas Hardy novel, which he found irritatingly dull. Curtis once asked Mr. Englewood why they couldn't read more enjoyable books. Mr. Englewood responded, "Curtis, you need to accept Tolkien, Wells, and Twain are for junior high students. You need to expand your reading capacity for growth and understanding."

After two hours of catching up and writing, Curtis looked forward to his third hour of World History with Mr. Erickson. They were supposed to cover Western civilization from the Greek Empire to the Vietnam War, but they were only on pace to get through World War I. Mr. Erickson spent too much time on the Renaissance and Enlightenment, which he considered the highlight of world history. There was another reason Curtis loved this class: His desk was in the direct sight line of Anna McCarthy. Curtis had shared many classes with her since third grade. Since her last name also started with "Mc," their pictures were always next to each other in the school yearbook. Anna grew from a cute girl he once played with at recess into a beautiful woman who did not know he existed. As a sophomore, she was invited to join the varsity cheerleading squad. Anna was the "girl next door" with enough charm to be elected to the student council and homecoming court. If there was a downside to Anna McCarthy, she ruined the bell curve for any class she took. Mr. Erickson was the rare teacher who adjusted his grades to the highest score. Because Anna was so perfect, there wasn't anything to change most of the time.

Between World History and lunch, Curtis had Woodworking, the second-semester follow-up class to Drafting. The high school shop building was the eminent domain of Mr. Oswald Gaffey. Apart from the superintendent, Mr. Gaffey was the school's most powerful and influential member. His longevity was undeniable and went far beyond tenure. His relationship with the school administration was bound by blood. He was a fixture of the establishment and ruled with the iron fist of a tyrant if you managed to get on his bad side. He measured his students by the strength of their handshake and the look in their eyes when he stared them down. He required more patience for losers, fakers, or wannabes, putting Curtis on shaky ground from the first meeting. Fortunately, Curtis had a firm handshake and fearless eyes that went a long way with a short man with a huge heart and aggressive demeanor.

By 1979, the school district was growing due to the development of many new subdivisions. With the influx of a larger student body, Mr. Gaffey used his age and influence to petition the school for an assistant. The school board adjusted its budget to comply with his request and hired an assistant for him.

Mr. Edwin Cannon, the man selected for that job, had started at the beginning of the school year. Mr. Cannon resembled a TV detective, but his attitude was pure Southern hillbilly, as only Kennett, Missouri, can create. His humor was mean and vicious. While his skills as a craftsman with wood were second to none, they made him arrogant. His expectations were exceedingly high, nearly to the point of perfection. Instead of teaching from his strengths, he critiqued anything that did not measure up. His criticisms were often harsh and mean-spirited, as if he delighted in giving bad grades. People who took the class without ever previously touching a saw were in for a rude awakening unless they had a substantial measure of natural ability. Students taking his Woodworking class discovered he would rather compete than teach.

The shop class was well stocked with the best commercial wood-working tools. Although the equipment was nearly twenty years old, everything was pristine. It was a woodworker's dream shop. All you had to do was pay for the wood and complete at least one project before the end of the year.

The shop class was where Coach Sydney Tyron went every day before lunch to read the newspaper. If Mr. Gaffey was the most powerful man on campus, Coach Tyron was the most feared. He lived for one reason and one reason only: to win football games. He had ten games scheduled every year, and the thought of losing any of them was unbearable. He was a mystery to most, and he liked it that way. Enigma tended to breed fear in teachers and students alike. While most students avoided him, his players loved and adored him, especially if they were seniors.

The students who ran his gauntlet from freshman to senior year and survived his crucible moved the world for him. The problem was, with over six hundred students in the high school, only a few dozen played football. From that minority pool of students, only the juniors and seniors mattered to him. Coach Tyron wouldn't give two squirts of piss for the other five hundred and fifty students even if they wore "W"s on their jackets or excelled in other areas of academics or arts.

Curtis was working on his project, a small lamp table he was assembling from pieces he had cut and sanded, when Coach Tyron strutted over to him and said, "I'm expecting to see you at football camp this summer. Stop by my office and get a physical waiver for your doctor to sign." Without waiting for a response, he approached several others and dictated the same instruction.

The coach saw freshmen and sophomores like a man raising piranhas sees goldfish. He wasn't looking for players; he was looking for fodder. The problem was, it wasn't a request, it was a demand. Curtis had seen *The Godfather* and knew the penalty for refusing to comply.

Curtis survived the morning. He found Brad, Marty, and Richie sitting in the cafeteria and joined them for lunch. Curtis had known Richie for a few years. They had sisters of the same age who took dance lessons together. Richie was tall and thin and played drums in the junior varsity marching band. He hoped to make it into the jazz band as a junior. The boys wolfed down the lunch consisting of Salisbury steak, applesauce, mashed potatoes, green beans, and a half pint of whole milk. Marty and Curtis filled the lunchtime sharing their Van Halen concert experience.

After lunch, Curtis went to his algebra class. He thought he had a eureka moment in which he suddenly understood quadratic equations. The short-lived feeling dissolved as he struggled with the next problem. He looked across the room and saw Anna scribbling away as she tapped her toes. She looked so splendid in her cheerleading uniform. Anna must have felt the stare because she turned toward him. She smiled and then went back to crunching numbers and solving the problem.

A pleasant surprise greeted Curtis when he learned his English Literature class would only be a half-hour. A mandatory assembly in the high school gymnasium would take the rest of the day. Once Curtis had ascended the hill to the large high school gymnasium, the bleachers were already packed. As he climbed the bleachers, he spotted his friends and wedged himself between Richie and Marty.

Curtis asked Richie, "What's this about?"

"The recruiters are here," he replied.

"Seriously?"

Richie countered, "Why would I lie?"

Curtis asked Marty, "Where's Brad?"

"He's skipping out. He's leaving early with his mom."

"That rat bastard," Curtis said.

Marty replied, "Like his mom will let him join the Army."

Richie said, "Brad's got skills like me. We don't need the Army."

Everyone agreed that Brad definitely had skills.

The next hour was full of patriotic speeches and calls for excellence. One by one, the recruiters came up and made their appeal for any who might be called to serve their country.

The Air Force captain appeared first, wearing a powdered blue work shirt and dark blue pants. He had a briefcase and opened it to remove a single sheet of paper. He spoke about the need for bright minds ready to tackle a technology-driven future. The Army sergeant followed him, wearing full fatigues. He spoke from his heart without notes and pleaded for people to consider the Army.

Then, a well-dressed Marine wearing his dress uniform came up to the podium. The regimentals consisted of contrasting light blue slacks and a dark blue jacket, separated by a white belt. His chest was full of decorations. He gazed onto the assembly, but he made it clear he wasn't there to talk to everyone. "I'm not here to talk to all of you. Most of you are not cut out to be a Marine. However, I think that in a group this big, a few of you would probably do well in 'my beloved core.' If you think you have what it takes, come see me." He pivoted on his left foot, marched back to his seat, and sat down, looking dead-eyed straight ahead.

Then, the Navy recruiter came up. He talked the longest but seemed to have the most fun of the four recruiters. His presentation was built around the call to "be someone special" and the numerous opportunities the U.S. Navy offered. While the other recruiters came alone, the Navy recruiter had four other sailors with him. Concluding his presentation, he told some sea stories centered on the South Pacific islands. He appealed to the students that the Navy was about working hard and having a good time. He laughed about all the good times he had serving and then introduced the other four guys.

The sailors, as it turned out, were musicians. While the recruiters talked, they had quietly set up drums, a keyboard, and several amplifiers. Everyone in the assembly watched as each sailor took their place, with one having a bass and the recruiter grabbing an electric guitar. Curtis anticipated they would play "God Bless America" or "The Star-Spangled Banner," but everyone was surprised when they began playing rock music. The keyboard player launched into a rendition of "Foreplay," making his keyboard sound like a Hammond organ. The solo segued into a loud and powerful version of "Long Time" by Boston, nearly as authentic as listening to the record. Only the vocals gave away the fact that it was only an excellent cover. No one could sing like Brad Delp.

Experiencing this performance was the first time Curtis saw a band play a cover song. It blew his mind that it was possible to perform the music of others. After the song was over to deafening applause and yells for more, the Navy recruiter spoke again and encouraged anyone close to graduating to talk with him about the benefits of enlisting in the U.S. Navy.

The principal dismissed the students after the assembly. Several students engaged the recruiters to discuss their future as others huddled in groups to listen in. Curtis grabbed his book bag and went outside to wait for the bus. He said hello to Mister Earl as he climbed the stairs but received an unwelcome stare. He walked to the back and found a seat. He looked out the window and recalled his confrontation with Mister Earl before the Christmas break.

Curtis wasn't sure where the idea had come from, but he thought it would be cool to fill a paper bag with ketchup and mustard packs from the cafeteria. It would not have been a big deal had he picked a few, but Curtis didn't do anything halfway. He took his time, saving packets in his locker after lunch. When many weeks had passed and the bag was halfway full, with a few mayonnaises added for color, he got off the bus clutching the bag. He tossed the bag under the rear wheel as the bus pulled away. It popped loudly, and red, white, and yellow streaks went everywhere, leaving a huge, colorful stain on the parking lot.

Curtis was surprised when he heard the loud screeching of the brakes as the school bus lurched to a halt. A moment later, an angry and irritated driver jumped out of the bus and ran toward Curtis. Curtis feared for his life but was too terrified to run. He had provoked Mister Earl, and the large driver grabbed Curtis and slammed him into the bus. "I don't know who the hell you are, but if you ever pull a stunt like that again, I will rip your nuts off, and you will choke on them so you will not breed any more stupidity into this world."

Many months later, Curtis stared out the window, wondering why he'd done that. Clearly, he had envisioned the laughter, but he didn't know the laughter would be directed at him. Instead of laughing with the other kids, he was being laughed at. It was embarrassing then, and that embarrassment followed him still.

When the bus returned to the Legion parking lot, he got off and walked home, talking with Elizabeth about the assembly. Fern listened as she strolled between her older sister and Curtis.

Elizabeth asked Curtis, "Would you consider joining the military after high school?"

"I don't know, Elizabeth. I don't think I'm the military type."

"Why would you say that? I bet you would look good in a uniform."

"I don't handle authority very well," he replied.

She said, "Who does? Isn't that what growing up is all about?"

"Yeah, you're probably right. It's still a scary thing to think about moving far away from friends and family."

Elizabeth stopped walking, turning to look at him. He saw her eyes sparkle as she said, "Yes, but fear and excitement are similar, aren't they? I mean, something can be scary and exciting at the same time, right? Like riding a roller coaster…or going on a date with someone for the first time."

The words "roller coaster" and "first date" reverberated through his mind. Curtis felt his heart up in his throat. He wasn't sure if she was hinting, teasing, or something else. Was his mind playing tricks on him? He tried to connect the dots of his thoughts and feelings but sensed coincidences were trapping him. In the moment, he understood courtship was the desire not to be alone, just as going away in the military was the yearning to be free from the prison cell of home and school. But life seemed to be playing a cruel joke on him by leading him on and then tricking him with reality. No matter how well he followed the moving cards, in the long run, the hustle of three-card monte always led to a losing bet.

They continued walking together until they arrived at the intersection of the small road that led to Curtis's house. Curtis said goodbye to the girls. Fern hugged Curtis and said, "You really would look good in a uniform." Elizabeth smirked at her sister and grabbed her hand as they headed home."

Curtis descended the small hill. The private gravel street connected four adjacent properties but was only used by three. In a few minutes, Curtis entered his home. His mother was in the kitchen preparing dinner.

She asked, "How was school today?"

"It was okay, I suppose. We had a substitute, so I had an extra study hall first hour. We had an assembly the last hour, so it was pretty easy."

"An assembly?"

"Yeah, a bunch of recruiters were there trying to get kids to commit to the military."

"Don't you get any ideas. You're a smart boy and will have no problem finding a good job if you get decent grades. You need to talk to your father. He'll tell you. You need to find a job that requires your brain, not your back."

Curtis tried to drift away, but she stopped him with another question. "Do you have to work tonight?"

Curtis answered, "Yes. They want me to come in at five this evening."

"How long are they going to make you work tonight?"

"It's a school night, so they usually let me leave around ten. I could probably leave earlier, but I need the hours."

"Do you have all your homework done for tomorrow? What about your paper…are you making progress on it?"

"Yeah, I was able to get it all done today in class."

"When do you think you're going to get your truck inspected? Those license plates are due for renewal."

"I know. I'll take care of it this week after I get paid."

Curtis went to his room and got ready for work. He tried reading *The Mayor of Casterbridge* but started dozing off. Putting the book aside, he stared at the flip clock until 4:30. Then he forced himself to get up, find his keys, and leave for work.

Chapter 6

A Day on the Meramec

Although the summer break was rapidly approaching, spring would not fully release its grip. A steady rain fell throughout the day. Curtis gazed out the rain-streaked bus window and noticed several cars and an old Chevy pickup waiting for the bus. Elizabeth and Fern ran to the truck and climbed in. Elizabeth rolled the window down. Fern yelled for Curtis and then pleaded with Roger, her stepdad, to give Curtis a ride home. There was no room in the cab, but Roger said Curtis could get in the back of the truck.

When Roger stopped at the top of the road, Curtis jumped out, waving goodbye as he ran down the hill to his house. He walked inside wet and cold but not nearly as wet as he might have been. After a hot shower, he changed into dry clothes and watched TV for an hour before driving to work.

Curtis arrived at work fifteen minutes early but went inside to escape the rain. He hung out near the storeroom beside the small office, trying to decipher the various withholdings of his paycheck. Mouse also came in early to pick up his paycheck and then quit without any notice. Steve wasn't happy Mouse had abandoned his job and made everyone working aware of it.

Before he left, Mouse gave Curtis a paperback copy of *The Late Great Planet Earth* by Hal Lindsey and encouraged him to read it. Mouse told Curtis he had another job lined up working at a church camp that summer and was quitting now so he could put more time into his finals at school.

Curtis was the first to clock in, and Steve had no choice but to promote him to the pizza oven for the night. Steve made the move permanent for Friday and Saturday nights before Curtis left at the end of his shift. Curtis was joyful because he could leave both nights at ten. On his way out, he said goodnight to the line cooks, who were starting their evening cleaning and prep work.

Tiny said, "Speedy, you keep getting promoted like this and you'll be running this place before the end of summer."

Leo retorted, "I seriously doubt that."

Curtis answered, "Leo, keep working hard, and one day, you will go far too. And when you do, please don't come back."

Tiny laughed at Leo because he knew Curtis had gotten under his thin skin, just as he had taught him.

The new job and schedule made the weekend fly by. He spent most of Sunday finishing his term paper on capital punishment and outlining an analysis for *The Mayor of Casterbridge*. The term paper was far more interesting. With less than two weeks before the end of school, Curtis would focus most of his attention on writing a short paper about the novel, studying for a few finals, and staining his table for shop class. The spring rains would not stop summer from coming. He sat at his desk, trying to come up with as many synonyms for "boring" as possible before starting his analysis.

On Tuesday, Curtis came home from school early to take a nap before work. Being older had its advantages, but having to go to work was not one of them. JoAnn tried three times to wake him up from his nap. He barely jumped out of bed before she could dump water on his head.

Curtis enjoyed his promotion, even though it did not come with a pay increase. Also, since he got off work at ten, he lost four hours of pay every week. The pizza oven was off in the corner of the kitchen, so he had a fair amount of privacy. The only interruptions happened when waitresses or waiters dropped off pizza orders.

The stunningly beautiful hostess, Celeste, would occasionally bring back pizza orders for carryout. She often wore a black shirt, matching slacks, and a red wool tuxedo jacket. She also displayed gold jewelry hanging from her ears and neck and a dainty Gucci wristwatch. Even after she left, the woody notes of cedar with a hint of honey remained. In another era, Celeste would be a debutante waiting to be introduced to society. In 1979, however, she smiled, seated customers, and handed hormonally driven teenagers pizza orders.

At ten o'clock, Steve came back and told Curtis he could leave. He caught lighthearted grief on his way out, which he took in stride. He said goodnight to Celeste as he left, and she smiled at him and waved.

He was in no hurry to get home, so he had no reason to speed. Most of the ride was spent listening to Traffic's *The Low Spark of High-Heeled Boys*, which was so mellow he was likelier to get a ticket for driving too slow than speeding. Yet as he exited the highway and turned left to cross over the bridge, police lights flared up in his rearview mirror. He pulled over and waited.

"Good evening," the police officer said. "Do you know why I pulled you over?"

Curtis had no idea what he had done and was afraid to say anything. The police officer continued, "Your license plates are expired."

Curtis grimaced when he realized he was already a week into the new month.

The cop took his driver's license and returned several minutes later with a summons. "Get your plates renewed and bring this ticket to any Arnold police officer on duty. Show them you have taken care of this, and they will sign this ticket. You'll still have to pay the court costs, but the city will waive the ticket charge. Have a good evening and drive safe."

The next day after school, he got his truck inspected, and on Thursday, he went to the license bureau after school and picked up new plates. When he got home, he removed the blue license plate and replaced it with a maroon plate. In place of "MISSOURI" at the bottom in white letters, the new license plate read "SHOW-ME STATE."

Curtis drove up to Arnold and found a police officer sitting in a bank parking lot and showed him the ticket. The officer walked around the truck and then signed the ticket.

When Curtis went to work on Friday, he was asked if he wanted to move to Saturday days permanently. He was told the day manager, Michael, would assign him to prep work in the morning and the pizza oven for a few hours during the lunch rush. Curtis would get two hours back, so he accepted. Curtis expressed his eagerness prematurely because Steve told him the new schedule would not go into effect until the following week.

When he got home from work, he gave his mom his paycheck and showed her the ticket. He asked her to cash his check the next time she went to the bank, take the money necessary to pay the court costs on the ticket, and write a check for that amount.

JoAnn was unhappy about the ticket, fearing it would raise her insurance rates. Still, she agreed to do it after verbally scolding him for procrastinating and not taking responsibility for the truck he was driving.

A few years after Curtis Sr. and JoAnn moved to Missouri, they purchased a 1965 Ford F-100 pickup truck. Ford introduced their Twin I-beam suspension, which allowed each tire to move independently, removing the bounce characteristic of many pickup trucks. Their advertising campaign promised, "Drives like a car, works like a truck." The catchy slogan enticed Curtis Sr. to drive to Dave Sinclair Ford with JoAnn and their young son after Christmas to look at the new trucks. The couple immediately fell in love with a two-tone Wimbledon White over Rangoon Red truck with a chrome front and painted back bumper. They liked the ride so much that when they returned from the test drive, Curtis Sr. negotiated the sale and drove back home in a new truck.

The eight-foot styleside bed pickup truck was handy for all the projects and upgrades their older home required. Ten years later, with two more children to take care of, they were back at the dealer to negotiate for a new Ford station wagon. Curtis Sr. had a company truck by this time, so his Ford pickup truck spent much of the time in the garage.

After Curtis Jr. turned fifteen, he began counting the days until his sixteenth birthday. His parents thought allowing him to drive the truck would give Curtis a chance to grow up and learn responsibility. He often drove the truck up and down the street "for practice." JoAnn took issue with it, overwhelmed with worry and fearing the worst. Curtis Sr. had started driving at a much earlier age—smoking too—he would remind his wife, but that didn't stop her from speaking her mind every time he did it.

On Saturday morning, Curtis was all set to go hang out with his friends before going to work that afternoon, but his dad was home and had several things he wanted his eldest son to do, which began with changing the oil on the station wagon and his truck. "Oil is cheap," his father was fond of reminding him.

Curtis changed the oil and filters on both vehicles then spent most of the afternoon helping his dad clean the garage. By the time they finished, he barely had enough time to clean up before work. He knew better than to complain.

The patriarch of the Grady family was Donald Grady. Don was a large, strong man with a clean-shaven head and face. He had cold, steel-blue eyes and was a man of the earth. Mr. Grady would have blended in with the migrant farmers of the 1800s. He hunted, fished, butchered rabbits, and tended to vegetable gardens to put food on his table. His property also contained many fruit trees and a small vineyard with half a dozen long rows of grapes he harvested yearly for making jelly and wine. Mr. Grady was the incarnation of frugal. He only went to the grocery store a handful of times each year to purchase essentials like sugar, flour, salt, and coffee. He did have a fondness for sugar cookies and chocolate.

Don was a gifted man—simple in his ways but not simpleminded. While not formally educated, he knew how the world worked and was exceedingly wise. Technology and an ever-changing world seemed to frustrate him, and the relief valve for his anger was a creative string of profanity-laced tirades at the smallest infractions of his perceived injustices, particularly when he felt them aimed at himself. Perhaps this was why he took his sons to Mass every Sunday morning.

He knew every square foot of the hundreds of acres of wooded land between his house and the Mississippi River. Don taught his sons how to hunt, fish, farm, and trap. Mr. Grady was more than capable of writing his own edition of the Foxfire books.

Although his anger could flare up occasionally, he was never a threat to his wife, sons, or their friends. His frustrations often became verbalized in a sting of profanity that was absurd to the point of being funny. Curtis spent so much time at the Grady's, an outsider would think he was family.

The previous year, Mr. Grady had come across a 1956 eighteen-foot Chris Craft Continental needing repair. He bartered, and in exchange for a piece of old farm equipment and a little cash, he had a boat to work on. As the weather improved, he worked on the boat every chance he could. After the engine was restored and running, he sealed the boat inside and out and painted it to make it waterproof. After the boat was licensed and registered—something he loathed the government for making him do—all that was left was to put it in the water.

The boat would comfortably seat five people, but only four seats were necessary that late Sunday morning when they put the boat in the river for the first time. Don drove, while Brad, Curtis, and Marty enjoyed riding along.

They went to put the boat in at Hoppie's Marina, but the Mississippi was up and running too fast because of the recent rains. They turned around, went back into Arnold, and launched the boat at Flamm City, a public ramp on the Meramec River. It was a beautiful day. The sun was shining, and the temperature was in the mid-70s by noon. They had no desire to get in the water, intentionally or otherwise. They had forgotten the life vests when they loaded up.

Like the Mississippi, the Meramec River was also up. The water was brown and provided poor visibility to underlying logs or debris. Don was careful with the speed, but riding against the current required a good amount of throttle. They went under the Route 231 bridge and soon lost sight of civilization. The river was lined with thick woods and steep banks along most of their journey upriver. Mr. Grady followed the river because the positions on a compass were meaningless with all the twists and turns. They went under the Frisco railroad bridge with only the roar of the boat motor echoing across the river. With Brad up front with his dad, Curtis and Marty sat back and enjoyed the scenery, drinking beers out of the cooler. Mr. Grady would occasionally stop to look under the floorboard and ensure the boat was not taking on water.

While the vessel had a sump pump, he never figured out how to get the automatic float to work. Any water that seeped in had to be pumped out using the push button he had installed.

Curtis found it challenging to track where they were. If not for the occasional bridge, he would have been lost. They went under the Lemay Ferry bridge, the interstate, and the Tesson Ferry bridge at Highway 21. Mr. Grady only went as far as George Winter Park, and once inside the small lake like enclosure, he let the boys take turns driving the boat around.

After everyone had a turn in the driver's seat, he took the controls, turned the boat around, and headed back to Flamm City. They made much better time going down the river with the current.

Mr. Grady explained the river was crossed using ferries back in the days before the bridges were built. He said Dougherty Ferry, Tesson Ferry, and Lemay Ferry all got their names from the men who had licenses to run the flat-bottom boats back and forth across the river before the bridges were built.

The boys enjoyed the boat ride and the history lesson. Mr. Grady was a wealth of information. The river gave them a different perspective on travel, time, and distance. What would typically take less than an hour to drive to and from George Winter Park took nearly the entire afternoon by boat. They returned to Flamm City, got the boat on the trailer, and headed home.

The people who lived in Jefferson County seemed more predisposed to contentment than the rest of the world around them. Searching for satisfaction was most often achieved in drowning worms, hunting critters, and boating. In such activities, the residents only needed a little to be happy: a fishing rod, a tackle box, and a .22 were sufficient on most days, provided they were dressed appropriately. Boating, similar to camping, was best experienced as a minimalist. They weren't working or buying things on a boat but simply enjoying being alive. Boating on the river was relaxing because the world slowed down and was quiet. Mr. Grady was onto something he could only teach by demonstration—a simple life delighting in undemanding and ordinary things that nature supplied free of charge. Mr. Grady was in no way a dull man, and his sons, even the adopted one, were never bored. He understood there was a joy to existing that money could never buy, no matter how hard it tried.

Curtis realized something new that day—relaxation was a worthwhile pursuit and a prerequisite for happiness.

When Curtis got home that evening, his mom was not pleased he'd been out on the river all day without letting her know. He had missed dinner, which also angered her. Curtis assured her they did not get in the water and the boat was safe, but she still had doubts and fears. Her anxieties were relentless and often unbearable when he was not home. His dad had tried to explain this to him multiple times and said his life would be easier if he just told his mother what he was doing.

He ate dinner alone like his dad often did. After his meal, Curtis went outside to go for a walk. The moon was full and bright in the evening sky. His understanding of the moon waxed and waned as the moon's phases did. On one hand, he believed in natural science because that was what he was taught. On the other hand, the moon inspired the wonder of the supernatural.

Something about the moon intrigued him enough to ponder its mysteries. He knew the moon caused the tides to ebb and flow, which brought life to the ocean. He wondered if, in some way, the moon also caused his life to ebb and flow. He asked himself if there was something to astrology. He reasoned that this seemed more like superstition and was leery of putting too much emphasis on it. Yet the moon seemed to follow him wherever he went, as if it were an eye in the sky slowly opening and winking at him before closing again.

CHAPTER 7

The Basement

The Basement existed for as long as Curtis could remember. His relationship with the Gradys went back to before he was old enough to have memories. As children, the Basement was the perfect place to hang out. Brad and Curtis created hideouts using boxes and furniture to imitate caves and tunnels.

For children growing up in Jefferson County in the 1970s, the outdoors was their domain, and the boundaries were limited to the range of a parent's yell. Living on top of a river bluff meant those screams could carry a long way. The Basement, however, was a wonderful place to escape extreme weather.

For many of those years, the Basement was a gathering place, a recreational playground only limited to the creative imaginations of Curtis, Brad, and his older brother, Gunner. When everyone grew old enough to ride bicycles, minibikes, and motorcycles, their world seemed small and restrictive. When parents could no longer yell, time restrictions became the norm.

As their territory expanded, so did the opportunity to meet others, particularly the new kids who moved into the area. Younger kids who grew up in their shadows also yearned for the freedoms of their predecessors. To the neighborhood, the Basement became an oasis, a haven, offering the comfort and security of a home away from home.

It was not like there was no adult supervision. Mr. Grady, who worked a late shift at General Motors, often put idle teenagers to work during the mornings. Brad and Gunner soon found out who their real friends were. While Curtis could never bring himself to slaughter a rabbit, he did more than his share of picking vegetables, stacking firewood, or helping drag some large treasure out of the dumps and landfills that sprung up in the numerous ravines.

The Grady home was a simple two-bedroom colonial-style house built on top of a walk-out basement and one-car garage, split by a single open staircase that ended at a single-step landing and opened to both sides. The garage section contained two old, well-used, and filthy workbenches drenched with years of blood, sweat, oil, and numerous unknown solvents. The oldest of the workbenches was constructed of coal-tar creosote timbers, the weight of which would be impossible to measure. It could catch fire and burn for hours before the wood would be in jeopardy. A large rusty toolbox with a broken hinge and drawers that no longer pulled out sat on one end of the bench. A dual-stone grinder was mounted on the other end. The centerpiece of the workbench was an antiquated steel vise on a swivel base that no longer swiveled.

There was no order to the various tools and toolboxes scattered over the area. Numerous boxes, bins, tin cans, and buckets of nuts, bolts, and miscellaneous hardware items were stored under the workbenches, with an occasional coffee can dumped on top of one. Looking for matching sets of hardware was a project in and of itself. The garage floor was littered with projects in various stages of construction or repair.

It would be unfair to call Mr. Grady a pack rat, but he saw a purpose for everything he dragged out of a junkyard or dump. He had more projects than time. His creativity at repairs knew no bounds. He had the imagination of an artist, the understanding of an engineer, and an uncanny ability to get almost anything to work.

The other side of the Basement was larger than the garage. The glass panels in the garage, entry doors, and a medium-sized picture window allowed in plenty of natural light.

In the middle of the Basement was an old cast-iron wood stove. During the summer, it was just another tabletop, but its usefulness in the winter made the Basement the best place to hang out after hours of sled riding and snowball fights.

Just inside the door of the Basement was an old icebox. The refrigerator had a small chest at the top, only big enough for a couple of ice trays. Over the years, the refrigerated storage box was used for many things, often as a cooler for the various fruits and vegetables Mr. Grady harvested. Sometimes, the refrigerator was full of five-gallon buckets of water containing the freshly cleaned catfish or rabbits waiting for the final steps of butchering. There were always the community gallon jugs of cold water for drinking. Most of all, the icebox was a great place to keep beer cold. Mr. Grady, of course, would tax a beer or two for this service, but nobody had reason to complain.

Because Mr. Grady worked a late shift and Mrs. Grady worked two jobs, the Grady Basement became the best place for teenagers to hang out, drink beer, and listen to rock and roll. Occasionally, Ronnie, an unruly, wayward classmate, would stop by to sell them pot. Nearly everyone who hung out was respectful of the Basement, and those who weren't found their Basement privileges revoked and their presence no longer welcomed.

The summer before Gunner went to college, he worked part-time and purchased a used pool table. A thick piece of roofing plywood, placed over the top, allowed the boys to play poker instead of billiards when they were flush with money. Old furniture dragged up from one of the dumps would be subjected to a good cleaning and reupholstered with an old blanket thrown over the top. The refurbished chairs and couch on the perimeter were remarkably comfortable. The Basement was complete when Brad brought his stereo downstairs and hung enormous speakers from the ceiling. Mr. Grady would occasionally stomp on the floor if the ruckus interfered with his television time.

The Grady household would not have been what it was without Mrs. Marge Grady, the eccentric, temperamental, and boisterous woman who was the glue that held everything together. Depending on her mood, Mrs. Grady would either come down and hang out with the boys or cuss everyone out and make them leave.

Everybody referred to Mrs. Grady as JoJo, probably because her middle name was Josephine. JoJo worked for Windsor School as the secretary and, like most mothers back then, knew far more about what was happening in school and outside of it. The boys of Imperial may not have feared death, Satan, or God, but they certainly feared the wrath of JoJo.

Because JoJo worked in the school, she had some influence on the assignment of teachers, so for nearly ten years, Brad and Curtis were never assigned to the same teacher until their shop class during sophomore year. JoJo gave Curtis a ride to school until he got to seventh grade, so the only time Curtis and Brad rode a school bus was coming home in the afternoons and on field trips.

When the boys entered junior high school, JoJo had to be at work an hour before school started, so Brad would have to sit in the office and wait. Curtis decided he would rather sleep an extra hour and started taking the bus in the morning.

When Curtis was fourteen, his mom and dad gave him a used Suzuki motorcycle for his birthday. It was the best gift of his life. The motorcycle gave him unspeakable happiness and freedom like no other possession he had ever been given. And his parents gave it to him two months before his actual birthday. Since his dad kept most of his tools in his company truck, any repairs done to the motorbike would be done at the Basement.

Unlike his dad, Curtis was not a natural mechanic, but Brad, Gunner, and Mr. Grady were. They would often watch him struggle for a while, and when the humor of his ineptitude wore off, someone would come to his rescue to save time and increase Curtis's never-ending indebtedness to his other family.

Down below the Grady and McGowan properties were over twelve hundred acres of Mississippi River floodlands, called Chesley Island, which extended from Kimmswick to the Meramec River. Every spring, the rivers would overflow their banks and keep the river valley from being developed. As the flood waters receded by early summer, the side channels, called sloughs, filled with water. The smaller one would dry up by midsummer, but the larger slough became a mile-long elongated pond. Although some of the land was used for summer corn, the boys built a lot of motorcycle trails among the trees and weeds or used the dirt roads the farmers made. An easement owned and operated by the Missouri-Pacific Railroad contained railroad tracks that separated the river valley from the upper bluffs along a long levy that created the western border of Chesley Island.

It was a Sunday afternoon, and the boys were hanging out in the Basement, drinking beer and getting high. Stoned people often get into the most interesting discussions, and a debate began about what is stronger: dark or light.

Travis, the youngest of the group, said, "Light is stronger than dark because when I hit the light switch at night, the darkness disappears."

Gunner refuted the statement, explaining, "That's because the room is relatively small to the amount of light from a light bulb. The larger the room gets, the less of an influence the light bulb has." Then Gunner started talking about black holes that prevented light from escaping. Whenever Gunner was not hunting or fishing, he read books…lots of them.

"It would suck to be blind," Curtis offered while taking a hit from the pipe they were passing around. Nobody argued with him over that.

Marty said, "I can't imagine total darkness. I close my eyes, and I still see images."

Brad, the only one not getting high, said, "No matter how dark it is, my eyes will adjust to the dark."

Gunner told his brother, "You only see in the dark because there's still some minimal amount of light. In total darkness, you would be as blind as a bat."

The discussion went from dark and bats to caves before Marty spoke up, saying, "Let's go. Right now. Let's go to Cliff Cave Park. There's a cave there, and we can see for ourselves."

Brad crossed to the other side of the Basement and found flashlights. Everyone grabbed a fresh beer and a flashlight before piling into Brad's car.

They drove to Oakville and found the Cliff Cave Park entrance. After they parked, Marty led them into the woods and a trail that followed along a small brook. The boys tread single file on the trail until the water pooled at the bottom of the hillside. The cave entrance was in the middle of the rock- and tree-covered hill. With some effort, they climbed over logs and large rocks to reach the cave's opening. The only other cave most of them had been in was Meramec Caverns. Cliff Cave was minuscule in comparison. The cave was only the size of a large cellar, although the tall ceiling made it appear bigger. The woods diffused the amount of light entering the cave, so the walls were darkened. Flashlight beams created more shadows, it seemed, than revealing details through illumination. It took five minutes to exhaust their survey of the cave when Marty found a smaller opening.

Marty yelled, "Hey, look! I found a small tunnel."

"Fuck that, I'm not going in there," Travis replied.

Gunner dropped onto his hands and knees and pointed the beam of light down the rocky hole in the wall.

Marty did the same, and then, to everyone's surprise, he crawled into the tunnel while holding his flashlight. Everyone watched as he pushed further into the tunnel. Marty yelled, his voice echoing, "Come on, you pussies."

Then, one by one, the others followed: Gunner, Brad, Curtis, and finally, reluctantly, Travis.

Curtis found crawling on hands and knees difficult while holding a flashlight. The rocks were cold and wet, and closer examination showed the water they were crawling through was shallow but flowing. Slowly, fear and claustrophobia made Curtis think this was not a good idea. There was no space to turn around, and moving backward would be awkward and require the skills of a crawdad. Yet the fear of death was nothing compared to the fear of letting friends down. Either they all went home together, or none would exit the cave.

Marty yelled back that he saw the opening. Curtis was glad because it seemed to him the ceiling of their tunnel was shrinking. A few minutes later, they all emerged into another cave about the size of a trailer home kitchen with a low ceiling that prevented them from standing up.

They huddled in a circle when Curtis said, "I bet nobody's ever been back here before."

Marty laughed and admitted he had been back here several times with other friends. The flashlights soon confirmed that the small cave was filled with chalk drawings and words carved and scratched into the stone walls despite its formidable terrors. The true mark of previous human visits was several crushed beer cans littered about.

Curtis said, "I don't know how you carry a six-pack back here."

Not forgetting the reason for their visit, Gunner told everybody to turn their flashlights off on the count of three. He also said they should see who would be the first to turn their light back on.

They all quickly discovered what it was to be in pitch-black darkness. There was no light for their eyes to adjust to. Curtis thought this must be what it was like to be blind. Ten seconds passed before Travis had had enough and turned his light back on.

"Told you," Gunner said.

"Yeah, so fuck you," Travis replied before crawling out of the cave as fast as he could.

On Tuesday, Curtis brought home the table he'd made. He was upset that he only got a C on the project. It looked good to him, and he was proud of it. JoAnn assured him that it was a lovely table, set it in the breezeway near her desk, and placed a houseplant on it.

Everyone was surprised when Curtis Sr. came home from work early. He had never come home from work in the middle of the afternoon. And certainly, nobody had seen him so visibly shaken up, which made everyone alarmed and anxious. In the privacy of his bedroom with his wife, it took some time for Curtis Sr. to get a hold of his emotions. Before dinner, he shared with the family that one of their neighbors was killed at work.

Curtis didn't know the Jones family very well. Bill Jones belonged to the same union as his dad. Curtis Sr. had been on the worksite that morning performing routine maintenance on a backhoe owned by his company. Just after lunch, Mr. Jones was crushed when the tractor flipped over while digging a trench. He left behind a wife and daughter. While the work done on the equipment had no bearing on the accident, the burden of guilt by association was considerable enough to render his dad into a state of grief that required him to take time off work.

Curtis knew Mr. Jones's daughter from school, but Mary Jones rarely rode the bus. When she did, she was more likely to have her nose in a book than to talk to anyone. Mary was a couple of years older than him.

Thursday was the last day of school. Most everyone was in shock and mourning over the loss of Mary's father, and it put a damper on the graduation ceremony being set up for that evening. Curtis cleaned his locker out and left early with JoJo and Brad.

Later that evening, when his dad came home from work, he said, "Curtis, don't make plans for Friday night." Curtis Sr. hardly ever gave his son commands of this nature, so Curtis knew he had no choice but to comply.

Friday was a strange day. While it was the first day of summer break, it didn't feel like it. Curtis waited and dreadfully watched the clock tick away the afternoon. His mother advised him to call his employer to let them know he would not be in that evening.

Curtis had one shirt with a collar his mom had bought him the previous year for school pictures. The shirt barely fit him. He could not get the top button done, so there would be no necktie. He wore a pair of black jeans and borrowed a pair of his dad's old dress shoes—which he had to dust off and polish—and wore an extra pair of socks to make them fit better.

At four thirty, Curtis left with his dad for the funeral home. JoAnn stayed home with the other two children. Curtis felt strange riding in his truck while his dad drove.

The younger McGowan had never been to a funeral before and had no idea what to expect. He had witnessed death of animals most of his life at the Gradys'. Curtis had seen catfish swim around in tubs of fresh water for a few days before being decapitated and skinned. He had heard the shrieks of rabbits being knocked senseless before they were butchered. It was not uncommon to see a deer suspended above the Basement drain. Yet none of these things prepared him to see the still face of a man appearing to be sleeping in a box and wearing heavy makeup. There was nothing natural about it. He had no response and felt overwhelmingly anxious when he heard people say things like, "He looks at peace," or "He looks good, doesn't he?" When he heard them, his inner voice erupted in a screaming, No! He looks dead to me.

While Curtis was in a room full of strangers, his dad seemed to know many union workers who showed up to pay their respects to the family. It was strange to Curtis to see nobody crying. He didn't see any outward expressions of grief, although boxes of tissues were throughout the parlor.

Mrs. Jones stood at the end of the line, greeting people as they passed by the casket covered with flowers and a table full of pictures.

When Curtis found Mary, she was busy talking to a group of older girls. He recognized a lot of them from high school. Most of them were seniors who had graduated the night before.

Mary spotted Curtis and excused herself from her friends. She came over and hugged him and would not let go. Not sure what to do, Curtis raised his arms, reached around her, and hugged her back. She pressed closer into him. He had never been this physically close to a woman before. To his complete horror, his body responded accordingly. When his brain registered what his body was doing, he broke the embrace, stepped back, and got lost in the words coming out of Mary's mouth.

"Thank you for coming," she said. "It means a lot to me. My daddy was a good man and is in a much better place now." Curtis studied her puffy eyes, an indication she had been crying. At that moment, he realized the incredible sadness she was still holding in and how much effort it took to control her grief. Slowly, Curtis began to understand the ritual at the funeral parlor was about the living and not the deceased.

Before they left, Curtis Sr. handed his son a small card. On the front was a picture of praying hands on a pale, gold-marbled background. The back side of the card said, "IN MEMORY OF Mr. William 'Bill' E. Jones" and the date of his birth and his death, "May 22, 1979." Underneath was Psalm 23.

Curtis Sr. said somberly to his son, "Memorize this verse because everyone dies…eventually."

The Lord is my shepherd;
I shall not want.
He makes me to lie down in green pastures;
He leads me beside the still waters.
He restores my soul;
He leads me in the paths of righteousness
For His name's sake.

Yea, though I walk through the valley of the shadow of death,
I will fear no evil;

For You are with me;
Your rod and Your staff, they comfort me.

You prepare a table before me in the presence of my enemies;
You anoint my head with oil;
My cup runs over.
Surely goodness and mercy shall follow me
All the days of my life;
And I will dwell in the house of the Lord
Forever.

CHAPTER 8

A Friday Night in St. Louis County

After leaving the funeral parlor, Curtis and his dad rode home in silence. The first thing he did when he got home was change shirts and take off the ill-fitting dress shoes. He put the memorial card in his Bible on the top shelf of other rarely read books. His mother told him that Steve had called and asked if Curtis would call him as soon as possible. Reluctantly, he called the restaurant and talked to his boss.

Curtis had worked at Riccardo & Lorenzo's for nearly a year and never called in sick. He was fearful that Steve would ask him to come in and finish the evening, but instead, Steve only wanted to know if he could still work his regular Saturday shift. Steve said he approved of his absence with a strong warning not to make a habit of calling in. His statement caught Curtis off guard because he would never have thought to fabricate a story that included a funeral just to get an evening off. Then again, Curtis had never managed a restaurant.

After he hung up the phone, he told his mom he was leaving and went to the Gradys'. When Curtis arrived at the Basement, there was already a gathering of cars, including one he'd never seen before. In the driveway was a brand-new white Ford Mustang II. Once inside, Curtis immediately spotted the new face.

Ronnie, their on-again-off-again friend, introduced Curtis to his new friend, Doyle, who went by the nickname Mick. Mick was a slender, well-dressed kid wearing loafers, pleated slacks, and a polo shirt. He had reddish-colored hair, freckles, and braces on his teeth.

Curtis asked him, "Is that your Mustang?"

Mick said, "It's a Mustang Two, but yes, that's my car."

"What year is it?"

"It's a '78, but I just got it a few months ago. It's practically brand new."

Curtis said, "It looks nice."

"It is. Do you want to come check it out?"

Curtis almost said no. He had had enough of Mick's arrogant responses and condescending attitude, but he was curious about the car Farrah Fawcett-Majors had made famous.

Ronnie spoke up, "Don't believe a word he says. The truth is, it's not a real Mustang; it's a glorified Pinto. Ask him…he'll tell you."

Everyone laughed, and Mick flushed with anger at the jab.

Curtis grabbed two beers out of the fridge, popped the tops off, and handed one of the opened beers to Mick.

Mick grabbed the beer from him and had a drink. "It's not true. It is a Mustang, but it does have some common parts with the Pinto."

From a distance, the car looked nice, but up close, Curtis thought it appeared to be an oversized Hot Wheel. He couldn't put his finger on it. The car just had a fake feel to it. Maybe it was all the plastic trim. The white vehicle was detailed with a large blue "COBRA II" sticker and blue cobras on the front quarter panels. The rear windows were louvered, the front end was cowled, and it had a hood scoop. It was a nice-looking car; however, the last thing Curtis wanted to do was feed the preppy kid's ego, but he did it anyway.

"Wow, that's a nice car," Curtis said as he trailed a hand over the hood. "It looks just like the one from Charlie's Angels."

"Yeah, a lot of people say that, but this is a '78 and hers was a '76."

He opened the front door and released the hood to show off the 302-power plant underneath. "It's a V8 with a lot of power. It's fast."

Curtis immediately noticed that the hood scoop was nonfunctional.

"How fast?"

Mick rolled his eyes and said, "I've had it over 100 a few times."

"No, not how fast can it go… How fast is it off the line?"

Mick thought about it briefly then answered, "I've never brought it to the racetrack, but I bet I could break fifteen seconds on a quarter."

Curtis said, "Bullshit. I'll bet you fifty bucks right now you couldn't beat that old Chevy sitting over there, and he can break fifteen," as he pointed toward Brad's '71 Chevelle.

Mick backed off and said, "I don't race. I can't afford a ticket, and truth be told, I can barely afford the insurance."

Curtis shut the hood. It barely made a sound compared to all the steel hoods around.

"So, what brings you out to Jefferson County?" Curtis inquired.

"I met Ronnie a few weeks ago at the roller rink."

"Rock Roll-O-Rena?"

"Yes, that's the place. Ronnie said if I ever needed weed, I could come out this way and ask for him."

They finished their beers and went back inside.

Curtis yelled to Brad, "Mick says he can smoke your Chevy. I told him fifty bucks says he can't."

Mick turned red when the fifty-dollar bet grew to over two hundred dollars by the other guys in the room. Brad smiled. He would race anyone, anytime, provided they weren't driving a Corvette or a Japanese import. Brad knew the odds of winning easy money were usually in his favor against other street cars.

"Come on, guys, don't be taking his money or he won't be able to get what he came for," Ronnie said.

Brad waved at Ronnie as he headed outside with Mick to conduct business. A short time later, the little Mustang drove away, and Ronnie came back inside to say goodbye.

Marty showed up around eight o'clock, and they sat around listening to the radio, playing pool, and drinking beer.

Marty asked Brad, "Where's your brother? I thought he would be home tonight."

Brad answered, "His last final was today, and they're going to celebrate in Columbia tonight. He should be home tomorrow for the rest of the summer."

Curtis spoke up, "Is anyone getting hungry?"

Brad said, "I feel like eating a Ford."

Everyone laughed as Brad turned off the stereo. He went upstairs to his bedroom to get some cash, and the others waited outside for him to return.

Marty asked, "You driving?"

"Yeah, I'll drive. Get in," Curtis said.

Travis got in Brad's Chevelle and sped along toward the interstate. Curtis and Marty did their best to keep up as they drove to South County.

South St. Louis County was a popular place for motorheads and gearheads alike. They came from all over the St. Louis Metro area, especially on the weekends. The police kept tight control on gathering vehicles to prevent crowds from forming. The caveat was if you parked, you ate. The police generally didn't mess with anyone if they stayed in their parked cars and didn't have music playing exceedingly loud. Eating a burger with the windows down allowed guys to talk to girls or other guys, depending on their interests. The guys would drive to McDonald's, get a burger and a small fry, and then talk to other people. Word got around that someone was looking to race, and if specific terms could be met, they would discuss where and when.

The safest place to race was the racetracks, of which there were two. People could go to Granite City, Illinois on Friday nights, and, for a fee, legally drag race on a quarter-mile strip. The entrants would wait in line to compete with a proper staging area, lights, and an uncontestable finish line. There was also an eighth-mile track in Pevely that offered the same features on Sunday afternoons. Then there were several locations where illegal racing was popular.

The four sat around for nearly an hour, but nobody was biting. Brad had collected some easy money over the past year, but now nobody wanted any part in challenging his Chevelle. An occasional Corvette or rice burner would try, but Brad shunned them as being out of his class. He was also wary of older men in their twenties, especially if he could hear the high-pitched whine under their hoods. Men with more money could turn ordinary cars into sleepers. Sleepers were regular cars with extraordinary power, acceleration, and speed kept hidden from spectators and competitors.

The trick of drag racing was consistent power transfer without breaking anything and keeping the car under control. The physics of racing and the forces involved were numerous and extensive. Although many high school mechanics understood their principles, they didn't often qualify and calculate them. They knew the preciseness because of their understanding and practical observations.

Men with excessive disposable income could spend thousands of dollars on fuel injection, nitrous oxide, blowers, or superchargers. Little did the teenagers know, but guys with that kind of cash would avoid hanging out with careless and reckless teenagers. They made good money by having excellent jobs and would not jeopardize their livelihood by going to jail. Still, you always had to be cautious of the sound and smell of a car that was looking to drag because, occasionally, a kid might get a hold of his dad's keys.

After spending some time at McDonald's, they drove up Lindbergh to White Castle. They all went inside and ordered drinks. Brad and Travis went back to Brad's Chevy while Curtis and Marty stayed inside because there was air conditioning.

When Marty and Curtis went outside, they noticed Brad was gone. Where the Chevelle had been parked, two girls were talking to some guys who seemed to be harassing them.

He recognized one of the girls as he approached his truck. He tried to place her face with a name. He glanced over again at the tall, skinny blonde. He was frustrated because he knew her face but couldn't remember her name or where he knew her from. Then it struck him: Kathy. Her name was Kathy.

By this time, the guys were yelling at the girls, and Curtis spoke up loudly, "Hey, Kathy, is everything okay?"

The two young ladies glanced over at him with bewildered looks on their faces. They turned toward each other and in silent agreement used the distraction to escape the belligerent guys.

The girls approached Curtis and Marty. Kathy said, "Thanks. We needed to get away from those assholes. I'm sorry I don't remember you, but thank you."

She grabbed her friend, and they scurried toward the green Gremlin on the other side of the parking lot near the exit. They did not turn around.

Curtis hollered over to them, "Kathy, I'm Curtis. We were in the same swimming class at Springdale a couple of years ago."

Kathy stopped, peered over her shoulder, and said, "Yeah, I think I remember. Sorry, we've got to go."

The two girls got into the car and left. Curtis started his truck, put it in gear, and drove after them. He barely made it through the intersection before the light changed. The little green Gremlin was fast, but Curtis kept the car in view without excessively speeding.

Marty asked, "Who are they?"

"I don't know who the short girl is, but I know Kathy. She has a brother a year older than us. She was just a kid the last time I saw her. I think she was only twelve or thirteen back then."

"You were just a kid a few years ago too." Marty laughed. "Most days, I think you might still be one."

As Curtis drove behind the speeding car, he remembered Kathy in detail as his memories all started to gel at once. It was the summer before he entered junior high. He was beginning to jump off the diving board in the deep end, and his mom wanted him to have proper swimming lessons.

The weather at Springdale could be cool in the morning, and the water was always cold because the pool was continuously filled with treated spring-fed water. Young kids often sat shivering on the pool's edge, listening to teachers talk about swimming and going over safety instructions before entering the pool. The kids wore colored ribbons around their necks, held together by safety pins. The colors indicated their age, water skills, and risk potential for drowning.

Curtis remembered that Kathy had worn a white cotton bikini to their swimming lessons. The cotton swimsuit was meant for a young girl, not a teenager. Kathy was thin for her age and had a tiny waist and a budding chest, but it was too revealing when that bikini got wet. The girl, without meaning to, launched Curtis into puberty before he had a single hair under his arms or anywhere else, for that matter.

Now, it bothered Curtis that she was avoiding him. He was curious and wanted to know why. He couldn't let it go, so he chased her from South

County through Affton and into Webster Groves. She drove through a red light, pulled into a Steak 'n Shake, and parked near the front of the building. Curtis didn't let the car out of his sight, and when the light turned green, he pulled his truck into the parking lot and got out.

Kathy also got out, reached back into the car, and grabbed a hat. She put the hat on before coming toward them. She yelled, "What do you want? Why are you chasing us?"

The boys stared at the tall girl with butter-blonde hair flowing from under a burnt orange Australian wool floppy hat. She appeared taller because she wore a pair of dark brown slip-on platform sandals. She waved her arms as she spoke. Large, gold hoop earrings bounced with her motions. She wore a floral denim jumper with all the colors of summer, yet despite the summer warmth her ensemble denoted, it fell short of inviting because of her agitated mannerisms.

The other girl got out and stood by the side of the car. Curtis saw she was dressed in a yellow ruffle-sleeved, pleated mini dress. Her long curly brown hair was fastened to her head with a white scarf hairband. He noticed she was wearing cowboy boots.

"Kathy, it's me, Curtis. I know you. I know your brother James. I know your mom." He had to think about it for a moment. "Your mom's name is Denise, right? We used to swim together at Springdale."

It was a relief for Curtis when he saw Kathy's face change. One minute, he was a stranger to her, and a moment later, she immediately recognized him as an old friend. She ran across the parking lot, hugged him, and apologized.

"I really thought you were chasing us to do us harm. We've been dealing with creeps all night long." The girl in the cowboy boots nodded in agreement.

Seeing the boys were no longer a threat, the brown-haired girl marched over and said, "My name's Francine. You guys really scared us."

"Hi, Francine, I'm Curtis, and this is my friend Marty." Curtis waved for Marty to get out of the truck. Curtis noticed that as he spoke to Francine face to face, she was not nearly as short as she had first appeared. However, Kathy was a few inches taller than everyone.

Marty greeted the girls, and just as everyone was feeling safe and secure with one another, a Saint Louis County patrol car rolled by slowly then stopped. The patrolman said, "Hey, you all need to go inside and get something to eat or leave. You can't be standing around in the parking lot." The radio squealed as the dispatcher checked in for the officer's status and location. The officer grabbed the mike, acknowledged the dispatcher, and provided an update before slowly driving away.

As they approached the entrance, Kathy said, "I work here. Let me talk to the manager. I'll get us a table, and I should be able to get us some food if they aren't too busy."

They sat at a table and enjoyed talking and catching up. The manager permitted Kathy to serve them free sodas if she wiped down the table before they left.

Curtis and Marty learned Kathy lived in Webster Groves with her mom, but her brother and dad lived in Des Peres. Their dad had bought him a car so James could drive himself to Webster to finish school. James was going to be a senior in the fall and had plans to go to Webster University after he graduated.

Francine shared that she was initially from Clayton but was living with her aunt in Brentwood and recently dropped out of school. There was an uncomfortable lull in the conversation, and the girls shared a look. It appeared as if they were talking in code with their eyes. Kathy excused herself to go to the bathroom, and Francine followed her without saying a word.

Marty was cautiously optimistic. "I got to hand it to you, Curtis, I'm impressed. I wish I had brought some condoms."

"Marty, I didn't pick them up. I know Kathy. She's like an old friend to me."

Marty replied, "An old friend with a beautiful ass."

Curtis shook his head at his friend.

The girls came back to the table and sat down. Curtis interpreted this as a good sign. He expected them to return and say goodbye, which would have ended the night. Yet here they all were, still talking.

Kathy asked, "What are you guys going to do now?"

Marty shrugged his shoulders. "We don't have any plans, really. Just came up to South County to—"

"I know," Kathy said with a smile, "you came up to South County to pick up girls."

 "Actually, no," Curtis objected. "We came up to South County to drag race."

Kathy laughed. "Seriously, you expect me to think you're drag racing an old Ford pickup. Francine, can you believe this? This is interesting. We've never been a guy's plan B before."

Francine said, "Okay, Curtis. If you didn't chase us down, what would you be doing right now?"

"Well, we would have gone back to Jefferson County to Grady's house and played pool and drank beer."

"Who is this Brady guy?"

"His name is Brad. Brad Grady. We hang out in his basement."

"Wait. Let me get this straight. You go to your friend's house and sit in their basement anytime you want and drink beer and play pool."

Marty added, "Yeah, pretty much. It's okay. His dad works a late shift, and his mother usually isn't at home on the weekends. It's just a cool place to hang out."

"That sounds interesting," Kathy said. Then she added, "Hey, Francine, do you want to drive out to the county tonight and play pool and drink beer with some cute guys?"

For the first time, Francine smiled, and her eyes lit up. She said, "Yes, I would like that a lot."

Kathy wiped down the table as Curtis gathered all the trash before leaving.

Francine hugged Kathy in the parking lot then looked at Marty and said, "You, ride with her."

Curtis unlocked his truck, and Francine climbed in and shut the door. Curtis did nothing but ask Francine questions about Kathy the entire drive back to Imperial. Every word he said was about Kathy. By the time they arrived at Grady's, she was hoping there would be a guy there who would take an interest in her.

When Curtis and Marty walked into the Basement with the two girls, it was like Christmas morning, and they were Santa Claus. Brad's eyes lit up. Travis revealed a wicked grin as he glanced over toward his friend Brian, who had come over with him to play pool. Brian showed indifference to the girls as he took his shot. Travis swung his head back around and made eye contact with Francine.

Curtis overheard Kathy whisper to Francine as she grabbed her hand, "We're either going to get killed tonight or have sex. Maybe both."

Francine replied, "I was kind of thinking the same thing."

Curtis and Marty watched in total amazement as the two girls worked the room. They hadn't been there fifteen minutes, and Travis had his arms around Francine, showing her how to shoot pool. Kathy was on the couch talking with Brad. Ten minutes later, they were making out. After people started to take notice, Brad headed up the stairs to his bedroom, leading the tall, butter-blonde girl by the hand.

Marty shot Curtis a perturbed look, shrugged his shoulders, and left. Curtis suddenly felt like the invisible man. He said goodnight, but nobody replied. He walked out the door in a state of disbelief and drove home. It was like a missing episode from the *Twilight Zone*, where nothing made sense.

When Curtis left for work early Saturday morning, the green Gremlin was still parked at the Gradys'.

CHAPTER 9

Springdale

Tuesday, July 19, 1954, was the second day in a row that temperatures in St. Louis exceeded 100 degrees Fahrenheit. Looking for temporary relief from the heat, Abigail Martin took her young family to Lincoln Beach on the Meramec River to cool off. Although the resort was in its waning years, Abigail had fond memories of her childhood splashing and playing at the river's edge. Many buildings were no longer in use, but the long concrete stairway was still there to get down to the beach. Unfortunately, most of the artificial beach had been washed away by regular flooding.

Abigail wanted to share her happy memories with her children: Rebekah (age six), Leanne (eight), Charlotte (twelve), and her son, John (fourteen). When they arrived at the riverside, she set her bags down and laid out a blanket. She took a hand from each of her younger daughters and told the older two children to stay where she could see them. The two young girls sat on the sand with little buckets and shovels and watched the water trickle into the small holes they made. Charlotte and John proceeded to splash water as they yelled names at each other. Charlotte soon grew tired of this. She joined her mother on the beach and played with her sisters for a while before returning to the blanket to read a book. Without her older daughter to help, Abigail swiveled her head, continually keeping an eye on her son while attending to the two young girls who grew tired of the bucket and shovels and began to explore the beach, looking for treasures.

John, being a teenager, walked out until the water was up to his chest. As he heard his mom call out his name, he tried to turn around to face her. When he turned, his foot slid down a steep, muddy incline and immediately slipped into the river. The boy, wholly immersed in the river, was no longer visible. His mother saw him disappear before her eyes. She jumped up and screamed for help, but that only drew attention to herself. Nobody understood what she was pointing to. By the time they figured it out, the young teenager was ten feet away from them and still completely submerged under the water, with the current dragging him further downstream.

The boy was not strong enough to get back to the surface. Unable to get above the surface to breathe, he drowned and lost consciousness. Two minutes later, he was twenty feet from the bathers, desperately looking for him, not realizing he was beyond their help. His young body, cloaked in the muddy water, went into a seizure. Within minutes, due to a lack of oxygen to the brain, he lost all bodily functions and died.

River drownings became all too common, and it didn't take long for people to start blaming the rivers. There's always an inherent danger when humans encounter oceans, lakes, or rivers. The idea of public swimming pools, with crystal clear water and full-time lifeguards, became popular, and large complexes began popping up all over the region. In 1960, fifty acres of land in Fenton, Missouri, were developed into a park with a 44,000-square-foot spring-fed swimming pool that contained over a million gallons of fresh water. A year later, Springdale Park & Pool was opened to the public.

Springdale was celebrating its ten-year anniversary when JoAnn was looking at apartments with her mother and father. Franz Bernhard and his wife, Clara, had recently moved after Franz retired as a motorman from the New York City Transit Authority. The only advertising required was the cool appeal of the aquamarine-colored pool filled with people on a hot summer day.

JoAnn had driven by the facility numerous times before stopping to find out the cost of admission. She learned that a season pass would be the best value for her family. After one visit, she returned with her mom and dad, and they also purchased one.

The pool and facilities were owned and operated by Louis "Vik" Papadakis, a retired teamster from Anheuser-Busch, and his wife, Agnes. Everyone called Agnes "Sunny." Vik sat, most days, shirtless on a chair in front of a small booth by the entrance. Season pass holders were waved through, but the others stopped by to add more bills to Vik's ever-growing wad of cash.

Sunny oversaw the work inside the bar and grill connected to the same building as the concession stand. The bar and grill were open all year and, from the public's perspective, separated from the park and pool. Like all public swimming pools, the swimming season started on Memorial Day weekend and lasted through Labor Day. The bar kept the Papadakis family busy in the off-season.

From Curtis's perspective, pool season didn't start until after school let out. School year length was often dictated by the number of snow days incurred. A light winter made for a more extended summer, making most people incredibly happy.

JoAnn had no trouble getting chores done during the summer months. Her "to do" items would be carried out while she packed a cooler and picnic basket with snacks and lunch. She had a few large pool bags for towels, sunscreen, and pool toys, most of the Nerf variety. Everyone would be in their bathing suits and flip-flops, waiting for her to go through her daily mental checklist.

Curtis went outside and started her station wagon. The morning sun had already heated the vinyl seats to a near-painful level of burn, but nothing like it would be on the drive home. Only the grace of a damp pool towel could prevent blisters from forming on exposed skin. The blast of cigarette smoke infused warm air blew out the vents. The smell would lessen as the refrigerant cooled the air, only to be infused again when his mother lit up before backing out of the driveway.

"Did you get the air mattresses out of the K-Mart bag like I asked?"

"Yes," Curtis replied.

"Both of them?"

"Yes."

The worst part of going to the pool the first time was blowing up rough, canvas-like rafts by mouth. JoAnn wouldn't get the cheap plastic ones anymore. Curtis knew his morning would be spent getting dizzy while huffing and puffing air.

He complained, "Why can't Dad get an air compressor?"

"Because we have to pay your truck insurance. Why don't you use a bicycle pump?"

"Because it's a raft, not a tire. The valves are different."

"There should be some kind of adapter. If not, maybe you can invent one and become a millionaire."

The pool didn't open until ten in the morning because private swimming lessons were offered. JoAnn had been a season pass holder for so long that she was known and loved by the Papadakis family. Vik had taken a particular liking to her dad as Franz spent many hours in a chair next to Vik at the front gate. Whenever Vik saw the Ford station wagon, he would wave hello and smile as the car rolled through to find a coveted spot with afternoon shade.

Vik allowed his friends to go in early, provided they kept their distance from the groups of kids, many of whom were covered in goose pimples and shivering with cold or fear. Numerous instructors worked with each group. For some, it was learning about how to overcome fear. Others would be taught how to kick or float.

When nobody was in the pool, it would be smooth as glass in the morning, filled with the most inviting element of the universe: water… and lots of it. Spring-fed 68-degree crystal-clear chlorinated water filtered into the million-plus gallons that filled the pool. A faded aqua-blue concrete basin with a smooth bottom formed the rectangular shape of the pool. A gentle slope started at the shallow end with three inches of water and dropped to over five feet at the other end. An even deeper section, roped off at the northeast corner, entrenched from ten to twelve feet of spring water to accommodate two diving boards.

The deep area was identified by the Capri blue-and-white twisted nylon rope floating on top of the surface supported by matching polyethylene buoys. Lifeguards strictly forbade anyone to touch the ropes or hang on to any of the white-capped steel pipe pylons that enclosed the deep end. Two stainless steel ladders, one on each side of the corner, provided egress from the pool.

The majesty of the pool's deep end was a pair of diving boards: a ten-foot diving board for the brave of heart and a three-foot diving board for fun-loving people of all ages. A lifeguard chair was positioned on the outside of each diving board. Like all lifeguard chairs, they were painted white with welded brackets to receive large umbrellas.

Behind the diving area was the pump house, a sizable tan building with a white gable roof. Broad sweeping letters in the shape of a wave spelled the logo SPRINGDALE in cobalt blue capital letters. Lifeguards could enter the secure building through a single-entry door to perform routine chemistry checks to ensure the water was safe. The pump house doubled as a storage facility and could be accessed from the park side through a roll-up garage door. Inside the garaged area was a tractor, trailer, and an enormous mowing deck.

The entire pool was encircled by a white concrete gutter built into its walls. Lifeguards could be assigned to pool maintenance and upkeep. It was common to see them scrubbing the gutters with thick bristle brushes and Comet.

Additional steel ladders surrounding the pool's perimeter allowed people to climb from the deeper sides. The swimming pool was surrounded by concrete topped with a sanded surface that was cooler to walk on and had enough texture to minimize slippage. Springdale had a strictly enforced "No Running" policy. Outside the concrete walkway, the surface gently sloped up to provide a comfortable angle for swimmers to lay out towels and sunbathe before dropping a couple of feet, which made the far edge a nice place to sit and watch people in the park. Between the edge of the concrete surface was more loose river gravel up to the base of a ten-foot-tall chain-link fence surrounding the pool.

Springdale Pool was the centerpiece of a lovely park that surrounded it. The park contained picnic tables, pavilions, barbecue and horseshoe pits, trees for shade, and lots of areas to park. The large open-spaced area was perfect for throwing a frisbee, tossing a baseball, or playing jarts. Vans and pickups often backed up to the chain-linked fence by the diving area and played music.

The only access to the pool for the public was through a massive brick building that contained toilets, showers, and changing areas with rentable storage lockers.

The last obstacle to face before entering the swimming area was an enormous shower spraying cold spring water in a full cone pattern from a single overhead showerhead. A small drain caused the cold water to back up in the basin. Showering and washing feet before entering the swimming pool was a matter of forced hygiene. Many tried to avoid the cold shower by clinging tightly to the chain-link fence and walking along the basin's edge. Unfortunately, leaving the pool at the end of the day, going to the concession stand, or simply using the bathroom required the same precautionary measures.

The Papadakis family were first-generation Americans. Vik and Sunny were the children of Greek immigrants who made their way to New York at the turn of the century. Vik moved to St. Louis with his wife and found employment with Anheuser-Busch. Sunny also worked at the St. Louis brewery during World War II. Vik retired as a member of the Teamsters and used a portion of his retirement savings to buy the park and pool. The couple remained childless until 1956, when Sunny became pregnant and gave birth to a son, Lucas Daniel Papadakis, whom everyone called Danny.

Danny, an all-American athlete, dropped out of college in his second year to return home and help his parents with the family businesses. Danny stood six feet, three inches tall with broad, muscular shoulders and back tapered down to a narrow waist. He was a natural swimmer and skillful diver with a lighthearted personality and a fondness for showing off. Danny rotated with the other lifeguards when not roaming the park on Springdale's groundskeeping tractor cutting grass or picking up trash. While he had no say in hiring or firing employees, he was responsible for their training and keeping the schedule.

Danny was engaged to his high school sweetheart, Samantha. In keeping up with the Papadakis tradition, everyone called her Sammy. Sammy also was a regular lifeguard at the pool in addition to serving drinks and burgers in the bar when Sunny needed to keep the concession stand in order.

From the start of summer until the end of it, Springdale had the vibe of a giant pool party that lasted for months. While the bar served beer and alcohol, the concession stand did not. And even though the sign at the entrance said, "No Alcoholic Beverages Allowed," nobody ever checked the coolers. Even Vic, by the end of the day, had a stack of red cups in his hand or sitting on the floor of the booth.

By 1979, women's liberation was recognized in the setting of public swimming pools as bathing suits, particularly the bikini, became more revealing. While scantily clad women were not in the majority, the uninhibited women stood out. From adolescent teenage boys to older men with one foot in the grave, men took notice. Because it was considered rude to stare, Ray-Bans became a popular accessory to provide a measure of anonymity to wandering eyeballs.

Just as women came in all shapes and sizes, so it appeared to Curtis that female breasts did as well. Objectifying women solely based on physical appearance was as problematic to the hormone-driven teenager as trying to differentiate between love and lust. And contrary to rational thought, having a grandmother, mother, and sister made no difference.

A few things in those formative years helped offset the tension. Recognizing that a woman could be sexy without being sexual was one of them. A woman sunning herself in public was worlds apart from a woman touching herself in public. Public decency and order could be maintained simultaneously for a time. In this situation, it was the best of both worlds. Women could feel good about themselves, while men could admire their beauty and move on with their day.

As a teenager still approaching his seventeenth birthday, sex and marriage seemed so far away. Long before he could see or touch a breast, Curtis had to get in the game, and that thought brought him fear. It would require getting to know someone, caring for them to some degree, and spending time with them. There were so many questions he did not have answers to. He was like a detective trying to solve a mystery with little evidence to clue him in. He wanted to get into the game but didn't know the rules or how to start. So, while he waited for the universe to clue him in, he hid in the darkness his Ray-Bans provided and carefully watched, daring to dream.

JoAnn was determined to keep her younger two children covered in suntan lotion and never let either one out of her sight. Around one in the afternoon, she made everyone get out of the pool to go home, ignoring their cries for one more hour. It would be a long summer, and she didn't want anyone getting a bad sunburn and ruining the rest of the week. To appease their disappointment, she stopped at the concession stand on the way out and bought everyone a chocolate-dipped ice cream cone.

CHAPTER 10

The Best Jukebox Ever

Franz Gustav Bernhard was born on the outskirts of Philadelphia, Pennsylvania, in 1906. He was fourteen years old when Prohibition was ratified. Franz was twenty years old when he moved to Queens, New York, near 234th Street in the growing neighborhood called Little Neck. Unbeknownst to him twelve miles across town in Astoria, a young Greek named Louis Papadakis was hustling to make his mark in life. During the 1920s, the population of Queens dramatically increased due to the massive improvements in transportation, particularly the approval of new bridges and roadways. Franz, or Frank, as he preferred to be called, started as a taxi driver shuttling people back and forth to Manhattan. In his twenties, he was thrust into bootlegging, which was dangerous and exciting. While it helped him pay his bills, it also hardened him in the way any illegal activity ruins an otherwise hardworking man. He eventually met and married the love of his life, Clara Mueller, the daughter of a German immigrant. With his hard work and connections with the network of gin runners, favors owed were called in, and he secured a job with the New York City Transit Authority. Frank would have this job until he took an early retirement in 1970 with a partial disability for a work-related injury.

Although the Great Depression of the 1930s slowed the rapid expansion of growth, the construction of the Triborough and Bronx-Whitestone Bridges and the construction of LaGuardia Airport allowed Queens to expand again. The farms disappeared and were replaced by new single-family homes on rows of newly poured streets. The security of the motorman job for the NYCTA could not have come at a better time for him. In 1939, on Christmas Eve, Clara gave birth to their third child, JoAnn

Colette. With the repeal of Prohibition six years earlier, the Bernhards could celebrate with a legal toast.

Curtis stayed up too late on Thursday and would not wake up when his mother called him. Instead of dumping water on his head, she left him alone and took his siblings to Springdale without him. JoAnn left a list of things for him to take care of before he went to work later that afternoon. Curtis woke around ten and saw the list when he went into the kitchen to make breakfast. The list was long, but Curtis dressed, went through each item, and was done before noon. Afterward, he pulled his motorcycle out of the garage, went down the hill to Chesley Island, and rode around for a while before returning to the Basement.

Pulling up, he saw the green Gremlin and Marty's car in the driveway. He was surprised to see everyone there so early. He parked his motorcycle in the shade and went inside. Brad and Kathy were upstairs, and Marty was playing pool with Francine.

Curtis asked, "Where's Travis?"

Francine missed her easy shot and glared at him. "You knew, didn't you?"

"What? What did I know?"

"You knew that kid was fifteen."

"Travis?"

"Yes, Travis," she said.

Only a week had passed, but Curtis was struggling with the details of the previous Friday night. He couldn't understand why she was upset with him.

"Of course, everyone knows Travis is just a kid."

"Well, just so you know, he ain't a kid no more," she yelled as she missed another easy shot.

Marty took a drink from his beer, shrugged his shoulders, and cleared the table. He looked at Francine and asked, "Do you want to play again?"

"Fuck you too. I don't know why I bother to come out here with you assholes."

"Because we really are nice guys when it comes down to it," Curtis offered.

"Yeah, nice guys that don't have a clue."

Curtis was sitting down reading through a week-old newspaper. "Hey, do you guys want to go see *Alien*? There's a three-dollar matinee today at two o'clock."

"Don't you have to work tonight?"

"Yes, but I don't have to be there until five."

Curtis went upstairs, but the door to Brad's bedroom was shut. He came downstairs and said, "They're busy and don't want to go."

Francine softened and agreed to go to the movies with Curtis and Marty. Curtis said he would drive himself so he could go straight to work after the movie.

"We'll see you there," Marty said.

Curtis took his motorcycle home, grabbed his truck keys, and drove to Mark Twain Theatre in South County.

Curtis went straight to work after the movie. While he loved science fiction movies, he was not a big fan of horror movies. Marty had convinced him to see *Phantasm* a few months earlier, and the movie gave Curtis nightmares. *Alien* was scarier, so he was glad he could go to work before driving home.

In between filling pizza orders, Curtis made it a point to go and tell Tiny about the movie.

"No shit?" Tiny laughed when Curtis told him about the gruesome scenes. "I'm gonna have to go see this movie now, Speedy."

"And that's not all; the hero in this movie is a woman. Bad to the bone and beautiful," he added.

Leo, always looking for a reason to insert himself, said, "If there is time to lean, there is time to clean."

Curtis returned to the pizza oven, and Tiny made obscene gestures as he returned to his grill.

Curtis finished the shift without further incident and left at ten. He came back the following day to work eight more hours. He looked forward to having Saturday nights off for the rest of the summer.

The convenient location of Springdale made it a popular destination in the summer months. There was nothing like the pool to beat the humid summer heat. Being near the intersection of Highways 141 and 21 was optimal since both roads connected St. Louis and Jefferson counties and drew people from both. The activities within the park were limited only by the imagination of the people who came.

No matter how much someone enjoyed the water, shriveling fingers and shivering bodies needed to escape the frigid waters for a spell. The magic of Springdale consisted of all the amenities that a spacious park could offer, so people took advantage of the acreage, sunshine, and fresh air of summer, knowing that they could always go back into the pool to cool off.

The park was perfect for physical and athletic souls, in large groups or small. People engaged in various outdoor activities, such as volleyball or softball. A few friends or couples could toss horseshoes or footballs. Outside the concession stand was a small arcade for the less athletically inclined.

The open-air enclosure housed half a dozen or more pinball machines and a couple of recently added video games. Seawolf, a submarine simulator, and Space Invaders enticed players to feed quarters into the machines.

Curtis would see how long he could stay out of the pool and play pinball with four quarters. While a dollar did not go far inside the concession stand, outside, four quarters could go a long way. By 1979, the pinball machines were getting more challenging to play. Sure, they had more lights, noise, and digital displays, but they also had steeper tables and a more sensitive tilt. Worse, the newer machines only offered three balls to play for the same quarter that used to get five shots. Still, Curtis found winning a free game playing pinball more satisfying than the challenge of typing his three initials into the top ten high scores of a video game.

Curtis didn't care for the video games, at least outside. The natural light glare made Space Invaders challenging to see, but he also found the game-play mindless, stupid, and a waste of time…and a waste of a quarter.

The covered arcade opened into a small, uncovered courtyard with a few picnic tables spaced apart along the far edge. The area was fenced off by a small brick wall topped with a wrought iron fence. People sitting at the tables could see the park entrance or the side pavilion that belonged to the bar and grill next door.

The food offered from the concession stand was limited but delicious as far as summertime food goes. Sunny Papadakis oversaw the concession stand and the bar and grill. A couple of dollars was all it took to get a burger or hot dog, a boat of french fries, or a giant, classic soft pretzel and a drink.

The biggest seller, however, was undoubtedly their soft-serve ice cream. A swirl of vanilla ice cream in a cone would be hand-dipped into a melted chocolate sauce that magically hardened into a delicious shell. Curtis would forgo every item on the board for one of their floats. The Springdale root beer float was second to none, made from traditional IBC root beer brewed locally in St. Louis. A large Styrofoam cup of soda topped off with a generous serving of vanilla ice cream was served with a straw, a long-handled spoon, and a handful of napkins.

Yet of everything in the open-air arcade, the best thing sat right next to the icebox in the form of a jukebox. The jukebox contained an impressive one hundred twenty songs and was remarkably cheap to listen to. The music was also wired into speakers around the concession area so everyone could hear it. A quarter would purchase three songs. And because it was so cheap, the jukebox often sang all day.

Many songs were played so often that they became embedded in the Springdale experience. It was impossible to walk from the park to the pool without hearing "Slow Ride" by Foghat, "Magic Man" by Heart, or Aerosmith's "Dream On." There were also a half dozen offerings by Elton John, Paul McCartney, and Fleetwood Mac that would be played several times throughout any given day. In 1979, two more songs made the rotation: "Rock 'N' Roll Fantasy" by Bad Company and "Dance the Night Away" by Van Halen.

Curtis spent more time playing the pinball machines. In previous years, he had to beg his mom for a dollar, but now that he was working, Curtis didn't have to ask anymore. His favorite pinball game was called Mata Hari. Curtis was not sure if he liked it because he was good at it or if he was good at it because he played it so often. It was a game he knew he could get free games on if he concentrated. Spending so much time outside the pool, he grew accustomed to hearing other songs like "Rock On" by David Essex or the Climax Blues Band's "Couldn't Get It Right." Dr. John's "Right Place Wrong Time" was also played quite a bit. These songs, played repeatedly, were engraved onto his mind.

After a joyful weekend, Curtis was looking forward to a day at the pool. His mother, however, was not having a particularly good day. She made the drive over to Fenton an unpleasant one. She ranted about many things for thirty minutes, primarily directed at Curtis. He knew that, for all intents and purposes, she was talking to herself. As most kids do, he had learned that it was best to listen with ears open and mouth shut. Each minute was a mile passed and closer to the pool. He closed his eyes and endured the tongue-lashing in silence.

He remembered a similar drive to the pool many years ago before he was a teenager. He received a tremendous dose of personal critique and admonition from his mother, and when he grew weary of it, he said something he would soon regret. With a cloudy mind, still groggy from sleep, he said, "Well, I didn't ask to be born."

JoAnn immediately pulled the car off the side of the road and took her flip-flop off her foot to beat her son senselessly with it.

Today, they arrived at the pool early. The pool was empty except for a couple of lifeguards milling about. Vik waved at JoAnn as she turned her car off the highway. She slowed and rolled down her window.

He asked, "Are your folks coming today?"

"Yes, but probably not for another hour."

"Okay, have a great day," he said as she drove in to find a parking spot.

Walking toward the pool, Curtis noticed a mist over the smooth surface of the water. Recalling a scene from Alien when a mist covered the alien eggs, a chill of fear went through him.

His grandparents arrived, but his grandmother entered the pool area by herself. His grandfather found a chair and would spend most of the day talking to Vik.

Thirty minutes later, several school buses parked near the front entrance. Dozens of black families flowed from the open doors, and an assortment of people, young and old, men and women, some with children grasping their mother's necks, and dozens of children, were running toward the pool. Mothers were shouting and trying to keep up with the anxious kids.

Curtis saw several teenagers run through the dressing area and come out the other side moments later. They ran through the cold shower and raced one another to see who would be first in the pool. The whistles immediately began blowing, but the young men plowed straight into the ankle-deep shallow end and raced each other, kicking up large rooster tails of spray behind them. Once they got past the slide, the depth of the water forced them to lift their legs higher, like hurdlers, until the water overwhelmed them, and they tripped, falling face-first into the pool. They began yelling and wrestling with each other before they realized the lifeguard was talking to them and cautioning them about the dangers of running. Until the time Curtis left, one side of the pool was filled with laughing black faces enjoying the cold water and having a wonderful time.

With what little money he had burning a hole in his pocket, Curtis got out of the pool and went to the arcade. He found the Mata Hari pinball machine available. The Bally pinball machine was his favorite. The game generated a loud knock when enough points were gained for a free game. The knock was pleasurably satisfying to hear.

Curtis was doing rather well on the game when a teenage girl wearing a sky-blue bikini and matching fingernail polish came into his view. She was tall with smooth skin, and her turquoise swimming suit contrasted wonderfully with her dark skin. She watched earnestly as he played the game, but her head was on a swivel as she glanced around, watching her peers as other black teenagers came around the corner with french fry boats and ice cream cones. Curtis noticed she had shoulder-length hair full of braids with white and blue beads. They rattled every time she swung her head.

She yelled, "Jamal, I'm over here."

Moments later, a tall, lean teenager with a white towel draped over his shoulders sauntered over. He was eating a giant soft pretzel. Curtis saw him tear off a large piece and offer it to the girl.

"Naw, I'm good. I might get me an ice cream, though."

He came back in a few minutes with an ice cream for her.

Curtis tried to focus on the game but was curious about the visitors. Up to this point in his life, the only black people he knew of were his childhood heroes, Bob Gibson and Lou Brock.

Jamal watched Curtis play and said, "You seriously bustin' at this."

Curtis replied, "I should be. I've put enough quarters into this game."

Curtis aggressively pushed the machine forward just enough to persuade the metal ball to fall back down the slot that led to the right flipper and timed it perfectly to knock down the remaining targets in the right bank, which caused them to reset. Six eyes followed the silver ball as it rolled back down. His attention was disrupted again by a dark hand placing a quarter down on the glass top.

Jamal said, "You might not get to play. This cat is slammin' hard."

As if in a trance, Curtis looked to his right and saw another beautiful black girl with dark eyes and full lips eating an ice cream cone. She was wearing a one-piece red bathing suit that appeared completely dry.

Curtis was nervous, and his attention was divided between glancing at her while trying to keep his eye on the silver ball, knowing he had the admiration of the other two kids on his right. He dreaded losing the ball down the middle; every second seemed like forever. He was anxious playing with all these eyes watching his every move. Every time he sent the ball back up to the top, he chanced a peek out of the corner of his eye.

When the score got high enough, he won a second game. The table knocked loudly, but the delight in winning a free game immediately disappeared when he saw the girl pick her quarter back up. He felt terrible because he knew she was waiting for the machine.

As she started to walk away, Curtis said, "Please don't go."

She turned around and stared at him.

"I've been here long enough. I want to go back to the pool. Go ahead and play. There's two games left."

"For real?" she replied. "Yeah, it's a fun game. I'm sure you'll like it," he said.

"Thank you," she said as she handed him the quarter.

As the courtyard filled up with more people, new songs emerged from the jukebox: the Commodore's "Brick House" and "Love Roller Coaster" by the Ohio Players, along with "Tell Me Something Good" by Rufus and Stevie Wonder's "Sir Duke." It was the last song that stuck with Curtis for a long time, with lyrics about music being a language everyone understood and the power of music to cause people to stand up and clap their hands. The music that day was both powerful and beautiful.

That hot summer day in June of 1979, Curtis learned a little about diversity, but the best jukebox ever was already one step ahead of him.

Later that night, he was back hanging out with his friends in the Basement. It was another typical Monday night in Jefferson County. A few friends drank beer, played pool, and listened to the radio. Ronnie stopped by to see if anyone needed weed. The radio was tuned to KSHE, and as they were playing pool, Curtis grooved to "Gimme Shelter" by the Rolling Stones. He was sharing a joint with Ronnie when the next song, "Walk on the Wild Side" by Lou Reed, began. All that could be heard was the occasional clacking of pool balls and the music.

Curtis began to listen to the songs differently. As the song ended, Ronnie said to Curtis, "You have to admit, those black girls sure can sing."

CHAPTER 11

Lumps in the Cream Sauce

The telephone rang and interrupted the McGowan family's breakfast. JoAnn slid out of her chair and grabbed the phone.

"Curtis, the telephone is for you."

Curtis chewed on a large bite of a maple syrup-drenched pancake as he got up from the table.

"Hello?"

"Curtis, this is Steve."

"Steve?"

"Yeah, Steve from Riccardo's. Listen, I know it's Sunday, but we're short in the kitchen today, and I was hoping you'd come in for a few hours to get us through lunch."

Curtis remained quiet, trying to figure out a way to say no without it sounding like complete bullshit.

"Curtis? Are you there?"

"Yeah, I'm here... I'd really like to help out, but I have plans today."

Both his mom and dad glared at him.

"I understand. I'm not asking you to work until close, just a few hours to cover lunch. I'll even pay you overtime today."

Between the glare of his parents and the opportunity to cash in, Curtis changed his mind.

"Sure, Steve. I'll get ready and leave shortly."

"Thank you. You're the man."

Curtis hung up the phone and returned to eat the rest of his breakfast.

"I have to go to work today," Curtis announced with a bit of annoyance.

His mother replied, "Well, you better get used to it. Your father works sixty hours or more every week, and he doesn't complain."

"Well, I wouldn't complain about it either if I made over twenty dollars an hour."

In a rare instance, his father spoke up. "Don't worry so much about the money, worry about doing a good job. The money will come once you prove you're a reliable worker. I used to pick cotton for two dollars a day when I was your age."

"I know…and you ate beans with bacon fat for dinner and walked everywhere uphill both ways."

"Yeah, you're right about that. And I was grateful for it too. You ought to be a bit more grateful for the opportunities you have."

Curtis quietly finished breakfast while his dad drank coffee and read the sports section.

"What time do you need to leave?" his mother inquired as she cleared the table.

Curtis checked the clock. "I have to be there at eleven, so I should get ready."

Curtis arrived fifteen minutes before eleven. Steve greeted him with a smile and a pat on the shoulder as he signed him in to start the shift. Curtis noticed the manager clocked him in at the top of the hour.

"Thanks for coming in. Go on back and make sure your pizza station is ready to go."

There was only one dishwasher working. It turned out Steve promoted the other dishwasher to make salads and help prepare food for the coming week. He had also called Gonzo, who would only commit to "I might come in if I feel better by noon."

Curtis headed down the waiter's side of the counter toward the pizza oven. Leo stopped him.

"What are you doing here?"

Curtis explained Steve had called him in to work the pizza oven for the lunch rush, then he would leave afterward because he was on overtime.

"Just think, if they offered you double time, you would still only make half as much as me." He laughed his way back to the pasta station.

Leo not only was a contemptible person, but he genuinely enjoyed being one.

Curtis ensured his pizza station was stocked and wiped down in time for the first pizza order. Just as he slid the well-crafted pie into the oven, Leo returned like a boomerang. "Just so you know, this is Sunday, and you'll have to do more than make pizzas. I'll need you to help Phil with food prep."

"Well, just so *you* know, Steve told me all I needed to do was work the pizza oven for a few hours to get through the lunch rush."

"Well, just so *you* know, I'm in charge of the kitchen, and I'll get this cleared with Steve right now."

When Leo found Steve sitting at the bar, trying to eat an early lunch, he whined to Steve. Steve walked back to the pizza station with Leo as Curtis was pulling a pizza out of the oven and sliding it onto a serving pan.

"Hey, Curtis, when I talked to you, I thought Gonzo was coming in and would be able to help with the food preparation. I'm not sure if he's going to make it, so I had to promote Phil from washing dishes to helping with salads. If you could help Phil, I would appreciate it."

Leo smirked, his eyes sparkling with delight at the annoyance written on Curtis's face.

The dining room placed a manageable number of pizza orders over the next hour, allowing Curtis time to help Phil break up heads of lettuce and peel onions for later slicing. Curtis browned fifty pounds of ground beef in the steam kettle for meat sauce. He also shredded a few cases of Provel cheese into stainless steel holding pans, covered the tops with plastic wrap, and stacked them crisscrossed in the walk-in cooler. Curtis watched the clock slowly tick toward one o'clock. He didn't mind working or helping Phil. He hated working with Leo and wanted to hang out at the Gradys' for a peaceful Sunday afternoon, drinking beer, getting stoned, and playing pool.

Curtis enjoyed making pizzas and was quite good at it. Leo always complained that Curtis put too much meat and cheese on the pizzas, but he was proud of the pies he baked and served. Curtis pulled them out when the cheese was more orange than yellow, and the thin crust was crisp without being burnt. He let the hot pizza set up for a minute or two before slicing. He always kept his oven swept out, his peel clean, and used the perfect amount of semolina under the pizza dough during assembly.

Leo came out of the walk-in cooler with a couple of trays of precooked pasta for his work station. He saw Curtis standing at the pizza station watching the clock.

Leo yelled over the counter, "Time to lean, time to clean."

Just as he began sweeping the floor, two pizza orders came in.

Curtis made the pizzas, while Phil was tossing a massive bowl of salad.

"Hey, Phil, you know you're supposed to have a nickname to work in the kitchen."

"My friends call me Filo."

"Seriously?"

"Sí, señor."

"Why are you working in an Italian restaurant?"

"Why do you have to hate, amigo?"

Phil and Curtis laughed.

The waitress came back and told Phil and Curtis that the pizzas and salads were to go. "I'm sorry, I should have checked that on the ticket," she added.

Phil flirted with the waitress in Spanish as he swiped the salads off the plates and into Styrofoam boxes.

Leo looked up and saw Curtis and Phil laughing with the waitress. He strolled down the aisle to witness Curtis boxing up two pizzas.

"You should cut them before you place them in the box."

"Do I tell you how to make fettuccini?" Curtis retorted.

Leo snorted. "When you're done there, I have something for you to do."

Curtis handed the pizza boxes to the waitress to go along with the two salads already boxed and bagged. Then Curtis found Leo lecturing the dishwasher on how to clean pots properly.

Leo turned to Curtis. "I need you to help me make some cream sauce. We're almost out."

"I've never made cream sauce before."

"That is why I said you need to help me. It's easy. I'll show you. Go grab two large stock pots and make sure they're clean. You'll also need five pounds of butter and ten gallons of cream."

Curtis walked back and talked with the dishwasher. He discovered his name was Julio, and he was one of Phil's cousins. Curtis encouraged Julio to ignore Leo and focus on what he was hired to do.

"You're alright, man."

Curtis grabbed two clean pots. Curtis chuckled as he imagined himself becoming like Tiny.

Curtis brought the pots, two large boxes of heavy cream, and five boxes of butter to the sauté station. He placed the pots on the large burners and set the butter and boxes of cream down on the counter. He carefully pulled the giant bag of cream out of the box and slowly filled the large pot through a long rubber hose extending from the bladder.

"Pizza order, Curtis," yelled one of the waiters as he waved the ticket while passing by.

"Give me that," Leo barked as he grabbed the bag from Curtis. "Go make your pizzas."

Curtis went to his station, quickly made the pizza, and slid it into the oven. He looked at the clock and noted the time before walking back over to watch Leo.

"Listen to me, you don't need to mess with the rubber hose." Leo demonstrated with his fist as he pushed all the cream away from the entry point of the bag, grabbed a pair of kitchen shears, and cut a sizable hole in the bag before dumping the cream into the pot. It took seconds instead of minutes.

Curtis lifted the other bladder out of the box and had similar results doing it Leo's way.

Leo instructed him to place the pots on low heat and showed him how to stir the cream with a long, thin, stainless-steel whisk. Leo had two large skillets with butter slowly melting away under low heat.

A waitress entered with an order for two lunch pizzas as Curtis pulled a slightly overcooked pizza out of his oven. He swiftly assembled the two lunch pizzas and slid them into the oven as he boxed up the other pizza.

The waiter walked back into the kitchen to check his pizza order. "This pizza isn't to go."

Leo yelled down the line, "Curtis, kill the heat on the butter, we don't want to burn it."

"Go take care of your butter." I'll unbox the pizza, the waiter offered.

"Thanks."

It was nearly one-thirty in the afternoon, and Curtis was overwhelmed. Watching the clock was mandatory when cooking pizzas but having an idea of the time accelerated his anxieties as his two o'clock departure became increasingly unlikely.

Leo returned and added flour to the melted butter to make a roux.

The waiter and waitress came back with multiple pasta orders for Leo.

"Curtis, get over here now."

Leo showed him how to stir the roux to keep the flour from burning and, at the same time, keep a good stir on the heavy cream beginning to steam as tiny bubbles burst at the surface. Like a mad chemist, Curtis alternated mixing two skillets of roux and whisking two giant pots of heavy cream.

Leo told him to take the roux off the heat, which he did immediately. Then he went over and pulled the two lunch pizzas out of the oven.

The waitress came in and was not happy to see these pizzas were also overcooked.

Leo yelled for him to keep stirring the cream.

The waitress cut her pizzas as Curtis abandoned his pizza station to care for the simmering cream.

"How's my cream sauce? Are you keeping it stirred?"

Curtis stirred the cream as it came to a steady boil, with large bubbles popping at the surface. He placed the roux back on the burners to reheat the mixture and stirred as best as possible.

More pizza orders came in.

"Leo, the cream is boiling, what should I do?"

"Turn the heat down, get a large whisk, and slowly add the roux and beat it into the cream."

Curtis did one pot and then the other, whisking them violently until his hands were numb. A few minutes later, the waiter came back in.

"Did you see my pizza orders? I know I waved them to you five minutes ago."

"Leo, I need help. I have pizza orders and can't do everything."

When Leo came over to the sauté station, his jaw nearly hit the floor.

"What did you do?" he yelled.

"I did exactly what you told me."

Leo yanked the whisk from Curtis's hand and whisked the cream sauce violently with bewildered eyes. Steaming, lumpy cream sauce fell off and back into the pot every time he pulled the whisk out.

Leo began to panic, screaming, "It's a fucking cream sauce. How can you ruin a cream sauce like this?"

Curtis returned to the pizza oven, ignoring Leo, and assembled two nice-looking pizzas. He opened the oven and broomed out the charred pizza dust before sliding the two pies into the oven.

"Curtis, get over here, now."

Curtis strolled over to the sauté station.

"Do you see this? This is ruined. You ruined five hundred dollars' worth of cream sauce."

Curtis turned back to the pizza station.

"I can't fix this," Leo sighed as his muscles refused to keep up the frantic pace of stirring.

He turned off the flames to both burners, walked out of the kitchen, and returned shortly with Steve following him.

Leo explained everything that had happened to Steve.

Steve looked over and saw Curtis cutting two pizzas already on trays.

"Curtis, get over here now," he commanded.

Curtis shuffled over and stared at Steve as the manager continued the interrogation.

"What is this? Do you have any idea what you've done here?" To make his point, he also pulled the whisk out of the cream sauce to watch the steamy, lumpy cream fall back into the pot. "Do you know what this is?" Curtis summoned his inner Tiny. "It's a lumpy cream sauce."

Steve's face flushed with rage, and he got angrier when Phil laughed out loud. When he couldn't control his laughter, he went inside the walk-in cooler and shut the door behind him.

Steve yelled, "This shit isn't funny," before unleashing a torrent of hostilities and insults at Curtis.

The waitress and the busboy exited the kitchen in an about-face faster than they'd entered.

When Phil was finished yelling, he glared at Curtis and said, "Can you tell me one reason I shouldn't fire you right now?"

Rage had been building inside Curtis for the last hour or so. He did everything in his power to try to defuse it. Distance could not relieve it, humor could not quench it, and silence was no longer an option. He wanted desperately to keep it inside. He dug deep for any possible way to bury his anger until he got home. He glanced over at Steve, who only hours before was shoulder grabbing and smiling at him for sacrificing his Sunday. And an hour or so before then, he had said all he needed to do was make pizzas for the lunch rush. Then he noticed the glaring smirk on Leo's face, arms crossed in a comfortable defensive posture, and he couldn't bear it anymore. Hell set fire to his tongue, and it was unquenchable.

"Fuck you both. I quit."

CHAPTER 12

Jailbreak

Several employees heard the confrontation, and as words heated in the kitchen, waiters, waitresses, and busboys gathered in the busing area to listen in. Curtis stormed out of Riccardo & Lorenzo Restaurante, not bothering to clock out. He didn't even say goodbye to the hostess when she told him to have a nice day.

Curtis's hands shook in rage. It took a concentrated effort to unlock his truck. He stared at the front door, waiting to see if anyone would come out. After five minutes of observing only customers emerging from the front door, Curtis started the truck. The radio played "Born Under a Bad Sign." As Cream blasted through the speakers, he pounded the steering wheel several times before speeding out of the parking lot.

Curtis knew he couldn't go home. His mom would ask questions about his day. He knew there would be hell to pay when his mom found out he quit his job. The best course of action, he thought, was to find another job. Curtis just needed some time to think; the Basement was the best place for that. When he arrived, Curtis noticed Gunner's Impala was there, along with the green Gremlin and Marty's car.

Gunner was showing Francine how to clean a rifle while Marty and Travis played pool. Gunner glanced up and said, "Hey, loser, what have you been up to all day?"

"I just quit my job."

Francine, looking concerned, said, "You what?"

All eyes were upon him as he told everyone the story.

Travis said, "What assholes. I'd quit too."

Gunner replied, "You have to have a job before you can quit."

"I have a job working for my dad, ya prick."

"What, working three days a week?"

"You have to start somewhere. Besides, I don't need a lot of money."

Brad said, "Not when you come over here and drink beer for free all the time."

Curtis asked, "Where's Kathy?"

"She's out shopping with my mom."

Gunner asked Curtis, "What's your mom going to say when she finds out?"

Curtis answered, "Nothing, because she isn't going to find out. I'm not going to tell her anything."

Curtis grabbed a beer from the fridge and sat beside Brad.

Brad said, "Thanks for getting me a beer."

"Do you want a beer? I'll go get you one."

"No, I'm just messing with you."

The anger in Curtis's heart dissipated with the alcohol as it seeped into his blood. He was on his third beer when Ronnie came walking in.

Everyone had to hear the story again as Curtis retold it to Ronnie.

"That restaurant work is bullshit. I wouldn't last a day working for people like that. I need to work for myself," Ronnie said.

Gunner replied, "You won't get fired, Ronnie. You're going to go to jail when you get caught."

"Not if I stay smart about what I'm doing," he replied.

Gunner said, "Prisons are full of people who knew what they were doing."

Ronnie ignored him and said, "I can't stay long. I saw all the cars and just wanted to stop by to invite anyone who wants to come to my sister's house. We're playing poker this evening."

Francine looked at Gunner before saying, "We're just going to stay home tonight."

When Curtis shot a look at Francine and Gunner, she said, "What?"

Curtis started to say something to her, but instead, he said to Ronnie, "I might come over, but I'm going to go home and eat dinner first."

Curtis left shortly after Ronnie and drove home. Curtis felt terrible for lying to his parents at dinner when he talked about his day at dinner, but that was the quickest way to get them to talk about something else instead.

His mom said, "Your sister has a dance recital next weekend. I'd really like you to go."

"Where's it at?"

"It's supposed to be on the *Admiral*, same as last year. Only this year, I don't think they're doing a river cruise. I heard on KMOX that they found bad leaks, and they might put an end to the excursions."

After dinner, Curtis went into his bedroom to read. He tried to get into the Hal Lindsey book Mouse had given him. After reading through the first few chapters, he concluded that worrying about the future was a waste of time. He thought fortune telling was a scam, and as far as astrology went, he figured it was a load of crap too. Curtis recalled when he read all twelve horoscopes in the paper and thought he could relate to nearly every sign of the zodiac.

The way Curtis saw it, life was a mystery. He saw good and evil in all things and people. He had read the Bible, and if Jesus had died for the sins of the world, what more did he have to worry about?

He tossed the book under the bed around seven thirty and wandered into the living room. His parents were cuddled on the couch watching television and paid no attention to him as he walked outside.

Curtis thumbed through his wallet and counted seventy-two dollars. His first thought was to go back in and give his mom fifty of it for his truck insurance. He would get one more check with some overtime, but who knew when he would get paid after that?

Then another thought occurred to him. He might be able to win more money if he took Ronnie up on his offer to play poker. There wasn't a need to take the truck as Ronnie's sister lived less than a half mile away.

Ronnie was glad when he saw Curtis at the door, relieved that he would not be the youngest one at the table. Ronnie introduced Curtis to everyone. Cassie was twelve years older than they were. She was a flower power girl from the '60s. Curtis would never say it out loud, but his first impression was she would fit in with the Manson family. Cassie's husband, Rick, had a state-of-the-art stereo system. Rick made good money working as an overnight mechanic. She entertained her guests with the improvisational, bluesy music of the Grateful Dead. If Curtis hadn't heard "Casey Jones," he might never have guessed what he was listening to.

Everyone was friendly. Curtis took advantage of the free beer and the occasional joint offered. Unfortunately, luck was not with him that evening. It seemed every hand he had needed to be better to win. When he drew three eights, he would lose to three jacks. When he pulled a flush on the last card, he lost to a straight flush. Those two hands cost him over twenty dollars. He would have lost more, but they had a ten-dollar limit on calls because they wanted the games to be friendly.

While the strangers he played cards with laughed and consoled his losses, he only became more depressed and switched to drinking Jack Daniels. By eleven, he was broke and excused himself to go into the living room, sit on the couch, and listen to electrified bluegrass.

By midnight, he realized he had drunk too much. The room would spin every time he closed his eyes, but every time he opened his eyes, he became nauseous. As his condition worsened, it became apparent to others because Ronnie said to him, "Hey, man, if you're gonna get sick, go outside."

Curtis barely reached the door and into the front yard before he began hurling. He lost balance as he stepped out of door and fell to the ground before stumbling towards the street. He looked up into the sky between his convulsions, hoping it would fall on him. Ronnie came out to see if he was okay. He stayed with Curtis for a while before going back inside. When Ronnie left, Curtis peered at the sky again, noticing the full moon. It seemed to be telling him to go home.

He never made it. Sometime before the break of dawn, Curtis woke up lying in a neighbor's front yard. He was cold and wet. He got up and walked the rest of the way home. Turning down the hill toward his house, he looked up just in time to see his dad backing his work truck out of the driveway. He hid behind Gunner's Impala as the truck passed by. He went home, snuck inside, and heard his mom down in the basement starting a load of laundry. Curtis took his shoes off, scampered in, and went straight to bed without undressing. The warmth of his blankets and the comfort of his pillow caused him to fall into a deep coma-like sleep. Curtis never heard his mother call him. His family left for the pool, and he slept another day at home alone.

When Curtis woke up, it was nearly one in the afternoon. A shower and brushing the socks off his teeth helped, but his stomach warned him not to try to eat anything. His lunch that day would be a can of his dad's Dr. Pepper.

As he was putting his shoes on, his eyes landed on the ticket still sitting on his mom's desk with the cash she had received from the bank when she had cashed his paycheck. She had never mailed a check to the city of Arnold.

Panicked, he grabbed the ticket and the cash and found his truck keys. His hungover mind was racing as he drove as fast as possible to the Arnold police station, which was a tiny building on the corner of Highway 141 and Jeffco Boulevard.

Curtis went inside the lobby, which was only big enough to contain two chairs with an ashtray-topped trash can between them. He approached the plexiglass window, which had many holes drilled into it for him to talk through.

The officer stopped writing in his book and asked, "May I help you?"

"Yes, sir. My name is Curtis McGowan. I have a ticket that I need to pay."

"I'm sorry, but tickets need to be mailed to the court direct. We don't take payment here." The man started paging through another book and said, "What did you say your name was again? McGowan? From Imperial?"

"Yes, that's me."

"Mr. McGowan, do you know there's a bench warrant for your arrest?"

"No, but that's why I'm here. I want to take care of this ticket."

"Hold on, please."

The officer got up from the desk and soon appeared around the corner. Curtis heard the door buzz before the police officer entered the lobby. "Curtis McGowan, I'm placing you under arrest for contempt of court."

The officer handcuffed and marched Curtis back through the door to be processed. He surrendered his wallet, keys, and shoelaces. He was read his rights and then fingerprinted. The last thing they did was take his picture before leading him to a desk with a phone.

"Call whoever you need to, and make it fast," the officer said.

Curtis knew his mom was gone for the day; the only number he could think of was the Gradys'.

The phone rang several times before Francine answered.

"Francine? This is Curtis. Listen, I've been arrested and locked up in Arnold."

"What? Where? How come?"

"Listen, I need someone to come with a hundred bucks to get me out. It must be cash."

"Don't worry, I'll take care of it. Bye."

When Curtis heard the phone click, he set the phone down in the cradle.

The officer led Curtis to what appeared to be an empty closet. "Step inside and make yourself comfortable."

The only thing in the tiny cell was a wooden seat that resembled a bookshelf. The door closed with a soft click.

Sitting down, Curtis could see nothing but the door and floor. He stood up to look out the small window and surveyed a few police officers in the tiny station milling about as they went about their workday, never looking at the cell door. The clock on the wall moved slowly.

At four o'clock, the arresting officer came back and opened the cell door. "Listen, do you have anyone else you want to call? If someone doesn't pick you up by five, we'll have to transfer you to the county jail in Hillsboro. If you go to county, you'll have to spend the night because they won't process you out until tomorrow."

Curtis told him he had nobody else to call, so he shut the door and returned to the chair in front of the window.

Curtis watched the clock tick away the hour. At 4:40, he was relieved when he saw Francine and Gunner enter the front door. Curtis watched Gunner count out one hundred dollars in cash and push the bills under the window. Fifteen minutes later, Curtis was outside with his friends with a new court date he needed to attend in person. He told them all about his day.

Gunner said, "You're lucky Mom was home. You owe her one hundred dollars, and she wants to talk to you immediately."

Francine hugged him and said, "I hope you didn't drop the soap."

CHAPTER **13**

A Weekend with Danny & Sammy

"**C**urtis, get your ass up here right now." JoJo's voice boomed throughout the house when Curtis entered the Basement.

"I told you," Gunner said. He immediately turned to Francine. "This won't be pretty. Let's get out of here." Francine, who had just bailed Curtis out of jail, left him to face the wrath of Mrs. Grady alone.

Curtis trod slowly up the stairs as if going up to the gallows. The door opened, and Brad and Kathy stared blankly at him before passing him on the stairs. Nobody wanted to be near Curtis as he faced JoJo.

Curtis stepped into the kitchen. JoJo was talking on the phone, and he heard her say, "He just walked in. I'll call you back later."

JoJo slammed the black phone into the receiver. "What the hell is your problem?"

Curtis focused on a stack of mail on the kitchen counter.

She yelled, "Don't you look away from me when I'm talking to you."

Curtis turned his face toward his other mother's brooding eyes.

"I just got off the phone with your mother," she said. Curtis felt the knot in his gut growing larger. The next fifteen minutes seemed like an hour as JoJo hammered him with the loving care of a marine boot camp drill instructor.

JoJo didn't relent until Curtis broke down and told her everything from the beginning. He promised to pay back the hundred dollars after he picked up his paycheck on Friday. Her face softened, and she said, "You better get home. You have some explaining to do with your mom."

Curtis descended the stairs and walked straight to the door without a word to Brad or Kathy. He drove home to experience the downside of having two mothers. Curtis went inside for a rinse-and-repeat cleansing of his soul. When he was afforded his turn to speak, Curtis took advantage of the time in the confessional to tell his mom that he got fired from his job on Sunday for ruining a large batch of cream sauce. Yet in his heart, he blamed his mother for all his woes. She was the one who made him go to work on Sunday. She was the one who didn't mail the check like she said she would, yet it was Curtis who was being punished for all of it.

Then she said, "If you don't get a job this week, I'm canceling the insurance on the truck, and it will stay parked in the garage for the rest of the summer."

Springdale was the only refuge Curtis had that week. Swimming, especially under the water, provided a quietness and peace that allowed him to think clearly. The shock of the cold water woke him up, body and soul. Comfort and pleasure came from a well-timed skill shot on his favorite pinball machine, the familiar music from the jukebox, and a foaming root beer float.

When they arrived Tuesday morning, Curtis saw Vik sitting in his chair. Barely one month into summer, Vik was suntanned like an ancient mariner. Because he refused to sit inside the hot shack, the only shade came from a visor he wore on top of his graying head. Vik appeared to wear the same shorts, sandals, and unbuttoned short-sleeved dress shirt daily. He proudly displayed his wealth in gold, with chains around his neck, a loose-fitting bracelet on one wrist, and a watch on the other.

Vik's pride and joy in life was his son, Danny. Curtis once overheard his grandfather tell the story about Danny being a "surprise child." The Papadakises were childless for many years and were told by different doctors they could not have children. It came as a complete surprise to everyone when Sunny became pregnant late in life.

Danny, like his father, was naturally athletic and strong. That paternal strength carried over into confidence, swagger, and what some would call chauvinism. In 1979, however, being hip, macho, and masculine were in-demand commodities. While numerous women attempted to gain his favor and interest, Danny only had eyes for his high school sweetheart, Samantha Stringer.

Samantha, or Sammy, was one of five lifeguards on duty when the McGowan family entered the pool area that day. The number of lifeguards on duty depended on the crowd size, primarily a function of heat and time of day.

Most mornings, four lifeguards were on duty, and each walked the perimeter of the pool, rotating every fifteen minutes. They would get a fifteen-minute break for each rotation before repeating it for the day. When it was jam-packed, there could be up to twelve lifeguards, and then they would rotate every five minutes.

That morning, Sammy was in the pool. Sammy was attractive, talkative, and outgoing. Curtis enjoyed conversing with her because her friendliness made her approachable. Since Sammy saw Curtis nearly every day, she greeted him by name like they were old, dear friends.

Sammy possessed a deep, gravelly voice that Curtis found authoritative, like a gym teacher's. She wore her sandy blonde hair pulled back into a ponytail, held in place with red beaded hair ties that resembled two Bing cherries. Sammy, like all female lifeguards, wore a one-piece bathing suit.

Curtis saw Sammy in the pool, working her way down the side with a stiff-bristled brush. He sat down next to the can of Comet and asked her how her day was going.

She wore oversized square-lensed sunglasses with gradient champagne-tinted coloring. She listened patiently to Curtis as he shared his summertime woes with her. As she worked her way down the side of the pool, Curtis would hand her the can of scouring powder, which gave observers the impression he was helping her.

She was standing in four feet of water, and Curtis, sitting on the edge of the pool with his legs in the water, tried not to stare at Sammy's jiggling breasts as her arms moved back and forth, vigorously attacking the green and black growth.

Sammy said, "Why don't you let me talk to Sunny? She's always looking for help in the concession stand."

"Actually, Sammy," Curtis said, "I'd like to be a lifeguard."

"In that case," she replied, "you need to talk to Danny. Speaking of the Beast…"

Danny jumped into the pool, splashing water and Comet residue onto Curtis and his sunglasses. He kissed Sammy before she could yell at him, as the blast of water nearly knocked her sunglasses off her face.

Danny inquired about their conversation.

"I can get you a job helping Mom in the concession stand, but you have to be trained and certified by the American Red Cross to be a lifeguard."

Curtis asked, "Is it expensive?"

"It can be, but I know someone who might be able to help," Danny said as he winked at Sammy.

"Really? Who?"

"Me. I'm a certified American Red Cross instructor. So is Sammy." Do you know CPR or basic first aid?"

"No."

"Well, lucky for you, we do. Sammy, what do you think? Should we help this young man become a lifeguard?"

Sammy appraised Curtis and asked, "Are you a strong swimmer?"

"I think so."

"You can't be thinking, Curtis," she said. "You need to have confidence that you are a strong swimmer. Are you afraid of the water?"

"No."

"That's a good thing."

Danny said, "Curtis, I need to check the water chemistry. Give me fifteen minutes then meet me down by the diving boards."

Curtis got up and went to put his sunglasses away. He told his mom he was going down to the deep end with Danny.

When Danny later exited the pump house, he went straight for the small diving board. He jumped high, spun around, and bent his knees to catch the board and stop it from bouncing. Satisfied with the board's response, he went to the back before taking a calculated step and skip into a spring so high up in the air, he had the time to execute a graceful dive into the water with hardly a splash.

Danny was strong and fluid in the water. Two kicks and a crawl and he was back at the edge of the pool, pulling himself out of the water in a single lunge without using the ladder.

Danny wanted to see Curtis jump off the high dive.

Curtis didn't want to protest but was not eager to jump from the tall board. "I thought we were going to see if I was a strong swimmer?"

Danny said, "Yes, that's important, but I also want to see if you're fearless."

Curtis's mind went into overdrive, remembering the first time he jumped off the high dive a few years ago.

Taking that first step required the most courage, but the most dangerous part for him was the climb up. The fear that began at the base of the ladder only got worse with each step. Each step above the concrete indicated a different level of potential risk, from sharp pain to a broken leg, and ultimately, the need for an ambulance or a hearse.

He tried to climb up the ladder without obsessing about it. At the last rung, he clung so tightly to the guardrail that his knuckles turned white. At the top, Curtis took little comfort in the anti-skid laminate covering the diving board's surface. He crept four feet out past the guardrail, with nothing but water below. As long as he jumped straight out, there was nothing to worry about. Impatient voices behind him amplified the pressure of the climb.

Other pressures faced the anxious adolescent. Curtis glanced down and saw one of the most gorgeous women in the world sunbathing next to the fence. Her oil-tanned body was adorned by two pieces of cotton, with nothing but beautiful curves extending from them. The distraction of the loud voices was enough for her to put her book down momentarily as she placed her hand up to her forehead to see what all the commotion was about. When she looked up and smiled at him, Curtis realized it was okay to die now. The presence of a real-life angel helped him overcome his fear long enough to walk to the edge and take that last step.

Immediately after hitting the water, the rush of the fall was replaced with a legitimate fear of drowning as gravity and buoyancy wrestled for control of the teenager caught in the crossfire of those forces. Curtis struggled through the long descent into the depths of the pool. Buoyancy eventually triumphed over gravity, and Curtis swam hard to the surface and gasped for air.

Yet even at the surface, the fear didn't dissipate. Curtis was terrified another jumper would land on him, so he paddled ferociously, swimming over to the ladder to get out of the way of the next diver. As reality returned to focus and he started to relax, he half expected to be greeted by the angel who gave him the courage to jump.

Instead, as Curtis grabbed the ladder to escape the pool, he noticed she was back reading her book and had already forgotten he existed. Curtis's stare and disappointment were interrupted by Danny shouting, "Not bad, Curtis. Now I want to see you dive."

Curtis had never dived off the high dive, but he knew his future career as a lifeguard depended on it.

This time, his heart was gripped with additional fears as he climbed the ladder and stepped out to the edge of the board. With Danny yelling encouragement, Curtis leaned over and fell into the water headfirst. His head smacked the water, causing an instant headache. The pain shot through his body, and for a moment, Curtis decided he'd rather drown than face Danny with tears in his eyes. When he came to the surface, he swam slowly toward Danny.

"Why did you pull your arms back? Keep your arms straight. Now, do it again."

That morning, Danny worked with Curtis until the crowd grew, and he needed to get into the rotation. Curtis gained more confidence with each dive, and the water stopped hurting.

When Danny started his rotation in the deep end, he watched Curtis tread water for ten minutes and tested his ability to hold his breath. Danny was impressed when Curtis demonstrated he could hold his breath for over a minute while swimming underwater.

Danny expressed the best compliment Curtis could hope for when he said, "Curtis, I think you have what it takes to be a lifeguard." Danny said he would be willing to train him, but he needed to talk to JoAnn to see if she was okay with her son going away for a weekend for training. "I also need to make sure my dad is willing to hire you after you have your certifications."

Later that afternoon, before they left for the day, Sammy came over and told him that Danny got provisional permission from Vik, but no promises of hiring him could be made because of his age. "Your mom said it would be okay for you to go to the lake with us to get certified, but we both have to work this weekend, so it'll be another week before we can get down to the lake."

Sammy gave Curtis two books from the American Red Cross. "You have two weeks to learn both of these books inside and out."

On Friday, Curtis drove to Riccardo & Lorenzo Restaurante one last time to pick up his last paycheck and say goodbye to Tiny. When he arrived, he had to wait up front, giving him a chance to talk with Celeste. She seemed genuinely sad that Curtis was leaving. It didn't go unnoticed that Steve did not bring Curtis his check; instead, the dining room manager brought it up to him. He said goodbye to Celeste and waited in the parking lot for Tiny to show up.

Tiny was angry when he heard what had happened. Leo had tried to make it seem that Curtis had intentionally ruined the cream sauce and was belligerent the entire day for having to come in and work.

"I'm not going to be here much longer, Speedy. My days here are numbered. I've been talking to Frenchie, and I think I may go to that culinary school too. It was nice working with you, Curtis. I hope you have a blast being a lifeguard."

Curtis drove back home and gave his mom the paycheck. It had over-time from the previous Sunday. He asked his mom to cash it for him so he could pay JoJo back her hundred dollars.

She asked, "What about your truck insurance? What about me, Curtis? When are you going to pay me?"

Sunday afternoon, Curtis rode with his parents and his sister, dressed in her dance costume, to his grandparents' house to drop off his brother. His dad drove the family station wagon downtown and parked near the Landing by the Gateway Arch. The sweet smell of licorice filled the air. They strolled along a cobblestone street and down the hill to the riverfront and boarded the *Admiral*. JoAnn pulled out four tickets provided by Denoyer Dance Studio for the recital.

Curtis thought he would be bored to tears, but his face lit up when he saw Richie. Richie's parents also forced him to come watch his sister, Lynn, who was best friends with Curtis's sister, Helen. The two boys stayed with their parents only until their sisters performed, then they escaped the crowd and made their way to the bottom of the boat, rich in diesel fumes and the smell of dead fish. They spent most of the afternoon playing games in the small arcade and talking about music. From their perspective, it didn't matter a single bit that the riverboat didn't move an inch during their time aboard.

Curtis spent more time in the pool the following week as Danny gave Curtis specific challenges to increase his swimming strength and endurance to prepare him for the weekend at the lake. When he was not swimming, Sammy challenged him with questions about first aid and water safety.

Saturday morning, Danny and Sammy picked him up at five. Curtis had packed an overnight bag along with a pool bag. He had seventy-five dollars in his wallet, which he hoped was enough to get by on. Curtis said goodbye to his mom when he saw them out the window. It was strange not seeing them in bathing suits. From where they stood on the driveway waiting for him, Curtis thought it looked like Burt Reynolds talking with Stevie Nicks.

Danny drove a 1970 Buick convertible. Vik and Sunny bought the car brand new and gave it to Danny when he turned sixteen. As Curtis put the bags in the trunk, Danny pulled the top down, and everyone waved goodbye as they left for the lake.

Curtis spent the three-hour ride to Lake of the Ozarks reading his American Red Cross books and listening to America. He heard "Ventura Highway," "Tin Man," and "A Horse with No Name" at least ten times. Curtis offered to pay for the gas when they stopped in Osage Beach. Danny accepted his offer, and while Curtis took care of the gas, they went inside to get the keys to the bathroom.

They were gone for over ten minutes. Curtis had already put the cap back on the gas tank and paid the attendant. He waited another five minutes before going to the bathroom to see if everything was okay. Curtis was surprised when he saw Danny laughing as he stumbled out of the women's bathroom, putting his belt back on. He handed Curtis the key and said, "When you're done, bring this back to the attendant."

Curtis walked into the men's bathroom. He heard the bathroom stall door open, and Sammy came out, holding her hat and brushing her hair. Her face turned red when she saw Curtis standing there, but she walked past him as if he were invisible.

Danny's parents owned a lake house near Sunrise Beach and shared a tiny cove with a few neighbors. Curtis quickly changed into swim trunks and followed his instructors down a long-wooded hill to the dock. He saw two small boats tied to the pier. Sammy stepped into the flat-bottom Boston Whaler.

Danny walked up behind Curtis and said, "Are you ready? Let's get going."

Before Curtis knew what was happening, Danny pushed him off the dock into the water and then jumped on top of him. Danny wrestled Curtis until he was gasping for air. Curtis fought Danny and swam away.

Danny said, "That is the most important lesson I can teach you. If someone has the strength to fight you, they have the strength to drown you. Get away until they tire; otherwise, the rescue team will likely pull two bodies out of the water."

After that, Danny went through all the different ways to approach a swimmer in distress and all the things to look for. During the rest breaks on the dock, Sammy would drill Curtis with questions about first aid, CPR, and water safety.

The morning went by fast, and after a quick, light lunch, they were back in the water until late in the afternoon. Most of the day was spent dragging Danny all around the cove. They went up to the house, and while Danny grilled dinner, Sammy brought in the Resusci Anne doll from the car and showed Curtis how to do chest compressions and mouth-to-mouth resuscitations.

Curtis was exhausted, so after dinner, he took a shower, laid on the bed, and fell fast asleep.

Danny woke him up a short time later to tell him he and Sammy were going out for drinks. Curtis barely acknowledged him before falling into a deeper sleep, never feeling the blanket Sammy threw over him or hearing her shut the door as they left.

Sometime during the night, he awoke to the sound of an unbalanced load in a washing machine. With all they had done, he didn't understand why someone would be doing laundry in the middle of the night. The constant knocking was loud and seemed to be getting louder.

Curtis got up, thinking he would find the washing machine and move the towels around so it would spin out quieter, but when he opened the door, the knocking stopped. As soon as he lay down, it started again. Curtis got up a second time and quietly walked down the hall before he realized the knocking was coming from the other bedroom.

Curtis was tired and sore and tried to fall back asleep, but sordid thoughts assaulted his brain with images he could not make disappear. Just as he fell back asleep, Danny knocked on the door loudly before opening it, saying, "Come on, Sport. We need to roll. I told your mom we would have you home before noon."

They drove back to Saint Louis, and the entire drive back was spent answering questions Sammy and Danny asked him about water safety and first aid. They were impressed by how much he had learned so fast. Danny and Sammy both agreed that Curtis would be a good lifeguard and that he would only get stronger and more confident with time.

Monday morning, Curtis was excited to go to Springdale. He was thrilled when Sammy gave him the American Red Cross certificates she and Danny had signed showing he was certified in CPR, First Aid, and Water Safety. Even though Danny had pushed the hard sell to his dad about Curtis's strength and exceptional knowledge, Vik would not hire him as a lifeguard because he was not eighteen. Neither Danny nor Sammy had the heart to tell Curtis that Vik had no problem ignoring the age restriction when he hired women, as some of the weekend lifeguards were still in high school.

Sammy encouraged Curtis to talk to Sunny and help in the concession stand. The thought of free burgers and root beer floats was enticing, but when Curtis talked to Sunny, he found out she expected a seven-day commitment, with hours based on how busy they were. When Curtis asked about wages, Sunny said they paid students a student wage, nearly a dollar less per hour than the minimum wage of two dollars and ninety cents. Curtis reasoned that it would not be worth having a truck if all he did was drive it to work. He turned down the job offer, which made JoAnn livid when she found out.

After they got home that afternoon, JoAnn said, "I'm not kidding, Curtis. You have one week to find a job, or that truck is being parked." Before going inside, she went to the mailbox.

JoAnn thumbed through the mail and found two pieces addressed to her son. The first appeared to be an invoice from Columbia House Record and Tape Club. The second piece was an invitation from Mary Jones.

"Who is Mary Jones?"

He said, "Do you remember the neighbor who was killed? Bill Jones was the man who worked with Dad and died in the accident. Mary is his daughter."

JoAnn handed him the two pieces of mail. Curtis ignored the bill and opened the pink envelope. Inside was an invitation with an attached note.

Dear Curtis, Thank you for coming to Daddy's funeral. It meant a lot to me for you to be there. I am having a birthday party at Rock Roll-O-Rena on Sunday, July 8, from 4 to 6 p.m. I hope you can make it. I would love to see you again. Sincerely, Mary

CHAPTER 14

L.A. Woman

In the late seventies, Lower Arnold was not the sort of place Windsor students wanted to be found alone. If you did not belong on Starling Airport Road or Hollywood Beach Road, it would be best if you didn't go there. Windsor was a small school compared to the massive Fox School District. The rivalry between Fox and Windsor was intense, and it was not unheard of for things to get hostile long after the games were over. Lower Arnold, jokingly, was referred to as L.A. in Jefferson County. It was a rough area, particularly close to the Meramec River. The most vicious residents lived close to the river and were affectionately known as "river rats." Some residents lived so near the river that their dwellings were raised above the ground on stilts. Eventually, the City of Arnold condemned all the houses closest to the river, and insurance companies denied coverage for new construction due to the regular flooding of the Meramec. L.A. had a reputation for being seedy. The notoriety was valid because everybody recognized it and residents even wore it like a badge of honor. Many pretty girls attended Fox School; some were from L.A., and a few became lost angels at night.

It was another typical hot and muggy summer day. Marty and Curtis spent most of Monday at Springdale for relief. Afterward, they drove to Mark Twain Theatre in South County to see the new Clint Eastwood movie, *Escape from Alcatraz*. After the film, they left the comfort of the air-conditioned theater to be assaulted by the relentless summer heat that baked the asphalt. The parking lot was hot enough to make the bottom of their shoes feel tacky. Traffic on the interstate was terrible, so they took the long way home. It was close to seven o'clock as they approached the Meramec River bridge and Curtis asked Marty if he was hungry.

"Pizza sound good?" Curtis asked.

"What do you have in mind?"

"There's a Lynn's Pizzeria right on the other side of the river."

"That works for me," Marty replied.

Curtis pulled the truck into the gravel lot and found no trouble parking. The hostess looked up from her magazine and asked if they were dining in or getting a pizza to go.

"Dining in," Curtis said.

"Follow me then," she replied, grabbing two bundles of silverware wrapped in napkins and two menus. She escorted them to a booth in the back of the restaurant. "A waitress will be with you shortly." The hostess sauntered back to the cash register by the front door and returned to her magazine.

A young woman approached them with a pleasant smile and a bobbing ponytail falling out of her red pizzeria cap.

"Hi there, I'm Brooke. I'll be your waitress. What would you two like to drink?"

Marty asked for a large Coke but was quickly interrupted.

"Is Pepsi, okay?"

They ordered a deluxe pizza and a pitcher of Pepsi.

While eating their pizza and talking about the movie, the owner, Lynn, walked over to see how they were doing.

It seemed to please Lynn to know they were happy with their service and food.

"Excuse me, Lynn…" Curtis caught her before she had walked away.

"Yes?"

"Are you hiring right now?"

"We're always hiring if we can find the right people. Do you have experience with making pizzas?"

Curtis briefly told her of his work experience at Riccardo & Lorenzo's. He fudged a little about his experience with the pizza oven. He knew the basics and figured he would catch on with whatever changes Lynn's Pizzeria required.

Lynn came back with an application. "Fill this out and bring it back tomorrow."

Curtis went back to Arnold the next day. He arrived midafternoon with a completed application. He sported the same dress shirt he had worn to his neighbor's funeral. He had lost weight from a month of swimming and the shirt didn't cling so tight.

The hostess introduced herself with a slight southern drawl as Mary.

"My mom…I mean, Lynn, will come get you in a minute. You really want to work here?"

"I need a job; I have truck insurance to pay."

"She doesn't pay much, and if you cook, you won't even get tips."

Before Curtis could ponder what Mary had told him, Lynn said, "Come with me."

Curtis followed her to a booth near the front entrance. Curtis waited for her to sit down. Lynn sat facing the lobby, and Curtis slid into the seat across from her. All the tables in the restaurant had a large centerpiece candle in the middle. On top of the candle was a black vent that looked like Lynn's Pizzeria hat logo. Lynn slid the candle to the side and placed his application before her. She surveyed it while pulling a pack of cigarettes out of her handbag. Lynn took a cigarette out, put it in her mouth, and lit it up. She carefully blew a large puff of white smoke away from the table.

"Do you want something to drink?" she asked.

"Can I have a cup of ice water please?"

Lynn looked around and spotted a girl wiping down the black-and-white plastic checkered table cover.

"Katie, can you come here for a sec?"

A young woman with short toffee-brown hair quickly finished wiping down the table and bounced over to them, flashing a contagious smile.

"Katie, would you be a dear and grab this young man a large cup of Pepsi with ice, please?"

"Yes, ma'am."

The waitress headed to the kitchen area and disappeared in back.

"Look," Lynn began, "I need a pizza cook, someone I can count on to show up, show up on time, and stay the full shift. It's only part-time, and you'll have to work the weekends."

Curtis asked, "What are the hours of the shifts?"

"Friday and Saturday are the same—five o'clock to midnight. Sunday is from noon to ten. You'll be scheduled as an assistant, which means, for the most part, you will prep, cook, and cut pies. Either Billy or Jeff will assemble until we can get you trained."

The pleasant waitress returned with a large soft drink, napkins, and a straw.

"Is there anything else you need?" she asked instinctively.

"No, sweetie, that's all. Thank you."

Curtis took the straw out of the wrapper and took a drink. He cleared his throat then cautiously asked, "How much does the job pay?"

Lynn took another large inhale off her cigarette and then flicked the ash into her ashtray while scanning the application.

"How much did they pay you at Riccardo & Lorenzo's?"

Curtis told her he made three dollars and fifty cents an hour as a cook.

"Seriously? Why did you leave?"

Curtis looked her in the eyes and lied. "They cut my hours way back, and it just wasn't worth it to drive all the way to South County for a partial shift."

"Look, I can only pay you minimum wage for the probation period, which is two months. That's two dollars and ninety cents an hour. I'll bump you to three and a quarter as soon as I can." She finished her cigarette and smashed the stub into the ashtray. "Plus, you can make yourself a free pizza to take home after your shift."

"Do we earn tips?"

Lynn met his eyes with a bewildered gaze as she considered the question.

"Did you get tips at your previous job?" Lynn asked.

"On the weekends we did."

"Hun, I can tell you that the only ones that earn tips here are my waitresses. You can ask them to share with you, but I don't think you'll like their answers."

Curtis asked, "What about waiters? Do you need waiters?"

Surprised by the question, she let out a hearty laugh. Lynn found this more amusing than asking about tips.

"Curtis, you seem like a likable guy, but to put it bluntly, you do not have the boobs, the butt, or the pretty smile that will get tips out of my customers. I only hire waitresses for my dining room."

Lynn got up from the table, picking up his application. She asked Curtis directly, "Do you want to make pizzas for me or not?"

Curtis hesitated as he thought about it. "Yes, thank you. I want the job."

She reached out and shook his hand. "Welcome to the Lynn's Pizzeria family. Stay here and drink your Pepsi. I'm going to bring you some paperwork to fill out. It shouldn't take long."

Lynn walked through the kitchen and back to her small office to get the packet for new hires.

Katie watched Lynn disappear into the back then made her way over to the table. She whispered, "Did you get the job?"

Curtis smiled at her and nodded his head.

She leaned over and whispered, "You're going to enjoy working here."

Katie spotted Lynn coming back, straightened up, and took Curtis's cup, which was still half full.

Lynn glared at Katie but didn't say a word.

"I just asked him if he wanted another Pepsi, that's all."

Lynn ignored the young waitress and returned to her seat. She went through the packet and explained things briefly. "Fill these out and give them back to me before you leave."

Katie returned with another Pepsi. Curtis felt her hand on his shoulder as she asked, "Is there anything else I can get you?"

Curtis sheepishly responded, "I don't have a pen."

Lynn excused Katie as she pulled a pen out of her pocket. "Here, use mine, but please give it back to me before you leave."

The pen was an attractive, light gold ballpoint. The black ink flowed smoothly as Curtis completed the forms. He drank the rest of his Pepsi and eased his anxiety by chomping on the ice. When he was through, he waited by the front for Lynn to come by the cash register. After a few minutes, Mary, the hostess, went back to get Lynn from her office then went into the kitchen and stopped to talk with Jeff, the pizza cook. Lynn met Curtis up front.

Curtis handed Lynn the completed packet. She thanked him and asked him to return the next day at four in the afternoon for orientation so he would be useful for Friday night and the rest of the weekend. Then she excused herself and returned to her office.

As Curtis left, he heard Lynn reprimand Mary for being back in the kitchen and not by the front door. She also chastised Jeff for his messy, understocked workstation and dirty floor. Mary came back and mouthed at Curtis, "She is such a bitch." Instead of responding, he said goodbye and walked out the door.

Curtis climbed into the truck and was immediately stabbed by the ballpoint pen he had stuck in his pants pocket. He sat in his truck, wondering if accepting the job was the right decision. He took the ink pen out of his pocket and threw it on the bench seat. He had every intention of giving it back to Lynn the next day, but the thought of the pen disappeared from his mind as the pen found its way under the back cushion. He took solace that his mother would be happy that he found another job. And the girl with a pretty smile assured him he would enjoy working there.

Curtis showed up at ten minutes before four the next day. He stood among some customers who were waiting for their take-out orders. Lynn came over and eyed him up and down.

"Please follow me," she requested, escorting him back to her office.

Sitting in the chair at the desk was a rather large woman with curly dark hair and a pleasant face. Lynn introduced Curtis to Georgia, her sister and assistant manager. Georgia was a kindly woman, but her weight and arthritic knees made getting around the restaurant challenging. This meant most of her time was spent sitting in a chair in the office. Georgia was great with numbers and had exceptional organizational skills. She also genuinely liked people and could handle customers when the need arose.

Lynn delegated all her administrative tasks, so Georgia handled all matters regarding payroll, ordering ingredients and supplies, totaling the daily receipts, and making the deposits. Georgia also managed all the scheduling. By assigning most of her duties to Georgia, Lynn allowed herself to do what she loved most: managing people.

After Lynn introduced Curtis to Georgia, she took him to the back storage area and gave him a red-and-white checkered shirt, a name tag with Lynn's Pizzeria logo, a white apron, and a Lynn's Pizzeria ball cap.

"I'm sorry, Hon, but I forgot to tell you yesterday that you need to provide your own black pants, socks, and shoes. Make sure you wear them tomorrow when you come to work."

As she turned to leave, Lynn added, "Take your name tag back to Georgia and ask her to make you a sticker. I think the label maker is in the desk somewhere."

Curtis went to the employee restroom, put on the shirt, and tucked it into his blue jeans. The apron was more challenging as it was difficult tying the strings behind him.

Curtis put on the hat and laughed at his reflection in the mirror. He had not had to wear a uniform since he was a Cub Scout in third grade. He went back to the office to talk to Georgia. She took the name tag from him, found the label maker, and typed in his name. She removed the plastic film that covered the sticky side of the label. After carefully and meticulously aligning the sticker to the center of the name tag, she pressed it firmly and handed it back to him.

Curtis struggled putting the name tag on, so Georgia kindly offered to help him. She lifted herself out of the chair with a grunt.

"Let me see this thing," she said as she got closer. She unclasped several buttons and ran her hand inside the shirt to prevent sticking him with the pin.

"There, that's a lot better," she said, admiring her work. She stepped back and noticed the disheveled apron ties.

"Oh, sweetie, you're a hot mess. Let me fix your strings too."

Curtis turned around, and Georgia cinched up the apron strings and tied them into a secure bow.

Georgia complimented Curtis as she sat back down in the chair with a sigh of relief. "You clean up nicely, young man."

Curtis headed to the prep area by the two large pizza ovens and introduced himself to Jeff, one of the pizza cooks. "It shouldn't be that busy tonight. The weeknights are quiet and usually pretty slow unless we get a softball crowd after the games…then it can get busy."

Curtis inquired about their process, and Jeff gave him the rundown.

Then Jeff whispered, "We're supposed to use the scale and weigh everything according to that chart on the wall up there. But that's the surest way to get behind on your orders. Make sure you use it from time to time so they see we're using it, but you'll get to know soon what three ounces feels like."

Curtis looked perplexed.

Jeff added, "Also, make sure you use it if Lynn is in the kitchen. Lucky for us, she hates the kitchen almost as much as she hates her office. She loves to hang out up front and talk to customers and order the waitresses around. She pretty much leaves me alone because I'm dating her daughter."

"Mary?"

"Hey, it's a family-owned business. Who knows? Maybe they'll franchise in a few years. One day, Mary and I could have our own restaurant."

Curtis was making mental notes of everything. So far, it appeared much more laid-back than Riccardo & Lorenzo's.

Jeff asked, "Do you have a girlfriend?"

"No," Curtis answered.

"Let me tell you, the girls that work here are easy. All you need to do is be nice to them, pretend you're listening, and if you go out with them after work, show interest in their silly little lives, they will reward you in ways you can't imagine."

"What are you telling him?" Mary queried from the cash register.

"Nothing, sweetheart, just telling him how we make pizzas, that's all."

"Um-hmm, that's what I thought."

"Mary and I have been together for the last three months." After a long, awkward pause, he added, "We're expecting a baby right around Christmas."

Curtis's felt butterflies in his stomach, and he wished he was drinking beers with his friends at the Gradys'.

Curtis observed for the next few hours. He quickly got the hang of everything that Lynn expected of him. By the end of the dinner rush, he was working the oven and slicing pizzas like he had worked there for weeks.

Right before ten o'clock, Lynn approached him and said, "I'm going to let you go early tonight." He walked to the back with her to clock out. She instructed him to hang up his apron and shirt. She added, "The first hat is free, but if you need it replaced, it will cost you three dollars, so don't lose it."

Curtis put the hat on the shelf where his shirt hung, but she stopped him. "Don't leave your hat here or it will be gone before you show up tomorrow."

Curtis placed his card into the time clock and pushed the large black button. He heard the stamp click but checked the card all the same.

Lynn took the card from him, put it on the desk, and scribbled a note for Georgia.

"Drive safe…and don't forget, black shoes, pants, and socks tomorrow, okay?"

Curtis acknowledged with a thumbs-up as he said, "Yes, ma'am."

Lynn smiled. She loved it when people did exactly what they were told.

The nighttime brought relief from the summer heat but not the humidity. Curtis didn't stop sweating even after leaving the pizza oven.

It was uncomfortable because the sweat laid on his skin and wouldn't evaporate. He felt clammy and wished nothing more than to drive over to Springdale, climb the fence, and jump in the pool.

"Air," he thought. "I just need some air moving." He rolled down the windows on both doors and headed for home, jamming out to "I Want You to Want Me."

CHAPTER 15

Sweet Hitch-Hiker

The next day, Curtis only worked a partial shift to cover the busy evening. Once things slowed down, he was told he could go home. He was ecstatic to get out of work early. With the radio up, he sang "Rock On" with David Essex as he sped home. He had only gone about a half mile when he saw someone walking along the shoulder of the road. As he got closer, he saw more clearly that it was a woman in a tight white dress stumbling in heels.

He slowed, turned the music down, and yelled out the passenger side window, asking her if she needed a ride.

Curtis pulled his truck over and came to a complete stop. The woman looked at him and waved. She approached the window and nervously peered inside. Not seeing any indications of immediate danger, she released an enormous sigh of relief and said with a raspy voice, "Oh my God, yes, please."

She struggled to get into the truck in the tight dress and heels. Curtis guessed she was in her early thirties or perhaps a little older.

"You're a lifesaver. Thank you."

Curtis asked politely, "Where do you live?"

"My old man has a house off Tenbrook. Do you know where that's at?"

"Yeah, it's not too far from here."

"It is if you're walking in heels. Oh my God, my feet hurt. Do you mind if I smoke?"

He didn't object to her smoking as she pulled a pack of Marlboros from her small purse.

"Do you live on upper Tenbrook or lower?"

"Hell, I don't know. I just know it's Tenbrook. I'll tell you where to turn."

She lit a cigarette and asked, "What's your name?"

"Curtis."

"Hi, Curtis, I'm Rita. Where you from? Do you live in Arnold?"

"No, I live out in Imperial."

"I know where that's at. I have a brother that lives in Barnhart."

As they approached the Fox School campus, she said, "Make a left at the light."

Curtis made the turn and followed the road. The silence was awkward.

"Why were you walking up the road alone?"

Rita inhaled her cigarette, and as she blew the smoke out the window, she explained her predicament. "Well, I was up at the Span Disco with my friend. She met some guy and left with him but forgot to give me the keys to her car. I was talking to a man who seemed nice enough, and he offered me a ride home when I explained I was left alone by my friend."

Her voice began to break as she continued, "But soon after we left, he asked me if I would go home with him for the night. When I told him I had a boyfriend, he offered me a hundred dollars to blow him. Can you believe that? I am not a goddamn whore!"

The word "whore" hung in the air for a minute. A half dozen ideas immediately entered Curtis's head, but Rita vocalized the only thought that came into hers.

"Prick! Who does he think he is? I told him to pull the car over to let me out. He kept driving, so I just started screaming. I was terrified of what he might do to me, so I reached over to grab the steering wheel. I'd rather take my chances bleeding in a ditch. He reached over and slapped me then pulled the car over to the side of the road. He called me a cock-teasing bitch as I got out of the car."

"I am so sorry, Rita. That's horrible."

"I should have walked back to the club to call my brother, but I was too upset and just wanted to get home." Rita was shaking as she wiped tears off her cheek. She took another long drag off her cigarette. "Guys can be such assholes—no offense. You're obviously one of the good ones. How old are you?"

"Seventeen."

"You're just a baby... Make a right here at the stop sign," she directed, pointing with her finger. "My house is just up here on the left."

Curtis pulled his truck up onto the steeply inclined driveway. Rita had a difficult time trying to open the heavy truck door. Curtis jumped out of the truck, opened the door, and helped her reach the concrete.

"Would you like to come in and have a beer or something?" she asked. "I'd give you some money for the ride home if I had any, but I spent all I had on drinks and cigarettes."

"Sure, that would be great." He knew his mom was not expecting him home until after midnight, so he had an hour or so to spare.

Curtis followed Rita to the porch as she fumbled around in her clutch purse for her keys. Upon finding them, she struggled to get the front door open. Once the door was unlocked and opened, she stepped inside and felt around for the light switch. Curtis followed right behind her and struggled to pull the door closed.

"I've asked Jimmy a dozen times to fix that damn door."

"Is Jimmy your husband?"

"No, he's my boyfriend. We've been living together for the last ten years."

"What time does your boyfriend get off work?"

"He works overnights at the brewery. He won't be back here until tomorrow morning. Hey, listen, grab a beer out of the refrigerator. I'm going to change and get out of these heels. I'm never wearing heels again."

Curtis crossed the tiny living room and found the nice-sized kitchen. He opened the refrigerator and laughed when he saw a Lynn's Pizzeria box on the middle shelf. There were about a dozen cans of Budweiser on the bottom shelf. He grabbed one, popped the tab off, and took a long pull.

When he returned to the living room, he saw Rita sitting on the chair, rubbing her feet with lotion. She was wearing red gym shorts and a revealing white spaghetti-strap camisole. She had pinned her hair up with a large hair clip.

"Do you want me to get you a beer, Rita?"

"No, I've had enough to drink for one night, but thank you."

She stood up. She was a lot shorter without heels on, and in the light, she looked a little older than he initially thought. Even from a few feet away, the smell of perfume was overpowering. The feminine textures hinted at through the fabric of the camisole left very little to the imagination. Curtis was anxious, confused, and a little fearful of the desires growing within him.

"I have another idea though." Then she turned to him and asked, "You're not a cop, are you?" It was the weirdest question anyone had ever asked him.

"No, I work at Lynn's Pizzeria and go to Windsor High School."

"Okay, cool. I figured as much, but I'd rather be safe than sorry."

She entered the kitchen, grabbed a chair, and reached into the cabinet above the refrigerator. Curtis could tell she was trying to get something far back in the cupboard.

"Do you need help?" he offered.

"No, but come over here and make sure I don't fall."

Curtis walked over but was unsure how to place his hands on the woman's legs without feeling weird. As she pushed up onto her tiptoes, she nearly fell off the chair. Instinctively, he grabbed her around the knees with his head almost in her butt to hold her steady.

"Got it!" she yelled triumphantly. Curtis helped her down and tried apologizing but couldn't find the words. She was oblivious to any of his transgressions toward her. He could hardly believe what he saw when he noticed what she had in her hands.

She held the biggest bag of the greenest pot he had ever seen.

"This is over a pound of the finest Mexican sinsemilla in the county!" she proclaimed boldly. "Please tell me you like to get high. Here, take this and go out to the living room."

Curtis walked into the living room without a clue that he was holding a twenty-five-year prison sentence in his hand. Rita came out with a giant red acrylic water bong and a BIC lighter. She sat next to him on the couch, filled the bowl, and handed it to him. "Be careful," she warned, "this is some potent shit." She took the lighter and held the flame to the bowl as he inhaled. Curtis heard the bubbling inside the large water pipe and, seconds later, was blasted to the universe's outer limits.

What seemed like hours turned out to be only a few minutes. When he regained his composure, Rita eyed him eagerly and asked, "What do you think?" Curtis was speechless.

"I know! Right?! Now it's my turn." She took the pipe, relit the bowl, and took an enormous hit. She closed her eyes and pedaled her feet like she was on a bike. When she could not take it anymore, she exhaled, set the pipe on the end table, curled up next to Curtis, and closed her eyes. When she opened them again, she asked, "How old did you say you were?" When he told her, she said, "You're just a baby," and closed her eyes again and started crying.

Curtis held her as long as he dared and drank the rest of his beer without disturbing her. When she'd gathered herself, she pulled away from him and sat up.

"I'm sorry, I'm acting like such a crybaby. I have had a horrible night, and now I'm tired and high. If you were just a little bit older, I would…" she caught herself and said, "I'm sorry, but I think it's time for you to go." Curtis was relieved because his thoughts and emotions had been racing since she'd changed her clothes.

He got up and went to throw the empty beer can away. Rita followed him into the kitchen, got a small sandwich bag, and filled it with the green reefer from the larger bag. She asked him to return the large bag to the back of the cupboard.

"I'm sorry I don't have any money for you, but this is probably better than money. You can smoke it or you can sell it. It's your choice. Please don't get caught with it, but if you do, you cannot tell them where you got it. Cool?"

Curtis agreed to her terms and carefully rolled the bag up. She helped him hide it in the waistband of his blue jeans. She walked him to the door and thanked him again for the ride home.

"You're a lifesaver."

Curtis went to hug her, but she threw her arms around him and kissed him on the mouth.

She pulled back, gazed in his eyes, and said, "If only you were just a bit older."

When Curtis got home, the house was dark and quiet inside. He locked the door behind him, put his keys on the kitchen counter, and went straight to his bedroom. He shut and locked the door, got undressed, and hid the bag of marijuana in one of the many puzzle boxes stacked on a shelf inside the closet. He was just about to climb into bed when he heard the door handle rattle then rapid, light knocks.

He went over to open the door. His mother stood in the doorway.

"I just wanted to see if you made it home okay. How was work?"

"It was fine. Mom, I'm tired and just want to go to sleep."

There was an awkward pause before she asked, "Why did you lock the bedroom door?"

"I don't know. It was an accident."

"Hmm…okay, good night." As she closed the door, she raised her head and began sniffing. "What is that smell?"

Curtis replied, "Mom, I work in a restaurant and I always come home smelling like pizza."

"I've never smelt pizza like this," she replied with a troubled look on her face as she closed the door.

CHAPTER 16

Another Story From the Window

Although not a pageant beauty, Katie wasn't ugly by any standard. The oversized Lynn's Pizzeria uniform hid her feminine curves and athletic frame. Katie, like Curtis, was diligent in her work. People from Arnold were usually uptight about anyone who came down from St. Louis County to work, but Katie seemed to blend right in. Her eagerness to work, delightful smile, and charm allowed her to work as many hours as she wanted. Her pleasantness caused older men to fill her purse with tips as she gently sidestepped unwanted solicitations and proposals.

Curtis was attracted to her, and his eyes followed her around every opportunity the time between pizza orders would allow. Katie was friendly toward him, and her genuine smile disarmed him, erasing any words he had formed in his mind to say to her. The other girls were continuously preening themselves for any advantage in an unspoken competition, but Katie simply didn't have time for it, at least not while serving pizzas to people not much older than her mom.

Perhaps it was Katie's short, unevenly parted hair that gave her a rugged boyish look, or maybe Katie's lack of makeup or overly sensitive skin, which the restaurant vapors occasionally aggravated with acute spots of acne, that made her seem ordinary, and therefore approachable, to Curtis. Confident and carefree, Katie was a good waitress and took care of her customers. As a result, they rewarded her for her service.

Thursday nights were hectic during the softball season. Carryout orders would overwhelm the kitchen. Patrons flocked to the restaurant after the games, and the workers stayed extraordinarily busy. That night, however, thunderstorms moved in and slowed things down. During the summer, thunderstorms caused flash floods, producing hail and damaging winds. Visible lightning was enough for an umpire to call off games and shut down the fields as people scampered to get far away from aluminum bats, chain-link fences, and open fields.

As the seven o'clock hour approached and the storms showed no sign of lessening, Lynn asked for volunteers to go home early. Curtis wasted no time to secure a night off.

Curtis changed out of his work shirt and took off his hat and the annoying hairnet. He stopped by Lynn's office to have his timecard signed but had to wait because Lynn was talking with Katie.

When Curtis came out to leave, Katie was in the foyer, peeking out the door waiting for a break in the downpour.

"Are you going to melt?" Curtis asked with a grin.

Katie smiled back, saying, "I doubt it. I don't want to drive home all dripping wet."

"What are you going to do when you get home?"

Katie replied, "I have no idea. I'll probably just watch TV or read a book. What about you?"

Curtis said, "I don't know, but I know I'm not going home right away."

"That's interesting. Why wouldn't you want to go home?"

"My mom will ruin the evening, and she'll yell at me for not working my shift."

"You should be grateful. At least your mom will be home."

Curtis saw the sparkle leave her eyes as her smile disappeared.

Hoping to see that smile again, Curtis asked, "Do you want to go hang out?"

Katie gave him a puzzled look. "Like go out on a date?"

"No, not a date. You know, just hang out and talk."

Katie frowned. "Do you hang out with just anybody, Curtis?"

"Yeah, I suppose I do. If I think they're interesting enough to hang out with."

"Interesting?" Katie replied as she peeked outside again to see the deluge of rain. "I don't know, Curtis, that sounds an awful lot like a date to me."

Curtis, slightly annoyed, said, "Okay, Katie, do you want to go on a date? Let's go back inside and get a table and order a pizza."

She laughed. "I'm hardly dressed for a date. I definitely don't want to eat here, but I think it'd be cool to hang out with you for the evening." She dug through her purse and asked, "Do you want a piece of gum?" She handed him a half-open pack of Wrigley peppermint. "Help yourself."

Curtis took two pieces of gum, opened the door, and was glad to see the rain lightening up. The thunderstorms had significantly cooled the evening air, but it still felt sticky. "Let's go," he said as he ran to his truck. She ran behind him before sprinting to her car, parked under a flickering dusk-to-dawn lamp.

Although the rain was letting up, it didn't stop completely. Curtis got into his truck and watched Katie dig around in the back seat of an old, sun-faded yellow Plymouth Satellite sedan. What he didn't expect to see was Katie peeling off her Lynn's Pizzeria shirt and revealing her bare back. She turned and said, "Don't be looking at my titties, Curtis. I know they ain't much, but this isn't a date. We're only hanging out, remember?"

Curtis didn't want to stare, but he couldn't make himself turn away from the silhouette of small breasts that didn't move as she bent over to get another shirt out of the car. She pulled on a white cotton shirt and changed her shoes. She dug some more in the back of the car and grabbed a bottle and her purse before locking her vehicle and running over to the truck to get out of the rain.

"Can you turn the heater on, please?" Curtis looked over at her and saw her shivering in a tight-fitting, faded Bud Man T-shirt, spotted with dozens of connected wet spots. Goose bumps covered her arms. Even though his body temperature was feverish, he turned the heat on as she'd asked.

Then, Katie did something else Curtis was not ready for. She leaned over and kissed him on the cheek. "First kisses are so awkward. Let's go find some orange juice. I'm thirsty and want to drink."

He stopped at a nearby gas station, and as he fueled his truck, she went inside and bought a large waxy carton of orange drink and paid for the gas with a ten-dollar bill Curtis had given her. When Katie came out, she complained that they didn't have real orange juice. She poured a sizable portion of the orange drink onto the ground to make room for vodka. "I was hoping for a screwdriver, but an orange whip will have to do." She drank from the carton and then passed it over to Curtis. "I am accustomed to drinking alone, but having a drinking buddy could have its perks."

The two laughed and talked as they shared the nasty, orange-flavored concoction. When Curtis took the time to taste the drink, he realized it was more potent than he initially thought. He wanted to stop while there was still time. The next time Katie passed the waxed box over to Curtis, he declined it. "Someone needs to be able to drive," he said.

"You're so boring and dreary," she said as she took her shoes off and put her naked feet on the dashboard. "But at least you're kind of cute. What kind of music do you like anyway?"

She turned the radio on and immediately started singing along with the Supertramp song she heard, not realizing it was a cassette and not the radio.

"It's weird. I don't even know who this is, but I know the song." She giggled. "It's strange I know songs…I know the words…I just don't know the bands." Immediately, she shouted out, "I have an idea! Drive us to Crestwood."

"What's your idea? What's in Crestwood?"

"I know a guy. You're going to like this."

On the drive up to Crestwood, Curtis learned three things about Katie: She went to Mehlville High School, her dream job was an actress, and she lived as an only child with "a bitch for a mom and an asshole for a stepdad." Any further questions Curtis asked seemed to make her drink more and talk less.

Curtis found himself in the parking lot of a radio station next door to the Crestwood drive-in theater. Even with the spotty thunderstorms, a few cars were waiting for it to get dark enough to watch *Corvette Summer*, even if it required the occasional use of their wiper blades.

The rain had filtered out all but the true die-hard radio fans who loitered about for an opportunity to talk to the DJ if he was in a social mood. The alcohol released Katie from acceptable social norms as she climbed out of the truck and immediately started singing, dancing, and twirling about.

Curtis followed her from a distance as she elbowed her way past people toward the window. Katie passed a tall, skinny girl wearing a black slip and over-the-knee leather boots under a clear vinyl rain jacket. The woman tapped Katie on the arm and said, "Don't bother, sweetie. They ain't giving nothing away tonight, so save your breath."

Katie replied, "Is that so?" before walking up to the window and knocking on it with an assortment of odd taps.

Curtis saw the DJ was wearing giant headphones and had his back to the window. He put his finger up, indicating to wait a minute. After a brief pause, he removed his headphones and went to the window.

"Katie! You came back," he said with a smile.

"I told you I would. I have a new boyfriend now."

"Lucky guy."

"Can I get two shirts and a song request tonight?"

"It will cost you. Will you pay?"

"Of course." Immediately, she lifted her shirt and revealed her breasts to the DJ.

The DJ said, "Katie, one day you're going to grow up and become a beautiful woman. When you do, dump this guy, or whoever you're with, and come find me."

Katie laughed and said, "And you're still going to help me get into the movies?"

The DJ laughed. "Sure. Maybe we can make a movie together."

The DJ tossed two shirts through the window and asked what song they wanted to hear.

Katie shrugged her shoulders and looked at Curtis. "What do you want to hear?"

Curtis had a brain freeze from the sequence of events he'd just witnessed. He stuttered incoherently, then blurted out that he wanted to hear "Fly By Night."

The DJ nodded his head and said, "You got it. I got to go, but thanks for stopping by."

Katie handed Curtis a shirt and kissed him. Then she stopped, leveled a gaze at the woman in the transparent raincoat, and said, "Sweetie, it's not what you got, but how you use it. Next time, spend a little more on water-resistant makeup."

They returned to the truck, and once inside, Katie took her T-shirt off and put on an oversized KSHE 95 T-shirt with a large-faced pig smoking a joint on the front. "Damn, mine's too big. I hope it shrinks when I wash it."

"I think it looks good on you," Curtis said.

"Thank you, Curtis. Let's go find some real orange juice."

She looked at him as he started the truck as if to say something, but she remained quiet.

Curtis headed toward Lindbergh Boulevard, and along the way, he stopped at a 7-Eleven and went inside to buy Katie some orange juice while she waited in the truck, singing along to the radio.

When he returned to the truck, he heard the DJ announce, "And by request, here's 'Fly At Night' by Chilliwack." It wasn't the song Curtis wanted to hear, but it became one he would never forget.

By ten o'clock, the vodka bottle was nearly empty. Katie was starting to become unmanageable to the point of being irritating. She began lamenting that she was out of vodka, but whenever Curtis tried to ask her personal questions, she only said, "You don't understand… Nobody understands."

Curtis didn't know what to do. He couldn't drive her back to her car; there was no way she could drive herself home. What was worse was that he didn't know where she lived. Every time he asked her, she would laugh. "Why do you want to know where I live, Curtis? So we can hang out and be friends?" Once a playful taunt, her words now had barbed hooks that pained him.

Then Curtis felt terrible that he didn't drink more of the vodka. Once afraid of drinking too much, he now worried about letting her drink so much by herself. His thoughts were interrupted by words no driver wanted to hear from their passenger: "I think I'm going to get sick."

Curtis pulled the truck over as soon as he could. It just happened to be a church parking lot. Katie opened the door and fell out, and then, for the next twenty minutes, he could only listen to the revolting, sickening sounds of retching and gagging as her body tried to detoxify itself. Curtis regretted not taking her to get something to eat before they went to the radio station. He knew all too well that feeling of trying to throw up when nothing was there.

It was almost eleven when Katie got back into the truck. Her ragged look, intensified by noticeable dehydration, removed the fullness from her face. She dug through her purse and found chewing gum, and only then did she tell him where she lived.

Curtis drove to the house near Suson County Park. He pulled the truck next to the driveway and parked on the tree-lined street.

"Where's my car? Please take me back to get my car."

"You left your lights on and the battery's dead. We'll have to get it tomorrow."

"You're a terrible liar."

Someone inside turned on the porch light. Curtis started to get out of the truck.

"No. You'll only make things worse than you already have. Please don't get out." She grabbed her purse. "Seriously, you need to leave. I'll see you at work tomorrow." She tumbled out of the truck.

Curtis watched her shuffle up the sidewalk from his perch in the truck. She was fumbling with the keys by the door when it opened. A bearded man with glasses and a full head of hair glanced around before locking eyes with Curtis. He felt his face burn as the laser-like glare cut him into ribbons. Then, to Curtis's horror, he saw him drag Katie inside the house by her hair before slamming the door shut and turning the porch light off.

The image haunted Curtis the entire drive home, evoking a mix of emotions he was not equipped to handle. When he got home, he noticed the empty vodka bottle and the balled-up Bud Man T-shirt lying on his "Little Devil Hot Stuff" floor mat. The shadows cast by the dome light transformed the charming character into something sinister. Curtis found the grin irritating. He turned the dome light off, and the floorboard became black as night.

Checking inside his house, he saw the light was still on in the living room, so he knew he had at least one parent to contend with. Whatever he faced, he knew it was nothing compared to the hell Katie was experiencing.

He grabbed the empty vodka bottle, walked to the wooded area behind the garage, and threw the bottle as far down the hill as possible. He returned to the truck, grabbed the KSHE shirt, and hid the Bud Man shirt inside it. He had every intention of giving it back to Katie the next time he saw her.

JoAnn met him in the kitchen as soon as he walked through the door.

"How was work?"

"It was okay."

"No pizza tonight?"

Curtis usually brought home a pizza from work because he could get a free pizza whenever he worked a shift.

"No."

The inquisition continued. "Why did you buy another shirt?"

"I didn't buy it. A girl gave it to me."

"Curtis, you need to stop lying to me all the time."

Curtis went to his room, wishing Katie had a parent who got angry at her in a different way. He counted himself lucky that his mother's anger was so manageable.

He couldn't stop thinking about her. He sat on the bed, pressing the cotton fabric of the Bud Man shirt into his face and inhaling the pleasant, aromatic scent of spice and fruit, a little heavy on the citrus. He could not verbalize or process his thoughts and feelings for the girl he barely knew. He could only convert his mixed feelings into tears as he cried for a girl who was living a life in such obvious pain. What he could not figure out was how she still managed to smile but considered it no small thing to hang out with a stranger and invited him into her world. The clues were there, but Curtis was not a very good detective.

CHAPTER 17

Lightning in the Sky

Curtis slept in on Friday and drove himself to Springdale after lunch with Santana's new song, "All I Ever Wanted," enticing him to drive faster than necessary. He wanted to swim for a few hours before going to work. Around three, Curtis took a shower and got dressed for work. He arrived at Lynn's Pizzeria twenty minutes before his shift and saw Katie's car still parked where she left it. Few cars were in the parking lot. He went inside and heard yells coming from the back.

Mary was sitting next to the cash register, paging through a magazine. She warned, "Don't go back there, Curtis."

"Why?"

"If you must know, Mom is having words with Katie."

Hearing Katie's name made Curtis forget about Mary. Ignoring her, he walked back to the manager's office.

As soon as Katie made eye contact with Curtis, she ran to him with tears in her eyes. Curtis immediately noticed Katie had a black eye and a busted lip.

Katie embraced Curtis, but before she could say anything, Lynn stood up and said, "Curtis, this conversation does not include you. Go wait outside. Your shift doesn't start for fifteen more minutes."

Katie interrupted, "She won't let me work tonight."

Curtis looked at Lynn, who said, "Look, I can't have a waitress looking like a battered sparring partner serving customers. I'm not firing her. She needs to take a week off to heal, and then she can come back."

Katie cried. "I can't take a week off. I need this job; I need the money."

"Well, sweetie, you need to think about these things before you get into a fight."

Curtis didn't want the situation to escalate, so he proposed a compromise. "Lynn, would it be okay if Katie made pizzas?"

Both Katie and Lynn looked at him like he had seven heads.

"Lynn, let me train her to make pizzas. The customers won't have to see her, and she can still get paid."

Lynn addressed Katie, "You understand, there's no tips for making pizzas."

"I know. I can accept that. Something is better than nothing."

Lynn sighed. "She's your problem now. Don't you screw this up or I'll fire the both of you."

When Katie looked at Curtis, her smile reemerged for the first time since she'd gotten sick the previous evening.

Their shift didn't start for another ten minutes, so Curtis asked Katie to follow him outside to his truck. He opened the door to retrieve her Bud Man T-shirt. She jumped into his arms and kissed him. The kiss surprised him, and he didn't know how to react.

Katie looked him in the eye and said, "You kiss like a dead fish. We need to work on that if we're going to continue hanging out." Katie thanked him for giving her back one of her favorite shirts and for saving her job.

Throughout the wonderful, fun-filled evening of making pizzas, she still refused to talk about her home life. She would not discuss her stepdad or how she knew the DJ from the radio station.

Even with a black eye and busted lip, there was something beautiful about this girl. She was zesty, a perfect mixture of sugar and spice, and, like the Opium perfume she wore, she was addicting. Something else he could not let go of was the memory of her bare breasts. Three times, she had revealed herself to him, and images of her nakedness were burned into his mind. Reality was a million times better than the glossy images in magazines. His mind was aroused, his love awakened and begging to be pleased. His eagerness, of course, was enflamed because he knew she would not object or deny his desires.

Before they closed the kitchen, they each made a pizza for the other to take home. After work, they hung out in the parking lot. She sat in his truck, and they briefly made out. The kissing was awkward because of the fat lip and cuts inside her mouth from the beating she had received the night before. She had to stop him when she felt his hand reaching under her shirt.

"Curtis, we can't do this tonight. Not tonight. I can't risk getting home late tonight, and I can't go home smelling like sex. Soon though… I am not saying no, just not right now." She kissed him, grabbed her pizza off the dashboard, and said goodbye. He watched her leave, listening to her sing. Curtis could only sit dumbfounded until her car left the parking lot.

Curtis drove home with his head in the clouds, wondering if he was in love with her. He didn't say anything when his mom met him in the kitchen. He handed her the pizza and headed for his bedroom.

His mom said, "Curtis, what is this?"

Curtis went over and looked at the pizza. Katie had used three times the amount of pepperoni he had trained her to use, and in the middle of the pizza were two pieces of raw anchovies shaped like a V.

"I'm sorry. I must have grabbed the wrong one."

JoAnn threw the anchovies into the trash and closed the pizza box lid.

Wednesday was July 4th, and Curtis arrived at work at eleven in the morning. Lynn treated the holiday like a Sunday and scheduled the workers to cover open to close. When he went inside to change, he discovered that Lynn would not let them work the pizza oven together anymore. Curtis surrendered his holiday hours to Katie so she could get the holiday shift, which she was grateful for. Curtis was thankful to have the holiday off. He gave Katie his phone number but was disappointed when she did not give him hers.

"It's not you, Curtis. If you call, Bill will only get angry when he picks up the phone. When Bill gets angry, he takes that anger out on my mom, or he'll take it out on me. When he takes it out on my mom, she takes it out on me, so either way, I get the painful end of it. I've already memorized it, and I promise I will call you."

Katie walked him to the front entrance and risked kissing Curtis goodbye. After three days, Curtis associated the taste of peppermint with her kisses. Katie's kisses to Curtis reciprocated what Curtis's hugs meant to Katie. Each one received from the other the perfect measure of affirmation they both so desperately wanted and needed.

Independence Day was one holiday the McGowan family did not go to Springdale for. It was too crowded, and the overwhelming amount of people made the pool unenjoyable. Giving up the pool one day over the summer was not so bad, even on a hot day in July. The holiday in Imperial was a massive event because the American Legion Hall sponsored a free firework show. It began years ago with a relatively small gathering of people comprising veterans from the local community, members of St. Joseph's Parish, and American Legion Post 283. Like all humble beginnings, they put on a fabulous party with barrels of beer, over-and-under tables, raffles, and other carnival-like games of skill and chance. Picnic-style foods, delicious barbecue, and vast tubs of Vess soda were available. The crowds grew exponentially with each passing year. By 1979, the crowd was so large that organizers needed to scramble to assemble transportation to get people from nearby Kimmswick to the Windsor School parking lot. Late arrivers had to park on the narrow shoulder of 61-67 and walk along Montebello Road with cars parked on both sides of the road, often in people's front yards. The only people with any advantage were the kids with bikes and motorcycles. The kids ruled as they rolled in and through the crowds. Curtis was among that brazen group, having long ago outgrown his banana seat Schwinn for his Suzuki motorcycle.

The neighborhood was packed by late afternoon, and people could easily get lost in the crowds. Nobody predicted the immense gathering of people. Some residents voiced concerns that fire trucks, paramedics, and police could not access the roadways. While nobody got hurt, and recent rains made wildfires improbable, the awareness created such pressure that the organizers had to agree this would be the last year. Still, the party would not end without a proper goodbye.

Curtis was motoring around when he spotted Elizabeth and Fern among a crowd of school kids. Elizabeth looked so out of place, being the oldest and tallest of the group.

"Hey, Elizabeth, do you want to go for a ride?"

"Really?"

He motioned for her to hop on. Elizabeth said something to Fern then walked over and slid onto the seat behind him. He felt her grab around his waist, and when he took off, she grabbed even tighter.

"Shouldn't we be wearing helmets?" she yelled into his ear.

"Probably, but I only have one, and I'm not even sure where it is."

"Should I be afraid?"

"No."

She held on tighter, wanting to believe she was safe.

A car started to pull out in front of him, but he saw it with plenty of time, and as he braked, the motorbike lurched. What he felt was unintentional but very real. Her breasts pressed into his back, which he felt even through their clothes. Focusing was going to be an issue, so he went slow until he cleared the cars. He gently accelerated around the corner and passed the graveyard, then rode up the hill and toward the water tower before braking again. Curtis negotiated the sharp left-hand corner like a pro, accelerating into the turn. The thrill of the motorcycle ride rippled from front to back as they raced down the hill, passing small groups of people laboring to hike up to the American Legion Hall.

Curtis took Elizabeth around Kimmswick a few times, going up and down the blocks of old houses. He drove around the small park and then across Rock Creek, going over a hundred-year-old bridge and onto Hoppie's Marina.

They strolled out onto the dock and stared at the river. The marina was quiet, and the awkwardness of being alone together became overwhelming. Curtis told her about the dozens of places he could take her if she wanted to see the river again.

As they returned to the motorcycle, she said, "Thank you, this is a lot of fun. I've been to Kimmswick before, but not this far."

Curtis drove up Windsor Harbor Road all the way to the school, but when Elizabeth saw the high school, she freaked out.

"Curtis! We shouldn't be here; we're trespassing."

"I know. I thought you'd like to see where we are."

"I see. Now, let's get out of here before you go to jail."

Instead of going back up Montebello Road, he took her on a more adventurous route. He cut under the railroad trestle at the edge of town and drove over an old dirt road overgrown with weeds. The road ran parallel to the railroad tracks for about a mile until he rode up a steep trail and crossed over two sets of railroad tracks. The sight of railroad tracks made Elizabeth scream, and she screamed even louder as he rode the motorbike hard up the hill that emptied into his backyard. He parked the bike beside his truck and walked Elizabeth back to the American Legion Hall.

They found more friends to hang out with, and Curtis treated Elizabeth to a BBQ hamburger and an orange Vess soda. As it grew dark, they waited anxiously for the fireworks to begin.

The fireworks were brilliant and loud. Initially, there was more waiting than oohing and ahhing. The increments built up to a crescendo that capped off the day. But as the day, so went the night, and it was over far too soon. If there was any consolation, Curtis knew he would be showered and asleep before many of the other people would even get back to their cars.

He walked Elizabeth and Fern home, but by the time they arrived, word had already gotten to her stepdad, Roger, about Elizabeth being on a motorcycle. Within Curtis's hearing, Elizabeth was strictly forbidden to "ever get on a motorcycle, or in a truck, or any other motorized vehicle driven by that boy."

After Roger went inside, Curtis apologized for causing trouble. Elizabeth assured him she would be alright and thanked him for an unforgettable day. Curtis walked home thinking about the day's events.

When he got home, his mom was waiting for him in the kitchen.

"Who's Katie?"

"What?"

"You heard me. Who is Katie?"

"She's a girl I work with and have been training."

"She called a few minutes ago. I told her you weren't home. She said she would call back, but I told her not to call so late, so she said she would talk to you tomorrow."

Only a few times in his life had Curtis ever raised his voice to his mother, and both times, she beat him severely for it. He was ready to add another tally to his count.

"Why would you say such a thing? It's not that late."

"You want a phone? You pay the bill. You're already behind on your truck insurance again. Katie said she would talk to you tomorrow. I don't need the phone ringing at all hours of the night." Then his mom stormed off to her bedroom and slammed the door.

Curtis took a shower and went to bed with Elizabeth and Katie on his mind. It was only natural for him to compare his thoughts and feelings about the two girls. Elizabeth, while younger, was far more beautiful. Elizabeth was the type of girl who would never have sex until she was married. Roger would see to that. He also realized that he valued his friendship with Elizabeth more than a romantic relationship with her. She was fifteen, and when he did the math, even if they fell in love and married, he'd have to wait three more years and seven if she went to college. Katie, on the other hand, was closer in age and had a mindset that was as daring and outrageous as his own. Her beauty was of a different type. Katie was feisty, strong, and resilient.

Even as he tried to fall asleep, he couldn't stop thinking about them both. He had to make a choice. What sealed the deal for him occurred when he imagined introducing each girl to his mother. He knew she would love Elizabeth. Her looks and her laugh would endear her to his mother. His mom would want to be Elizabeth's friend. Curtis could imagine his mom taking Elizabeth to the store to shop for clothes. On the other hand, Katie would be met with stiffness and hostility. The phone call was proof that JoAnn did not have any tolerance for Katie.

Then his mind raced, as did his heart, that Katie was stronger than Elizabeth. She wouldn't close her eyes in fear. She might even influence Curtis more because she was more demanding and resilient through her pain and suffering. There was a beauty in that trait. Curtis saw freedom from his mom in Katie. The more he thought about it, the more he saw his mother as the one who kept him too close, trying to hold him too tight, refusing to let him grow up. He wanted to be who he wanted to be.

After all the mental gymnastics, Curtis realized he did not have to choose at all. The choice had already been made for him. With peace in his heart, he fell asleep thinking of incense burning, heavenly spices and fragrances dominated by citrus fruits, and peppermint-flavored kisses.

Chapter 18

Aja

In 1971, Curtis was a Cub Scout, and JoAnn was his den mother. At a pack meeting, the leaders decided to gather magazines and newspapers to deliver to veterans returning from Vietnam. The various troops would collect what they could, and members with vans and trucks would take the kids and the collection to a meet and greet with veteran liaisons at Scott Air Force Base in Belleville, Illinois.

Brad Grady was never a Cub Scout, nor would he have reason to be. While JoAnn's den was busy making leaf rubbings, learning about songbirds, and making messes with papier-mâché, Mr. Grady taught his boys how to hunt, fish, and tend a garden. On Saturday, young Curtis was assigned to collect magazines. Brad was willing to walk with him to help. The boys took turns pulling a wagon and knocking on doors to collect what they could.

The last house they visited was a lonely old house set back off the road by a long gravel driveway. The house was dark, well-worn, and needed a new roof. Brad pulled the wagon down the long driveway, and Curtis climbed the porch stairs and knocked on the door.

Brad followed him, saying, "I don't know why we're even here. We don't even come to this house on Halloween."

The door opened, and the boys saw a long, gray-haired, unshaven man with a cigarette hanging from his mouth. The man was wearing boxers, barely covered by a bathrobe, and slippers. He was harsh and without manners or courtesy. "What do you kids want?"

"Sir, we're here to collect magazines—"

"What kind of magazines? Who are you collecting magazines for?"

"Vietnam veterans coming back home, sir."

"Is that so? Wait right here. I'll be right back."

Neither boy had any plans of stepping into that house.

He came back with a grocery sack loaded with magazines. He set them on the porch and said, "Here you go, now get!" then he abruptly closed the door.

Curtis picked the bag up and set it down in the wagon. When he looked down, his jaw dropped. On the cover of the top magazine was a picture of a naked woman. The woman was propped up on the back of her elbows, with the bottoms of her feet nearly touching, like she was giving birth.

Brad pointed as he said, "Look, I can see her butthole."

Curtis woke up Thursday morning to a quiet house. He was glad he had the day off, but there wouldn't be any time for lying around. There were chores to do. He knew he was on thin ice, so he planned to buckle down for a day. His mom wanted the grass cut, and his dad had brought home ten gallons of driveway sealer and a few bags of sand to coat the blacktopped driveway. While anxious to get outside and take advantage of the cooler morning weather, he didn't want to miss Katie's phone call.

It was only nine-thirty, so he went into the kitchen to make himself a peanut butter sandwich for breakfast, but when he went to get the milk out, he saw the pizza box and changed his mind. He had two large slices of pepperoni pizza instead. While eating his pizza, he pulled the newspaper apart, looking for the comic section. Then the phone rang.

"Hello?"

"Curtis?"

"Yes, it's me. Is this Katie?"

"Are you expecting someone else to call?"

"No, not really."

"Did you have fun watching fireworks last night?"

"Yeah, it was a very nice display, but it didn't last long enough."

"The good stuff never lasts long, Curtis. Hey, listen, sorry I called so late. I hope you didn't get in trouble. Your mom didn't seem very happy with me."

"Yeah, but she'll get over it. I'm glad you called."

"Well, I can't talk very long. I have some errands I need to run, but the good news is the swelling in my lip is almost gone, and the bruise around my eye is only yellow and green now. I think with some makeup, I can go back to waitressing before the weekend."

"I can't imagine you wearing makeup."

"What are you trying to say, Curtis? Are you saying I need makeup?"

"No, not at all, but—"

"Can I tell you a secret?"

"Katie, you can tell me anything…"

"I'm not kidding, Curtis, but I have serious makeup skills. When I have time, I can make myself look like I'm in my twenties."

"Really? Why would you do that?"

"Well, sometimes I get dressed up and put makeup on, and I'll go to a bar. Grown men will buy me drinks all night long. I don't do it all the time because, between you and me, many men are ignorant pricks. I can't tell you how often I've been groped, molested, and harassed."

"No kidding…all that for a free drink, though?"

"Yeah, drinking is expensive. I really should cut back. Sometimes I just want to wipe off my makeup and give the old geezers a heart attack when they find out I'm only sixteen."

"Katie, I thought you were seventeen."

"I am. I just wanted to see if you were really listening to me. Anyway, I really like you. I don't want to tell you everything because I don't want you to hate me, but I would like to share some things with you about me."

"Katie, I don't think I could ever hate you."

"Curtis, trust me. I know boys better than you know girls. I think your innocence makes you the most attractive guy I know."

Curtis had no response to her, so he remained quiet.

"Maybe innocence is the wrong word. You're clearly naive, especially about girls, but that's a good thing, provided you don't let the wrong one take advantage of you. You're honest and trustworthy, Curtis. That makes you rarer than a four-leaf clover."

"It's funny you say that because my mom thinks I'm a liar."

"That's because you have secrets, and you hide them well. Our moms just have this God complex that makes them think they have to know everything all the time. It's their last chance to have a measure of control over our lives. Listen, Curtis, I wish we could talk all day, but I need to go. I'll see you at work tomorrow. Bye."

Curtis hung the phone up after hearing the click on the other end. He was sad that the call was so short, but he wanted to make the most of the remaining time, so he threw himself into his chores to free his mind from the infatuation growing in his heart.

He entered the bedroom, made the beds, and straightened everything up. Then he went into the kitchen and cleaned everything up there. He dug through his closet and found an old pair of shoes to match his old pair of shorts. Entering his parents' room, he dug through his dad's closet until he found one of his old work shirts.

He went outside and was pleasantly surprised to feel the twenty-degree drop in temperature from the previous day. He backed his truck off the driveway and pushed his motorbike back into the garage. He wondered if he should tell Katie about Elizabeth…or maybe he had it backward. "You're naive," touched a raw nerve with him. He wondered why he was the way he was. It felt like a game was being played, and he didn't know all the rules. It was like he was a detective trying to solve a mystery without any clues. And what was this thing about going to bars just to get free drinks from guys? He stood gazing over the lawn where it connected to the woods and saw a rabbit eating clover. He thought of Alice chasing the rabbit down the hole into Wonderland. He thought of Katie and wondered if he was similarly in pursuit of her. Were Katie and Alice the same person?

He grew weary from his thoughts, took his shirt off, and went back to work.

Curtis pulled the lawnmowers out of the garage along with the gas can. Then he carried the two five-gallon buckets of driveway sealer out and set them apart at each end of the driveway along with three bags of sand. Curtis spent the next two hours sealing the driveway, pouring, pushing, and pulling the syrup-like substance with a squeegee, working diligently to remove the forming ridge lines.

When finished, he hammered some old tomato stakes around the perimeter to rope off the driveway. The work made him tired, hot, and sweaty. Taking a thirst-quenching drink and long summer shower from the garden hose helped him cool off and refresh himself enough to cut the grass.

Brad rode down on his motorcycle. "Your dad's going to be happy with that. It looks good. You should consider doing this for a living."

"I can't imagine having to do this every day, from sunup to sundown no less," Curtis replied.

Curtis told him about Katie.

"Katie, huh? You need to bring her over. You can't keep a secret like that to yourself."

"I'd love to, but the thing is, this girl drinks like a fish. And she doesn't drink beer either."

"Well, she's welcome to drink dad's wine!"

The boys laughed. Mr. Grady's wine would make any rational person want to quit drinking.

Brad said, "Speaking of wine, are you going to help cut grapes this year? A few more weeks, we're going to press out another barrel."

"I don't think I've missed but one time in the last ten years. But now I need to get this grass cut before my mom gets home."

Brad started his motorcycle and waved goodbye as he headed down the hill to the river bottom area to enjoy the peace of summer.

Curtis nearly had all the grass cut when the station wagon returned around five o'clock. JoAnn rarely said anything nice, but today, she complimented Curtis on the driveway and the yard.

When his dad got home about an hour later, Curtis was just putting the lawn mower away. His dad smiled and thanked him as he put his hand on his son's shoulder. That was even more rare than a compliment from his mother.

He regretted putting the motorcycle in the garage because he wanted to go for a ride. He put his dad's old work shirt back on and considered for a second taking the motorcycle out for a ride down to the river, but he wasn't willing to put a tire mark on the driveway or take down his barrier, so he went inside.

Curtis took off the soiled shoes caked in tar and grass, threw them in the trash can, and went inside to shower. His mom was in the kitchen making dinner and talking on the phone when he walked by her. Curtis got in the shower and realized that everyone had already taken a shower, so no hot water was left.

After dinner, Curtis was so tired that when he tried to read, he just fell asleep. Even though his kid brother, Garrett, had a friend over, Curtis was fast asleep by seven o'clock. He didn't wake up until the following day. His mom made him breakfast, which put him in a good mood. He decided to drive himself to Springdale and spend a day at the pool before going to work.

While at the pool, he did something he had never done before. He borrowed his mother's raft. JoAnn had a nice raft made of canvas. Unlike the cheap plastic rafts, this raft never lost air and was comfortable because it was firm like a good mattress. It was expensive, but she liked laying out on it. While she was reading on a chair, he went to the pool and took a nap floating on the water. When he woke up he added a waterbed to his ever-growing list of wants.

After his mom took his brother and sister home, he showered in the dressing room and got ready for work. He arrived at work a little early, and when he went inside, he saw Katie, but he hardly recognized her. She was true to her word. She had put on makeup and looked ten years older than any other waitress.

Lynn was astonished and had no choice but to let her return to waiting tables. Lynn looked at Curtis and said, "Curtis, it looks like the pizza oven is all yours again."

Before the shift started, Katie pulled Curtis aside and said, "The bad part about wearing all this makeup is when we smooch, you'll be full of lipstick." Then she whispered seductively, "I won't mind if you don't."

Katie kissed him just gently enough to leave a slight waxy print on his lips before grabbing a stack of menus and heading back out to the front of the restaurant.

Curtis stood there, wanting to wipe the lipstick off his lips, yet at the same time, wanting to keep it there. Ultimately, he wiped his mouth on the back of his hand, where a light red swipe appeared.

All through the night, Curtis kept up with the pizza orders. Carry-out orders were heavier than average, but the dining room looked full, so he didn't have to worry about Katie being sent home. Curtis watched her work and noticed she was always playful with the customers. He would notice the subtle things, like how she gently touched a customer on their shoulder or how she would help move a chair or table to accommodate a special request. He knew she was doing it for the tips, but she did it flawlessly.

When he wasn't being mesmerized by her, he focused on making quality pizzas. He went to the busing area and helped himself to a cup of ice and filled it with Pepsi. It was always "all you can drink," and he knew they still were not paying him much, so he tried to take advantage of free drinks and food as much as he could.

As he drank his Pepsi, he noticed two speakers mounted to the ceiling at each end of the prep station. He listened hard, barely making out the music playing in the dining room. Customers routinely shoveled quarters into the small jukebox. Unfortunately, the exhaust fan drowned out the music in the kitchen. When his orders slowed, Curtis traced the wires to the back and found a little amplifier by the electric panel next to the alarm box. The knob labeled "kitchen" was at the lowest setting, so Curtis moved the knob to the middle position. It made a noticeable difference and made his work more enjoyable.

While at Lynn's Pizzeria, "Night Moves" was the clear winner, with "Heart of Glass" not far behind. A month after working there, he never cared to hear "The Gambler" or "Lonesome Loser" ever again.

After work, Katie told Curtis they could hang out for an hour, but she had to be home before one in the morning. Curtis waited patiently in his truck while she went to her car. Katie returned with a small shopping bag. He noticed she hadn't changed out of her work shirt.

She got into the truck and said, "Let's go somewhere a little more private." She directed him to Meramec Bottom Road, which wasn't far from the restaurant. He drove over the interstate, and the road soon became dark as it cut between two fields and distant woods behind them. She guided him to a hidden trail, a type of overgrown dirt road that she said returned to the river to an excellent fishing spot. They didn't go very far when she told him he could stop.

Curtis parked the truck and turned the motor and headlights off.

"Katie, why do you cut your hair so short?"

She said, "Do you want to know?" as she pulled a pint-sized bottle of Southern Comfort out of the bag. She took the top off, drank, and handed the bottle to Curtis. He cautiously took a sip and found it sweet, like warm, thick, spicy apricot nectar. He tilted the bottle back and enjoyed a longer drink.

"Hey now, save some for me," she laughed as he handed back the bottle.

"Yeah, I want to know." Curtis reached over and ran his fingers through her hair.

Katie scooted herself over on the truck seat so he could rest his arm across her shoulders as he massaged the top of her head.

"I have short hair so I can wear wigs."

"Why would you do that?" he asked.

"So I can pretend to be somebody I'm not."

Curtis turned the engine off but left the accessories on so the radio would still work.

"Oh," Katie said as she reached into her bag. "I bought this for you yesterday." She handed him a brand-new cassette tape. "Do you want to hear it?"

"Yes. Who is it?"

She took the tape back from him because he was struggling to open it. She used her teeth and fingernails to tear into the plastic to remove the plastic wrap. Then she continued, "It's a group called Steely Dan. It's one of the only bands that I know and like. This is my favorite album. It's kind of a long story, but I was in a record store and saw this album called Katy Lied, it made me laugh so hard I almost peed. You made me think of this when you said your mom thought you were a liar. My mom has thought the same thing about me for years. The difference is I do lie to her because the bitch doesn't deserve the truth. That's a different conversation for another time. When I saw an album that said, 'Katy Lied,' it didn't matter if I liked a single song on it; I was going to have it. I didn't even buy the tape; I bought the album because I wanted my mom to see it. If I were a millionaire, I would build a billboard so my mom would see it every day when she went to work. Then I listened to it, and it was terrific. The album cover still makes me laugh. And the thing was, I really enjoyed the album so much I bought another album and then another one, and then I discovered this one. It's my favorite one out of all of them."

Katie took the Supertramp tape out, dropped it into the bag, and pushed the new tape into the player. She took another drink of Southern Comfort and handed the bottle to Curtis, then rested her head on his chest while he held her close and the music played.

Curtis experienced an overwhelming and heavenly serenity as he got lost in the music, feeling her next to him. He sat there wondering what a "Black Cow" tasted like. As if reading his mind, Katie turned and offered her mouth to him. She seemed to delight in his adaptability, proving he was a quick learner.

Katie, always full of surprises, beat him to the punch, and she reached her hand up under his shirt and massaged his belly and then his chest. Then her hand roamed up and over, until her fingers began to play with his nipple. She stimulated it until it was rock hard. She backed off the intensity of her kisses then worked sensual magic with a dozen shorter ones over his face with moans of affirmation and whispers of encouragement.

It was all so much for Curtis to take in. He had played this scenario out a hundred times, and here it was, nothing like he had expected it to be. By the time "Aja," the title track, began, he was straining in the seat with relentless waves of desire building up with nowhere to go.

Katie was curious and withdrew her hand from under his shirt and reached down to touch him where his hope lay, and immediately, with just a single touch, his body tensed as giant spasms of erotic seizures he could not control took over until he collapsed. She never moved her hand as she whispered in his ear, "It's okay, Baby, don't worry about a thing. You'll be okay."

She held the quivering young man in her arms, but tears ran down her face. She thought in quiet despair, how was it possible for falling in love to hurt this bad?

They listened to the cassette's entire first side before either one moved.

"I'm sorry, Katie. I'm not sure what to say."

 Katie said, "Don't think too much about it. We'll have other chances." They passed the bottle back and forth until it was gone.

"Curtis, I think if we're going to make this work, we need to promise to be patient with each other."

"Okay, I promise."

"You say that, but you've probably never had to deal with an ugly truth in your entire life."

"What are you talking about?"

"Okay, Curtis, here's an ugly truth for you… But first, let me ask you a question. We can't lie to each other. Ready?"

"Yeah."

"How many girls have you had sex with?"

Curtis had no response.

"Yeah, I thought so. Okay, now ask me."

"Ask you what?"

"Ask me how many times I've had sex."

"I don't care."

"Ask me."

"It doesn't matter."

"Ask me, dammit."

"Katie, how many times have you had sex?"

"I don't know."

"What?"

"See? That's what I'm trying to tell you."

"I don't understand."

"No. No, you don't."

There was an awkward silence, and she held Curtis as they embraced.

She said to him tenderly, "Listen, Curtis, please don't hate or judge me, but I've been sexually active for a long time. And from when I was twelve to the time I was fourteen, I had no say in it. It wasn't my choice. That's an ugly truth, and there's nothing I can do to change it. All I can do is try to forget."

Katie looked at her watch and saw what time it was. "Oh crap, look at the time. Curtis, I'm sorry, but you need to get me back to my car. I need to get home, or my ass is grass. As much as I like to make pizzas with you, I like making the extra money." She didn't tell him she made more with tips than she did with her wages, but he already knew that.

When Curtis dropped her off, she instructed him to wait before he left. She put her belongings in the front seat, then dug around in the back until she found small packets of towelettes. She grabbed a handful of them and brought them over to Curtis.

She handed him a dozen packets of KFC hand wipes. "Curtis, listen to me. What you need to do before you go home is stop at a gas station and clean yourself off with these, so you don't walk into your house smelling like sex."

Curtis felt a little trepidation as she looked at him.

"Then throw away your undershorts. Just go commando until you get home. It'll feel weird, especially in those work slacks, but it will be easier than the alternative—explaining to your mom what happened tonight."

Curtis handed her the empty case for the Supertramp tape. She took the tape case from him, leaned through the window, and kissed him gently without rushing. "Curtis, a couple days ago, you kissed me like a dead fish, and now you have me purring like a kitten." She kissed him again and then broke free to run to her car. "Drive safe, Baby. I'll see you tomorrow."

Curtis did precisely what she had instructed and then came home. As usual, his mom was waiting in the kitchen, but as he walked through the kitchen, she stared at him without saying a word. It was weird, but he kept walking. He went straight to the bedroom, got a clean change of clothes, and then went into the bathroom to shower.

When he shut the bathroom door and saw himself in the mirror, he understood his mother's worried face. Katie's red lipstick was smeared all over his face and neck.

CHAPTER 19

Watershed Moments

On Saturday, Katie traded to work an earlier shift. When Curtis told her what happened, she laughed and said, "I gave you all those wipes. I thought you would surely wipe your face off with one of them."

Katie left right after the dinner rush ended, and Curtis finished the evening with thoughts of her overwhelming him. It was strange to him how tedious the job was now that he could not lose himself watching her.

After eleven o'clock, everyone was busy cleaning. The restaurant closed at midnight, and nobody liked to stay later than they had to on a Saturday night. Thirty minutes later, two young men in their twenties came in together. Mary walked over and hugged the tall, wide-shouldered man wearing cowboy boots and blue jeans and yelled for her mom. Curtis overheard Mary introducing everyone to her older brother, Gary.

Lynn came out and greeted her son and the shorter man with him. Curtis could see that Gary was wearing a black shirt with a Caterpillar logo embedded on the front with a matching belt buckle and hat. The diesel logo was familiar because his dad worked on their equipment and Caterpillar stickers were on his toolboxes.

The two men sat at a table in the corner, and Gary ordered a large pizza. One of the waitresses offered to bring out pitchers of soda, but Gary pointed to a cooler and said they brought their own drinks.

Lynn came back into the kitchen. She told Curtis to continue cleaning and that she would take care of making her son's pizza. Curtis pulled his free pizza out of the oven and boxed it up.

After the restaurant closed, Curtis was all set to leave when Gary yelled, "Hey! Where do you think you're going? You got a hot date? Get over here and be sociable."

Curtis did as he was told and went over and pulled up a chair, and a strange sensation overwhelmed him. It seemed weird that the waitresses were still hanging out. Gary asked the waitress to close the curtains and instructed another one to turn off the dining room lights. Gary reached into the cooler, pulled out a Busch beer, and slid it across the table. "What's your name?"

"Curtis."

"Curtis, we're family here. How long have you been working for my mom?"

Curtis replied, "About a month."

Gary said, "That explains why you look new to me then. Curtis, this is my friend Neil."

Neil was quiet with dark, darting eyes. He wore a tight-fitting, open-collar white shirt tucked into dark slacks. Neil hid his face behind a well-kept but extremely short beard and had wavy hair that tended to fall over one eye.

"Drink that beer, Curtis. You want some pizza?"

"No, thanks. I eat too much pizza."

"I can only imagine. If I worked here, I'd be bigger than a poisoned dog."

Curtis surreptitiously glanced around and didn't see Lynn.

As if reading his mind, Gary said, "Mom's gone. She left with the deposit." Gary jiggled the keys and said, "This is my office now. Where you from, Curtis?"

As Curtis continued the impromptu interview, several waitresses watched the exchange with eager eyes.

"Imperial."

"Imperial… You don't say. That makes you a Windsor Owl. You son of a bitch! How's your basketball team these days? Years ago, I used to play those courts, and I recall you guys always played us tough. You still lost, but they were good games."

Gary guzzled his beer, exaggerated his burp, and crushed the can with his fist before announcing, "Now, the reason we're here… Neil and I are business partners and looking to expand our business. We want to make you an offer. Now, I understood there was a young lady who works here that goes to Mehlville. Where is she?"

One of the waitresses spoke up, "You're looking for Katie? She got off early today."

Gary opened another beer and shook his head. "I'm sorry to hear that. I really wanted that fine, silver-tongued honey pot to be here tonight because she's included in this offer too. Mom says she is cool as a cucumber with customers."

"What offer are you talking about?" Curtis was growing impatient, and the insinuations he was making about Katie were making him angry.

Gary laughed. "Simmer down, lover boy. Mom says you're sweet on that girl. I'm not out to wreck your marriage. We're family here, you got that?"

"I was just curious what the offer was, that's all."

"Drink your beer, and I'll tell you. Can you do that for me?"

Curtis popped the top and drank without any enjoyment. The beer was warm, causing it to take on a metallic taste, which annoyed Curtis. Curtis looked at Gary and said, "Next time, can you bring bottles?"

Gary paused midthought with his mouth wide open before he started to laugh.

"You see, Neil? This is what I'm talking about. Leave it to someone from Imperial to tell me what he wants. Neil, write it down. Per Curtis, no more cans, only bottles."

"Done," the quiet man replied.

"Okay, this is why we're here tonight. Neil, go ahead and show them."

Neil pulled a plastic bag of what looked like a pound of green marijuana from his coat. Curtis immediately thought of Rita, the hitchhiker. The similarities of the bag and the color were identical. It was too much to be a coincidence.

Neil spoke up and said, "This here is the finest Mexican grown and imported sinsemilla. You won't find a better buzz or mood enhancer than this."

Gary said, "Neil and I will front you up to eight ounces at thirty dollars per or you can pay cash and make an extra ten dollars yourself. It makes no difference, but if you owe me money, I want my money back by your next payday. Don't be stupid or I'll be out some money and you'll be cut from my family, and I won't be able to protect you anymore."

Neil said, "If you're smart, you find some people at school and get them to sell for you. You know how a pyramid works, right? Do you know people who sell Amway, Tupperware, or Avon? If you're bright, you can be fronting like we are in a few years."

Gary stood up and looked Curtis dead in the eyes. "Listen to me now, because this is important. If you're stupid and get caught and I get called in to be questioned by the law, you need to know that I operate a bulldozer for a living and I can hide things nobody will ever find."

When Gary sat down, Neil got up, removed his coat, and retrieved a set of nunchucks from one of the inside pockets before presenting a powerful display of kobudo.

After the demonstration, Gary said, "Neil's my friend, and I work for him. Neil knows people I don't know. Frankly, I don't want to know them because they're scarier than him. "There you have it. Does anyone have any questions?" The waitresses seemed eager to leave. Curtis finished his beer and stood up. "Curtis, what do you think? Do you think we can work together?"

Curtis said, "I think I might be interested, but I definitely would pay cash up front after I get paid."

"See, Neil? I told you he was a smart one. These Imperial Owls are wise." Neil stared at Curtis in a manner that was supposed to be intimidating. Curtis imagined Neil was trying to read his mind, but if he were, he would only see an image of Katie.

When Gary put on his hat, Curtis immediately noticed the Local 513 union badge pinned to it.

Curtis was never so glad as to get out of the restaurant. He thought about the money he might make but decided to talk to Ronnie first. If given a choice, Curtis would rather sell for Ronnie. Then he thought of the enormous difference in quality between the pot Ronnie sold and what Gary was offering. Yet, for all his faults, Ronnie wasn't nearly as arrogant as Gary. The more he thought about Gary and his friend, Neil, the angrier he got. He wanted to push all the thoughts out of his head, so he turned on the radio and drowned them out, cranking ELO's "Don't Bring Me Down" to an ear-hurting level.

Seeing all the lights out when he got home, Curtis sighed in relief. He paused before going inside and stared at the full moon. That large eye in the sky was open wide, and Curtis knew the universe was watching, but for what purpose? Ignoring the question, he went inside quietly. Curtis put the pizza on the counter before showering and going to bed.

Before falling asleep, he thought about Gary and Neil and had a premonition more strange days were to follow. He recalled reading that full moons were often a precursor to craziness. The whole world seemed crazy to him.

He woke up Sunday morning tired and in a daze. He went into the kitchen to pick through what was left over from breakfast. He noticed Mary Jones's birthday party invitation on the refrigerator door and decided he should go.

Buried deep in the back of his closet was an old, well-worn kelly green carrying case. Curtis had spent a lot of time going to the roller rink but stopped going shortly after he turned sixteen. As he pulled the case out, he recalled when he was younger that it had seemed to be the size of a steamer trunk.

Inside were his roller skates, a bag of tools, and several sets of wheels kept together by old skate laces. The black leather low-top Riedell skates were a gift from his parents for Christmas years ago. As his foot grew, the skates accommodated a larger boot.

The boot's two off-white leather racing stripes reminded him of a time when speed skating and chariot races allowed him to go fast. His love for speed never faded but was replaced by his motorcycle and truck.

Curtis wasn't sure they would still fit, but they did, even if tight in the toe box. He went to his parents' room and borrowed a pair of his dad's ultra-thin dress socks, and they felt much better.

He took the skates into the dining room and put down a towel. He was replacing and oiling the wheels when JoAnn walked in carrying bags from K-Mart.

"Seriously, Curtis? My good kitchen towel? What is wrong with you? Take that downstairs to your father's workbench right now."

Curtis quietly gathered his things, holding his tongue from speaking the numerous hateful thoughts he was thinking.

"Curtis, I swear you don't have the good sense God gave you." As he gathered everything up, she said, "Before you go downstairs, help me bring in the rest of the bags from the car."

He lost thirty minutes between carrying in several bags full of clothes and school supplies and cleaning off a place to work on the workbench. He grumbled to himself, "I could have been done by now if she would just leave me alone."

Immediately, he heard his mother slam a kitchen cabinet door before yelling downstairs, "Curtis, if you have anything to say to me, get up here and say it."

When he completed his task, he went upstairs with his cleaned and oiled skates. JoAnn said, "You've already ruined that towel now. You might as well take it with you or put it in the rag bin."

He avoided his mom for the rest of the afternoon, and when it was time, he put his skate case in his truck and drove to the roller rink. He showed the invitation at the front door and was waved inside.

The matinee crowd was leaving as the party crowd was coming in, so chaos ensued for the next fifteen minutes while groups gathered and sorted passing near the entrance.

Curtis went to the back bleacher section to put his skates on. The air conditioning made the building feel like an ice rink. He was delighted that his sense of balance had not abandoned him. After a few strides, it was like he had never stopped skating.

He barely made it a lap around when he was yelled at to get off the floor. The large man who yelled at him said it was a private event and didn't start until five o'clock. Curtis found the clock on the wall, which showed 4:55.

A skate guard wearing a gold button-down shirt raced laps around the arena for the next few minutes pushing a large dust broom, and at five o'clock sharp, the announcement was made that party attendees could skate.

Curtis skated around a few laps, looking for Mary. She was surrounded by her girlfriends. Curtis saw the tall, bulky man who had yelled staring at him as he exited the floor. The man walked over and said, "What's your name, son?"

"I'm Curtis. Curtis McGowan."

"Hi there, Curtis. I'm Ben Dunham. I'm the pastor at New Life Assembly of God."

Curtis shook his hand and was relieved when Mary came over.

"Oh, Brother Ben, this is Curtis. He's the boy I was telling you about."

The man replied, "We just met. I look forward to talking to you later, Curtis." The pastor excused himself to go speak to Mary's mother.

"Curtis, thank you for coming to my party. I hope you have a good time," Mary said before leaving to get her skates from the counter.

The skating rink was full of strangers. Apart from Mary, Curtis didn't recognize anyone else. Apparently, she invited her church friends and not anyone from school. He skated around by himself and felt miserable. Curtis regretted coming and wished he had just stayed home.

When he thought it couldn't get any worse, they announced it was time for a "couples only" skate. Curtis saw Mary and skated over to her since she was the only girl he knew. Mary politely declined his offer to skate with him. Curtis went and sat on the bleachers and noticed that the only people skating were older married couples.

At six o'clock, they stopped the music and asked everyone to gather in the back for cake and ice cream. Mary opened a few presents people had brought and read the cards people gave her. It had never occurred to Curtis to bring a present or a card to the party.

Brother Ben prayed for the group after the presents were open as if the cake and ice cream were a Thanksgiving feast. Then, he preached for about fifteen minutes about God's gift to humanity in the person of Jesus Christ.

"Before you can know the good news, you need to understand the bad news…"

It was as if the pastor lit himself on fire as he preached some more on the wrath of God on sinners. Every word he spoke seemed directed at Curtis. Brother Ben's narrow eyes burned directly toward Curtis. The longer the pastor talked, the more irritated Curtis became and he longed to be anywhere but the skating rink attending the party. Curtis regretted going to the funeral, and he regretted talking to Mary at all. Curtis's rage matched the anger he heard in the pastor's voice. An image of the card his dad gave him at the funeral entered his mind, and he regretted taking that home.

Curtis looked at the faces around him. Some held their heads down, and others looked up at the ceiling. He felt like they were all aliens from another planet. Even when the pastor's tone softened, his words of love and acceptance reached Curtis's heart, but only as a sense of yearning. The rest made no sense to him. It was only noise to Curtis, and he was greatly irritated by it.

When the pastor finished speaking to the group, he made a point of finding Curtis and asked him if he was interested in having a personal relationship with Jesus. Curtis said that was something he needed to think about.

As soon as everyone returned to skating, Curtis went to the back area and removed his skates. He did not want to make a scene, but after putting on his shoes he tried to leave without saying goodbye to anyone. Mary skated up to him, and asked, Curtis are you okay. He replied, "I'm sorry, Mary, but I'm not feeling well."

Mary's eyes watered up and she said, "Did I do something wrong?"

"No, it's not your fault. I need to go home."

Curtis left the skating rink and drove back to his house wondering why Mary would cry over him leaving her party early.

CHAPTER 20

FM

A package from Columbia House Record and Tape Club hung on the mailbox with a large rubber band. Curtis grabbed his package, and the other mail stacked inside. He went inside and tossed the mail on his mother's desk. He knew she would not be home from Springdale for a few more hours, so he went inside his bedroom and shut the door to celebrate an early Christmas. He tore into the package and out fell twelve brand-new cassette tapes. He could not imagine getting such a bargain for only a penny and a stamp, which he took from his mother's desk a few weeks ago. He unwrapped each tape and admired the glossy, new look. Curtis lamented the small writing and the loss of detail in the artwork the record albums had. Curtis gathered all the trash and placed it in one of the many paper grocery bags his mom stashed behind the refrigerator. He balled the bag up, went out to one of three burn barrels in the backyard, and set it on fire to destroy the evidence.

Curtis went back inside and spent the rest of the afternoon listening to all his new albums through his dad's headphones. A few hours later, his younger brother came in to change out of his swimming shorts and then left to play.

Curtis was in his room enjoying *Don't Look Back*, his new Boston album. He liked how the headphones accentuated the stereo effect and drowned out the background noise. Also, he didn't have to worry about his mom yelling for him to turn the music down, which she often did. He hated her double standard. When she cleaned the house on Saturday mornings, she would have the music so loud it would wake him up. Even if he were out in his truck, she would yell at him, "Turn that noise down before you go deaf." He would pretend not to hear her, which only aggravated her more when he didn't respond.

JoAnn scared him with a flustered look when she burst into the bedroom splattered with flour and holding a hand towel. "You have a phone call. I called your name a half dozen times. That music is too loud. You need to turn the volume down."

Curtis entered the kitchen, picked up the phone, and said, "Hello?"

"Curtis, this is Katie. What are you doing?"

"I was listening to my new Boston album."

"Boston? Are they like Chicago?"

Curtis saw his mother eyeing him, so he stretched the curly cord out so that it was nearly straight so he could talk in the dining room with a measure of privacy.

He laughed at her and replied, "No, not really."

"What's so funny? Are you making fun of me?"

"No, it's just they sound nothing alike."

Katie said, "Hey, listen…I know it's last minute, but I was wondering if you wanted to go to the movies with me tonight?"

Curtis eagerly accepted her invitation. He asked, "What time do you want me to pick you up?"

"The movie starts at seven, so I'll pick you up at the restaurant an hour before."

Curtis looked at the clock. It was a little after four o'clock. "Okay, sounds good."

"Curtis…"

"Yes?"

"Never mind, I'll see you in a couple of hours and we can talk then."

Curtis hung the phone up and tried to leave the kitchen unnoticed.

"Curtis, who was that?"

"That was Katie."

"Are you going somewhere tonight? Are you going to be here for dinner?"

"No, I won't be here for dinner. I'm going to leave in about an hour."

She said, "I thought Katie was just a coworker."

"She is, but we're friends too."

JoAnn sighed and turned her back on her son.

Curtis took a shower and got dressed. The only cologne in the bathroom was his dad's Old Spice aftershave, which he applied liberally.

Anxious to see her, he drove up to the restaurant and arrived thirty minutes early. Katie's car was already there. She got out of the car and came over and kissed him. She looked spectacular in her all-over print, tie-back halter dress. The dress appeared to be all the colors of random toucans on a field of teal. She was wearing white flat sandals that buckled around her heel. He noticed she wore several brass ring bracelets that jingled on her wrist.

"Curtis, I hate to tell you, but you smell like an old man." She laughed and gave him another kiss to assure him it didn't matter as much as he thought.

Then she said, "Maybe we can hang out one afternoon, and I'll take you to Famous Barr, and we can pick out a scent just for you."

He returned to his truck and asked her, "Where's the theater?"

She replied, "Don't worry about it. You're not driving. Get in."

He protested, "Seriously?"

"Seriously. Lock your truck. Hurry up, we have to go."

Curtis double-checked that he had his wallet and keys and locked his truck. He went and got in her car. It smelled like vanilla and jasmine.

"Sorry it's such a mess, but sometimes I have to live out of this thing."

The front wasn't so bad, but the back had a blanket, pillow, several soft luggage pieces, an assortment of shoes, and a makeup bag. Those were just what was visible on top. All these things appeared to be on top of two laundry baskets. The items that caught his eye were a pair of books tucked into one of the baskets. He saw clearly written on the spines, *The Joy of Sex* and *Sex and the Single Girl*.

Katie turned onto the road and asked him about his day as she drove north toward the city.

"I think my mom wants to meet you."

"Oh no," she laughed. "Are you ready to introduce me to your mom? We might have to start dating more and hanging out less."

"Why did you feel the need to drive tonight?"

"Need? I didn't need to do anything. I wanted to," she replied.

"I've never ridden with a girl driving."

"I'm sure there are many things you haven't done with a girl before," she teased.

Curtis felt his face flush but found no words suitable for a reply.

Katie broke the awkward silence by asking, "So, do you want to know what we'll see tonight?"

"*Alien*?"

"No, silly. I don't like horror films. We're going to the Hi-Pointe Theatre to see a movie called *FM*. You're going to love it, and it's my treat."

While they were driving into the city, Curtis told Katie about the offer he was given to sell weed for Lynn's son.

"Curtis, let me be frank with you. Don't do it. You'll get caught up in something and be over your head. It's a game, and the game is rigged. In the end, you'll either get beat up, go to jail, or worse. I know Lynn's son… and many guys like him. He uses people to get what he wants."

Curtis was silent as he reflected on her words.

Katie added, "I didn't take you for a stoner. You seem to be level-headed and have your shit together, at least when you're with me."

"Do you get high?"

She replied, "I prefer to drink. You know that. But can I tell you something? I haven't had anything to drink since Friday. I've been completely sober for three days. Isn't that something?"

"You know, the only reason I smoke pot is because it's simple to get and easier to hide. Whenever we get caught with beer, the cops either take it or make us pour it out and then send us home."

"Yes, but if you get caught with weed, you're going to jail. And if you have a lot of it, you'll be in jail for a long time."

"It seems silly to me. Alcohol and pot…one is tolerated and sold everywhere, and the other isn't."

Katie said, "The world's a mystery, Baby. I just know if you go to jail, your life will be different forever."

They made it to the movie theater. Curtis held her hand as they walked. They went inside, and she purchased two tickets at the counter but realized the movie didn't start until eight o'clock. They had over ninety minutes before the movie started, so she convinced him to walk with her to The Parkmoor to get something to eat.

The restaurant was slightly over a mile away, but the excellent food was worth it. They ordered King and Queen burgers and shared a basket of onion rings. Curtis paid for the dinner, and then they walked back to the movie theater.

When they entered the small theater, it was empty. With only a few people in attendance, Curtis and Katie sat in the back row next to the wall for heightened intimacy. The movie began with the music of Steely Dan, so Curtis immediately knew why she liked the film. He sneaked a peak at her and saw her moving her lips, silently singing along. He enjoyed the movie and was delighted feeling her arm on his.

The movie reminded him of *WKRP*, a show he watched occasionally on television. He suffered a moment of anxiety when he saw scenes of a woman seducing a disc jockey. He wondered about Katie's mysterious connection with the radio station disc jockey. The soundtrack to the film was full of recognizable songs, and the numerous cameos entertained him.

After the movie, Katie drove to downtown Clayton to show him where the St. Louis County Courthouse and jail were. She said, "You need to know where these places are because you might have to come to bail me out one of these days." Then she added, "Just like I may have to come and get you."

Curtis began to worry for her. She had convinced him that he should not get involved with selling pot on the side. She was right. He would get caught. He had no idea where his life was going, but jail would be a setback. He'd watched the documentary *Scared Straight* and knew prison must be avoided at all costs.

"Everything okay over there, Baby? You're kind of quiet." Katie reached her hand over, and he accepted it.

He said, "Katie, this has been a fantastic night. Thank you for the movie."

"Well, thank you for dinner," she replied.

"I know it was a lot of money, plus gas…"

"Curtis, don't worry about money. Do you have any idea what I make on tips? I make decent money, especially on the weekends."

Curtis felt uncomfortable talking about money, but he didn't have time to think about it because she said, "I have almost two thousand dollars saved up."

"Seriously?"

"Yeah. I'm thinking hard about something, Curtis. I need to get away from my mom and her pervert boyfriend. If I don't, I think I'll do something horrible to him."

Curtis didn't know how to respond. He just held her hand and squeezed.

"I keep thinking that maybe I should make a change, you know?"

"What kind of change?"

"Like, leave here and move. Go somewhere else and start over."

"You don't want to finish school first, then go off to college?"

She laughed. "Curtis, you are so adorable, but I don't think you understand how bad things are for me. I'm not sure I can finish school, and I don't plan to go to college."

Curtis asked, "What do you think you're going to do then?"

"You'll laugh if I tell you."

"No, I won't."

"I think I'm going to go to California and try to get into the movies."

There was a long pause, and the silence only created tension. She pulled her hand back.

"I know it's crazy. It sounds unbelievable even as I hear myself say it. You must think I'm a freak. I just don't know what to do anymore."

Katie dropped Curtis off at his truck. She kissed him on the cheek when he leaned over to say goodbye.

He stood there watching her car leave and felt an emptiness he knew he should not feel after such a fabulous date.

Curtis woke up and looked at the flip clock on his nightstand. It was 3:16 in the morning. He thought he heard a phone ringing. Two seconds later, it happened again. When his mind registered that it was the phone in the kitchen, he listened as his mom banged the door open from her bedroom. He jumped out of bed and ran into the kitchen just in time to see JoAnn pick the phone up.

He heard her say, "Just a minute…"

She handed the phone to him and growled, "This is totally unacceptable."

"Curtis?"

It was Katie. She was crying.

"Yes, it's me."

"I'm sorry. I had to talk to you. I needed to speak to someone."

"Is everything okay?"

"No, nothing is okay. I thought I could do it."

"Do what, Katie? What are you talking about?"

"I thought I could stay sober. I thought I could stop drinking. I thought if I just had something to live for."

"You can, and you do," he replied.

"We had such a good time tonight. What's wrong with me?"

Curtis could feel the glare from his mother, who still stood in the hallway listening.

"Curtis, I'm sorry. I know it's late. I'm scared, and I don't know what to do."

"What can I do? Do you want me to come over? Do you have somewhere you can go?"

He could see his mother shaking her head no.

"No, Curtis, I just wanted to hear your voice."

Curtis glared back at his mother, and she returned to her bedroom and slammed the door shut.

"I had a great time tonight, Katie. I hoped we could do it again."

"I know…me too," she said as her voice cracked.

He could hear her words slurring as they talked. She confessed she had drunk most of a bottle of peach schnapps since she got home. "Just to take the edge off," she added. She started just sipping while listening to her Steely Dan records, but now she was drunk, scared, and alone.

"I wish you were here to hold me," she said.

"I don't know what to do. Do you want me to come over?"

The silence was gut-wrenching.

"Curtis, are you still there?"

"Yes."

"Do you think I'm ugly?"

"No, not at all."

"I know I can be pretty if I work at it, but I feel fake when I wear wigs and makeup. My mom is gorgeous without makeup, but she is an ugly person inside."

Curtis listened to her talk and cry for over an hour. She kept repeating herself and refused any offer he made to help. She sounded exhausted, but he didn't know how to end the call.

After several minutes of awkward silence, Katie said, "I know it's late. I don't want to get you into trouble. I'm going to go lie down and try to sleep."

"Okay. I hope you feel better when you wake up."

"Curtis?"

"Yes?"

"Thank you for being a good friend. Goodnight."

Chapter 21

Blue Mist

On July 11, 1979, Skylab fell back to earth and disintegrated in the atmosphere. The debris from NASA's first space station scattered throughout the Indian Ocean and Western Australia. Curtis felt his heart being similarly pulled and fractured.

He drove to work early and was extremely anxious to talk to Katie. It wasn't like her to be late. He had so many things he wanted to ask her. Mary yelled at him and said he had a phone call. "Make it quick," she ordered. "This is our main line."

Curtis ignored her and picked up the receiver.

The raspy voice on the other end said, "Curtis, this is Katie. Listen, I'm very sick and can't work today."

She sounded terrible. "Can I bring you something when I get off work?"

"No, Baby, I just wanted to hear your voice." He could tell she was crying.

The second phone line rang, and Mary yelled at him, saying, "Hurry up, we're missing sales."

Katie heard her and said, "Tell that bitch to shut up. I'm sorry. I don't want you to get fired, Curtis. I won't stay on the phone. I just wanted to hear your voice. You mean everything to me. I hope you believe that. We'll talk again soon."

Katie hung the phone up, and Curtis handed it back to Mary.

Mary snapped at him and said, "I hope that call was important because it cost us a sale."

Curtis completely ignored her because Lynn's Pizzeria was now costing him something much more.

The evening went by slowly, and his mind was everywhere but making pizzas. Lynn had hired two more pizza cooks, and he was training one of them. Keith had previously worked at Pizza Hut and understood what Lynn expected. As the night went on, he did more, so Curtis did less. Lynn was so impressed with Keith that she told Curtis he could have Friday night off if he wanted it.

Curtis did not go to Springdale on Wednesday because he hoped Katie would call. She didn't. Later that afternoon, he left for work early and drove by Katie's house. His heart sank when he saw her car was not there. Curtis drove to Lynn's Pizzeria to prepare for work. He was in the back getting dressed when Lynn came over to him.

"Curtis, I don't know how to tell you this, but Katie no longer works here."

"What? Did you fire her?"

"No, I didn't fire her. I talked to her mother this morning, and Katie has some problems she needs to address. I shouldn't even be talking about it because her mother asked me not to. But I know you're sweet on that girl, and between you and me," Lynn whispered, "and this is not to go any further than the two of us—but Katie admitted herself into an alcohol treatment program in Texas."

"What?" Curtis felt the tears welling up in his eyes. "Why Texas?"

"From what she told me, her daddy was a veteran, and she's getting some kind of assistance from the government to pay for it. I'm sorry, but the girl is an alcoholic. From what her mom says, a pretty bad one. Christ Almighty, I don't even think she's seventeen yet."

Lynn offered Curtis the night off. "Keith can handle it. I'll see you Saturday. Go hang out with your friends for a couple of days. You're young, and there are plenty of fish in the sea."

For all her kindness, Curtis hated Lynn but took her up on the offer for the evening off. He drove home, took the bag of pot Rita, the hitchhiker, had given him, and went up to Brad's to hang out and get stoned in the Basement.

Kathy and Brad were gone, but Francine and Gunner were happy to hang out. The quality of the weed blew everyone away, and when Curtis showed them how much Rita had given him, they were impressed all the more.

Curtis opened up about Katie. Francine was upset that Curtis never brought her over to meet everyone. "She sounds like a super cool chick."

"It's strange that I've only been at this restaurant for about a month, but it seems like I've known this girl my whole life."

All the while, Curtis lamented his pain and loneliness; it only seemed to drive Francine and Gunner closer to each other. The three sat there smoking and drinking beer while listening to Steve Miller Band's *Fly Like an Eagle* album. They listened to the entire album twice, but as they got incredibly high, it stayed on side one for the rest of the evening. As time continued to slip into the future, Curtis lost track of the number of times he heard "Wild Mountain Honey."

Sometime during the evening, Brad and Kathy came in and joined them. Sometime around midnight, Gunner turned the music off. Curtis asked him if he would stash the weed, so he didn't have to bring it home again. Gunner took the bag from him and hid it behind the stereo. Curtis walked home, staring at the moon as it disappeared into the clouds.

Friday morning, Curtis woke up early enough to ride to Springdale with his family. He found Sammy sitting up on the lifeguard chair by the deep end. Curtis talked to her and kept following her as she rotated around the pool. He told her about his job making pizzas, his feelings for Katie, and her alcohol problem. When he shared his grief about her moving to Texas, Sammy said he was too young to be serious about one girl. She pointed at ten different young teenage girls around the pool. "Curtis, go! Quit complaining about one troubled girl and go find a good one." Curtis found himself now hating Sammy.

He went out to the concession area but couldn't get an ice cream float because the soft serve machine was down. He got change for a dollar only to discover that his Mata Hari pinball machine was out of order because someone had broken the glass. He found a new machine called Future Spa and went to work, trying to learn and master it. Yet for all his efforts to stop thinking about Katie, the jukebox was relentless at keeping her in the forefront of his mind with songs like "Baby, Hold On," "Some Kind of Wonderful," and Andy Gibb's "I Just Want to Be Your Everything." After he was down to his last quarter, Curtis went over to the music box, looked at all the songs, and then selected "Peg" to play three times.

Things didn't improve when he got home. His mom began grilling him. "Aren't you supposed to work tonight? Did you lose your job?"

Curtis wasn't sure how to reply to his mother. On the one hand, if he told her the truth, it would be another strike against Katie. Curtis hoped she would return from Texas so he could introduce her to his mother. On the other hand, she saw right through it whenever he lied to her. The obvious answer was to tell her a partial truth. "Lynn wants me to take the evening off to ensure our new pizza cook can work without my help."

His mom rolled her eyes and said, "If you lost your damn job, just tell me so I can cancel the insurance on the truck." Then she went into the kitchen to start dinner.

Frustrated by the exchange, Curtis rode his motorcycle to clear his head. After his ride, he stopped at the Basement to see what was happening. Brad, Gunner, Travis, and the girls discussed going to the drive-in.

Curtis asked, "What's showing tonight?"

"It's a double feature: *Animal House* and *Up in Smoke*."

Travis complained because he wanted to go, but neither Brad and Kathy nor Gunner and Francine wanted a third wheel. Curtis said he would be willing to go and drive, and Travis could ride with him.

Francine said, "Travis, you're too young to go to rated R movies."

"I'll just hide under some blankets with the cooler."

Curtis invited Travis to ride with him to Arnold to get his paycheck and the bank so he would have cash. He took his motorcycle home and exchanged it for the truck.

Travis stayed in the truck when Curtis went inside. Lynn immediately walked over to greet him. "I'm so glad you're here. I need you to work tonight."

"Lynn, I just came here to pick up my paycheck. I can't work tonight. I have plans."

"Curtis, I really need you. That new hire, Keith, only came here to leverage the Pizza Hut manager for a raise. I wouldn't match that offer, so he quit."

"I'm sorry, Lynn, but I'm not working tonight. I have plans. I just need my check."

Lynn was desperate. "I need someone to help Billy in the kitchen tonight. You know how crazy it gets on Friday nights."

"Can I please have my check?"

"Curtis, if you walk out on me now, don't ever come back."

Lynn stormed back to her office and returned with an envelope with his paycheck.

"I can't believe you're doing this to me after all I've done for you. This is how you thank me?"

Curtis took the check and marched back to his truck. Driving to the bank, he realized he would miss making pizzas. He would even miss the little jukebox with its limited selection of good songs, but he would not miss working for that dysfunctional family.

When he told Travis about all that took place, he said, "You should apply for a job at Pizza Hut."

After he cashed his paycheck, he headed to the Basement. They hung out drinking beer. Curtis watched as Francine took the bag of pot that Gunner had stashed and rolled up a dozen large joints to take to the drive-in. Curtis marveled at how fast the bag of weed was emptying.

Curtis left to go home and eat. He arrived just after his dad got home from work.

"Hey, Dad, I've been meaning to ask you something…"

Curtis Sr. regarded his son with concern, unsure what would follow his son's inquiry.

"Do you, by chance, know a guy named Gary Payne? He's a member in your union."

Curtis Sr.'s look immediately went from concerned to troubled. "I don't know him personally, but I know something about him. Why do you ask? Do you know him?"

Curtis answered, "Gary is the son of the woman I work for. He came in to eat the other night, and I saw a Local 513 pin on his cap."

Curtis Sr. said, "He's trouble. Avoid him if you can. Some people think he drinks and does drugs on the job. I met him one time on a job site, and he thought he knew everything."

"You should have said, 'Since you know everything, what am I doing here?'"

Curtis Sr. laughed. "Yes, I suppose I should have."

Curtis told his dad, "He's extremely arrogant. I noticed that when I talked to him."

"Like I said, Curtis, he's a troubled man. He is in the wrong profession to not have his mind fully engaged when on a piece of heavy equipment. For the life of me, I don't understand why the good Lord takes a good man like Bill Jones while letting men like Gary Payne jeopardize everyone around him."

When Curtis Sr. went inside to clean up, Curtis realized he would never do anything with or for Gary. If he needed to secure good pot, he would drive to Arnold and ring Rita's doorbell.

After dinner, he drove back to the Basement. Around seven-thirty, they headed down to Pevely in three different vehicles. They stopped for gas, beer, soda, and snacks to avoid the high cost of the concession stand.

Travis got in the back of the truck and hid under a stack of blankets covering the cooler. They arrived early and had to hang out, waiting for the sun to go down. Everyone made fun of Travis, who had to stay hidden until it got dark enough for him to come out without being noticed.

Curtis had backed his truck into the spot and put the tailgate down. When it became unbearable, Travis crawled out of the blankets. The old pillows and blankets made an excellent, comfortable seat as they leaned their backs against the cab.

Up in Smoke started just after nine, and Francine brought over several joints and exchanged them for a couple of cold beers. After a short intermission, *Animal House* started just before eleven. It was well after midnight before they left, and Curtis got home an hour later.

The next day, JoAnn knew something wasn't right when Curtis didn't go to work again. She confronted her son. Curtis told his mom that he quit because Lynn's Pizzeria was a drug den. He didn't want to get involved in selling drugs just to keep his job. JoAnn picked up the phone to call the sheriff's office after he told her everything.

Curtis yelled at his mother, "Go ahead and call the police. This Gary guy will bury me with a bulldozer after his friend bashes my brains in with his nunchucks. Then you'll never have to see me again. That's what you want anyway."

JoAnn put the phone down and went to her bedroom in tears, slamming the door behind her.

Tensions were high in the McGowan house, and nerves were wearing thin. Curtis made himself scarce for the rest of the day, riding his motorcycle the length and width of Chesley Island before retreating to the Basement for the remainder of the afternoon.

That evening, Curtis went with his family to his grandparents' house for dinner. After dinner, the adults started drinking highballs and playing cards with poker chips.

Curtis asked if he could join. His request was deferred to his grandfather, who decided it would be okay. They moved the chairs around, making room for him. While they excluded Curtis from drinking highballs with them, he settled for drinking Dr. Pepper with his dad.

Curtis enjoyed listening to his grandparents talk even as he was losing his chips. He was dealt plenty of good hands, just not good enough to win. He learned quickly that his grandfather didn't bluff. He also noticed his father folded too soon. Curtis, on the other hand, took chances but paid accordingly.

During the evening of card playing, Curtis heard a familiar story. It was a story that made his grandmother smile whenever she told it. She recalled meeting Stan Musial. Everyone at the table, except for Curtis Sr., was a native New Yorker. Clara grew up a die-hard New York Giants fan until they moved to San Francisco. Everyone at the table, except for Curtis Jr., had fond memories of seeing games at the Polo Grounds.

In the spring of 1954, the adults recalled watching a doubleheader on television. The Cardinals and the Giants played in St. Louis, where the all-star Red Bird slugger hit five home runs in a single afternoon.

Twenty years later, Franz took Clara to an early dinner at Tony's Restaurant for their 45th wedding anniversary. Vince Bommarito welcomed them and checked on them multiple times as they celebrated. To her surprise, their table was next to a larger table, and they found themselves in the near company of Stan "The Man" Musial.

When Vince Bommarito stopped by, Franz asked if it would be possible for him to introduce his wife to Mr. Musial. When Vince made the request known, Stan stood up and walked over to greet the couple.

Clara remembered the delight of meeting the legendary baseball player. Stan sat at a table with August "Gussie" Busch Jr. and two Cardinal broadcasters, Jack Buck and Mike Shannon. When Gussie heard the German accent, he got up, came over, and introduced himself. When he learned they were celebrating their anniversary, Gussie promised them two tickets to a Giants-Cardinals game in his private box. While Franz recalled the wonderful time he had chatting with Mr. Busch, it was the memory of meeting Stan Musial that made Clara swoon.

Curtis was the first to lose all his chips. He didn't sulk or complain. Instead, he drank Dr. Pepper and watched his grandfather win it all.

Whenever Clara overindulged in bourbon and soda, she was prone to saying outrageous things. When their poodle, Yahtzee, kept barking for no reason, it agitated her. She yelled at Franz, "Would you please kick that dog in the nuts so he keeps quiet?! I can't stand all that yapping."

"Mother!" JoAnn scolded her mom for her outburst. "Not in front of the kids."

Curtis could not figure out why his mom yelled at his grandmother. His younger brother and sister were fast asleep in the living room, and Curtis had heard far worse things.

Before they left, Curtis's grandfather commended him for being a good sport about losing. He told his grandson that poker was a life skill and was more than luck. "Once you know how to read people, you will win more than you lose."

Franz disappeared and returned with a square-looking Ball mason jar full of coins. "Curtis, I started collecting silver coins before you were born." His grandfather gave it to him and said, "Put this away for college." He hesitated then added, "And take care of that Lucky 13 mason jar. It's probably worth more than the coins that are in it."

Curtis went home that night and dumped the coins on his bed. They didn't sound real to him. He turned on his flip clock radio and listened to music as he meticulously looked at all the coins before putting them back in the jar. He kept a large 1921 silver dollar out for good luck and then put the jar on the top shelf in the closet.

He turned the lights off and lay down, listening to the music playing quietly on the radio. The last thing he remembered hearing were the lyrics from "Blue Mist."

Chapter 22

A Shed, a Pipe, & Led Zeppelin Too

Curtis was hanging out at the Gradys' shooting pool alone while Brian and Travis were on the other side of the Basement working on Travis's motorcycle. Gunner was upstairs with Francine, and Brad was nowhere to be found. When Curtis heard a car pull up, he put the cue stick down on the table and looked out the window. He saw a familiar white Ford Mustang parked outside.

Stepping outside, he immediately noticed the car was no longer in pristine shape. A large crack crossed the windshield, and the plastic induction cowl appeared broken and held in place by thick wire and duct tape. The engine seemed excessively loud, making him think something was wrong with the car's exhaust. He saw Mick staring off into the distance, oblivious to Curtis's presence or aware of the annoyance created by the noisy vehicle.

Curtis approached the driver's side and knocked on the window. Mick rolled the window down.

"Hey, Kirk…"

"Curtis. My name's Curtis."

"That's right…Curtis. Sorry about that."

Curtis noticed the preppy sweater was gone and was substituted with a well-worn Jimi Hendrix "Bold as Love" tie-dye shirt. Cutoff blue jeans replaced the pleated pants, and flip-flops instead of loafers. Mick's hair had grown out quite a bit, but poor testosterone levels frustrated his attempt to grow a beard and mustache. The smile that once showed the brightness of silver braces that gleamed in the light was now dull due to a lack of personal hygiene.

Curtis looked inside the car and saw a smelly mess of fast-food bags, empty beer cans, and crushed cigarette packs. He asked Mick, "Why is your car so loud?"

Mick smiled and bragged that he had replaced the catalytic converter with a test pipe and installed new Thrush mufflers. To make his point, he pressed down on the accelerator, and the engine roared in response then popped several times as unburned fuel ignited inside the exhaust manifold.

"I'm looking for Ronnie. Is he around?"

"I haven't seen him today," Curtis replied.

"He lives around here, doesn't he?"

"Yeah, he lives up the street, not very far from here."

"Get in," Mick said. "Show me where he lives."

Curtis did as he was told. Mick tossed everything from the front seat into the back to make room. Curtis got inside and shut the door, but the door wouldn't shut completely.

"You gotta lift it up to close it. I think I might have bent the doorframe a few weeks ago when I went over a curb."

Curtis pointed out the windshield crack. "You need to get your windshield fixed because the cops will pull you over and give you a ticket."

Mick laughed and showed him the ticket tucked away inside his visor. "Yeah, they already got me. I need to get the windshield replaced and then they'll sign off on the ticket and I'll just pay the court costs."

Curtis advised him, "Don't wait until the last minute to try to get that taken care of. I got arrested on a bench warrant for something similar."

Mick laughed again. "No shit? You got arrested?"

Curtis told him how he got arrested for not paying his license plate renewal on time as they drove toward Ronnie's house.

When the loud car pulled up next to the house, Ronnie burst through the screen door and came running outside. "Damn, dude. Turn that engine off. I can't hear myself think." He stuck his head in the window. "Man, your car reeks. How can you stand this stench?"

Mick replied, "Yeah, I know I got a lot of things to do. Listen, Ronnie, I'm dry. Can you help me out?"

"I can, but you need to take a whole lid. I'm not nickeling-and-diming anymore."

"No problem. Still twenty per?"

"Yes, sir."

"I'll do two," Mick said, handing Ronnie two crisp twenty-dollar bills.

Ronnie looked over at Curtis. "You good? Do you need anything?"

"No, I'm good," Curtis answered.

Ronnie said to Mick, "You need to replace that windshield before you get a ticket." Ronnie disappeared inside and came back with two sandwich bags of brown weed.

Mick said, "Is it good?"

"Good enough," Ronnie replied.

"Hey, listen, Ronnie, do you want to hang out with me and Curtis today?"

"I can't. I have places to go and people to see. Maybe another time."

"No problem." Mick started the car.

Ronnie yelled, "You need to get out of here before the neighbors complain. I don't need cops coming over here to investigate a noise complaint. Get that muffler fixed, or the cops will pull you over for that too."

Mick laughed as he backed out of the driveway, waving goodbye.

As they drove down the road, Mick dug through some cassette tapes in the center console.

"Do you like Led Zeppelin, Curtis?"

"I know a couple of their songs."

"Yeah? Which ones?"

"'Stairway to Heaven.'"

"Everyone knows that song. It gets played all the time. What else do you know?"

"I don't know a lot of songs by their name," he replied. Curtis continued embarrassing himself by misnaming songs. "Don't they sing, 'Hey, hey, mama, the way you move'? I don't know what it's called, but they play it all the time too."

Mick laughed and said, "That's 'Black Dog.' I can't believe you don't know their songs. They have so many."

"I only hear what they play on the radio."

"Oh man, the best songs are the ones they don't play on the radio." Mick kept digging around and finally found the tape he was searching for. He handed it to Curtis. "Here, put this in."

Curtis looked at the tape and read, "Houses of the Holy." He took the cassette from the case and pushed the tape into the player. Mick heard the song and pushed the button to rewind the tape.

Mick had upgraded his factory stereo to an Alpine system with a graphic equalizer mounted below the dashboard. Curtis saw all the little green function lights and a red power light. When Mick heard the tape click, he hit play. Curtis was mesmerized by all the little green LEDs as they bounced around as "The Song Remains the Same" drowned out the exhaust sound. The little white Mustang bounced down the road, leaving a sonic music trail and exploding gas fumes in an invisible wake to the annoyance of everyone they drove by.

Curtis had not planned on spending the day with Mick and even thought that he probably should call his mom in case she should come looking for him, but instead, he let the music carry him away. Thirty minutes later, they were on the other side of the river and heading toward Mick's dad's house in South County.

When they arrived, nobody was home. Mick pulled the car into the driveway and parked it in front of the garage. He gave Curtis a tour of the modest ranch-style home with a finished basement. The basement had a large sliding glass door that opened to a stone and concrete patio with a gas grill, tiki lamps, and an assortment of lawn furniture. Off to the side was a fair-sized private swimming pool with a large utility shed next to it.

Mick disappeared and came back in with two cold Busch beers. The two boys went out to the shed, and Mick turned on a fan to move the air around and turned on a large stereo system. Curtis didn't hear any music, just a loud hum. Mick disappeared a second time and came back with a box, a couple of cassette tapes, and a water pipe.

He pulled one of the bags of recently purchased weed from the box and handed Curtis another cassette. "This, my friend, is Zeppelin's best album."

Curtis looked at the cassette cover and saw a black and white photo of an aircrew and a whited-out Zeppelin airship. "Led Zeppelin" was written in faded warm-colored block letters surrounded by cloud effects.

Mick filled the water bowl with fresh water and crumbled dried leaves into the bowl. He held a lighter up to the bowl and inhaled the smoke. Curtis heard the familiar gurgling sound and watched Mick inhale until his face turned red. While still holding his breath, Mick pushed the tape into the player and then turned the volume up.

By the time Curtis took his hit from the water pipe, the music had progressed to a sequence of hypnotic rhythmic drumbeats and the tapping of various cymbals. Swirling guitar noises and wails that suggested sensual bliss reverberated around the shed in stereo. All the music that went back and forth inside the tiny shed entered his ears and rolled around inside his buzzing head.

The water pipe made the hot smoke more like a cool vapor, and the effects were immediate. Curtis sat back into one of the comfortable lounge chairs he'd dragged into the shed and fell into a mellowness that erased all the anxiety.

Curtis was facing Mick; both seats were in the center of the shed. They were close enough to pass the water pipe back and forth. There were speakers in every corner of the shed. Curtis noticed that the speakers weren't very large, but he could see through the gray cloth enough to identify outlines of the woofer, midrange, and tweeter speakers.

Maybe it was the pot. Perhaps it was the stereo and the authentic reproduction of music by high-quality speakers. Or maybe it was the perfect assembly of gifted musicians at the peak of their craft in the form of one of the greatest rock bands of all time who could capture the magic of their music on tape. Whatever it was, it all came together for about an hour in a shed in St. Louis County that summer day in late July of 1979.

Mick was generous with that first bag and filled the bowl multiple times when perhaps only one or two were all that was necessary. Not a word would be shared for most of the hour. The experience was like an episode of the *Twilight Zone*, outside the realm of time and space. Mick broke the silence when he asked Curtis if he wanted another beer.

As soon as Mick left, Curtis heard a beautiful song piping through the speakers. It made him think of Katie. He wished more than anything she was there with him to share the experience. It felt good to be so relaxed and calm in his feelings for the girl that any sadness he'd felt was transformed into joy. Although he was as high as a kite, the song brought him down to earth for a moment. He felt alone, but he was glad that he had found her, even if for such a short time. The song ended like a carnival in a music box. She was a part of him now, and his longing for her found a new expression. The music, almost prayer-like, drifted up through the roof of the shed toward the sky and sun. In time, he believed the prayer would return to him in the form of rain.

Mick came back with two cold beers, and when "Heartbreaker" broke through the reverie, it was deafening. Mick turned the volume all the way up. Curtis watched tools vibrate and fall off the workbench and dust fall from overhead. Mick demonstrated his knowledge of guitar by playing an invisible one. The song culminated in an amazing guitar solo. Curtis thought it was clean and perhaps not as electrifying as Eddie Van Halen's "Eruption," but this solo was mesmerizing and possibly had more soul. In the end, it didn't matter. Whether by rocket ship or freight train, the ride these musicians took him on was otherworldly.

Mick turned the music down after the song. "What do you think, Curtis?"

Curtis could only smile. There were no words to capture his feelings and thoughts. Curtis enjoyed the cold beer, the cool buzz, the breeze from the fan, and the incredible gift of music. He thought Mick might be a bit of a burnout, but he is a likable guy.

When "Ramble On" started playing, Mick traded his invisible guitar for an invisible microphone and sang from his heart for the next four minutes. It turned out it would be the only song Curtis would remember from that afternoon when he was at a record store looking for his own copy of the tape a few weeks later. Despite listening to the tape dozens of times, he would never be able to recapture the magic of the first time he heard it.

The boys spent the rest of the afternoon in the pool. While frowned upon in public pools, cutoffs brought no objection from Mick.

"Hey, Mick, I want to ask you something… You go to Mehlville, right?"

"Yes, I've been there my whole life."

"Do you, by chance, know Katie Adams?"

Mick was taken by surprise.

"Fish Bait? You're talking about Fish Bait?" Curtis was confused. "What are you talking about?"

"Yeah, I know Katie. She's a strange girl. We all call her Fish Bait. I don't know anyone that calls her Katie. I don't think she has any friends."

Agitated, Curtis asked, "Why would you call her that?"

Mick drank his beer. "Wow, I don't even know where to start. That poor girl never had a chance. She had a difficult time in school for as long as I can remember. I could look back in yearbooks to see when, but I know I had a couple of classes with her. I'm not sure if it was third or fourth grade when it happened."

"No kidding? What happened?"

Mick stared at him then turned away. "She pissed herself in the middle of class one afternoon. She just sat there at her desk and peed. We might not even have noticed if she didn't start crying and making a scene."

Curtis stared back at Mick in horror.

"Yeah, they got her out and cleaned her up. The school nurse and principal came. It was weird. She wound up spending the next couple of years in special education classes."

"Seriously? That's crazy."

"Yeah. I know. It turns out her dad was killed in Vietnam when she was little, and her mom just had trouble raising her. The thing is, that wasn't even the worst part. Most people forgot about that day in elementary school. Most of the kids in our school didn't even know her back then. What they don't forget is what happened when she was in eighth grade."

Curtis felt his stomach tighten. "What happened in eighth grade?"

Mick smiled and said, "She got caught in the boy's restroom with two boys in one of the stalls. She and the boys were suspended. The boys pretended it was no big deal, but she never lived that one down, and nobody ever forgot."

Curtis felt his stomach tightening up to the point of almost getting ill.

"Do you want another beer?" Mick asked as he climbed out of the pool.

"No, I think I'm good."

Curtis had so much on his mind. Every question he got answered seemed to leave him with ten more he wanted to ask. He had too much information to deal with, and he was tormented by it.

Mick came back with two beers. "You really look like you can use this. If you don't want it, I'll take care of it."

Curtis changed his mind about the beer.

As he popped it open, Curtis asked him, "Mick? Why Fish Bait? I still don't get it."

"I guess you don't fish much, do you?"

"No, not very much."

"Well, if you did, you'd know fish bait is nasty."

Chapter 23

Cornell '77

As the Grady brothers became more enamored with Kathy and Francine, the Basement became less and less the go-to place on the weekends. Marty saw Gunner and Brad as pussy-whipped, which caused everyone to become more temperamental. It became so much of an issue for Marty, he stopped driving up to Imperial altogether on the weekends. Curtis had no interest in going to Auto Auctions every weekend and found himself hanging out with Ronnie and Brian instead.

Even though Curtis was the same age as Ronnie, he had never hung out with him much because Ronnie came from a troubled home, which made him more of a loner and a rebel. Ronnie was also not afraid to occasionally experiment with real drugs. Ronnie learned that by selling drugs, he could have others subsidize his growing appetite for them. As Ronnie became more comfortable selling weed to the kids he knew from school, he seemed to enjoy people needing to come to him. Never shy, he carefully vetted and brought people into his little network. On more than one occasion, he tried to convince Curtis that selling a nickel bag was a way to get a doobie or two for free. "Talk to Brian or Mick. They'll tell you what a good deal it is."

Brian was a loner. He was a couple of years younger and stayed to himself most of the time. Brian loved coming to the Basement to play pool and drink free beer. Nobody at his home ever knew where he was, the Basement being unknown to his parents. This made it the best hideaway to get out of homework, chores, and beatings, even if for just a little while.

Curtis never stopped going up to the Basement. The Gradys had always been more like family to him anyway. But in the evening when he found the little Green Gremlin there and noticed the lights were off inside, he would feel a bit dejected then go for a walk. It was on these walks in the cool of the evening, under the moon and stars, that he would occasionally run into Ronnie or Brian doing the same thing.

Ronnie's sister, Cassie, lived with her husband, Rick, in a quaint two-bedroom house they rented. The 800-square-foot home sat back off the road about one hundred feet with a gravel driveway that ended under a dilapidated lean-to carport that kept blanket-covered laundry equipment, a rusting engine stand, and a doghouse out of the weather.

Cassie's Texas yellow 1968 Karmann Ghia was sitting in the driveway and blocked in by several vehicles when Curtis and Ronnie stopped by on Friday night. They walked in without knocking, and everyone seemed to know who Ronnie was as he greeted each person by name. Cassie sauntered over to Curtis with outstretched arms. She was wearing a colorful, oversized, one-piece kaftan with sleeves that ended just above her elbows.

Cassie hugged Curtis and after he sat down, she offered him a glass of wine. Surprising himself, he accepted her offer. Up to then, his only experience with wine was either the hootch Mr. Grady made every summer or Mad Dog 20/20, which was equally toxic. Cassie's face showed signs of disapproval as he emptied the glass with a single drink.

She whispered something to Ronnie, and Ronnie pulled Curtis aside and told him, "I need to tell you, we can hang out here, but my sister has a few rules we need to follow."

"Rules? What kind of rules?"

"Well, for one, we can't get drunk here. She doesn't mind us hanging out and drinking, but she will not tolerate people getting sick or passing out."

"That sounds reasonable."

"And also, she asks that we go out in the backyard behind the trees to piss. She has a thing about people using her bathroom."

Curtis wondered what else was coming.

"And we need to stay out of her kitchen. She knows we smoke weed but doesn't want to have to go to the grocery store more than once a week."

Curtis laughed and agreed to the terms. Cassie walked back over, took his empty glass, and handed him another, saying, "Slow down and enjoy." Then she swirled her own glass and closed her eyes before taking a deep breath. She drew all the fruity fragrances into her nose. "Life is about peace and pleasure. Don't go too fast or you'll miss it."

After dinner one evening, Curtis couldn't decide if he wanted to get high or get drunk. He stole a bottle of wine stored in the bottom section of his mom's china cabinet when she was down in the basement doing laundry. He went outside and hid the bottle behind the garage and waited for it to get dark outside.

When his parents were watching television, he snuck out through the kitchen, grabbed the bottle, and walked up to the Basement. The Green Gremlin was there, and the lights were off, so he kept walking.

He continued to Cassie's house and knocked. She answered the door and was surprised to see him there with a full, unopened bottle of wine, which she assumed was a gift.

"Thank you, Curtis, that is so sweet of you." She hugged him and then introduced him to her husband, Rick, whom he had never met. The older man shook hands with him and smiled. A few women were in the kitchen talking, and another couple was sitting on a couch in the small living room.

Cassie opened the wine and poured a few glasses. She smiled as she smelled the wine, which made her smile disappear. She picked up the bottle and read the label. It was just an average, table-variety Cabernet Sauvignon, more suitable for cooking with than drinking. She recorked the wine and added stew meat to her shopping list before opening a bottle of hers.

In the meantime, Rick was showing Curtis his stereo system. Rick, apart from knowing cars, was also an audiophile and had spent a small fortune putting together a high-fidelity stereo system.

"Curtis, don't get started with this madness. It's always changing; it's a relentless pursuit of perfect audio reproduction. It requires an ear even to know the difference, but once you hear it, you gotta have it."

Rick explained how superior reel-to-reel was over cassettes and 8-tracks, which he considered to be a waste of money. "I'd rather hear leaves rustle or wind blow over tape hiss any day." Rick showed Curtis his Marantz reel-to-reel but would not tell him what it cost. He pointed to Cassie. "She would divorce me if she knew what I spent on this."

Curtis was overwhelmed because he didn't have an inkling of the difference between high fidelity and low fidelity. He was still listening to most of his music through a single-speaker flip clock. Everything sounded better than that. He just didn't have the courage to say it.

Rick explained how phonographs worked and took the lid off his Stanton player as he did a show and tell with the needle, the tonearm, and the platter. The needle was worth more than one of Curtis's paychecks. Rick said he preferred the belt drive models because he had too much money invested in vinyl.

"None of this is worth a damn without these," he said as he pointed to the four large Polk speaker cabinets that sat in the corners of the living room. "And this is where the magic happens," he said as he turned on the Pioneer tuner and amplifier, which also powered up a Technics equalizer.

Digging through his stack of albums, he pulled out *Cornell '77*, a Grateful Dead album, with a cover of a turquoise blue square within a square with an orange and red flower-like symbol in the middle—very psychedelic in design. He carefully extracted one of the vinyl discs out of the protective sleeve, placed it gently on the platter, and, with surgeon-like precision, lowered the needle onto the revolving disc. Immediately, everyone in the house stopped what they were doing and started smiling and dancing. It was the wildest thing Curtis had ever seen. Rick smiled and winked at Curtis, rotated the volume knob to four, and joined the happy women dancing with glasses of wine in their hands and smiles on their faces.

While everyone was dancing, Curtis sat down and started going through the stacks of records. He only recognized one of every ten albums. The Rolling Stones and Eric Clapton seemed to be the only albums he recognized. Curtis had no idea that the Grateful Dead had made so many records. The only song he was familiar with was "Truckin'." There also seemed to be a lot of Frank Zappa albums in those stacks. He recalled conversations he'd had with Gonzo while working at Riccardo & Lorenzo's about Frank Zappa. Those conversations had been one-sided because Curtis had no clue who Frank Zappa was. Even now, as he stared at the album cover and the picture of a dark-haired man with brooding eyes, a wide soul patch, and a full mustache that extended downward past the corners of the mouth, Curtis could only think of the words Roger Daltrey recently shouted on KSHE: "Who are you?"

CHAPTER 24

Kimmswick

Curtis sat on his motorcycle, reminiscing about his fourteenth birthday. So much had changed in the last three years. The day Curtis turned fourteen was the happiest day of his life. His parents had changed their minds and given him a motorcycle for his birthday. JoAnn reluctantly yielded to her husband's overriding vote to get it for him. For years, his friends had rode around on go-carts and minibikes. When they got older, Brad and Gunner had motorcycles. Even Travis, who was younger than Curtis, had a small motorbike. All Curtis could do was watch with envy from the banana seat of his shrinking Schwinn bicycle.

For a teenage boy in rural Missouri, the motorbike made all the difference in the world. Without it, there was no keeping up with friends. Having a motorbike, a sense of balance, and a heart yearning for adventure, Curtis felt bonded once again with his friends and realized an independent spirit through his newfound freedom. The motorcycle was his ticket to the great beyond. And Chesley Island was that great beyond.

His mom had picked out a bright yellow Suzuki TM125, a lightweight and durable motorbike explicitly made for off-road use. His mother only had two stipulations: first, he stayed off the streets, and second, he always wore a helmet. While Curtis intended to obey, he was on the road within a week, and the helmet was often left behind in the garage.

The boy on a motorcycle never confused reality with make-believe, at least not for long. Reality had a way of teaching a boy real fast. Physical laws applied to everyone, without exception. Gravity would quickly correct a careless attitude. The rider learned that centrifugal force was an ally, loose gravel was to be respected, and heat shields would only afford so much protection from burns. The spark plug was also known for occasionally biting a careless, gloveless finger.

His reminiscing dissipated when he kicked the motorcycle into gear. Even though he spent less time on the motorcycle now that he had a license to drive, riding it reminded him of happier times when the summer was all his to enjoy. Going for a motorcycle ride after coming home from the pool was about as close as he could get to the "good old days."

While Curtis was out riding around, he noticed his front tire needed air. He saw his neighbor, Mr. Fernbeck, hosing down the back of his truck in his driveway. Mr. Fernbeck and his wife, Mae, lived across the street from the Gradys. Curtis's dad often walked up the street to talk to Mr. Fernbeck because he had a no-nonsense country view of life and knew life was precious and fleeting.

Curtis assumed the neighbor would help him because he was friendly with his dad. Mr. Fernbeck had an air compressor, and he figured it would only take a minute to shoot some air into the tire. Curtis pulled his motorcycle into the driveway, but to his surprise, Mr. Fernbeck immediately turned the water off and jumped off his truck, yelling, "Get that fucking Japanese abomination off my driveway right now, Curtis! I'm not messing around with you. I mean it."

Dumbfounded, Curtis hastily made a U-turn and rode to the Phillips 66 station by the highway. The full-time mechanic, Jody, took a break from the muffler he was replacing and let him wheel his motorcycle inside so he could look at it. Jody brushed soapy water over the wheel and determined Curtis had a bad valve stem core. He replaced it, refilled the tire with air, and sent Curtis on his way without taking a dime from him. Before Curtis left, Jody told him a crack in the front fender was about to cause it to fall off.

When his dad got home from work, he mentioned Mr. Fernbeck's outburst. His dad told him Mr. Fernbeck was a marine who'd spent a couple of years in the South Pacific at the end of World War II, and he had no love for the Japanese people or their products. Curtis brought it up with Mr. Grady, who had a similar attitude. Mr. Grady lamented how well Japanese companies were doing in America. He was a UAW card-carrying member, and his union was hostile toward foreign cars. Mr. Grady had a bumper sticker on his car that read: HUNGRY? EAT YOUR IMPORT.

July once again proved to be a hot, muggy month with no job schedule to worry about. Curtis spent all of the time inside the pool area because he was broke and had no money to play pinball.

Tuesday afternoon, Curtis went to the Basement to hang out. JoJo looked mad as hell as she stormed out of the house when he arrived. She tore out of there in her white Thunderbird. Mr. Grady's car was gone, so he assumed he was at work.

Curtis walked into the Basement and noticed Francine and Gunner sitting on the couch, holding hands. He could feel the tension in the room.

Curtis asked, "What's going on?"

Francine cried, saying, "It's all my fault."

Gunner said, "No, not all. She's mostly mad at me."

"Because of me," she cried.

Curtis said, "She sure seemed mad to me. I saw gravel flying everywhere as she left. Where's Brad? Is he at work?"

Francine said, "No, he's upstairs. I wouldn't go up there. It's been a bad day for everyone." Then she lowered her voice and said, "Kathy broke up with him. He's not handling it well."

"Really? What happened?"

Francine replied, "I'm not going to say. If Brad wants to tell you, he will."

When Gunner pulled out the nearly empty bag of pot, Francine said, "I'm out of papers."

Gunner got up, rooted in a box, and found an old corn cob pipe. He triumphantly said, "Where there's a will, there's a way."

The radio was playing, and the DJ was spinning new music. A year earlier, a band from Boston called The Cars released their self-titled debut album. Many of the songs from that album were in regular rotation. The band had recently released a new album, *Candy-O*, and their song "Let's Go" seemed to pick up where "Just What I Needed" left off.

Also, just a year ago, an English band called The Police released their album, *Outlandos d'Amour*. Their song, "Roxanne," was an ear-candied contagion that could stay in your head for days. While they sat around getting stoned, KSHE played a song by the band Sniff 'n' the Tears called "Driver's Seat."

The best part about KSHE was that the DJs always seemed to find the deep cuts—one-off tracks from bands nobody had ever heard of. They played new bands without forgetting the old ones, even if they changed names or members. KSHE unapologetically embraced the new British Invasion as punk rock-influenced bands went mainstream and progressive bands became more popular.

Change is only partially accepted when people have choices, and the radio dial spun quickly to other stations. Other times, putting on a record or pushing in a tape was the preferred route. That evening, when the DJ played a David Bowie song nobody recognized, Gunner got up and said, "Enough of this bullshit." He dug through his ever-growing record collection and pulled out a well-worn Ronnie Montrose album.

As the night went on and everyone mellowed out, Gunner told Curtis that JoJo was so upset because he had informed her that he wasn't going back to finish his degree in the fall. Although Francine was a factor in his decision, he said it wasn't the only one.

JoJo told him he needed to find a job because if he didn't return to school, she would take the money they saved to put him through college and use it to start her own business.

Brad eventually came downstairs and sat in silence. He had no desire to drink or get high. Gunner turned the music off and went back upstairs with Francine. Curtis asked Brad if he wanted to go for a walk. The two friends walked down the hill to the railroad tracks. Curtis didn't say a word as they hiked along the empty auxiliary tracks that paralleled the main line. Curtis hoped Brad would want to talk, but he never did.

As the sun started to set, the bluffs cast a deep shadow over Chesley Island. They turned around to go back. Brad finally spoke up, "She's gone, and there's nothing I can do about it." Curtis knew precisely how he felt but kept his thoughts to himself.

They walked back up the hill, a hill they had walked or ridden a thousand times before. It was always a steep climb, but it reinforced the notion that moving away from something was always easier than returning to it.

That Thursday, JoAnn took his truck keys from him and said he could not drive it again unless he was looking for a job. He was so angry at his mom that he refused to go to the pool with the family. After they left, he completed his chores and walked up to the Basement to hang out with his friends.

He told Gunner he needed a new front fender for his motorcycle. Gunner said he needed a new chain and sprocket for his bike. Gunner offered to drive to High Ridge to Hide-A-Cycle. He had read about the business in the *Trading Times*. He had been there before to check them out and testified they had a lot of used and new motorcycle parts.

The morning was stunningly gorgeous. The temperature was in the low 70s when they loaded into Gunner's car. Francine sat in the middle, playing with the radio as Gunner drove toward Antonia and House Springs. Curtis rolled down the window, singing along to "Running On Empty." It was a twenty-minute ride, but it took another ten minutes to find the location.

Inside the building was a bonanza of motorcycle parts and accessories. Curtis found a suitable replacement fender and was dismayed he didn't have enough cash to buy all the cool things he discovered. Gunner found his needed parts. Gunner paid for everything with cash put aside to buy textbooks. "I'll pay you back just as soon as I find another job," Curtis promised.

The weather was beautiful, so Gunner took the long way home and drove toward Cedar Hill on the way to Hillsboro. As they drove through Morse Mill, they saw many kids standing around watching others take turns jumping off the Big River bridge.

After they got home, Curtis went to get his motorcycle, and Gunner helped him replace the fender and then replaced the chain and sprockets on his motorbike. Francine sat on the ground, pulling ticks off Gunner's beagle and smashing them with a hammer. By the time she finished, the concrete had turned crimson and looked like a crime scene.

While they were sitting in the shade working on their motorcycles, Richie drove up in a ten-year-old Camaro. Richie hardly ever came over, but he wanted to show off his new car. Curtis was envious when he saw it because it was a beautiful automobile.

Richie bitched about the band camp that started earlier that week. He loved playing the drums, but he hated marching. When Gunner and Francine went inside, Richie took Curtis for a ride down the street and back and promised a longer ride when he had more time.

Friday was cooler than the day before. Since rain was in the forecast, JoAnn didn't take the kids to the pool. Curtis spent the morning doing the chores his mother assigned him. She made him try on all the clothes for school she had purchased, which he loathed doing.

Then his mom decided to do a deep clean of his bedroom. She was livid when she pulled the bed away from the wall to vacuum and saw books, trash, dirty clothes, and a gym bag. She opened the gym bag and had a fit about her son's laziness in not even putting his dirty clothes and towels into the laundry.

She called for her son to carry his mess downstairs to the washing machine when she discovered a box of magazines. Curtis entered the room and stood in horror as he watched her dump the magazines out onto the bed. "Do you really need to keep all of these?"

She never understood why her son wasted money on *Mad*, *Cracked*, and *National Lampoon*. As JoAnn sorted through the stack, she found several issues of *Penthouse*, which she confiscated immediately. Without saying a word, she stormed past him and straight to the trash can in the kitchen.

After lunch, he ran out of the house before she could add more things to his chore list. He walked up to the Gradys' and discovered they were all going to Wet Willies in Fenton. Brad was sent home early because he had too much overtime for the week. Without Kathy, he had turned to his work and stayed in the shop as long as possible.

Curtis said he had no money, but Brad told him not to worry. Curtis and Travis rode with Brad. Gunner and Francine drove separately.

Wet Willies was a curving, partially tunneled water slide extended from a support tower atop a hill. The kids rode down on color-coded foam mats so the attendant could keep track of riders and when to send the next person down. Like sled riding in the winter, it required a long, steep climb up to the top for the payoff of a short ride down. The slide ended abruptly, sending kids tumbling into a large pool of water below. The girls that had been there before knew to wear T-shirts or one-piece bathing suits. The girls new to the water slide quickly learned that rapidly falling into a pool of water occasionally ripped bikini tops off. It turned out, Francine was new to the water sliding experience and would remember to bring a T-shirt next time.

About an hour into their fun on the slide, it began to rain, and at the first sign of lightning, the facility closed for the day.

Curtis spent Saturday morning riding his motorcycle, and when he rode up the hill from Chesley Island, he saw Richie's Camaro in his driveway. Richie had brought his sister, Lynn, over to play with Helen for the afternoon.

Curtis offered no objections when Richie asked him to go for a ride. Before they left, Richie gave Curtis a closer look at the Super Sport Camaro. Electric blue metallic paint covered the car over a black vinyl interior. Richie said his dad would help him rebuild the 350-cubic-inch engine over the winter. The car was spectacular, inside and out. Curtis couldn't imagine it looking any better, but Richie had plans for it.

Richie drove to Kimmswick, a small but historic town hemmed in between Imperial and the Mississippi River. Like many small river towns, Kimmswick was prone to flooding, so large piles of sand were all over. Whenever the call for help went out, volunteers came to pack and stack sandbags. While the Missouri Pacific Railroad easement provided a decent levee, the Mississippi River would backfill nearby Rock Creek, allowing floodwater to enter the town from the south.

Kimmswick was also the center of two annual celebrations that drew people from all over. The Apple Butter Festival was popular with the older crowd in the fall, but the St. Joseph Parish Picnic in early summer appealed to everyone.

Richie drove his car over one of the oldest bridges in existence. Everyone who crossed over Rock Creek on it marveled that they survived the crossing since the bridge was so old and rickety. The iron span bridge was built sometime in the 1800s to cross the River des Peres in St. Louis. Sometime after the Great Depression, they relocated the bridge to Kimmswick.

An old, historic home sat on a corner about a quarter mile past the bridge. A beautiful stone wall separated Windsor Harbor Road from the private property with a strip of lawn extending down to the roadside. A small grove of assorted oak, cypress, and elm trees lined the edge of the property. The trees were perfect for shade, which made the corner a popular summertime hangout for teenagers. Bikes would lay on their side as kids sat on the wall with watchful eyes on the road, the railroad tracks, and the Mississippi River.

When Richie drove past, he recognized some of the kids from band camp. He pulled his car off to the side of the road, and a crowd gathered around to admire it. Curtis didn't know anyone, so he sat in the car as Richie got out and talked to some band members. Curtis observed Richie talking to a short blonde girl with large breasts. She seemed to laugh at everything he said.

Standing beside her was a much smaller girl wearing white overalls over a deep yellow shirt. Her curly, reddish-brown hair fell to her shoulders. As she stood with her hands in her pockets, fidgeting, she peered in the car and spotted Curtis. She smiled then turned away, but occasionally, she glanced back at him. Curtis could not stop staring at her. Finally, she took her hands out of her pockets, tapped her friend on the arm, and said something to her. Richie got both girls to laugh at something he said before he returned to his car.

He fired up his Camaro and revved the engine as he waved goodbye. Curtis waved out of sheer politeness, and his stomach knotted when he saw the cute red-haired girl wave back.

Curtis asked, "Who were you talking to?"

"I was talking to Theresa. She's a drummer in the band, but they have her on cymbals for marching. I'm on the snare, so I stand close to her most of the time. We rip on each other at band practice."

"Who was the girl standing next to her?"

"I think her name is Rhonda. She plays clarinet. I don't know her well, but I think she's close friends with Theresa. You should've come over; I could've introduced you to them."

CHAPTER 25

Football Camp

The Montana State Bobcats were 7-2, coming off a crushing victory at the expense of Northern Arizona with a 45-0 rout. A week later, on November 10, 1973, Montana State Senior Sydney Tyron, middle linebacker, put on a stunning defensive performance with fifteen tackles and two sacks. The Bobcats had a three-point lead going into the fourth quarter.

The Fighting Hawks of North Dakota were not going to go down easy. On a second and five, from their 30-yard line, the Hawks offense ran a sweep to the right. The quarterback tossed the ball to the running back. The tailback followed the guard and bounced off the defensive tackle toward the middle of the defense. Tyron had his eyes on the ball carrier and never saw the tight end. The blindside chop block ended the game and the promising football career of the Big Sky All-Conference player. As the medical attendees carried the injured player off the field, an NFL scout watching from the stands circled a question mark next to Sydney Tyron's name on his report card. The North Dakota Fighting Hawks would score two touchdowns and win the game 41-30.

On Wednesday morning, JoAnn drove Curtis to see Dr. Herbert Matthews, the family pediatrician. It was unusual for Curtis to see the family doctor because, for the past several years, he received most of his shots at the emergency room as he was a most curious and fearless child prone to severe lacerations, punctures, and concussions. As a teenager, it was embarrassing to see a doctor accustomed to seeing younger children, a doctor who preferred to be called "Doctor Herbie."

It was a relief when the nurse instructed JoAnn to remain in the waiting area as Curtis went back alone to see the doctor for his physical.

The nurse appeared to be the same age as some of his teachers in school but was quiet and withdrawn as she weighed him and took his temperature. "The doctor will be with you shortly," was the extent of their interaction.

Dr. Matthews came into the room a short time later, pulled out the rolling chair, and glanced through the folder.

"So, Curtis, I understand you're here for a physical to play football this year."

"Yes, sir," he replied.

"Do you know what position you'll be playing?"

"No, sir, I have no idea."

"Whatever position you play, you'll find it is all about teamwork." Dr. Matthews listened to his heart and had him breathe in and out as he positioned his stethoscope around his chest and back. "Do you smoke?" "No, sir."

Then he asked casually, "Are you experimenting with any drugs or alcohol?"

"No, sir," Curtis replied while checking the clock to see what time it was.

The doctor wrote in the charts as he asked, "Are you sexually active?"

"No, sir."

The doctor wrote some more and then had Cutis lie down on the table as he felt around his stomach and groin. "Do you feel any pain or soreness?"

The doctor instructed Curtis to stand up and remove his underwear. The doctor proceeded to thoroughly examine his genitals before holding his testicles in one hand and instructing him to turn his head and cough.

"You can get dressed. I see no reason you cannot play football. It's important that if you do choose to become sexually active, you take precautions against venereal disease and unwanted pregnancies."

"Yes, sir. I understand."

Dr. Matthews left the room, and just as Curtis finished getting dressed, the nurse came in with a few booklets for him to take home with him. As JoAnn talked with the nurse, Curtis glanced through the brochures, covering topics such as diet and exercise, drugs and narcotics, and sex. The nurse gave JoAnn the form signed by the doctor for Curtis to return to the high school.

After the doctor's visit, they stopped at K-Mart so JoAnn could buy Curtis additional pads and safety equipment not supplied by the school, including a mouth guard, a jockstrap, and a cup. The ride back home was a quiet one as Curtis thumbed through the pamphlets. He resisted reading them sitting next to his mother, fearing she might initiate a conversation he did not want to have with her.

Later that afternoon, Curtis brought in the mail. He pulled out two pieces addressed to him. One was an invoice from Columbia House Record and Tape Club for seventy-six dollars for some tapes ordered to complete his membership obligation. He was tired of hearing his mom bitch at him anytime they sent him anything.

The other envelope was from the City of Arnold, advising him of his upcoming court appointment on Tuesday, August 14, 1979. The court costs and fees associated with his license plates were one hundred twenty-five dollars. The letter stated: "Cash required for all transactions."

They went to Springdale the next day. Curtis overheard his grand-mother telling his mother about a wedding invitation she'd received for Sammy and Danny in early December. JoAnn frowned and said she was disappointed she hadn't received an invitation.

Curtis dreaded going to football camp on Monday. The football camp, he was told, would consist of two practice sessions, Monday through Friday. The morning practices would start at seven and end at eleven. The evening sessions would start at six and end around nine.

Part of his apprehension was having to go to bed early so he could get up at six in the morning. Apart from roller skating, Curtis had never been involved in sports. Besides Cub Scouts, he had never been part of a group. His dad assured him everything would be fine. He gave him twenty dollars to put gas in his truck so he could drive himself to school in the morning. JoAnn had no desire to drive back and forth to the school four times a day, so she reluctantly gave in to letting him drive his truck to school for football practice.

He arrived early and parked close to the high school. Whatever dread he carried was confirmed when the first thing he heard from Mr. Collier, one of the assistant coaches, was, "Hey, numb-nuts. You can't park here. Go park where you're supposed to."

Curtis moved his truck to the student parking lot and reluctantly walked toward the school building. The school letter had provided times, dates, and a reminder to turn in a signed medical form. It said nothing about where to park.

That morning, Coach Tyron and his assistants stood with clipboards in hand and whistles on cords around their necks. Everyone gathered in a circle and separated according to their class. Curtis noticed what a couple of years' difference made as some seniors looked like grown men, some even sporting beards and mustaches.

Curtis spent the morning doing various drills, most of which included some form of running. Afterward, the coaches separated everyone into two groups: backs and linemen. The coaches instructed the players to follow them back to the school so they could issue equipment. They gave oversized, meshed red shirts to the backs and receivers and yellow ones to the linemen. The coaches gave everyone a pair of game-day jerseys.

Curtis was designated a lineman and then issued shoulder pads and a helmet. Curtis didn't know it, but with absolutely no football experience, there was no way he would ever play a single down in a real game. He, along with several others, was recruited into the football squad for one reason only: to hold canvas dummies for the varsity players to hit in practice.

British drunks were often impressed into the Royal Navy. When they eventually sobered up, they found themselves separated from the comforts of their beloved taverns by a dozen leagues of cold Atlantic Ocean. Likewise, Curtis and several other underclassmen would quickly discover the terms of their conscription.

His helmet had a single plastic bar that went over his upper lip. All the other linemen had full caged masks over their faces, but Curtis looked like a punter. When he protested that he'd received the wrong helmet, he was laughed at and told that was all that was left.

Curtis found the evening workout equally unpleasant. There were obstacles to jump over or sidestep around. There was more running. When his body adjusted to the running, they increased the intensity or muscle-numbing frequency. Curtis had heard whistles at the pool, but they never annoyed him. Now, the whistle was like nails on a chalkboard. Someone was constantly blowing a whistle, and the yells were never constructive. The first day set the pattern; as the week continued, conditions worsened.

The mornings began with group calisthenics and stretching. Curtis found lying on the cool, damp grass to stretch the only part of the four hours he would enjoy. After that, it was all pain and misery.

After a brief water break, the older linemen climbed to the top of a nearby hill. The younger linemen, who had to wait in line to drink water after the older linemen had their fill, had to run up the mountain under a chorus of verbal assaults initiated by Coach Tyron. The head coach was present with the linemen every morning. In the first half of the drill session, players pushed the coach around thick, tall grass on a sled. When the sled went straight, he was pleased. When the sled went in a circle, he was not.

The morning dew evaporated as the sun crept higher in the morning sky. The humidity raised the heat index, and everything was harder to do as the practice went on. Curtis directed his thoughts to shade trees, water sprinklers, and swimming pools, but these thoughts only made things worse. Every chance Curtis had to disassociate from the physical pain was interrupted by continuous cursing and blasts from the annoying whistle.

The first time they walked down the hill, Curtis had this idea that the hard part of the practice session was over. He couldn't have been more wrong.

The water break during the second session seemed to be for the upperclassmen only because the coolers were empty by the time Curtis and the other junior varsity players got their turn. The varsity team ran practice plays for the rest of the evening. Curtis was assigned to hold a heavy canvas bag called a tackling dummy. The dummy bag resembled a boxing bag with handles. While the coaches designated the evening practices as "no contact," the players were encouraged to hit the dummies as hard as possible.

And woe to the junior varsity member that got knocked over. As Curtis soon found out, the only thing worse than getting knocked over was to turn loose of the bag and let the other guy fall. In that first session, Curtis managed to do both.

When he got knocked off his feet and fell, the running back carrying the ball narrowly avoided stepping on the younger classman with steel cleats as he sprinted by.

"The next time you fall like that, he's gonna step on your face," Coach yelled.

Later, they ran a play toward Curtis, and two large seniors came running toward him with the running back right behind them. Curtis held onto the dummy as long as he could, but when he saw them charging like enraged bulls, he stepped to the side, and when the first senior hit the dummy, it fell to the ground, and he tripped over it. The other lineman and the back had to jump over him to avoid stepping on him.

Luther Conrad, the varsity player who fell, got up, slapped Curtis's helmet, and cussed him out for not holding the dummy correctly. Coach Tryon came over screaming, "What the hell is your problem, McGowan?" Then he picked up the dummy and told him to hold it, threatening him within an inch of his life if he ever dropped it again.

Every day was more of the same, and the more he practiced, the more he realized he did not know anything about the game. After the evening practice on Thursday, he approached Coach Tyron and said, "Excuse me, Coach, but do you have a playbook for me to study, so I know what these plays are?"

"Playbook? Are you kidding me? You don't need a playbook. You need to pay attention."

Friday night, as he came down the hill for the last part of practice, the field was split down the middle as the band camp was practicing marching on half of it. Curtis spotted his friend Richie. Everyone in the band wore their marching band uniform tops and hats. Richie had his back to him, but Curtis could see he was talking to a short girl holding a pair of cymbals. Her cute red-haired friend was standing next to her, but she appeared to be uninterested in what her friend had to say. Then she made eye contact with Curtis, smiled, and waved. Curtis smiled and waved back.

Jordan Reynolds, one of Curtis's many varsity nemeses, saw him and said, "Hey, look at this, gay boy McGowan is rutting for a squeeze."

Jordan's taunt brought the angered glare of Coach Tyron upon Curtis. "McGowan! Knock that shit off right now and pay attention. You might learn something."

If the first week of football camp taught him one thing, it was a new appreciation for sleep. Curtis rarely went to the pool on the weekends, but he'd missed the pool all week long. On Saturday, he disappeared for a couple of hours, but when he came home, he got an earful from his mother for driving the truck to the pool without permission.

That afternoon, he walked to the Basement to talk to Brad. Several people were there as word had gotten out that Mr. Grady would be crushing grapes for his new batch of homemade wine. Because Curtis had been in football camp all week, he had missed the annual harvesting of grapes. Francine had had her first experience picking grapes, and the Basement was full of five-gallon buckets and large steel tubs of enormous purple grapes.

Mr. Grady owned a cast-iron, turn-of-the-century winepress. Everyone liked to turn the crank, crushing grapes dumped into the hopper. The juice from the crushed grapes was directed into a clean white bucket by a plastic sheet that acted as a funnel. Curtis learned long ago it was unsettling to see bees, grasshoppers, and other insects go to their doom with bellies full of grape juice.

After the initial crushing, a disc would screw down by turning a massive wheel. The pressed disc would squeeze most of the remaining juice out of the pulp. Mr. Grady had a large wood cask on a wheeled base he'd made, and he transferred the grape juice into it before adding his sugar and yeast. The remaining juice went into empty plastic milk jugs. They removed large wheels formed from the pulp and rolled them away like tires until they disintegrated in the backyard, much to the delight of legions of honeybees that swarmed to the messy feast.

Travis and Brian had stopped by to help with the winemaking, and Marty was also there. Curtis had not seen Marty in a long time. Marty said he had been working at the Imperial Auto Auction all summer and was seeing a girl named Becky, who worked there too. Marty said Becky's father owned property at Lost Valley Lake, and they spent a lot of time out there on the weekends. A tall, gangly-looking man walked in while he was talking with Marty about the lake property.

Marty said, "Marvin, where have you been?"

"You know, here, there, and everywhere…"

Marvin went to school with Gunner, so, like Gunner, he was several years older than everyone else. Marvin lived in a trailer near Antonia, where he volunteered as a part-time fireman. Marvin had a full-time job as a maintenance man at the school, but he was quick to point out he was not a custodian and didn't have to mop or sweep floors.

Marvin drove a 1972 blue and white Chevy Suburban with flood lamps on the front bumper and a blue and white emergency light that could be placed on the dashboard, and he had it equipped with a two-way radio and scanner. He was the go-to guy when details about an accident or fire that were not published in the local paper were needed. Whenever he was off work, he drove around Jefferson County but never overstayed his welcome in any one place.

"What have you been doing? It smells like a candy store in here."

"Crushing grapes all day long," Travis said. "Can't you tell?" Travis held out his arm to show all the welts from bee stings.

Gunner heard the voice and came downstairs, with Francine following him.

"Hey, loser. Where have you been?"

"I know, I've been wanting to stop by, but it's been busy at school getting everything ready for when these boneheads return next month."

While Brad and his dad cleaned up the mess and hosed down the winepress to put it away for another year, Gunner, Francine, and Marvin went outside for privacy as everyone else hung around drinking grape juice.

After Marvin left, everyone sat around the pool table talking. Travis let it be known that his grandparents would be out of town in two weeks. Marty suggested that they throw a back-to-school party.

It didn't take much persuasion to get him to agree. Travis thought it would be okay if everyone stayed outside. "I can't have people going into their house." He said he would speak with his mom about it because she was the one house-sitting for her parents.

Sunday, Curtis found Brad and pulled him aside.

"Brad, I need help. I need some money for that ticket I got."

"How much do you need?"

Curtis said, "The court instructions I received in the mail says I need a hundred and twenty-five dollars."

Brad went upstairs and came back and gave him two crisp hundred-dollar bills.

"Thank you. I'll pay you back."

"You'll need a job first," his friend replied.

"I know. I think I'd rather make pizzas than play football."

"Me too."

On Tuesday, Curtis put on the same clothes he wore to Mr. Jones's funeral. Gunner had no interest in going to court with him, but Francine said she would go. She dug through JoJo's closet to find something nice to wear.

Curtis waited over an hour before he went up before the Honorable Judge Lois Goeke and pleaded guilty to his failure to appear in court charge. The judge read over the paperwork and then counseled him on the need to be attentive and responsible for all licenses and restrictions enforced by the State of Missouri and the City of Arnold. She dismissed the case, directing him to the court clerk to pay the associated court costs and fees.

Curtis was pleasantly surprised that the City of Arnold had already applied the hundred-dollar bond, so he only needed to pay twenty-five dollars. When they left, Francine hugged him and said, "Please don't get in trouble with the law anymore. I don't ever want to go to court again."

Later that night, after Brad came home from work, Curtis returned the hundred and seventy-five dollars. Brad asked him if he wanted to keep the money to get by until he found another job. Curtis accepted the offer.

Travis came over later that evening and told everyone he'd asked his mom. While initially hesitant, she knew they would go somewhere else if she said no. Reluctantly, his mom told Travis he could have a yard party but stipulated there better not be any drugs or hard liquor. She also warned adults would be out and about watching things.

"How many people do you think will come?" Travis asked.

"I don't know…maybe a dozen or so?" Curtis offered.

"How many girls do you think will be there?"

"I don't have a clue," Curtis replied.

"You can say that again," Gunner said.

Curtis asked Travis, "Do you think you could ask your sister about calling some of her friends?"

Everyone in the Basement thought this was a great idea.

Travis got defensive and snarled, "You need to leave my sister out of this, you bunch of pervs."

"I wasn't talking about your sister, dweeb; I was asking about her friends."

Everyone laughed, and Travis said he would bring it up with her when he got home.

CHAPTER 26

Fumble Recovery

Friday was the last day of football camp. Although Curtis hated every minute of it, the strength and conditioning of the challenging workouts twice a day during the summer months had melted the softness of his core right off his body. When his mother had to go to K-Mart to get him new clothes that fit him properly, she worried she was not feeding him enough.

Curtis drove to the workout and parked in the back of the high school parking lot. He changed in the parking lot to avoid going into the locker room. The smaller underclassmen were subject to frequent verbal insults and painful hazing, especially if their last name was McGowan. For whatever reason, it seemed to Curtis that Coach Tyron had marked him for harassment, more so than any other sophomores or juniors practicing with the varsity squad. The reality was that he did not play football anyway. It was all physical brutality on an individual level, even though several times, he was told there was no "I" in "team."

He would participate in daily practices after school if he made the team. He sat in his truck listening to *Hemispheres*, an older Rush album he recently acquired. When he saw Coach Tyron walking toward the football field with his goon squad of blood-lusting seniors, he let out a deep sigh, rolled down his window, and tossed the keys on the floor mat before slamming the door shut. He did not want to be labeled a straggler, so he grabbed his helmet, quickly jogged toward the field, and arrived only moments after they did. He kept his distance from the main group whenever possible to avoid verbal and physical harassment before practice.

When the three coaches agreed that most of the team was there, Coach Tyron blew his whistle and screamed, "Gentlemen, listen up. Today is the last day of summer camp." He paused when an uproar of clapping and cacophony of cheers flooded the field. He motioned with his hands for the team to quiet down. "It will be hot this morning, so make sure you drink plenty of water on the water breaks. I want everyone to give me 110% this morning. We have our first game against Ste. Genevieve in three weeks, and we will win that game." Another round of yells and screams erupted before the coach blew his whistle again and shouted, "Let's line up and get going!" He blew his whistle repeatedly as the team captains ordered the large group and spread out over the field to do calisthenics.

Allen Tanner, the senior quarterback, started the count-off: "Jumping jacks. Ready. Begin. One, two, three, four. Two, two, three, four..."

Before the ends and backs split off from the linemen, they went through a series of stretches on the ground. It was easy to feign a stretch and enjoy the contrast of the cool ground to the hot summer air. Still, if Tyron saw one of his players relaxing, he made sure they had something to think about. Coach Tyron roamed around and critiqued, kicked, and slapped, as appropriate, to ensure everyone was doing what they were supposed to be.

As the players were stretching, Coach Tyron taunted the junior varsity members while he attempted to enrage the varsity players. The coach paced through the rows of young men going through their exercises with the intensity of a rabid marine gunnery sergeant.

"Allen, Travis Sweet here says he's going to kick your ass and take your quarterback job before the end of the year."

"Oh yeah?" the senior captain replied. "Well, Coach, tell him good luck with that." His response made the varsity members laugh.

"Jordan Reynolds, Charlie Butler says he's going to smash your mouth today because you suck at defense."

"Coach, is it okay if I fuck him up this morning?"

"Conrad, McGowan here says you're a pussy."

The massive all-state senior responded, "Well, tell that dick you are what you eat."

And on it went until the coach was satisfied that the team—well, the varsity team—was warmed up and ready for practice. Tyron instructed the assistant coaches, Collier and Donnelly, to work with the backs and receiver corps, and he was going up on the hill with the linemen. He grabbed his clipboard and yelled at the guys in yellow shirts to hurry up at the water station.

"Just a sip. If you drink too much, you'll get sick."

As usual, the last few guys in line did without because all that was left in the large plastic buckets was dirt, grass, and tiny dead bugs floating in spit. And Curtis was always one of the last in line.

Coach Tyron put the linemen through the paces, hitting dummies and pushing the sled up and down an uncut hill with tall grass. He would go livid when the lines were unequal, and the young junior varsity members pushed the sled with the varsity members because, otherwise, the sled just went in a big circle. The last drill they performed was a fumble drill. The coach would call five guys into a small circle and have them hold their hands out and chop their feet. When he was satisfied they had lifted their knees high enough and long enough, he would throw the football down in the middle of the circle. Whoever got the football was done with the hill workout. They could go down the hill and catch their breath with the water buckets. The others had to return to the end of the line and try again. The longer the exercise went on, the more painful it was for those who remained. Coach Tyron loved survival-of-the-fittest workouts because he enjoyed watching the younger kids suffer at the hands of their older classmates.

Because Curtis was at the end of the line, he was grouped with four of the most prominent varsity members: Luther Conrad, Woodrow Walls, Jonathon Livingston, and Jeff Cole. Jeff Cole had no business being on a high school football team because he was a grown man nearly twenty years of age. It seemed nobody remembered him failing both third and fifth grade. Coach Tyron had a fierce and sadistic look as he blew his whistle and yelled, "GO!"

"Get those feet up, McGowan. Get those feet up... That's right. There you go."

Coach Tyron spiked the ball into the circle with great force. Curtis, embracing the inevitable and expecting to be battered, knew this would be painful, but the bounce caused the ball to go up higher than anyone expected. The four big brutes collapsed into an enormous heap, fighting for the ball, which squirted out, and Curtis bent over, picked it up, and tossed it over to the coach.

"Get the fuck out of here," he yelled at Curtis, who was already sprinting and halfway down the hill.

After practice, Curtis headed straight to Springdale to shower and cool off in the pool. His mother was already there with his brother and sister.

"Where's grandma and grandpa?" he inquired.

"Your grandma isn't feeling well today, so they stayed home. … Did you put sunscreen on?"

"No. Do you think I need it?"

"Do you want to burn? Get over here."

As she applied the greasy white lotion onto his neck, shoulders, and back, he saw a stunning blonde lifeguard with a trendy shag haircut patrolling her area. She wore a red one-piece bathing suit that clung tightly to the curves of her body. She cupped her hands around her mouth, blew her whistle, and waved to a pair of young boys wrestling in the water over a ball. It seemed strange to be a grown teenager and still having his mom care for him like this. Curtis wondered what it would feel like if the lifeguard put the lotion on him instead of his mother. His fantasy balloon popped when his mother tapped him on the shoulder with the bottle of lotion.

"Here…you do the front part yourself." He took the bottle, and she headed for the ladder to get into the pool.

After spending the afternoon at the pool, he left when his mom did but arrived at their house ten minutes before her.

"You're going to get a ticket, Speedy Gonzalez," his mother warned.

JoAnn made a delicious dinner that night for the four of them: pork chops, creamed spinach, mashed potatoes with brown gravy, and dinner rolls and butter. It was one of Curtis's favorite home-cooked meals. She put a large portion of the vegetables and two pork chops on a plate. She covered the food with plastic wrap and set it under a heat lamp on the kitchen counter. After taking care of her husband's plate, she called the kids back for dessert, a delicious family favorite: peanut butter sheet cake with homemade chocolate buttercream frosting.

After dinner, Curtis took another shower to remove the residual sunscreen and chlorine from his body. He quickly got dressed for the party. His mom inquired where he was going.

"I'm just going up to the Gradys'. I'm not driving anywhere tonight." JoAnn was relieved to know her son would be nearby on a Friday night.

Curtis wore the new jeans his mom bought him. They were a bit tight because he'd asked her to wash them every day for a week to soften them up, even adding a little bleach with the detergent to fade the blue denim. She was not happy about doing it, but he said he wouldn't wear them if they were stiff and stained his underwear blue. She softened and did as he'd asked. JoAnn also purchased a brand-new pair of tanned leather Dunham boots he'd requested. She thought the bright red laces were over the top, but Curtis liked them and wore them every day that week to break them in. He called them his "waffle stompers." He decided to wear his Van Halen concert shirt. It was the first time he'd worn it since April, and it hung a little off his shoulders now, but it felt comfortable.

"Aren't you going to wear a belt?"

"No, these pants are tight enough without one."

"Those pants would look better with a belt."

"I'm not going on a date, Mom. I'm going up to the Gradys'."

She left it alone at that.

Before he left, he grabbed his brown leather biker wallet, stuffed it in his back pocket, and snapped the chrome chain to a belt loop. He left his truck keys on the dresser.

"Mom, please don't lock the door tonight. I'm not taking my keys."

"Okay, have a good time. Please be home by midnight."

"Mom, it's Friday night," he pleaded.

"Alright, one o'clock…but not a minute later."

Curtis reluctantly conceded.

He walked up the gravel street to the Gradys' house. Curtis could see everyone was already inside, talking and drinking beer as he opened the door.

"It's about time, slug," Gunner yelled from across the room.

Curtis opened the refrigerator door, grabbed a remaining beer, and said, "We're almost out of beer."

"No shit. We were waiting for you, moneybags. Didn't you get paid today?" Travis asked.

"No, I haven't had a paycheck since July."

"What? How many jobs have you had this summer?" Marty asked.

"Just the two... I'm not worried; I'll get another one soon."

"Does your mom know?"

"She reminds me every day."

The group continued talking and drinking until everyone was empty. The steel trash can was overflowing with semicrushed aluminum cans.

"Where's Brad?"

"Oh, he's upstairs watching TV."

"Is he going to the party?"

"He said he might. He said he has a headache and isn't feeling that well."

"He ain't drinking, that's why," Travis diagnosed.

"We need more beer. Gunner, take us to the liquor store so we can get some beer."

"I still need to take a shower and get cleaned up," he retorted.

"Marvin?" Curtis pleaded.

"Hey, man, I'm not drinking. I'm on call tonight."

"Well, we're not asking you to drink, we're asking you to drive."

Marvin was hesitant. He didn't mind buying a six-pack for a few of the younger guys to drink with him if they weren't driving, but asking him to buy a few cases for a party—his gut told him not to do it.

"I'm sorry, guys, but I really don't want to go right now. Maybe later." Marvin thought if he could delay for a while longer, Gunner would take his shower, get dressed, and then take them.

Travis said he had to head home.

"Hey, see everyone tonight. This is going to be great."

Curtis asked Marty to go to Jeffco Market to buy beer.

"That would be too damn expensive," replied Marty.

Gunner offered, "Hey, my dad has a whole barrel of wine we could tap into."

Everyone let out a huge guffaw and made sick faces at that suggestion. Mr. Grady's red wine was known to be mean and potent. Some years were better than others, but this year's batch was still fermenting, and last year's batch was extraordinarily tart and toxic. It worked, but you paid a considerable tax to your body that the porcelain god usually collected. It was getting close to six in the evening, and Marvin said he needed to prepare for work.

"I thought you were just on call tonight?"

Marvin blushed. He was busted, and he knew it.

"I'll get you two cases of beer, but that's all. And then I'm going home. Who's coming with me? I'm not going by myself."

Curtis and Marty volunteered then collected cash from the group. They walked out to Marvin's truck. Curtis got in the front seat and handed Marvin the money. Marty had to move some of Marvin's stuff out of the way before getting in the back.

"Your truck is a pigsty," Marty muttered.

Several people were already walking around as they drove past Travis's grandfather's house. Travis, his sister Rita, and their mom talked by the trailer. Marvin honked the horn, and everybody waved.

Marty rolled down the window and yelled, "We'll be right back."

Marvin drove to Imperial Main Street and parked on the side parking lot next to the feed store. "You guys just stay in here. I'll be right back."

Curtis and Marty stayed in the truck and talked about the party. Curtis asked Marty if he recognized any of the people who were already there.

"A few," is all he would offer.

Marty rolled down the window, lit a cigarette, tilt his head to the sky, and waited. Curtis watched two cats chase each other over by the Imperial Feed Store. Marvin still wasn't back when the train signal began banging the alarm, and flashing lights dropped with the arms to stop traffic on Main Street. The roar of three Frisco engines was deafening as the locomotives crossed the intersection heading north with an assortment of boxcars, gondolas, and covered hoppers. Marvin came around the corner carrying two cases of canned Busch beer in his arms, carefully stepping down off the sidewalk to make a straight line back to his Suburban. Marty got out of the truck to grab and hold the cases of beer so Marvin could open the tailgate.

They had to wait several minutes for the train to pass and for the line of cars to clear off Main Street. Marvin made the left when he saw an opening, crossed the tracks, and hurried through the changing light at the state highway. They were back on Montebello Road a few minutes later, heading back to the Gradys' to put the beer in the cooler.

As they approached Travis's house, Curtis was the first to see that the crowd of people had more than tripled since they'd left. Marty was the first to spot a pony keg sitting in a blue tub on the driveway.

"Hey," Marty yelled to Marvin. "Stop here for a minute."

Curtis saw kids walking around with beer in plastic cups. As Curtis was prone to do, he acted without thinking. He reached over and flipped on Marvin's flood and flashing lights, grabbed the microphone, and switched the radio to the PA function:

"EVERYONE, FREEZE! STOP WHERE YOU ARE AND GET OUT YOUR IDS."

Immediately, people started throwing their beer cups down on the ground and running. It was one of the funniest things Curtis had ever seen. Marty laughed hysterically, but Marvin found no humor in the situation as he angrily grabbed the microphone and turned off the lights. Travis found no humor in it either.

Travis came running over to them, shouting, "You assholes! That was some pretty mean shit you did there."

Curtis took all the blame—or credit, depending on who you asked—for the prank.

Curtis stayed, while Marty rode back to the Gradys' with Marvin to put the beer in the cooler. A long line formed at the pony keg as the kids returned to refill their cups. Marvin left as soon as possible, wanting to get far away from the party. Marty walked back with Gunner and Richie to join the large gathering that must have included over forty people by now.

Richie was talking to a couple of girls he knew from band camp. Curtis came over, and Richie nodded as he joined them. "Nice shirt. I wish I could have gone to that concert."

The girls nodded their heads in agreement. Richie didn't bother introducing the girls to Curtis, so he asked them their names.

"My name's Theresa, and this is my friend Rhonda."

When Rhonda looked at Curtis with large brown eyes, her cheeks flushed a bit.

Curtis responded, "Hi, Theresa. Hi, Rhonda. I'm glad you could come. I hope you have a good time tonight."

Rhonda smiled then put her hand up to cover her mouth out of habit.

Theresa elbowed Rhonda lightly.

"What?" Rhonda said with a grimace that contained a remnant of her smile.

Theresa said, "We'll see you guys around." She grabbed Rhonda by the wrist and led her away.

After they left, Curtis asked Richie, "What was that all about?"

"Dude, I think she likes you."

"Theresa?"

"No, Rhonda, you dumbass."

From across the lawn, Curtis noticed Theresa and Rhonda talking. He slammed his beer and tossed the plastic cup in a trash bag hanging from a low-lying tree branch. Fueled with sixteen ounces of liquid courage, he approached the two girls.

Gazing into Rhonda's eyes, he said, "On a hot summer night, would you offer your throat to a wolf with a red rose?"

Rhonda blushed, and Theresa rolled her eyes and said, "Seriously? Can't you come up with anything better than that?"

Theresa grabbed her friend by the arm and said, "Let's go before he says something really stupid."

Curtis watched the two girls join another group of girls, and when Theresa saw he was still looking at them, she said something to the group to make them laugh. Curtis could not believe how badly he'd fumbled trying to impress Rhonda with his not-so-witty charm.

Fewer things sting like the pain of rejection. Nothing multiplies that ache like the fear of blowing something perceived as significant. As Curtis wandered away, he pondered why he'd said what he had and why he felt the way he did. His actions always seemed to go differently than how he'd expected.

He ended up in the shadows and considered just going home. He could not bear the thought of seeing those lovely brown eyes scornfully looking at him. Peering into the sky through the trees, he asked the universe what he needed to do for a second chance.

Just then, he felt a light touch on his shoulder.

After a gentle laugh, she whispered in his ear, "Can I tell you a secret?"

"Yes, of course you can."

"I freaking LOVE Meatloaf. Give me a few minutes to shake loose from my momma bear, and I'll come and find you."

<h1 style="text-align:center">CHAPTER 27</h1>

<h1 style="text-align:center">Party</h1>

Rhonda Mead was a petite, winsome girl with curly, shoulder-length auburn hair that hued closer to brown than red. She was just two months shy of her sweet sixteen birthday on the night of the party. She had a beautiful smile, but for the time being, she was reluctant to share it because of her braces. Her large brown eyes were open to seeing things others couldn't. Like most teenage girls, she longed to be accepted by her peers.

She wanted the other girls to see her as "normal." She was terrified that her desire to get good grades and her participation in choir and band would make her seem "geeky." Most of all, she wanted a boyfriend. All the girls she looked up to had one. When she heard rumors about a party on Friday night, she called her best friend, Theresa, to confirm and gossip.

Theresa and Rhonda were at band camp when they learned more about the party from Richie. Not only did Richie confirm the reality of the party, but he outright offered them an invite. Rhonda thought about it for the rest of the morning and on the way home. She decided that she wanted to go, but not by herself. When Rhonda called Theresa, she convinced her to accompany her. Rhonda knew better than to ask her mom if she could go to a party when her mom had no idea who would be there, and certainly not if the party would be outside with no adult supervision. So, Rhonda did what most teenagers do—she asked to spend the night with Theresa. Her mother had no problem with that, completely unaware of any party.

Theresa was a voluptuous young woman with blonde hair and a pretty face and a loud mouth who could be harsh and bold. Like Rhonda, she would be entering high school as a freshman this fall. Since she developed early, she had to contend with an assault of trash talk thrown her way from boys and girls alike since she was twelve years old. And being from Jefferson County, she often had to verbally defend herself against men twice her age. She had excellent musical abilities and fit in perfectly with the Windsor High School marching band. She was also active with her friends at Windsor Baptist Church.

Theresa had no problem getting boys to go out with her. The problem for the boys was when they tried to get physically intimate with her. Any rush to do anything more than hold her hand during couples skating at the roller rink was swiftly rebuffed, likely resulting in her calling her mom to pick her up early. When that happened, there was never a second date.

Her parents trusted her so completely that they rarely, if ever, said no to her. When she told her parents she was going to a party, her mother mildly protested.

"Mother, you know I don't drink. Besides, if I'm not there, who is going to watch over these people? I would rather help drunk kids get home than read about my classmates dying in a car accident." Theresa whittled her mother down with enough good excuses to get permission. She said nothing about Rhonda spending the night, though.

By eight o'clock, the party was in full swing. Cars lined the street on both sides. Some people, including Theresa, parked in the American Legion lot and walked a few blocks to the party. Travis had brought out his grandparents' large stereo into the garage and had it playing very loud. There was constant arguing about what to play on the radio. The girls wanted to dance, and the boys wanted to rock. Initially, they would take turns. One minute, they would listen to "Who Are You?" and six minutes later, they would listen to "Le Freak." Eventually, a consensus was reached, resulting in many Boston, Supertramp, and Fleetwood Mac songs.

Curtis couldn't get Richie's words out of his head, plus Rhonda had sought him out and whispered in his ear. Had that really happened or was he losing his mind? Were there really such things as miracles, and had he experienced one? He could not help but notice his breathing was rapid and his palms were sweaty. He was on a roller-coaster ride of emotions. He constantly scanned the crowd for Rhonda and Theresa. He spotted Theresa, but she was by herself. Theresa would look his way, but she turned her head away whenever he made eye contact with her.

Curtis ran into Elizabeth and Fern. Elizabeth was wearing white jeans and a dark blue tank top with "Super Groovy" in yellow lettering. Her hefty bust line made the words challenging to read. Fern was a year younger, but having an older sister caused her to be mature for her age. Fern was slightly envious of the older kids. She anxiously waited for her own chest and hips to develop, but in the meantime, she relied on her wit and smart-aleck mouth to draw attention away from her young age.

Curtis chatted with Elizabeth for a bit, while Fern just listened. Elizabeth spotted someone else she knew and excused herself to go catch up with them. Fern rolled her eyes, hugged Curtis, and quickly followed after her sister.

As Curtis loitered about, he noticed the line at the pony keg was gone. He walked over, grabbed a clear plastic cup, and went to fill it, but only a trickle came out. He pressurized the keg with the attached pump and tried again. This time, the beer flowed nicely with added foam.

"Would you pour me one of those, please?" a voice said from behind.

He turned around. It was Rhonda.

"That girl is driving me crazy tonight," she said apologetically.

Curtis said, "Here, take mine," and handed her his cup. He grabbed another plastic cup and filled it up.

"I'm not much of a beer drinker," Rhonda confessed. "I really don't like it, to be honest."

"It takes some getting used to," Curtis offered. "It's better when it's cold. I think a partially numb throat makes it go down better."

There was an awkward silence but not for long.

"I got the *Bat Out of Hell* album for my birthday last year and have played it a thousand times. I've been a Meatloaf fan ever since."

"Seriously?"

"Seriously. I know every word to every song."

"No way."

"Curtis, I can prove it to you right now…"

"How would you do that?" Curtis inquired.

"Well, first, you owe me more than one rose. If you listen carefully, he says, 'red roses.' Second, it wasn't 'a wolf' but 'the wolf.' But most importantly, Curtis, you are not a wolf…unless you're a werewolf, and since there's no full moon tonight, I'm not worried."

Curtis stared again into her brown eyes; their delightful twinkling matched her silver smile.

"Have you ever heard of the *Rocky Horror Picture Show*?" she asked.

"No, what's it about?"

"Well, from what I heard, it is weird and disturbing. My cousin told me about it. She said I should go see it because Meatloaf plays one of the characters in it and sings."

"Is it a movie?" Curtis asked.

"I think it is a play and a movie…at the same time…but I haven't seen it, so I'm not sure."

"That sounds interesting," Curtis replied.

"I think it sounds silly, but I'd still like to hear Meatloaf sing. …Do you live around here?"

"Yeah, my mom and dad have a house down the hill right over there." Curtis pointed in the general direction until he realized he was pointing into darkness across the road.

"How long have you lived here?"

"As long as I can remember. I think my mom and dad moved here when I was in first grade."

Rhonda and Curtis strolled around talking and sipping their beers. When Curtis finished his beer, Rhonda said, "Here, take mine. I really don't like it." He saw the lip gloss prints on the plastic cup and turned the cup so he drank from the same place. Rhonda kept forgetting about her braces and smiled for the rest of the night. She reached out her hand, and he accepted it. They continued mingling and talking to other people as a couple.

Eventually, they ran into Theresa. Theresa saw Rhonda was genuinely happy and chose to ignore the person who was the reason for it. Realizing she had lost her friend for the evening, she went back with the other girls to dance and gossip.

"That was awkward," Curtis confessed.

"She'll get over it. She's so bossy sometimes."

They shared another moment of awkward silence.

Rhonda turned and locked eyes with him. "Do you know if there's anywhere we can go where there are fewer people?"

Curtis thought for a moment. "We could walk over to the American Legion Hall. They have swings over there and—"

"Curtis, I don't want to swing…" She leaned up into him and kissed him on the lips.

Instantly, the universe felt aligned with rightness and blissfulness.

Curtis scanned the property, and the only thing that came to mind was the backyard. The problem was that Travis's mom was carefully guarding the gate to the backyard. She had brought out her portable lounge chair and was doing her best to chaperone the party from that chair. Keeping the kids restricted to the lit part of the shared front yards made her job easier.

After careful thought, Curtis figured out another way. He took Rhonda by the hand and said, "Come with me."

Curtis and Rhonda weaved in and out of the crowd of people and made it over to the back of the trailer where Travis and his family lived, right next door to Travis's grandparents. They were about to disappear into the shadows when Curtis heard a familiar voice.

"Where do you two think you're going?"

It was Fern. Curtis smiled at Fern, but Rhonda frowned at her. Fern rolled her eyes and said, "Whatever. Have fun." Fern turned and, with drooping shoulders, walked slowly away.

Curtis and Rhonda crept carefully down the fence line in the darkness. They could still make out the music, but the voices from the party were faint. The waxing crescent moon only provided enough light to make the shadows darker.

"How are we…" Rhonda hadn't finished the question before Curtis lifted her and set her down on the other side of the small chain-link fence. She almost yelled when he lifted her because it was so unexpected.

Curtis ensured she was clear then grabbed the top of the fence and pulled himself up and over. He landed on his feet and was quickly next to her again.

There was a small barn in the back of the yard, and from within it came some hissing and cackling and a single honk.

"What is that?" Rhonda said as she clutched Curtis tightly.

"It's okay. They have geese. It's a good thing they're put away, or they would chase us right out of here."

"Seriously? Do they bite?"

"Yeah, they'll nip you if you get close enough, but what you have to worry about are their wings. They will flat-out bludgeon you with them if you get too close."

Curtis muttered, "I wish we had a blanket."

Rhonda hugged him tightly, whispering, "We don't need a blanket." She kissed him passionately and without reservation.

Curtis had kissed other girls, but none ever kissed him back like this. Being in uncharted waters was terrifying and exciting at the same time. As he tended to do, he tried to think through what was happening. How could he lead when he didn't know where he was going? How far was this going to go? He could only hold on for dear life and enjoy the ride. His knees began to buckle, and his body started responding to the emotional and physical stimulation as hormones surged through his body. Rhonda sensed this and guided him down to the ground, placing his hand on her right breast outside her shirt as she overwhelmed him with her relentless wet kisses.

They lay on the ground side by side as they kissed. Rhonda's hand rubbed his thigh and began exploring. She aggressively rubbed the bulge she discovered inside the stonewashed blue jeans. Curtis slipped his hand from on top of her shirt to inside it, then under the lacy bra, touching her breast. She let out a soft moan and pulled back. Curtis fumbled around her back, trying to figure out how to unhook her bra. Rhonda stopped long enough to sit up and do in an instant what he had been trying to do for several minutes.

Curtis was mesmerized by everything he felt. He was eager to enjoy with all his senses. Her kisses had a metallic taste. With every part of her body he touched, his mind screamed for more.

Realizing he was approaching the point of no return, he stopped what he was doing.

"Are you okay?" Rhonda asked.

Curtis confessed that he felt out of control.

Rhonda laughed, hugged him, and snuggled her head under his chin.

They talked as they held each other closely. Curtis began to share all the things he wanted to do with Rhonda. His list was nearly endless: He described dates to the Pevely drive-in, to Imperial Bowl, to Rock Roll-O-Rena, putt-putt golf, motorcycle rides to the Mississippi and Kimmswick. There was the approaching Apple Butter Festival. Rhonda laughed and accepted all the proposed dates.

"What about kissing Rhonda?" she asked.

"Oh yeah, a lot of that," he agreed, and just like that, the young lovers were into round two.

The kissing led to more heavy petting, and as Curtis embarked once again into uncharted waters of intimacy, he let his hands dare to explore further. When his hands found the waistline of her jeans, she instinctively lifted her hips up as Curtis attempted to maneuver his hand under the tight denim fabric. Proving too tight, he found the brass snap with his free hand, popped it out of the socket, and then pulled the zipper down. Once again, she lifted her hips and helped him pull the jeans down off her hips. His hand found the lacy fabric of her underwear much easier to slide underneath, and with her help guiding his hand from outside her underwear, he found himself touching her most intimate area with moans of approval.

Her other hand was not idle, rediscovering the bulge pressing into her leg. The young lovers' passions were so engrossed in their pursuit of more pleasure that they didn't hear the music stop or the screaming of people from the front yard where the party had taken a turn for the worse.

Curtis liked this girl and didn't want to rush things. He also imagined having sex for the first time should be in a bed, not a back seat or in a backyard next to a barn. Rhonda showed him clearly that a girlfriend would make his dreary life more exciting. It seemed to him this was a match made in heaven. Meanwhile, they enjoyed the pleasures of touching and pleasing each other while they kissed.

Curtis continued to fondle and rub the tender and silky-smooth areas of Rhonda's body but immediately stopped what he was doing when he heard the latch of the gate release from up by the house. He rolled over to his side and saw the tiny figure of someone in the shadows swiftly drawing near.

"What is it?" Rhonda asked as she got to her feet, pulled her pants back up, and snapped them tight. She bent over to pick her bra off the ground and crumbled it into her hand.

Fern approached them less than a minute later, slightly out of breath because she had run down the hill.

"Guys, you need to get back up there. One of the girls was throwing up before she passed out. They called the police, and paramedics are on the way."

Curtis ascended the hill with Fern as Rhonda got her brassiere back on, brushed out her hair, and dusted the grass off her jeans the best she could. Rhonda ran to catch up with them.

As soon as they got to the gate, Curtis was met with an angry stare from Travis's mom. Theresa came up to them and snatched Rhonda by the hand.

"Rhonda, we have to go."

Rhonda tried to hug Curtis and kiss him goodbye, but Theresa wouldn't release her vicelike grip on Rhonda's wrist.

"Now, Rhonda! I'm not kidding. We have to leave NOW."

Rhonda called back to Curtis, "Can I call you tomorrow?"

"Yes, I'd like that," Curtis yelled back.

Theresa pulled Rhonda down the street toward her car like a toddler who didn't want to leave the swimming pool. Rhonda tried to talk to Curtis while looking back over her shoulder.

"What's your number?" she shouted.

Realizing the futility of yelling a telephone number at her, he replied, "It's in the phone book. I have the same name as my dad."

Rhonda smiled again at him before slapping Theresa's hand to let her loose. "I'm coming, I'm coming," is all Curtis heard before she disappeared into the evening darkness.

Several minutes later, an ambulance and a Jefferson County deputy showed up.

The paramedics identified the young girl, and after she threw up several more times, they correctly diagnosed her with acute alcohol poisoning. When she demonstrated she could hold down water, they called and released her to the care of her parents, who were unhappy with what had happened. The paramedics left about an hour later, but the sheriff's deputies remained and took statements from the few people lingering around. They spent most of the time talking to Travis's mother, and after hearing what she had to say, they issued a warning, not a summons.

Curtis offered to stay and help clean up. His offer was appreciated and accepted. He left shortly after midnight and would be home well before his curfew.

Despite how it had ended, it was the best night of Curtis's life. He walked home high on the memories of Rhonda's touch, which was better than anything he could ever have eaten, drank, or inhaled. He felt like he was floating on the moon instead of walking the short distance to his house.

He entered the house and passed through the living room on his way to his room. His mother was curled up next to his father on the couch watching a late-night movie. Observing them, he began to understand what it meant to be in love. He stared at his parents with a dazed smile and didn't even hear his mother when she asked him a question. He went into the bedroom, shut the door, and got undressed. The mirror attached to the bureau he shared with his brother reflected his image, and for the first time in his life, Curtis liked what he saw. He turned out the light, got under his blanket, and thought of Rhonda. Thinking about someone other than himself was an incredible and freeing feeling. He fell into a deep and dreamless sleep. His reality was now better than any dream he could have had.

As Curtis walked out of the living room, he heard his mother say, "I think you need to talk to your son. I think he's doing drugs or something. Did you see that look on his face?" Curtis Sr. remained silent and went back to reading his book.

Chapter 28

Telephone Line

Rhonda did her best to keep up with Theresa as they returned to her car.

Theresa's unfiltered thoughts interrupted the allegro rhythm of their footsteps as she frantically dug around in her purse for her car keys.

"I can't believe what happened tonight. Can you?"

Rhonda replied, "I'm still not exactly sure what happened. I heard a girl was poisoned, and someone called an ambulance."

"It was alcohol poisoning, Rhonda. Someone brought a bottle of liquor. A small group of them were passing the bottles around. I mean, I knew there would be some beer, but I saw three different kinds of booze."

The girls got in and buckled. Theresa pulled the car out of the American Legion parking lot and headed for home. They passed two Jefferson County police cars with flashing lights heading down the darkened street they'd just traversed.

The experience was surreal, and Rhonda was in emotional freefall. Her life had changed so much in the last hour, going from newfound blissful pleasures and longing to a frantic and worrisome emergency she had no control over. She felt frustrated, sad, and disappointed. She wanted to go home and call Curtis to ensure he got home okay.

Theresa continued caustically, "I knew someone was going to get sick when they started chugging Southern Comfort. I tried to get them to slow down, but they just laughed and made fun of me because I wouldn't join them."

"I think people just wanted to have a good time and drank too much too fast," Rhonda offered.

"Well, since you mentioned good times, where were you? I searched all over for you and couldn't find you anywhere."

"I was hanging out with Curtis in the backyard where it was quiet."

"I thought they said the backyard was off-limits?"

"Well, no one stopped us from going back there."

Theresa drove in silence as she turned toward her home.

"Are you taking me home?"

"No, you're spending the night just like you told your mom."

"I'd rather go home, if that's okay."

"Rhonda, you can't go home. If your mom finds out you were at a party with boys and alcohol, your summer is basically over."

"Yeah, you're right, I suppose."

They arrived at Theresa's house, and her mother, Mrs. Shewey, met them at the door in a faded pink, quilted housecoat and fuzzy slippers.

"You girls are home early tonight. Did you have a good time?"

"I did," Rhonda said with warmth returning to her face.

"It was okay, but there were more people there than I thought would be there," Theresa added.

Mrs. Shewey frowned. "Were there a lot of boys? How much alcohol was involved?"

Theresa replied, "It was about fifty-fifty, wouldn't you say, Rhonda?"

Rhonda sheepishly nodded in agreement.

"Well, I'm no fool, and if there was a party with teenage boys, there is going to be alcohol. I'm just glad you're both home for the night."

"We're going to get cleaned up and ready for bed."

"Okay, good night, girls."

The girls walked to the end of the house. Theresa went into the bathroom, and Rhonda went into Theresa's room to get her things out of a grocery bag. Theresa came into the bedroom while Rhonda was getting undressed, just in time to see dry grass fall out of her shirt as she pulled it off. Both of their faces flushed in unison.

"We need to talk, Rhonda. Tell me…where did you and Curtis wander off to?"

"We just went for a walk, that's all."

"Rhonda, you're such a liar. I can tell when you're lying because you look down at your feet and rub your wrists."

"We just went back by the barn where it was quiet so we could hang out and talk."

"Did he try to kiss you?"

Rhonda blushed again.

"He kissed you? Oh my God, he kissed you!"

Rhonda tried to look her friend in the eyes, but her neck muscles wouldn't lift her head, and in a frozen, downward stare, she replied, "Yes."

"Wow. Unbelievable. I'm shocked, really. Do you even know who this guy is?"

"I really don't want to talk about it right now."

Theresa got off the bed and started pacing around the room, scratching her head. Rhonda was quiet as she gathered her thoughts, knowing that every answer she gave would lead to more questions. She excused herself to go to the bathroom.

When Rhonda came back into the bedroom, she shut the door.

Theresa continued her questioning. "Did you kiss him back?"

"A little."

"Oh, no, Rhonda…you didn't actually…like, make out with this guy?"

Rhonda's eyes watered up as she told Theresa, "I like him. I really like him."

"Rhonda, he's a nobody. He's not in the band; he's not in any of the honors classes. I bet he doesn't even make the football team this year."

"So? What has that got to do with anything?"

"Let me get this right: You make out with a guy who's basically a stranger. What's next? Are you going to go steady with him? Are you going to let him ask you to Homecoming?"

Rhonda's frustration gave way to anger, and she smacked her friend across the face. Startled by the sudden outburst, Rhonda stammered, "I'm sorry, Theresa. I want to go home. Please take me home."

Theresa let the sting dissipate from her cheek. Then, calmly, she said, "Now, Rhonda, we've already talked about this." She sat Rhonda down on the bed and joined her. The two girls hugged and cried, and then Rhonda told her everything.

For all the talking Theresa had done, she was now speechless. Rhonda was sure her friend would see that she had genuine feelings for Curtis. They had a connection that was more than physical.

The girls finished getting changed. Theresa put on a blue cotton night-gown, and Rhonda changed into bright yellow sweatpants and a brown Windsor Owl T-shirt. The two girls shared the twin-sized bed. Theresa reached over and turned the light out.

Theresa spoke into the darkness, "You know you can't see him anymore, right?"

Rhonda squeezed her eyes tight, but not tight enough to keep the tears from running down her cheek.

"Did you hear me?" A few minutes went by. "I know you're not sleeping. Rhonda, trust me…you don't know boys the way I do. My mother told me all about their wicked ways. They start with promises and kisses, but before you know it, one hand is up your sweater, and their other hand is trying to pull your pants off. You'll wind up pregnant before you can finish school."

Rhonda replied, "Can we please talk about this tomorrow? I'm exhausted."

"Sure. Rhonda, you're my best friend. We've been friends since first grade. You're smart and talented. You're a pretty girl with a future. I don't want to see you throw it away for a loser burnout from Imperial. You just met him." The room was quiet when she continued, "You know what I think? I think he was drinking and took advantage of you."

"He had one beer."

"At least two beers. You said he drank yours. And who knows how much he drank before coming to the party."

Rhonda turned her back to her friend and stared at the clock radio on the nightstand. A couple of hours ago, she thought she was in love. Now she was confused, and her best friend was breaking her heart.

The next morning, the girls woke up and took turns taking showers before getting dressed. Theresa made her bed while Rhonda dried and brushed her hair.

Rhonda's tired face was reflected in the mirror. She didn't want to rush Theresa and appear rude, but she wanted to go home to think things through on her own. She loved Theresa but knew how dominating and demanding she could be. Rhonda figured she would stay to eat breakfast and then call her mom to come pick her up. She just wanted to go home and call Curtis. She needed to hear from him what his thoughts were about her and what his plans were beyond high school.

They went down the hall to the dining room and discovered Mrs. Shewey had made scrambled eggs, bacon, and toast with fresh-squeezed orange juice. Mrs. Shewey served the two girls and asked, "Did you girls stay up all night? You look kind of tired this morning."

"No, not all night, Mother. We talked for an hour or so."

"Really? I love gossip."

Rhonda's heart melted when Theresa said, "Mother, I think you need to explain some things to Rhonda. She won't listen to me."

"What kind of things, dear?"

"Birds and the bees kind of things…especially the part about pretty girls getting stung."

"Oh, dear…"

Theresa shared what she knew, and Mrs. Shewey listened attentively without interruption. She didn't say anything until the girls finished their breakfast. Mrs. Shewey whisked away a nearly uneaten breakfast from Rhonda and cleared the rest of the table. A short time later, she returned with her Bible. She spent the next hour with both girls and explained God's plan regarding purity, sex, and marriage before praying with and for them. "Trust me, dear, it's for the best for you and the boy."

Theresa pulled the phone directory out of the closet, found the number, and wrote it down. She handed the piece of paper to her friend. "Do you want to call him or should I?"

JoAnn was at the table balancing the checkbook when the telephone rang. She got up to answer it.

"Hello?"

"Hi. Is Curtis available? I really need to speak with him."

"May I ask who is calling, please?"

"My name is Theresa."

"Hold on a minute, Curtis? You have a phone call…"

"Who is it?"

"A girl named Theresa?"

"Hello?"

"Is this Curtis?"

"Yeah, who's this?"

"This is Theresa. I'm calling to tell you that Rhonda can't see you anymore. Last night was a mistake. Please do not call her."

Curtis heard the phone line click before it went silent. His mind raced with a dozen questions that would go unanswered.

JoAnn noticed the blank stare on her son's face. "Are you alright? Is everything okay? Who is Theresa?"

Curtis ignored his mother, slammed the phone down, and stormed out of the house. He was consumed by inexpressible torment. Last night, everything had been so perfect until the ambulance came.

The summer sun was rising high into the late-morning sky, radiating relentless heat. He had nowhere to go. If he went back inside, he would face his mother and a barrage of questions. The anguish in his soul begged for relief, but there was no one to talk to…no one who would really understand what he was going through. The bitterness of loss overwhelmed him, and behind the garage, he cried in an uncontrollable state of rage and without relief.

CHAPTER 29

Turn to Stone

A Monarch butterfly landed on a tiny branch of an elm tree on a warm day in mid-September 1979 as JoAnn was taking down sheets from her clothesline. The elm tree was letting go of its yellow leaves in preparation for winter. Below the butterfly, a stubborn leaf dangled from the branch hanging by a dried-out thread. The leaf vibrated in the autumn breeze until the thin stem broke. The leaf flittered down and disappeared within the mass of foliage accumulated below. In time, the leaves would decay and enrich the soil from which new plant life would eventually emerge. The butterfly opened its wings and caught the last wind current heading to Mexico. She hurried along as fast as she could flutter to become part of a beautiful pillar. Having fulfilled one purpose, the butterfly would one day return to fulfill another by giving life to new butterflies, oblivious to hurricanes wreaking havoc in Florida.

The new school year started on Monday. Officially a junior, Curtis began counting down the days until he graduated. The previous year, the school counselor persuaded him to fill out his schedule. His mother had made it clear that he could not attend college without scholarships, so Curtis gave up on pursuing higher education. Instead of taking college preparation courses, he only signed up for the classes he was interested in.

His morning classes were broken up with a study hall period before lunch. He enjoyed English, history, and natural science classes but only took the math courses required to graduate. Curtis front-loaded his schedule so only three classes remained after lunch: Physical Education, Advanced Woodworking, and English Composition. Curtis looked forward to Miss Jackson's English Composition class because she included creative writing and poetry. Curtis heard rumors her classes were challenging. Since it was an elective class, few people signed up for it.

His mother allowed him to drive the truck to school, provided he continued looking for a part-time job. Curtis agreed to look but didn't know where the time would come from between school and football commitments. He hoped he would see Rhonda around, and she would give him some clarity on what he could do to see her again.

While it was nice to sleep in thirty minutes, he discovered the congested traffic near the school and the crowded parking lot took exponentially more time to negotiate the longer he waited to leave. In addition, he had to walk further to get to class on time. By the end of the week, he adjusted his thirty-minute morning snooze to ten minutes to avoid the hassle of dealing with late-arriving cars.

Time spent at football practice after school was streamlined. Unlike the two-a-day summer camp conditioning sessions, the after-school practices were more gamelike and took significantly less time. He was home before six o'clock and would often eat dinner with his dad.

All week long, Miss Jackson's English Composition class was the perfect class to end the day. Curtis's initial impression of her was a short, tired-looking elderly woman counting down the days to retirement. However, when she stood in front of the class, her energy pulsed through the classroom with enthusiasm as she talked about the elements of short stories. Miss Jackson passed out two papers listing novels and short stories. The first list was labeled "required reading," and the second was "suggested reading." While the suggested readings were college-level books and stories, she said she would give extra credit to students who accepted her challenge.

The in-class discussions were lively, with no homework. That changed on Friday when she told everyone to pick a short story and write an essay on any element that interested them. Kyle Cooper, a senior, raised his hand in objection. Curtis was having similar thoughts but kept them to himself.

Miss Jackson said, "This is an elective class, Kyle. It's for people who enjoy reading. Don't think of reading as homework. Reading and writing aren't homework if you enjoy them."

The class became awkwardly silent. Miss Jackson broke the silence by adding, "Look, teachers have been telling you what to think and how to write for the last ten years. I'm challenging you to express yourself to justify your thoughts and ideas. Please don't deprive me of learning from you."

While Curtis was at school, JoAnn went out to the mailbox. As she retrieved the mail, a fragrant scent from the mailbox reached her nose. JoAnn thumbed through the stack of mail and found an invoice from Columbia House Record and Tape Club. She ripped it open and cursed out loud when she saw a bill for one hundred and seventeen dollars and cursed again louder when she saw the big red bold-faced letters saying PAST DUE. Then she saw a letter for Curtis without a return address. She held the envelope to her nose and recognized it as the source of the floral and citrus scent. Her curiosity got the best of her, and she opened the letter. She skimmed the single-page letter, front and back, then read it again, slower. While she was reading it, her hand began to shake. The letter was signed "All My Love, Katie." JoAnn momentarily forgot about the invoice. Her rage intensified as she tore the letter and envelope into tiny pieces and dropped them into the trash can before walking into the house sobbing.

Curtis approached the Basement and saw a brand-new red Porsche 911 in the driveway. Going inside, he found Ronnie and Mick. Mick wore a pair of tan chinos and an unbuttoned white dress shirt revealing a thick gold rope chain hanging from his neck. His left arm was in a sling.

Curtis looked past Ronnie and asked, "Did you trade your Mustang?"

"Totaled it," Mick replied.

"Seriously? What happened?"

"I got T-boned going through an intersection over in Richmond Heights. I never saw it coming."

Ronnie said, "This lucky bastard only survived because he was drunk."

"Yes, but so was the guy that hit me. I don't remember much. I was hanging out with some friends at Forest Park. I left, and one minute I'm driving home, and then I wake up in a hospital bed at Saint Mary's."

Ronnie said, "This lucky bastard hit the jackpot and goes out and buys that turbo Volkswagen parked out in the driveway."

Mick glared at Ronnie and said, "You don't even know what you're talking about."

Ronnie said, "I'll let you figure that out when you have to start buying parts for it. I got to run."

Ronnie left, and Curtis asked, "Where is everyone?"

"It beats me. I saw Ronnie when I pulled up and we've just been hanging out here. Do you want to see the car?"

Curtis went outside with Mick and admired the car.

Mick said, "I can't do much driving because of my left arm, but hopefully the cast comes off in a few more weeks. But check this out."

Mick had wasted no time in upgrading the car stereo system. Mick turned on the radio, pushed in a tape, and twisted the volume nob. Curtis's ears tingled with the sounds of an electronic wind, like the exhaust of an alien spaceship. The eerie sound was reminiscent of the beginning of Montrose's "Space Station #5," but then echoing guitars broke in. For the next twenty minutes, Curtis sat mesmerized by the sounds bouncing around the speakers and the flashing lights on the graphic equalizer.

The opening song was enchanting, full of hyperkinetic drumming and otherworldly sounds held together by booming bass and pulsating guitar chords. He took the cassette case from Mick. The artwork revealed a red star inside a circle lit underwater with stars in the background. "Rush 2112" revealed the album's artist and title. Mick did his best to air drum with a broken arm.

The song told a story about a future that struggled with freedom, control, and beauty, using religious imagery and ending in sadness.

After they listened to the album, Mick told Curtis he promised his dad he would go into alcohol rehab. When Curtis asked why, Mick said his dad retrieved all the car's contents before it was towed away to the scrapyard; he was unhappy with what he found inside.

"The way I see it, Curtis, I don't need to get drunk anymore. I just want to experience the freedom of driving fast, enjoying the music, and, on occasion, smoking a little reefer in the evening to chill out. I think the car accident was a wake-up call of sorts for me to get my shit together."

Curtis got out of the car. He felt envious of the rich kid from the county as Mick fired up the beautiful German sports car and drove away. Mick's life was getting better while his was falling apart. Curtis contemplated the fairness of life and what he might do to tip the scales in his favor.

Due to Labor Day, there were no classes on Monday, so Curtis went to Springdale one last time before they closed for the season. He spent most of the day in the pool but couldn't resist playing his Mata Hari pinball game one more time or drinking down one more root beer float while listening to "So Into You." He never got a chance to say goodbye to Sammy or Danny.

Curtis's enthusiasm and happiness for his junior year was short-lived. The first week of school had been uneventful. Except for Advanced Woodworking, he liked all his teachers. Mr. Cannon removed all the fun out of woodworking. It seemed unfair that some kids could work on their project and Mr. Cannon never said a word to them. Whatever Curtis did was critiqued harshly, loudly, and publicly. It was frustrating to be constantly called out and critiqued instead of taught.

Kyle and another student dropped Miss Jackson's class, but their departure did not hinder her from moderating a lively, thought-provoking discussion about Shirley Jackson's "The Lottery."

Curtis went to football practice after school. Everyone was eager for the first game of the season scheduled for Friday night. The Windsor Owls would host the Hillsboro Hawks, and Coach Tyron would not tolerate a home-opener loss. The intensity of his remarks carried over into overly aggressive actions during the practice, and Curtis McGowan was the first to physically suffer from the Coach Tyron's command..

Jordan Reynolds came off the line on the first play, and as he hit the practice pad Curtis was holding, his arm slid up and his forearm smashed Curtis in the throat. The punter's helmet offered little protection to his face or neck, and for weeks, he had suffered hands getting through to his nose and mouth, but this was different. The hit was so violent, he fell to the ground and vomited.

Coach Tyron blew his whistle and stormed over to the junior varsity player rolling on the ground, yelling, "What the fuck, McGowan? Are you puking on my field? What the hell is wrong with you?"

Oscar Collier, the assistant coach, realized the situation required more than a scolding and called the trainers over to look at the hurting player.

"Get him out of here and clean this mess up," Coach Tyron said as he returned to the other players.

The trainers helped Curtis off the field, and when they were sure he could breathe okay and swallow, they let him sit there holding an ice pack against his throat.

As Curtis watched the team practice, the lights in his brain turned on. He realized he was a square peg trying to force himself into a round hole. Maybe for a better man, Curtis might be willing to give a part of himself up, but he looked at Coach Tyron with rage and hate. He hoped he would lose every football game he ever coached. Nobody said a word when he grabbed his helmet, slowly walked to his truck, and drove home.

He skipped practice on Wednesday, which didn't go unnoticed. When he came to school on Thursday, a group of seniors were waiting for him when he arrived.

Luther Conrad said, "Your ass is grass if you aren't at practice today."

Jordan Reynolds added, "You need to toughen up, you fucking pussy."

After lunch, Curtis went to his truck, gathered all his football gear, and went to the locker room. He entered and heard a radio somewhere playing "Long Haired Country Boy."

Curtis saw Luther and Jordan in the coach's office. Curtis noticed the fire escape door was propped open, and other varsity players were standing around smoking. Curtis recognized the weed smell, but he ignored it. He entered Coach Tyron's office and set the equipment on the floor.

Luther said, "Awe, you are going to be a baby and quit?"

Jordan said, "Good fucking riddance."

Coach Tyron finally spoke up, "What the fuck do you think you're doing, McGowan? You pick that gear up, and you better be ready to play hard this afternoon."

"I quit," Curtis replied.

The coach stood up and leaned over his desk, demanding, "What did you just say?"

Jordan began to laugh, which angered Coach Tyron more, and he said, "You two, get out of here and close the door."

Jordan said, "See ya, wouldn't want to be ya," as he shut the door behind him.

Coach Tyron said, "You can't quit. Nobody quits on me. I've been coaching for five years, and nobody has ever quit on me."

Curtis didn't reply, which seemed to irritate the coach more.

"Do you have something to say? If not, pick your shit up and get out of here, and I'll see you this afternoon at practice."

Curtis opened the door and walked out without picking up the football equipment.

"You get back here and pick this gear up. Nobody quits on me, McGowan."

Curtis kept walking and never looked back.

"If you quit me, McGowan, you will be a quitter for the rest of your life."

Curtis went to the cafeteria and ate a quick lunch before returning to the locker room to dress out for gym class. The equipment he turned in was gone, and he felt relief that his life would move on without football.

That evening, he saw a full moon and thought of Rhonda. He went to his room and wrote her a letter and tried to figure out a way he could get it to her.

CHAPTER 30

Love Hurts

In 1979, speculative investors began leveraging their positions with precious metals, particularly silver. For most of the year, silver prices fluctuated between four to five and a half dollars. By the last quarter of the year, however, increasing demand caused the prices to jump between fifteen and twenty-five dollars per ounce. As the year came to a close, the Hunt Brothers, heirs of a Texas oil tycoon, used their vast fortune in an attempt to corner the market, driving the price of an ounce of silver to nearly fifty dollars.

Curtis took the bus to school on Monday to talk with Elizabeth. He told her about the party's events as they walked to the bus stop. He shared how much he liked Rhonda and how difficult it was to understand why she didn't want to talk to him anymore. Fern said, "I think you can do better than her. She seemed kind of mousy to me."

Elizabeth said, "I'm not sure what you want me to do."

While they waited for the bus, Curtis handed Elizabeth a crisp, folded letter in the shape of a triangle. Elizabeth reluctantly took the paper football from him and stuffed it into her coat pocket. "Curtis, I don't know her very well, but I'll see what I can do."

The morning moved along smoothly, and Curtis was optimistic the rest of the day would follow suit. Geometry was the last class to tackle before lunch. Mr. Donnelly, who was also an assistant varsity football coach, approached Curtis and said, "I heard you quit the football team."

"Yes, sir, I did."

"Well," he said, patting Curtis on the shoulder, "football isn't everybody's cup of tea." Curtis took his seat and dug out the homework he had completed in study hall.

After lunch, Curtis ran into April, the classmate who introduced him to Van Halen earlier in the year, while heading to the locker room to change for gym.

"Hey, April."

She stopped and looked around to see who called her name. "Kurt?"

"Curtis. It's been a while."

"Yeah, I remember now."

"Were you able to see Van Halen earlier this year? I thought of you when I went to the show."

Her eyes dropped. "No, I was supposed to go, but I broke up with my boyfriend and he took someone else."

"I'm sorry to hear that."

"I bet they rocked," she said. "I sure missed seeing their show. They used to be my favorite band."

There was an awkward silence, and just as she was about to turn and leave, he asked her, "So, what other new bands do you know about?"

"Well, I'm not sure if you'd like her, but Joan Jett is going solo. I loved her with The Runaways. I think you would really like Tom Petty. You should check out his new album."

"Tom Petty…he was in the movie *FM*, right?"

"Yeah, that was him. He's right up there with Bob Seger, as far as I'm concerned. He's such a wonderful songwriter and has a fantastic band. Hey, listen, I need to get some lunch, but it was good catching up with you."

April turned and headed down the hill to the cafeteria. Curtis walked up the hill with his books in one hand and his gym bag in the other.

Curtis entered the double doors that led into the high school from the bottom floor. He climbed up the short set of stairs that led to the lower level but had his head down so as not to make eye contact with the high school seniors who lined the long hallway. This area was premium real estate as some seniors claimed the lockers close to the exit doors.

Curtis heard a familiar voice saying, "Who are you looking at, fucker?"

Curtis did his best to ignore the taunt, but more name-calling from other varsity members continued. He needed to make it fifty yards to get to the safety of his literature classroom. The hallway had suddenly morphed into a gauntlet.

Someone grabbed him from behind. It was Luther Conrad. "Hey, he asked you a question," he shouted as he shoved Curtis against a locker. The blow loosened his grip on his books. Conrad slapped his arm, causing them to fall to the ground, and then he kicked the books and notebooks, sending them down the hallway like hockey pucks on an ice rink.

Curtis saw two teachers standing in the hallway. When they heard the commotion, they retreated into the security of their classrooms and shut the doors. It seemed even teachers were afraid of Coach's wrath.

The hallway became Curtis's Via Dolorosa as he received numerous slaps and punches he didn't deserve. His gym bag absorbed most of their strikes as he endured the hostilities and did his best to deflect their blows.

When he cleared the mass of people, he dropped down to his knees to pick up his books and notebooks, but his assailants' feet kicked and scattered them away from him.

In addition to the physical abuse, the worst part was getting back on his feet to see the happy faces of pretty girls, some wearing bright yellow sweaters with a big brown Windsor logo. These same girls who were smitten by the security of their alpha male protectors were the same girls who would cry if a German shepherd chewed up a declawed cat.

Gathering the strength he needed, Curtis broke free with what books and papers he could gather and ran the last few yards to Miss Jackson's literature class. He stumbled into the quiet, darkened room and saw his teacher at her desk, eating her lunch in solitude.

She told him to close the door, and then he came and sat at a desk in front of hers.

"Tough day, I hear."

Miss Jackson gave Curtis the time to calm down and gain his composure. She had been around teenagers long enough to know the brutality the alpha males inflicted on the more sensitive boys.

Curtis tried to gather his papers together and panicked when he couldn't find his paper on "The Most Dangerous Game."

"Miss Jackson, I read the Richard Connell short story and swear I wrote a paper on the theme."

"And what was your conclusion of the theme, Curtis?"

"I wrote about the connection between the hunter and the hunted, and that people could use fear and power to dominate other people."

"I have no doubt that you wrote a very fine paper on that subject. Now my eyes show me evidence that such learning of the mind has been translated to the reality of your soul. I do not need to read the paper now. I will give you the A you deserve, so please stop worrying about looking for it."

Coming around to sit on the front of her desk, Miss Jackson said, "Listen, young man. I'm going to tell you something very important."

Curtis met her gaze and took the tissues she offered him.

"Those boys out there who abused you the way they did, and the girls who watched and said nothing, you need to understand that these are the best years of their lives. No matter what else they do in their life, they will look back to their high school years as the highlight of their life. Do you understand?"

"No, not really."

"I've seen this behavior for over twenty years, Curtis. I can tell you that the boys who excelled in high school grow up and grow old, reflecting on the good old days. Only they found out they weren't so good, but that is all they have. There is a sense in which you, and people like you, have better days to come. You will look back into the days of your youth as the springboard they were supposed to be, not the end of all, as some foolish people think they are."

"I don't even think about the future all that much, Miss Jackson."

"Of course, you don't. That is why you need teachers who guide as much as they teach. The choices are always yours. We can only offer advice, but most of us have all lived out what you are going through."

Curtis excused himself so he could read as she finished up her lunch. Curtis lost track of time until she reminded him the bell was about to ring. He went to the locker room to change clothes for gym.

Walking home from the bus stop, he shared with Elizabeth all he'd suffered after lunch.

Elizabeth said, "I'm sorry, Curtis. I don't get why people need to be so mean and hateful."

Fern hugged Curtis, and he awkwardly hugged her back.

Elizabeth said, "I know you don't want to hear this, but when I gave Rhonda your letter, her friend grabbed it out of my hand and wouldn't give it to her."

Fern said, "It looks like the bullies always win."

Curtis walked the girls to their house. He had a lot on his mind as he walked home and was overwhelmed with gratitude that there was one teacher in the school who cared about him. He determined to read as many books on her list as he could before the end of the school year.

When he got home, he gave his mother a long list of books he wanted. JoAnn never said no to books. Her eldest son frustrated her with his lack of drive to get good grades, but he never stopped reading, and she found solace in that.

Curtis was mindful anytime he walked the hallways alone and avoided any gathering of upperclassmen. He experienced a brief reprieve and didn't have to deal with any hostile acts for a couple of days. That changed on Thursday.

Curtis changed into shorts and a T-shirt for gym class. He entered the gymnasium earlier than usual. Curtis's Physical Education class was taught by Ms. Mayfield, who also coached several of the girls' high school sports teams. Ms. Mayfield wheeled out two basketball carts and had one of her junior varsity volleyball players add air to the basketballs that needed it.

As more kids entered the gym, it became noisy. Ms. Mayfield called for everyone to get in, quiet down, and gather around. Curtis had noticed Jordan Reynolds lurking in the hallway but didn't see him double back through the side door. Jordan picked a basketball up off the cart, and as the kids were heading toward Ms. Mayfield, Jordan threw the ball toward the back of Curtis's head. Curtis caught sight of the movement out of the corner of his eye and instinctively twisted and ducked as the basketball violently struck his upper right arm.

The ball ricocheted and hit another student in her face, and a third student knocked the ball away before it could hurt anyone else. Curtis received a bright red spot on his arm from the impact, but the girl got a bloody nose.

When the girl screamed, Ms. Mayfield immediately spotted Jordan running toward the door. She ran after him and then escorted him to the principal's office. Other girls attended to their classmate's bleeding nose and led her to the nurse's office. Jordan Reynolds received a three-day suspension from school for his actions and was not eligible to play football when the Owls traveled to Festus. Windsor nearly lost their second game of the season because they played without their all-conference varsity player.

When Curtis got home, his mother handed him a pair of George Orwell books, *1984* and *Animal Farm*. She said she would get him two more when he finished those.

He took the books into his room and began to read *1984*, wondering what the world might look like in five more years. He turned on his radio and heard a new song by The Police called "Message in a Bottle." The song seemed to be written just for him.

Over the weekend, Curtis realized he needed to get active. As much as he hated the football workouts, his fitness had improved from all the exercise. He didn't want to lose all that hard work, so in the evenings, he began running. Initially, he ran up and down the hill, but as he adjusted to the hill, he took off down the street and ran down to the bus stop and back. When that didn't seem so far, he ventured out to the highway and back, and once he ran the entire mile, he started running for time.

The weekend went by in a hurry. Curtis read another short story on Miss Jackson's list and drafted an essay on "The Monkey's Paw" by W. W. Jacobs. He also put a sizable dent in *1984*.

On Monday when he went to leave for school, he noticed he had a flat tire. His stomach churned when he confirmed that he had two flat tires. He knew something wasn't right, so he circled the truck and noticed all four tires were flat. Worse than being flat, he could see that someone had cut the sidewalls of each tire with a knife. They were beyond repair and would need to be replaced.

He wasn't sure what to do, but he feared whoever vandalized the truck might have done more than the tires. He got in and turned the engine on, and the check engine light immediately came on. The engine ran rough for less than a minute before it howled, screeched, and stopped. The starter clicked when he turned the key.

He went inside and told his mom, and she came out and saw the tires. Profoundly distressed and unsure what to do, she called the Jefferson County Sheriff's Department. She took Curtis to school then stayed home waiting for the police to arrive. The deputy that drove out took pictures and wrote up a report. He said it looked like vandalism, but it was doubtful that someone would be prosecuted without hard evidence or a confession.

After he left, JoAnn was livid and called the school to talk to JoJo. As the school secretary, she knew of the trouble Curtis was in for quitting the football team as information had come to light when one of the vital varsity players got suspended. Coach Tyron had been in the office raising hell that if the school wanted to win, they needed to be able to "look past these things all kids do." JoJo assured JoAnn that when Elroy Powel, the principal, heard about a student's truck being vandalized, the school would have to respond decisively.

The administration called Coach Tyron into a closed-door meeting with the principal and the school superintendent. He came out of the meeting in a foul mood and stormed back down to his office.

When Curtis took the bus home in the afternoon, he stared out the window as the bus rolled down the highway. He saw a sign in front of a small jewelry store with large letters, "WE PAY TOP DOLLAR FOR SILVER COINS."

When Curtis Sr. came home from work that evening, he opened the truck's hood and found that the air filter had been taken off and fine sand poured into the carburetor. The gas cap was also gone, so he assumed the same sand would also be found inside the gas tank. He pulled the dipstick and noticed the oil had been drained. He crawled under the truck and saw the plug missing from the oil pan. Whoever did this was determined the truck would never run again. JoAnn called the insurance company, and they said they would send an adjuster out to look at and assess the damage.

Curtis went back to walking to the bus stop with Elizabeth and Fern every morning. As Friday approached, Curtis asked Elizabeth if she would go to the Homecoming dance with him. She politely declined his invitation, saying someone had already asked her.

Curtis wanted to ask who but remained quiet.

As if reading his mind, Fern blurted out, "That burnout Ronnie asked her."

Curtis burned with envy but kept his thoughts to himself.

It had been months since he had received a paycheck, and he was still on the hook to Brad for the money he let Curtis borrow. When Brad got home from work, Curtis asked him for a ride to the jewelry store. He pulled out the mason jar full of silver coins his grandfather had given him for college. They went inside, and the man went through the jar and pulled out all the silver coins, leaving only buffalo nickels, wheat pennies, and some Canadian coins. He counted the coins and offered Curtis four hundred and fifty dollars for all the coins and another hundred dollars if he could keep the mason jar. Curtis left the store with more money than he'd ever had in his life, even after he gave Brad back the hundred and seventy-five dollars he owed him.

After dinner, he finished *1984* and began drafting an essay about the book. When he finished the essay, he went for a run and felt good about himself. After his run, he went inside and showered. He counted out the money he owed Columbia House and set it aside. He would ask Brad to take him to the bank for a money order. He did not want to explain where he got all the money from to his mother.

He lay in bed with the lights out, listening to the radio. He found, once again, that the radio knew the songs he needed to hear as he listened to the lyrics to "Rosewood Bitters." He made a mental note to see if Columbia House offered the Michael Stanley Band album in their catalog. He knew for sure Tom Petty's *Damn the Torpedoes* was offered and wanted to add that record to his collection too.

Then he thought about Ronnie and Elizabeth together. That unpleasant image ruined the peace he was looking for to fall asleep. Then he wondered if April would be willing to go with him. He conjured up a plan to ask her if she would draw another Van Halen emblem to replace the drawing ruined by the washing machine. Everything he touched, it seemed, fell into ruin. That sad rumination carried him to sleep.

Chapter 31

Another Brick in the Wall

The juvenile horned owl sat perched and hidden in the tree line, the trees not yet cleared of all their darkened leaves. The owl, hidden in the shadows of a full moon, focused on the movements of two rabbits foraging along a culvert. The nocturnal bird of prey gazed upon the rabbit grazing outside the shadows, every movement as clear to the winged predator as if it were daytime in spring. Now was the perfect time for one to die so another might live.

The owl slipped off the branch and swooped toward the earth without making a sound, and with a few powerful thrusts of her stealthlike wings, her accelerated movement had her on top of the rabbit, which she struck with the precision of a thunderbolt. The strike was nearly perfect as three of the four talons pierced entirely through the tender flesh of the herbivore. Each puncture by itself would have been lethal, but together, the rabbit was dead before the owl landed on the road to consume her late evening meal.

With rapid, short stabbing motions, her sharp, curved beak ripped and violently tore into the nourishing protein she needed. While eating, the owl sensed tremors emitting from the ground. Something unusual alerted her to the threat of danger. Her head swiveled over a hundred degrees in both directions, but no visual signs of trouble caused her enough concern to abandon her catch. The tremors were increasing, which caused her to be distressed and stop eating. She swept her field of vision a second time, but this time, her eyes caught sight of a source of light. An unusual, seemingly unnatural light. The owl focused enough to see there was not one but two lights, like small moons on the horizon, growing larger and brighter with each passing second. Momentarily paralyzed by the blinding light, the two moons became like suns, and her primal fear gave way to a loud squeal that silenced her own cry as she tried to leap into the night sky and the safety of flight. In a moment, as fast as lightning crosses the sky, the young owl was mangled and dead in a ditch.

Homecoming week was the worst; everything reminded Curtis he was alone. His thoughts of asking April to the Homecoming dance disappeared when he saw her eating lunch with another boy. They laughed and took turns feeding each other like a bride and groom eating cake after a wedding.

When Curtis spotted Ronnie sitting with Elizabeth, his heart ached. He knew enough about Ronnie, but he could do nothing about it. He didn't think anything could be worse than knowing something to be true but not having the courage to do anything about it.

After lunch, Curtis walked up to the high school but chose to walk the long way around the building to enter from the top floor. He entered Miss Jackson's room as she ate lunch and read a magazine at her desk.

She looked up and waved him over as she finished her sandwich.

Curtis asked her, "What are you reading?"

Still chewing, she flipped the magazine over to show him the cover. Curtis saw a watercolor illustration of people holding colorful umbrellas and walking across green grass. Typed top and center were the words *The New Yorker.*

Miss Jackson took a sip of her tea and then pointed to a stack of magazines on a table by the window. She told Curtis he could help himself to her old copies.

While Curtis thumbed through the pile, she said, "Truman Capote worked for *The New Yorker* briefly before he got fired."

"What did he get fired for?"

She laughed and said, "He upset Robert Frost."

Curtis asked, "Who's Robert Frost?" as he dug through the magazines.

Miss Jackson stood up and said, "Curtis, forget the magazines." Going to a bookshelf, she pulled a book and sat back at her desk. She opened the cover and signed: "To Curtis, Let me have the pleasure of introducing you to Robert Frost. You need to stand on the shoulders of giants for a sharpened view of life. Gloria Jackson."

She handed the book to him and encouraged him to read it.

"Thank you, Miss Jackson. I haven't read poetry before."

"Sure, you have. Everybody's read Dr. Suess, wouldn't you agree?"

Curtis sat down and flipped the book over to read the back flap.

She broke the silence and asked him, "Have you read anything by Truman Capote?"

"I read *In Cold Blood* last year," he replied.

"I'm impressed," she said.

"My mom said it was one of her favorite books."

"Well, what did you think of it?"

"I liked the movie better."

"Curtis!"

Walking home from the bus stop, Curtis finally couldn't help but share what he knew about Ronnie with Elizabeth.

"Don't worry, Curtis. I don't do drugs, and he promised to bring me home right after the dance. I can assure you there will not be any hanky-panky going on. He's just a friend to me, like you are."

Friday night, Curtis stayed home after dinner. His relentless thoughts about people having fun at the school dance he wasn't a part of were unsettling. Curtis sat at his desk reading through the Robert Frost book. Poetry intrigued him, but he grew bored of it quickly. The poems, Curtis thought, were like songs without music. He would rather listen to music, so he closed the book and turned on the radio.

He got lost in his thoughts, trying to connect poetry and song lyrics. He wondered if Miss Jackson could explain it to him.

Curtis grabbed a random volume from his encyclopedias, let the pages fall open, and started reading about lighthouses. While reading, he wondered if he was closer to the Atlantic Ocean or Pacific and if he would ever see the ocean or a lighthouse. As he pondered these questions, he heard the DJ say, "Now, by special request from a listener in Shrewsbury, here is 'Kashmir' by Led Zeppelin on KSHE 95 FM."

Immediately, as if a gong went off in his head, his mind recalled the day he spent with Mick listening to all those Led Zeppelin songs. The more he listened, the more he realized this song differed from the others. Curtis had never heard a song like this before.

"Kashmir" was hypnotic, and Curtis found his mind drifting away, captured by the sounds and the lyrics. The lyrics enhanced the music he heard, but the music magnified the lyrics. He wondered what strings and brass instruments were doing in a rock and roll song. The music and lyrics carried him away, even though he never left the chair. He closed his eyes and felt stoned, even though he hadn't smoked anything in weeks. And the singer's wailing voice profoundly touched his soul.

Curtis felt the tension building. He felt torn between focusing on the experience or letting go into a different one. Eventually, the song seduced him into letting go.

He found the hair on his arms and neck standing up as chills flooded his body and goose pimples broke out. What was this? What was going on? No other song had ever caused him to respond this way. The lyrics captured his mind, and the music pleased his ears, but the experience transcended both. Rhythm and melody carried him away, and he didn't want it to end.

Nevertheless, the song ended. The short-lived experience faded, feeling distant almost immediately. The next song, "My Sharona," brought him back to Earth in the most irritating way.

Like girls, music was another mystery to be solved, with pleasures to be explored and company to be enjoyed. He already knew girls were a blessing who extracted a price, but could music do the same?

Sunday was one of the saddest days of Curtis's life. Those bastards had ruined his truck, and there wasn't a thing he could do about it. Despite having more money than he'd ever had, it was barely enough to replace the tires and not nearly enough to replace the engine.

That afternoon, a man drove over the river from Illinois with a truck and trailer. He hauled Curtis's truck away, and Curtis never saw it again.

Curtis stood with his dad and said, "I loved that truck. I really did."

"I know, son. I did too."

His dad gave him five hundred dollars and said, "Take this and put it away. We'll find something else for you to drive."

Later that evening, Curtis went for his run. The temperature had fallen, so running in shorts and a T-shirt felt inadequate, but he was too lazy to turn around to get a jacket. Instead, he ran faster to stay warm.

Curtis made it down to the gas station in record time, but as he came around the last corner, he saw a man standing near the pay phone. It was unsettling, but wanting to run to his turnaround point, he ignored his apprehension. He was determined to complete his run; no stranger would keep him from it.

Curtis ran up the small hill and into the gas station parking lot. The stranger stood under the dusk-to-dawn light, illuminating the man's body. The man appeared to be wearing a hooded jacket that kept his face in shadow.

"Good evening, friend."

"Hi," Curtis replied.

"Quite a night for a run. It's chilly, isn't it?"

"Yeah, I guess so."

The man asked, "Why are you running?"

"I'm exercising to control my weight."

"I see. Are you afraid?"

Curtis was not afraid until the man had asked that. Then, unspeakable fear gripped his heart. He wanted to turn and run, but he couldn't move. The voice wasn't threatening, and the stranger made no movements toward him.

"No, I'm just cold."

"I see," the man said.

"I guess I should be going. My mom might start to worry."

"Before you go, I'd like to ask you one more question. What is holding you back?"

"Holding me back? Holding me back from what?"

"You better get home to your mom before you catch a cold."

Curtis turned and ran away as fast as he could. Just before he turned the corner, he looked back. The stranger was gone.

Monday, Curtis, suffering from a head cold, walked with the girls to the bus stop. He asked Elizabeth about the homecoming dance.

"I don't want to talk about it," she said.

Fern shouted, "Curtis warned you, but you're so stupid."

Elizabeth started to cry, which made Curtis feel awkward, so he held out his hand. Elizabeth held his hand as they walked. Curtis held out his other hand to Fern, leading the two sisters toward the bus stop as Elizabeth shared her worst night ever.

"Oh, Curtis, why couldn't he be more like you?"

The words were from her heart. While they were authentic, her words had the opposite effect of what she'd intended. She meant them as a compliment, but they hurt Curtis deeply.

As they approached the bus stop, a car sped past them, honking repeatedly. Curtis caught Ronnie's angry face glaring at him from the car window.

Later that afternoon, as Curtis walked the girls home, Ronnie ambushed him. Curtis wasn't much of a fighter, and Ronnie was unrelenting as he beat Curtis senseless with both of his fists.

When Fern tried to intervene, he knocked her down. Fern, however, distracted Ronnie long enough for Curtis, mustering every fiber of his body, to throw and land one punch. It landed squarely between Ronnie's left eye and ear. Ronnie fell sideways then tried to stand up. His legs buckling, he fell again then struggled to get up on one knee. Mr. Fernbeck ran down his driveway shouting and stopped the fight before things really got out of hand.

The girls walked Curtis down the hill to his house and knocked on the door. When JoAnn saw her son bleeding, she panicked. Elizabeth and Fern came inside as JoAnn made him lie down and put bags of frozen vegetables on his face to stop the swelling.

Elizabeth explained what had happened. "It's all my fault. I should never had gotten Curtis in the middle."

Fern came to the defense of her sister and said, "It was not your fault. This is all Ronnie's fault."

Elizabeth called her stepdad, and he drove over to pick them up. Later that night, Elizabeth telephoned Curtis to see how he was doing.

"Roger was livid. After he brought us home, he said he was going to go over and teach Ronnie a lesson about putting his hands on his girls." Elizabeth then told Curtis, "If he knew what Ronnie tried to do with me on Friday, my stepdad would go to jail. I'm sorry I got you mixed up in all this. You're a sweet boy and don't deserve any of this."

"It's okay, Elizabeth. I think the world of you and your sister."

"I know you do. When Fern told Roger what you did to Ronnie for pushing her down, he thinks differently about you now."

Curtis didn't sleep well. He woke up in the middle of the night trying to recall the details of a dream. He vaguely remembered hearing a voice, and suddenly, he was in the back seat of an old sedan, necking with a cheerleader wearing a purple high school sweater at a drive-in movie theater. He tasted lipstick as she smothered him with kisses as The Ronettes sang in the background. He remembered trying to reach up under the cheerleader's sweater, but then suddenly he was in a gymnasium playing basketball while a dozen cheerleaders wearing purple sweaters yelled his name. He took the shot, and when he looked up to see if the ball had gone into the basket, he woke up again.

The following week, Curtis asked Elizabeth to go on a date. He suggested going to the varsity football game on Friday night. He was nearly certain she would say yes, and she did. It was a warm evening when they boarded the spectator bus. They rode down to Herculaneum with the varsity cheerleaders leading chant after chant.

During the game, the temperature dropped as a light rain started falling. The Windsor Owls went on to destroy the Herculaneum Black Cats. Everyone was glad when the game was over so they could get out of the rain. While the bus offered shelter from the rain and wind, everyone still had to endure a cold, wet ride back to the school.

Curtis was in high spirits but not from the football game. He couldn't care less who won or lost. He was happy to be with Elizabeth. Cold and shivering, she snuggled up close to Curtis for warmth.

As the bus approached Barnhart, it slowed before coming to a complete stop. Curtis could see lots of flashing lights through the giant school bus windshield. The police had shut down all but one lane as they directed traffic around an accident.

As the bus drove past, Curtis stared through the rain-streaked window and saw a light tan Chevette with the front end wrapped around a telephone pole. He saw flares and flashing lights and caught a glimpse of a familiar Chevy Suburban.

Immediately after that thought entered his head, he saw a group of paramedics wheeling a gurney with a covered body toward an ambulance.

Elizabeth said, "Oh my God, I think somebody was killed."

Curtis held on to her tightly as a chill ran down his spine.

Rhonda Mead was a petite, winsome girl with curly, shoulder-length auburn hair that hued closer to brown than red. She was barely sixteen when she was killed in a single-car automobile accident driving home from work on a rainy Friday night. The police report stated, "Evidence indicates an adolescent female swerved to avoid hitting wildlife. Evidence also suggests the inexperienced driver overcorrected in wet conditions and veered off the road, impacting a utility pole. The victim was dead on arrival and likely died immediately on impact. There were no drugs or alcohol present in the vehicle."

Chapter 32

Time Passages

The news of Rhonda's accident traveled fast, and her death took its toll on all who knew and loved her. When the reality of it sank in, Curtis cried so hard he could not catch his breath. He buried his face deep into his pillow to muffle uncontrollable sobbing. He had told his mother just enough so she would not ask him questions, but that did not stop her from entering the room to check on him.

When he thought he couldn't cry anymore, he only needed to look out the window and see the waning moon, with just a sliver of darkness on the edge, to remind him, and the deep wells of his soul would unleash a new round of tears.

By Sunday, he felt well enough to call Elizabeth. They talked for an hour, and Curtis learned that Rhonda was being buried in Mountain Home, Missouri.

Windsor was somber for those who knew Rhonda. It was just another day for those who didn't. The days were slow and dreary, but Curtis tried to escape them by focusing on his reading assignments and running in the evenings.

Gazing out his bedroom window, Curtis observed the signs of autumn. It wasn't even close to dinner time, yet the sun hung low in the sky. Ginger-colored leaves fell off the oak trees and fluttered to the ground like moths with torn wings. Still other leaves clung to the nearly naked branches with various shades of green showing, but the brown edges hinted at their rapidly approaching demise.

Curtis went out to the kitchen. His mother was preparing dinner.

He asked, "What time are we eating?"

"Soon."

"Okay, I'll be back soon," Curtis replied as he grabbed his jacket and went out the door. He heard his mom yell something, but he was halfway up the street before she could dry her hands and go to the door.

Curtis saw Brad by Mr. Grady's pole barn. Curtis walked through the beaten-down path to see what he was doing. Brad was carrying a five-gallon bucket.

"What's going on?" Curtis inquired.

Brad replied, "Check this out."

The two boys climbed around an old tractor, and back in the corner of the barn, they heard a shrieking, whimpering sound. Brad pulled out a flashlight and shined it in the corner. Tiny pink bodies lay squirming over each other on a dirty carpet.

"There are four of them," Brad said.

"Where's the mother?"

"I think Travis's grandfather killed her."

"What? Why would he do that?"

"Travis said his grandfather heard a commotion in his barn and thought a fox was going after his geese last night. He went out with a flashlight and his shotgun. He noticed that her teats were swollen with milk only after he shot the poor bitch."

"So, what are you going to do?"

"My dad said they would starve to death and told me to put them out of their misery. I figured I'd put them in the bucket and put the bucket in the freezer."

Curtis was horrified, and his face could not conceal it.

"We can't just kill these puppies. We need to try to save them."

Curtis walked into his house and straight to the basement with a five-gallon bucket of four crying, blind, hairless, and very hungry puppies. JoAnn came downstairs to see what her son was doing, and when she saw the puppies, she said, "Hell no." She told Curtis it was a foolish and selfish effort. "Without a mother, those puppies are going to die."

Curtis had enough of death and dying and would not listen to reason.

"Curtis, your dinner is getting cold," she hollered.

Curtis grabbed a clean towel from the dryer, found one of his dad's old drop lights, and tried to keep the puppies warm. Curtis watched the four tiny creatures roll into a little ball until he heard his mother yell again.

Curtis went upstairs, wolfed down his cold meatloaf, ate a spoonful of applesauce, and chugged the glass of tepid milk.

"Mom, can I borrow the car? I want to go get some baby formula."

A week later, against all odds, the puppies were still alive. Their eyes were open, and they waddled around in the warm enclosure Curtis had created. Elizabeth and Fern came over to see the puppies. Fern asked if they could have one when it got old enough. Curtis did not object. Fern was so excited and asked if she could use the phone. She came back downstairs heartbroken because her stepdad had said no.

Elizabeth asked, "Do they have names yet?"

Curtis answered, "Not yet."

"Well, they need cool names."

By the end of the month, raising four puppies was starting to take a toll on Curtis, so Brad said he would take two of the puppies. Curtis kept the little brown male, naming him Bear, and the little furry black female, named Black Betty. Brad named his tan-and-white male puppy Bandit. He named the solid black male Black Sabbath but then shortened it to Sabbath.

It rained on Halloween, and for the first time in his life, Curtis did not get dressed up or go out. Elizabeth called him, and when she found out he wasn't doing anything, she invited him over for pizza. They started to watch a movie, but Roger said the film would have to wait another time since it was a school night.

It had been almost a month since the fatal car accident. Curtis was trying hard not to think about it. He was in his bedroom reading when his mother said he had a phone call. "I think it's Elizabeth," she said as she handed him the receiver.

"Hello?"

"Curtis? This is Elizabeth. Are you busy?"

"No, what's up?"

"I hate to bother you, but I have some algebra that I can't figure out. Do you think you can come over to help me? I only have a couple of worksheets to finish."

"Sure. What time are you thinking?"

"Anytime. My stepdad is out in the garage working. Just knock on the door when you get here."

"Okay. I'll come down in about an hour."

"Do you have a date?" JoAnn asked as he hung up the phone.

"Elizabeth needs help with her math."

"Is your homework done?"

"Most of it. I don't have much left."

"Well, finish it first. Will you be home for dinner?"

"I think so."

Curtis enjoyed seeing Elizabeth but was always nervous when Roger was home. He entered the open garage and saw Roger welding with his back toward the opening. Roger didn't even look up when Curtis knocked on the door that opened into the kitchen.

Elizabeth opened the door and smiled as Curtis came in and shut the door behind him.

"Thank you for coming over. I really need to figure this math out. It's the only class I struggle with."

Elizabeth wore white-trimmed blue gym shorts, a T-shirt with a Windsor Owl logo across the front, and anklet socks. The white shirt was not opaque enough to completely hide the darkened silhouette of her bra.

Curtis removed his jacket and shoes before going inside. She motioned to a chair beside her and showed him the problems she needed help with.

"Would you like something to drink? We have Coke, Diet Coke, tea, and water."

"A glass of ice water would be great."

Elizabeth pulled out an ice tray and twisted it, causing some ice to fall onto the floor. She filled a cup with ice cubes and bent over to pick up the ice on the floor. Curtis watched until he realized he was staring, and then he focused on the math worksheet before him.

The math problems looked easy enough. Word problems were always tricky for any algebra assignment, but he liked the challenge. He enjoyed demonstrating his mastery over numbers but loved that he was able to spend time with Elizabeth because she was such a beautiful girl who was kind to him.

She paid attention as he showed her how to work through the math problems. She rested her chin on her folded hands and followed his pencil marks with her eyes.

"Are you paying attention or sleeping?" Curtis asked. His voice startled her, as she had not realized she'd shut her eyes. "Do we need to take a break?"

"I'm sorry, Curtis. I followed along and only closed my eyes for a second."

Elizabeth jumped up, which startled Curtis. "Maybe I just need to get some blood flowing." She started doing some jumping jacks in the living room. Curtis watched as long as he dared then left the dining area and found the bathroom.

He returned to find Elizabeth sitting on the couch with her eyes glued to the television.

"Curtis! Do you see what is happening in Iran?"

Curtis went over to the couch and sat down next to her. It was all over the news. Iranian students had seized the United States embassy in Tehran, Iran's capital city. The students captured and held more than fifty Americans as hostages.

Curtis stared at the television, recalling the movie *Raid on Entebbe* from just a couple of years ago. "This is not good."

Elizabeth started to feel anxious and turned the television off. "No, it's not. I'm so scared for those hostages. Do you think they will die?"

"It never ends well when terrorists are involved."

Just as they got back to the kitchen table to work on the remaining problems, Roger stuck his head inside the kitchen from the garage and yelled, "Elizabeth, I have to run out to the hardware store. I expect your homework to be done and dinner ready when I get back."

"Okay," she replied. "We're almost done with my last worksheet for math."

Roger started to shut the door but stuck his head inside again and added, "Curtis, I need you to get going. Elizabeth needs to finish that homework and complete her chores. It's a school night." Roger shut the door before Elizabeth could respond. He was not in the mood to argue.

Elizabeth sighed, and Fern came out of her bedroom to find out what all the yelling was about.

Elizabeth sat at the table, chewing on her pencil as Curtis went into the living room to get his shoes. She heard Roger's truck back out of the driveway. "Come on, Curtis, help me with these last two problems before you leave."

"You should do your own homework," Fern said. "I don't have anyone help me with mine." She stormed back to her room and slammed the door shut.

Curtis said, "Those last problems are the same as the other ones. Whatever you do on one side of the equal sign, do to the other until you figure out what the X is."

Elizabeth got up from the table and said, "You make it seem so easy."

Curtis put his shoes on then leaned over to tie them.

Elizabeth walked behind him, saying, "Why are you in such a hurry to leave?" as she bumped into him hard with her hip. Curtis lost his balance and fell over.

Elizabeth laughed.

Curtis looked up at her, towering over him. She leaned over him, and her dark hair fell off her shoulders and enclosed her face. Curtis saw her face as if at the end of a tunnel. Her eyes sparkled, and her mischievous grin broke into contagious laughter. She pointed her finger at him and taunted, "The larger they are, the harder they fall…"

"Oh yeah? Is that so?" Curtis answered as he grabbed her wrist and pulled her down. She lost her balance and fell on top of him.

Elizabeth shrieked as his arms wrapped around her, and they wrestled to see who could get up first. The wrestling was innocent enough, but Elizabeth quickly yielded, and Curtis rolled her over and pinned her to the floor.

"You win. Let me up," she said.

"No."

"Let me up, please."

Curtis noticed how her hair spilled over the floor in every direction. After an awkward silence, she smiled up at him. He misread the smile.

"I'll let you up for a kiss."

"I'm not kissing you. Get off me."

Curtis looked down and saw the same grin as before.

"Curtis, I'm not even joking. Let me up."

"Neither am I," he replied.

"Okay, just one kiss, but that's it."

Curtis leaned down and kissed her.

With all her strength, she heaved and pushed her pelvis off the floor with her legs, bucked to one side, and sent Curtis tumbling to the other side.

"I think you need to go now," Elizabeth ordered with a sigh.

Curtis observed the ravished, tussled hair, the hurt look in her eyes, and the flushed face. Her beautiful honey-colored skin was closer to umber, reddened by blood flushing her cheeks with anger and embarrassment.

"I'm sorry, Elizabeth…"

"Yes, so am I. Please get your shoes on and leave."

Curtis finished tying his shoes on and walked out the kitchen door. He had a lot to think about on the slow walk home.

After Curtis left, Fern came out of her bedroom.

"You are in so much trouble when Roger comes home," she said.

"Fern, no. Please don't say anything."

"I'm telling him everything. You are such a bitch, Elizabeth."

"Fern, please. I'll do anything you ask. Just leave Roger out of this. He'll kill Curtis if he finds out."

Fern looked at her older sister. One part of her was envious of how easily she could win a boy with her looks and charm. Another part of her hated her sister because she could be so callous about the destructiveness of her coquettish behaviors. And still another part of her was angry because Fern could never count on anyone to help her, so she worked twice as hard to ensure nobody needed to. Yet she could not help but think that if given the chance, she would pretend to be stupid if that was what it took to get someone like Curtis to notice she was alive.

"I won't say a word if you do the dishes for the rest of the week."

"Okay, I can do that. Thank you."

"And make my bed too."

"Okay, I'll make your bed every morning. Anything else?"

"Yes. You apologize to Curtis tomorrow for being such a bitch." Fern slammed the door again and flopped on her bed. She stared at the book she still needed to read for her book report.

Elizabeth felt the sting of her sister's words. Was she a bitch? Did she add confusion to everything and everyone she knew and cared about? She pushed these questions into the recesses of her mind and went into the kitchen to brown ground beef and prepare dinner.

Curtis stared at the full moon in the new evening sky as he headed home. Was the moon to blame for his animal behavior? Did he misread Elizabeth's eyes and face? He wondered why someone would say yes and no at the same time. Once again, he found himself confused and conflicted, but now that conflict may have destroyed the relationship with the one girl he thought understood him. He would see Elizabeth again in the morning on their way to the bus. Would she talk to him? He could not bear the thought of her not talking to him, especially after all they had shared the past few months.

The following day, Elizabeth put Curtis's worries to rest when she apologized to him as they neared the bus stop. She did not want an awkward kiss to ruin their friendship. To make her point, she kissed Curtis awkwardly while waiting for the bus.

Elizabeth and Curtis went to the last varsity game of the season together. Fox clobbered Windsor to end their bid for a perfect season.

On Friday after lunch, Curtis talked to Miss Jackson about love. "Curtis, you are an intelligent boy but very emotional about life. I can see this in your writing. That passion and zeal for life will get you in trouble with the girls. You must start thinking about love on a grander scale and not just focus it on one person. Your heart is a laser, and you will burn people who get close to you. For heaven's sake, write your experiences in a journal. You will discover that your emotions and thoughts are more manageable through an inkpen."

Elizabeth came over on Saturday afternoon. It was a beautiful day as the temperature outside warmed. After playing with the puppies, Curtis and Elizabeth went into the backyard and played catch with a frisbee. As they grew bored of easy catches, they began challenging each other with throws that required some running and jumping.

Elizabeth overthrew the disc, and Curtis jumped and fell short before tumbling across the grass. Elizabeth ran over to see if he was all right. When she leaned over, he pulled her down to the ground. She screamed as she fell, but it quickly turned into a laugh.

They lay beside each other, staring into the autumn sky and watching the clouds drift by. Elizabeth discussed her expectations for the remainder of the school year and plans for next summer. Curtis convinced her she should train to be a lifeguard. He told her about Danny and Sammy and how much fun they were to train with. She did not believe him when he said he was certified in CPR, First Aid, and Water Safety.

Curtis said, "I could give you mouth-to-mouth to prove it."

Elizabeth teased and said, "Maybe later."

Curtis enjoyed that afternoon with her. He found her voice comforting.

She was full of curiosity about things like he was. She had more hope for the future than he did. Then his mind recalled what Miss Jackson had said to him. Would he burn Elizabeth if he got too close? Her words ran circles inside his brain, but Elizabeth silenced them as waves of delight and joy rushed through his tender and reckless heart.

"Look," Elizabeth said, pointing her finger, "up in the sky." Above them, a red-tailed hawk was surfing the late autumn breezes in a loose spiral. The bird came out of the spiral and hung in midair.

"Curtis!"

Although Curtis heard his mother calling his name, he pretended not to.

"Curtis, would you please come here for a minute?"

Irritated by her dream-ending voice, he sighed and pulled his ball cap down over his eyes.

Elizabeth sat up and said, "I guess I need to be going."

Curtis stood beside her and helped her knock the grass off her pants.

He walked with her to the end of the driveway. He offered to walk her home, but she kissed him and said she would be okay. "I'll call you later, okay? You better see what your mother wants."

Curtis watched her walk up the hill, and when she turned the corner, he went inside to see what his mom wanted. JoAnn was in the kitchen making dinner. She turned and asked, "Do I need to set another plate? Is your friend going to stay for dinner?"

The week after Thanksgiving, Curtis came home on Monday to find out his mother had given Black Betty a new home. Whenever he thought his life was going well, something occurred out of his control and broke his heart. Curtis tried to understand the logic, but his brain was not equipped to heal his heart with reason. His mom was right when she said he could not afford to care for two dogs.

"Mom, I never got to say goodbye. She was my baby."

JoAnn apologized and said she would take care of the veterinarian bills so Bear could get all the necessary shots to live a long life as an indoor pet.

On Saturday, Richie drove his Camaro over to drop his sister off for the day. The two boys talked briefly, and Richie said, "Curtis, I don't know if you'd be interested, but I have an extra ticket to see Styx and April Wine tomorrow night. Do you want to go?" Curtis was ecstatic to go to a concert. He remembered clearly the last time he saw a live band. The next night, Richie picked him up, and they had a great time. Neither band disappointed.

December arrived under the light of a glorious full moon. The radiant light shone, and the world seemed brighter even at night. Curtis continued running in the evenings, and every time he made it to the payphone, he hoped the faceless man would be there to talk to. He never was, and Curtis felt disappointed whenever he turned around.

On Monday, Elizabeth was ecstatic about a new album she bought over the weekend. "Curtis, you must listen to this album. I've never heard a record that expressed my thoughts and fears of being alone like this."

Curtis asked, "What is it?"

"It's by Pink Floyd. It's called *The Wall*."

That Friday night, Curtis went down to hang out with Elizabeth. She played the album all the way through on Roger's nice stereo. He had to come in several times to tell them to turn it down because it was too loud. "You need to get a copy of this. It's even better to listen to with headphones."

The following two weeks were wonderful. Curtis was enjoying school as things wound down for the holidays. Coach Tyron was fired after the football season, not because they lost the last game of the season, but because word got out that he had gotten a student pregnant. Curtis knew only four months remained after the Christmas break, and most of the vicious bastards that had ruined his truck would graduate and no longer be around to torment and abuse him.

On the last day of school before the break, the girls were unnaturally quiet as Curtis walked them home. When he asked Elizabeth what was wrong, she began to cry and reluctantly told him Roger got a new job and they would be moving out of state before the end of the school year.

On Saturday, Curtis borrowed his mom's car, drove to Street Side Records, and purchased *Stranger in Town* by Bob Seger and *Aja* by Steely Dan. He had them gift-wrapped and made a tag for Elizabeth. Then Curtis drove to Waldenbooks and bought Fern a box set of the *Little House* books by Laura Ingles Wilder. Later that afternoon, he gave the girls early Christmas presents. Elizabeth gave Curtis his own copy of *The Wall* from them both.

After dinner, Curtis walked up the hill toward the Gradys'. His heavy coat blocked the wind but not the bitter cold. Halfway up, he stopped and turned around. He surveyed the tree line that encircled his parents' yard. The trees, stripped of their colorful leaves, filled the woods with more space than substance. The cold winter would stunt their growth for a season, and another ring inside their trunks would form. The trees revealed nothing but bareness with nothing to give. Nature was teaching him something, but he couldn't fully grasp it. A chill ran down his spine, and the frigid air stung his face, shattering his contemplative thought. The familiar smell of burning wood called him to warmth as smoke poured from the Gradys' chimney. A few minutes later, he walked through the door to the Basement and the coziness of fire and friends.

Curtis spent the rest of the day with Brad, Gunner, and Francine. That afternoon, he opened up to his friends about Elizabeth and Fern moving. His words were awkward, full of pauses from incomplete thoughts. His friends listened attentively as he spoke of his feelings toward Katie, who left his life as quickly as she entered it, and all without saying goodbye. If Katie broke his heart, then Rhonda shattered it by making herself permanently unavailable.

Francine offered several loving platitudes to break the silence, but the more Curtis spoke, the more Curtis observed her falling into Gunner's arms. Curtis's feelings of grief now mingled with envy, and the pain became unbearable.

Brad didn't say a word, but his eyes followed every word of the conversation. In the background, the radio continued to pile on their heartaches. The music reminded Curtis that love was a dangerous game. "Sara" was drowning in seas of love, "Layla" was running and hiding, while "Jane" was playing unwinnable games. Curtis had been enticed to pursue love at whatever cost.

The game of love was worth playing, he decided. Curtis just had to figure out what the rules were. The radio seemed to understand this hopeful change of mindset as Boston advised him "Don't Look Back," REO Speedwagon encouraged him to "Roll with the Changes," and Tom Petty counseled him not to live his life like a "Refugee."

The door opened, and JoJo yelled down the stairs, "Who's down there?"

Brad yelled back, "It's just us and Curtis."

"It's time to eat. Curtis, are you staying for dinner? Get your asses up here. I don't have all day."

Curtis replied, "No thank you. I need to get going. As his friends went upstairs, he put on his coat as the radio played "Listen to the Music."

Curtis stepped out of the warm Grady basement into a freezing December wind. New falling snow swirled and blew all around. He was careful not to slam the door behind him. He walked from the snow-dusted sidewalk toward the street as snow accumulated on the naked branches of trees and covered the ground with sparkling beauty. The full moon brought light and heavenly grace into the dark, cold world of his existence. He delighted in the delicate crunch as virgin snow gave way to his steps. He stood quietly under the streetlight and fixated on the dizzying array of snowflakes falling like stars. It was so quiet he could hear them bounce off his jacket.

Passing the streetlight, he observed the moon, mesmerized by its colorful halo. A single crystal of ice struck his eye. He wiped his eye, turned around, and saw smoke and sparks flying into the night sky from the Gradys' chimney. Another sudden chill provoked him to head home, where his mother was listening to Charley Pride's *Christmas in My Home Town* and baking cookies with a brown puppy running around her feet.

The World's Greatest Jukebox

A1	Jackie Blue	The Ozark Mountain Daredevils	Better Days	B1
A2	Couldn't Get it Right	Climax Blues Band	Sav'ry Gravy	B2
A3	Right Place Wrong Time	Dr. John	I Been Hoodood	B3
A4	Dance the Night Away	Van Halen	Outta Love Again	B4
A5	Dream On	Aerosmith	Somebody	B5
A6	Rock 'n' Roll Fantasy	Bad Company	Crazy Circles	B6
A7	Tell Me Something Good	Rufus featuring Chaka Khan	Smokin' Room	B7
A8	Sir Duke	Stevie Wonder	He's Misstra Know-It-All	B8
A9	Dream Weaver	Gary Wright	Let it Out	B9
A10	Magic	Pilot	Just Let Me Be	B10
C1	Listen to What the Man Said	Wings	Love in Song	D1
C2	Fly Like an Eagle	Steve Miller Band	The Lovin' Cup	D2
C3	Slow Ride	Foghat	Save Your Lovin' (For Me)	D3
C4	Rhiannon	Fleetwood Mac	Sugar Daddy	D4
C5	If You Leave Me Now	Chicago	Together Again	D5
C6	Mr. Blue Sky	Electric Light Orchestra	One Summer Dream	D6
C7	Mr. Jaws	Dickie Gordman	Irv's Theme	D7
C8	Bennie and the Jets	Elton John	Harmony	D8
C9	Magic Man	Heart	How Deep it Goes	D9
C10	Dreams	Fleetwood Mac	Songbird	D10

E1	Life's Been Good	Joe Walsh	Theme from Boat Weirdo	F1
E2	Still the Same	Bob Seger	Feel Like a Number	F2
E3	Cocaine	Eric Clapton	Lay Down Sally	F3
E4	With a Little Luck	Wings	Backwards Traveller/Cuff Link	F4
E5	Love is Like Oxygen	Sweet	Cover Girl	F5
E6	Don't Look Back	Boston	The Journey	F6
E7	Thunder Island	Jay Ferguson	Magic Moment	F7
E8	Peg	Steely Dan	I Got the News	F8
E9	Baby Hold On	Eddie Money	Save a Little Room in Your Heart for Me	F9
E10	Doctor My Eyes	Jackson Browne	Looking into You	F10
G1	Tonight's the Night	Rod Stewart	Fool for You	H1
G2	I Just Want to be Your Everything	Andy Gibb	In the End	H2
G3	Don't Give Up on Us	David Soul	Black Bean Soup	H3
G4	So Into You	Atlanta Rhythm Section	Everybody Gotta Go	H4
G5	Takin' Care of Business	Bachman–Turner Overdrive	Stonegates	H5
G6	Live and Let Die	Wings	I Lie Around	H6
G7	I Heard it in a Love Song	The Marshall Tucker Band	Life in a Song	H7
G8	The Rubberband Man	The Spinners	Now That We're Together	H8
G9	Nobody Does It Better	Carly Simon	After the Storm	H9
G10	Turn to Stone	Electric Light Orchestra	Mister Kingdom	H10

J1	Hold Your Head Up	Agent	Keep on Rollin'	K1
J2	Go Your Own Way	Fleetwood Mac	Silver Springs	K2
J3	Play That Funky Music	Wild Cherry	The Lady Wants Your Money	K3
J4	Love Rollercoaster	Ohio Players	It's All Over	K4
J5	Let Your Love Flow	The Bellamy Brothers	Inside of My Guitar	K5
J6	Rocket Man	Elton John	Susie (Dramas)	K6
J7	Fox on the Run	Sweet	Miss Demeanor	K7
J8	Rock and Roll, Hoochie Koo	Rick Derringer	Time Warp (instrumental)	K8
J9	The Joker	Steve Miller Band	Something to Believe In	K9
J10	Another Park, Another Sunday	The Doobie Brothers	Black Water	K10

Author Acknowledgments

I'm grateful that my mom and dad demonstrated a love for reading and never said no to books. I struggled with reading due to transitioning to a new school for first grade because the initial school taught using the Initial Teaching Alphabet. ITA was a phonetic reading method that used a 44-character alphabet. Fortunately, I had a caring first-grade teacher, Miss L. Kottwitz, now Linda Miller, who worked with me to unlearn all those extra characters. By the end of second grade, I was earning Reading Circle Certificates. I am also extremely grateful to Ms. Davidson, my freshman English teacher, for encouraging me to write when I was her student over forty years ago. If students only listened to their teachers the first time, right?

I began journaling and extensive letter writing when I was in the US Navy. The journaling habit carried over into my adulthood. And when the world shut down for COVID-19, I started filling notebooks with stories. I signed up for evening creative writing classes at Meramec Community College. I joined the St. Louis Publishers Association and the St. Louis Writers Guild.

I am thankful for Andy Doty, former president of the St. Louis Publishers Association (SLPA), for his understanding and promotion of self-publishing as well as his continued encouragement over the years.

I am indebted to my creative writing teacher, Jeffrey Penn May, for his kind insights, gentle rebukes, and a coffeehouse demeanor for constructive criticism. I benefited from every class he offered. While Jeff has retired from teaching, he has compiled many of the topics he covered in his excellent book, *Finding Your Fiction: Concise Steps to Writing Successful Fiction.*

With more notebooks, index cards, and ink pens than any one person should have, and with somewhat of a clue of what I wanted to do, I went straight to work putting ink to paper. The problem I had—and it's not a complaint—is I started way too many stories with incomplete character backstories, timelines, and chapter outlines. In a word, chaos. I had a huge mess and was compelled to bring order to it.

It turns out, neurodivergent minds love dopamine, and starting a new project was easier than finishing an old one. My counselor, Sandra Smith, offered the best advice a writer with ADHD needs to hear: "Pick one of your projects and discipline yourself to the task of finishing it." I am grateful for my counselor, who has helped guide me through the labyrinth of my mind into fresh air. Becoming aware of my tendencies to avoid the difficult, our sessions became focused on how to work through my tendency to procrastinate. Within six months, I had a completed first manuscript.

Taking ideas and putting together a story to completion would not have been possible without Sandra and Jo Lena Johnson, my book coach and copy editor for my first draft. I met Jo Lena through the SLPA. She provided gentle nudges in the right direction. Jo Lena now serves as the president of SLPA.

So many times over the past three years, I found myself way in over my head, wondering what I was doing. Getting a story out of my head and onto paper was more difficult than it initially seemed. "Just write…," I was told. As a former long-distance runner, it reminded me of something that the running coaches said repeatedly: "Left foot, right foot… repeat."

Then, I met Karen Tucker at an SLPA event. She offered to look at my manuscript and encouraged me to make some changes. We went back and forth, and she became my editor and proofreader. Her thoroughness and commitment to excellence and being extremely patient with this first-time author were appreciated. "Write. Rewrite…repeat."

Karen introduced me to Carolyn Vaughan, who took my manuscript and cover art and transformed them into a beautiful book. Thank you, Carolyn, for your attention to detail, suggestions for clarifications, and willingness to work through my overactive imagination and nearly impossible schedule to make the book I wanted to write a reality.

Speaking of cover art—and so much could be said about this topic, but sufficient for now—I offer special thanks to Lisa Pomerantz, Artists' Representative @ ILLUSTRATION ONLINE LLC, for negotiating and introducing me to one of her illustrators, Ester Cuesta De La Mata. I am amazed by her vision and talent for the book cover artwork of this novel.

If the reader only knew how little I gave her to work with in the form of a sketch and what she produced for me from it! We can reminisce the mysterious details of the wonderful album cover art of the 1970s, which inspired the idea. ¡Muchas gracias, mi amigo talentoso de España! Enjoy this video of her working on the book cover! https://www.youtube.com/watch?v=Gxxqi89DBpI&t=3s

I am grateful for the friends who encouraged me at one time or another over the past few years of this journey. George Foley, while patiently sharing his wealth of knowledge about racial issues he dealt with in the 1970s and his love of music, movies, and football with me, demonstrated that we have more in common than our differences. Dan Vores, a fellow Navy veteran and self-published author, for his numerous emails of encouragement, phone calls, and insights for authoring a novel for the first time. Tim Belford, for the time he spent sharing memories of high school several years ago when this book was in the planning stages. Last, but certainly not least, my dear friends Lisa Goeke and Dawn Cierpiot for beta reading, making suggestions, and providing me with hours of encouragement when I really needed it.

There are a few more people who may not be aware of their importance in the work I have completed: Nigel Watts, for authoring the fantastic book, *Writing a Novel*. Anne Lamott, for writing an equally enlightening book, *Bird by Bird*. d-maps.com for the free map of Jefferson County. Wikipedia, the free encyclopedia that anyone can edit, for the picture of the Meramec River. Helen Sedwick, for her fine article, "Book Disclaimers: Everything You Need to Know." Patti Smith Jackson, for inspiration drawn from her book, *St. Louis Arena: Memories*. Joe Holleman, for inspiration drawn from his book, *Rollin' on the River: The Story of The Admiral in St. Louis*. Ron Stevens, for producing an excellent and epic documentary on KSHE, *Never Say Goodbye*. The memories I have of KSLQ, KWK, and KSHE radio in those formative years when music gave me context for my conflicting feelings took me decades to put back into a story. Thank you.

About the Author

Carl L. Bost Jr. was born in Queens, NY, and survived growing up near the Mississippi River in Imperial, Missouri. He graduated from Windsor High School in 1982 and Jefferson College in 1983. Carl is a Navy submarine veteran, and he has completed five marathons, both accomplishments arming him with the mental fortitude he required to write his first novel. He currently resides in the City of St. Louis with his three cats: Azir, Nidalee, & Baby Rengar.

*Author photo taken
by Anna Barton.*

If you enjoyed this book, please give it a favorable review on Amazon and Goodreads and drop me a line at owlsongsllc@gmail.com.

Thank you!